HOT SPELL

HOT SPELL

Emma Holly
Lora Leigh
Shiloh Walker
Meljean Brook

BERKLEY SENSATION, NEW YORK

THE BERKLEY PUBLISHING GROUP
Published by the Penguin Group
Penguin Group (USA) Inc.
375 Hudson Street, New York, New York 10014, USA
Penguin Group (Canada), 90 Eglinton Avenue East, Suite 700, Toronto, Ontario M4P 2Y3, Canada
(a division of Pearson Penguin Canada Inc.)
Penguin Books Ltd., 80 Strand, London WC2R 0RL, England
Penguin Group Ireland, 25 St. Stephen's Green, Dublin 2, Ireland (a division of Penguin Books Ltd.)
Penguin Group (Australia), 250 Camberwell Road, Camberwell, Victoria 3124, Australia
(a division of Pearson Australia Group Pty. Ltd.)
Penguin Books India Pvt. Ltd., 11 Community Centre, Panchsheel Park, New Delhi—110 017, India
Penguin Group (NZ), Cnr. Airborne and Rosedale Roads, Albany, Auckland 1310, New Zealand
(a division of Pearson New Zealand Ltd.)
Penguin Books (South Africa) (Pty.) Ltd., 24 Sturdee Avenue, Rosebank, Johannesburg 2196,
South Africa

Penguin Books Ltd., Registered Offices: 80 Strand, London WC2R 0RL, England

This book is an original publication of The Berkley Publishing Group.

First edition: November 2005

Library of Congress Cataloging-in-Publication Data

Hot spell / Emma Holly . . . [et al.].— 1st ed.
    p. cm.
    ISBN 0-425-20615-7
  1. Erotic stories, American. 2. Occult fiction, American. 3. Supernatural—Fiction.
I. Holly, Emma.
    PS648.E7H677 2005
    813'.0850837—dc22

                                                                        2005020265

PRINTED IN THE UNITED STATES OF AMERICA

10 9 8 7 6 5 4 3 2 1

contents

THE
COUNTESS'S PLEASURE

EMMA HOLLY

one

Everyone said what happened in Bhamjran stayed in Bhamjran. Despite this universal assurance, Georgiana DuBarry, the dutiful widowed Countess of Ware, wasn't sure she was ready to put the claim to the test.

Bhamjran might be the Aedlyne Empire's capital of sensual enlightenment, but Georgiana had only been here a week. One did not throw off the restrictions of a well-bred lifetime as soon as that. One did not even throw off one's corset.

She stood now, face shielded by hat and veil, in the secret heart of the desert city. This was a sweltering warren of sandy alleys west of the *chowk*, or central square. Bhamjran's elaborately carved sandstone buildings rose four stories above her, rich merchants' mansions rubbing elbows with narrow shops. The little *jali*-screened balconies—their stonework as fine as lace—lent the mansions an air of mystery. Pampered male consorts might be peering out from them secretly, whiling away the bright, hot hours until their mistresses returned to take their pleasure in the *zenan*. As interesting as this reversal of the usual patriarchal pattern was, what intrigued Georgiana most was not the idea of harems, but the prosperous-looking establishment directly opposite her watching post.

A steady stream of local women, both alone and in groups, filed beneath the pointed archway to The Ladies' Lotus. Wrapped in colorful saris more appropriate to the climate than Georgiana's heavy gown, each woman handed a silver coin to the turbaned guardian at the door. All were smiling faintly as they passed inside, as if their anticipation of what was to come was too delicious to suppress.

Georgiana could join them if she found her nerve. Two years had passed since her husband's death, all the mourning decency required. Her parents had been gone since before her marriage, and she owed Jonathan's memory nothing but discretion: to keep his secret as she had when he was alive.

At the thought of that secret, she pressed her white sweat-dampened gloves to the waist of her lilac gown. To have never known true conjugal pleasure, to have been twenty and full of life and in love with her handsome husband, only to discover he could not provide her that private joy, was a disappointment she had never imagined she'd experience. That her disappointment was too shameful to be shared with anyone she had understood at once, even without Jonathan's tearful pleas not to expose him. To this day, his family did not know the truth. His mother, God heal her bitter soul, still blamed Georgiana for their marriage's childless state.

I am free now, Georgiana reminded herself. *I have money and position and no one about me with the right to tell me what to do. I can explore any side of life I wish.*

"He is worth it, *memsahib*," said a soft, lilting voice at her shoulder.

An older woman had come up beside her on the pourstone pavement, a richly dressed, golden-skinned Bhamjrishi with merry eyes. When she rubbed one knuckle beneath the curve of her teasing smile, silver and ruby bracelets clinked down her arm. From the look of her, Georgiana suspected *her* harem was well cared for.

"Bhamjran has not seen Iyan Sawai's like in a dozen years," the helpful stranger continued. "A shameful admission, considering he is a foreigner, but there it is. Certainly, you will not find his equal in a tourist trap."

Georgiana cleared her throat and hoped the shadows on this side of the street hid her furious blush. "I *have* heard he is a graceful dancer."

The other woman laughed. "Grace is only the beginning of that demon's charms. Iyan Sawai can make *every part* of his body dance."

Georgiana struggled not to picture too clearly what this emphasis must mean. She leaned closer and dropped her voice. "I have sometimes wondered if demons' . . . I mean the Yama's bodies work the same as ours."

"Better," the woman said with a grin, not the least scandalized. "Which isn't to say I'd want one in my bed. Parvati forbid I'd ever take a consort who equated smiling with a sin. However, to look at, the Yama are all any goddess would find divine. Go along now. You'll forget you are embarrassed the moment his tunic comes off."

Georgiana wasn't as sure of this as the stranger, but it seemed more embarrassing to stay with the older woman urging her on. Smiling weakly and nodding her thanks, she took a breath, smoothed her constricting bodice, and strode across the dusty street.

Thankfully, the male attendant took her coin without comment and waved her down the stairs.

It was cool and dark inside The Ladies' Lotus, and Georgiana's eyes required a moment to adjust. Cheerfully painted columns split the sunken space, allowing the audience to form small groups. Comprised entirely of women, they sat on the floor on jewel-colored satin cushions. Here and there, low tables held coffee cups and samovars. The sweet scent of cinnamon rode the air, so rich and heady it seemed as if the sun-kissed skin of the women must give it off. They all looked so comfortable in their surroundings, so natural and free, that Georgiana felt even more out of place than she had feared.

For the first time since disembarking from the train at Victoria Station, she wished she had a female friend with whom she might enjoy this adventure. That being out of the question, she looked for a place to sit.

A few cushions remained unclaimed. Unfortunately, the only one Georgiana thought she could get to was in the right-front corner next to the half-moon stage. The last thing she wanted was to sit that close, but the prospect of climbing over the others in her awkward skirt and petticoats was even worse. Resigned, she continued up the aisle and then arranged herself and her gown as best she could on the floor.

A mirror-spangled curtain veiled the platform in smoky blue. Georgiana tried to pretend she wasn't furiously wondering what it would reveal.

Clearly used to such things themselves, the group beside her wished her a casual good day in her own language. Georgiana had heard that by the age of ten most Bhamjrishi had mastered three dialects. Her husband had liked to say the Queen's Ohramese was the noblest language, and only savages need speak more, but today she found herself wishing she could return the greeting as considerately.

At least she would not have felt she was the backward one.

She was saved from her self-consciousness when a hush descended over the gathering. A trio of musicians had begun to play in an alcove opposite her seat. Their flute and sitar twined like snakes with the rhythmic pattering of an animal-skin drum. The music was unlike anything she heard at home, wild and worldly at the same time.

Georgiana's heart began to thump faster. Mindful not to prick herself with the hat pins, she removed her little satin toque. She was really here. She was really doing this. Shades were lowered until the room was black, after which a light swelled from the foot of the stage, a newfangled electric light that was not, strictly speaking, permitted to shine in Bhamjran. Queen Victoria's agreement with the Yama dictated that their technology be sold to Ohram alone and barred in its protectorates.

But she had no leisure to be offended on her country's behalf. The spangled, smoke-blue curtain was rising.

Georgiana's helpful stranger had been mistaken about the tunic. The tall male figure whose form was being revealed from the ankles up was completely naked—and completely breathtaking. He was facing away from the crowd, as motionless as stone, his every muscle thrown into relief by the bright artificial light. Georgiana's mouth went dry. It seemed wrong to stare, despite having paid for the privilege, but she could not help herself. Symmetry and strength united in the figure's back, in his long, athletic legs, in the lovely, cuppable rounds of his bum. His hair, which was as black as the proverbial raven's wing, fell in glossy waves to brush a pair of broad shoulders. Even his arms, body parts Georgiana had never thought of as objects for admiration, brought an odd ache of longing into her chest. His hands hung relaxed and long-fingered by his hips.

He might have been a statue in a museum. Nature simply did not make men as wickedly beautiful as this . . . at least, human nature did not.

For thousands of years, the Yama—or demons, as humans liked to call them—had lived in scrupulous isolation in the icy northern wastes beyond the mountains of Yskut. There, they had been sufficient unto themselves, developing their highly stratified society and their amazingly clever science without the humans who lived around them suspecting they were there. One of Georgiana's distant cousins, an adventurous captain of the guards, had been the first to stumble across their existence, more than a generation ago now.

Many changes had followed for both races, especially after

Queen Victoria signed the infamous Avvar Accord, an agreement allowing the Yama to exile certain of their undesirables in Ohram's capital. In return, the Yama had given Ohram access to enough of their technology to assure Victoria's superiority over the less secure of her possessions, thus establishing peace throughout her empire. Some of the compromises involved had been uneasy, but given the Yama's dramatic effect on human fortunes, none could deny a fascination with the empire's newest visitors.

Yama were so like humans, after all. They simply were more: more beautiful, more intelligent, more perfect. They lived longer than humans, healed faster, and had more strength. Humans might want to deny it, but in their hearts they knew the truth: had the Yama not been so intent on distancing themselves from what they saw as the human taint, they could have ruled the world.

Luck alone saved Georgiana's kind. The biggest difference between the races was the very one Yama feared. Humans were emotional beings. Sorrow and joy, lust and longing were an accepted part of their lives. The Yama, by contrast, shunned all the fiery issues of the heart. Control was their god, the chill of their icy homeland their ideal. Human nature filled them with disgust. Worse, because of their unusual sensitivity to human auras, the human taint could literally rub off on them.

As a result of this quirk in their constitution, the opportunity to see a demon in an intimate setting was extremely rare. That this demon must be a *rohn*, or lower-class Yama, was guaranteed. No self-respecting *daimyo* would ever display himself in this manner, and few enough *rohn*, either. Had more of Georgiana's countrywomen enjoyed her advantages, she suspected the most conservative would have had difficulty walking by The Ladies' Lotus without a pang. The thrill of the forbidden was enough to assure they'd wish to go in.

Which wasn't to say that the demon who posed before her needed any more allure.

Georgiana's gloved hands pressed her folded legs, now as hot as if she'd baked them beneath the sun. The demon had begun to move. One isolated muscle flicked behind his thigh and then one in his lower back. He made his delectable bottom flutter, then the ropy muscles of his shoulders. This was not a dance; artistic expression was as alien to the Yama as emotion. No, this was an explicit demonstration of physical control as, one by one, he shook the various parts of himself alive.

It wasn't long before Georgiana was barely breathing. She *had* forgotten to be embarrassed. She had not seen her husband naked often enough to take such displays lightly, and this man . . . Oh, this man was so beautiful, so strong, it would have been a sin *not* to look.

And then he turned just his head, his chin coming to the line of his shoulder. To her amazement, his eyes locked onto hers as if magnetized.

She realized her hands were fisted at her breast when her heart tried to leap out.

His were not human eyes. Bereft of whites, they were silver from rim to rim but for the swell of his black pupils. In a face as smooth as a mask, those eyes glittered like icy fire. They were alive and, therefore, *he* was alive. The knowledge came home to her that she was staring at a thinking, breathing person and not a thing.

Her blush seared across her cheeks, but even then she could not tear her gaze away.

His body followed the turn of his head, slowly, calmly, drawing out the tension. As he faced her, her eyes drifted irresistibly to the revelation that was his chest. A shading of black hair could not obscure the beauty of its shape. His ribs moved upward with a breath. Losing her nerve, she looked at his face again. His tongue came out to wet his upper lip. She had heard that Yama did not often do this. Their tongues bore a natural marking that made them seem forked, the very mark that had caused her race to label them demons.

The gesture had a strange effect. Georgiana was no longer merely hot. A pulse as insistent as the goatskin drum thrummed between her legs, centering on the small, tight bud her departed husband had never thought it decent to acknowledge. An image flashed into her mind of the demon's tongue stroking her there. The ache of longing that stabbed through her was as unprecedented as it was strong. She had desired her husband, but not like this.

"Oh, my God," she whispered, unable to keep her shock at herself inside. "Oh, my God."

As if he heard her above the music, the demon's eyes went momentarily black.

Sweat trickled down Georgiana's back. The demon's lips moved soundlessly. *Look,* they said. *Watch.*

Gooseflesh prickled the nape of her neck. Her blood was rushing so loudly she barely noticed the audience begin to softly chant, "Sawai."

The demon deliberately lowered his dark-lashed eyes, not so much acknowledging the others as compelling her. This time, Georgiana obeyed temptation. The front of his body was as lovely as the back. He was lean, symmetrically muscled, and well over six feet tall. She tried to skim past his most blatant attraction by admiring the shapely length of his thighs. It was no use. What hung between them was impossible to ignore.

His sex was as perfect as the rest of him.

He was slack but large, thick of girth and round of head. One strong, blue vein led down the front of his shaft, branching twice to circle him. As she followed this vital conduit to its termination, she saw he was uncircumcised. This gave her another unexpected sexual jolt. She bit her lip and prayed she wouldn't gasp aloud.

"Sawai," sighed the audience with a definite note of praise.

His sex had begun to swell.

A moan caught in Georgiana's throat. He wasn't even touching himself, and he was rising in smooth, hypnotizing surges. The skin of his penis grew darker, the covering over the head drawing back. Considering the size at which he started, she wouldn't have thought he could get much larger, but he did, growing ever more impressive until his now-bare crest approached the curve of his navel.

He grew so stiff the blood could only shudder within his engorged flesh, an absolute hammer of stark male strength. No one could think him incapable of penetrating his mate, of riding her deep and hard. Georgiana had never seen anything like this prodigy. She would need two hands to stroke him. She would not be able to fit even half of him in her mouth—

And she did gasp then, because she realized what she was thinking and what this said about her sanity.

The demon's eyes were waiting when hers flew guiltily up. Any human male would have smiled in triumph, but the demon's expression remained serene. His lips were parted and his pupils large, but by no other means did he betray his interest in her reaction.

Georgiana jumped as someone tapped her shoulder. A pretty young local woman, dressed in the Lotus's signature smoky-blue, was offering her a shallow bowl. The oil inside it smelled of almonds.

"You must do the honors," she said. "Sawai has chosen you."

Georgiana's jaw dropped in confusion. "The honors?"

"You must bring Sawai the oil. He will apply it, *memsahib*, unless you wish to do that, too."

"No!" she said, and the server's pretty eyes widened.

Georgiana supposed the woman was unused to anyone refusing, but if she touched the demon, even with her gloves, she feared her etheric-force would transfer over. This was one of the problems of association between the races. The Yama could draw energy from humans. Slightly different from their own life force, it acted upon them like a drug—pleasurable, but potentially addictive, and saturated with emotion. Lower-class demons, whose self-discipline was less developed, had occasionally gone mad from overindulging. The donation of energy left signs on humans as well, thinning them, refining their looks, until they resembled Yama a bit themselves. Georgiana wasn't ready to commit herself to that. Watching this demon's performance was more than daring enough for her.

"I will give the bowl to him," she said more calmly. "If you would help me up."

As her legs were nearly asleep from their uncustomary posture, this was a necessity. The young woman gave her a hand, then carefully handed her the oil.

Luckily, the stage was only a foot away. Georgiana's arms trembled wildly as she lifted her offering. The demon watched her shake for a moment, blinked inscrutably, and then cupped his hands beneath her gloves. Her knees threatened to buckle at the tingling wave of sensation his touch inspired. His fingers were long and surprisingly hot; his hold gentle but sure. She was almost sorry when he pulled the bowl away.

"Stay," he said. His voice was low and had a roughness she did not expect. "Please."

The "please" was grudging. *Rohn* or not, it seemed his pride did not bend easily.

Georgiana swallowed, then nodded in agreement. She could not bring herself to touch him, but she could stay. To do otherwise would probably be an insult. In any case, she was not sure her knees would allow her to sit again. If she tried to bend them, they might collapse. Instead, she braced her hands on the stage's edge.

The demon did not dip his fingers into the oil. Still facing her, he brought the bowl to his breastbone, tipped it back, and let the almond-scented stream run down his stomach muscles to the base of his cock. When the rivulet split and rolled over his testicles, he cupped them before it could drip. As if he wanted everyone to notice how full he was, he massaged his scrotum, pulling its swollen roundness out from his body. His fingers were expert and shining.

Oh, God, Georgiana thought, and prayed she had not spoken aloud again.

He handed the bowl back to her. "Hold this," he said. "I want to coat my shaft."

Not understanding what he meant for her to do, she stood frozen where she was. When he knelt, bringing their eyes to the same level, it felt unbearably intimate.

"Hold the bowl firm," he said, angling it upward in her hands, "and I won't have cause to touch you again."

Then he slid his erection into the bowl, using his hips to work it over the oily curve of the well-worn wood. Over and over, he pushed his crest to the rising edge, compressing it until his veins shone dark through his skin. Without consciously deciding to do so, Georgiana soon went beyond holding the bowl. Rather, she began to maneuver it in opposition to his strokes, to exert pressure and rub it over him.

From his soft gasp for air, she could hardly have done better if she'd used her hands.

She knew what men liked. Jonathan had taught her to please him as much as he was capable of being pleased, and this obviously healthy male suffered no lack of responsiveness. Indeed, allowing for the differences in the races, this demon was most receptive to her efforts. His cock grew redder and fuller until, like the plucking of the sitar's string, a subtle shudder vibrated through his frame.

"Good," he whispered as he pulled back.

When she lifted her gaze to his, she was almost ready for the inevitable jolt of shock.

"Shall I finish here," he inquired softly, "or would you prefer I rise to my feet again?"

Three choppy breaths were required before she could answer. "Here," she said, every scrap of her failing courage in the word. "I want to see from as close as I can."

A muscle flickered in his cheek. She did not know if this were simply tension or an aborted smile. When he spoke, his tone was calm.

"I shall use two hands," he said. "Because this afternoon's excitement has made me so very large."

His words seemed to suggest she was the reason for this circumstance, but it was impossible to guess what went on behind those silver eyes. Would a demon use flattery to please a customer? Did he resent his audience and, by association, her? Did he find this exchange as extraordinary as she did, or was it perfectly pedestrian for him?

But these were foolish questions. No human would ever understand the demon mind. Certainly, Georgiana wouldn't, not when he wrapped his length in both hands and robbed her of the power of thought.

She knew this act was not meant to be a dance, and yet it was—a beautiful, erotic dance in which every muscle and joint of his body became involved. He made a tunnel of his oiled hands by lacing his fingers together and pairing his thumbs on top. His body undulated as he pulled his hold along his rigid length, dragging his organ out and down—slowly, firmly, as if every inch of every pull must be enjoyed.

He used his foreskin to rub the tip. Each time the pressure of his fingers crossed that sensitive area, his buttocks tensed and pushed forward. His grip was tighter than any Georgiana would have dared employ, though her husband had liked it tight enough.

As his pulls increased in speed, the demon closed his eyes—for privacy, perhaps, or because his blindness let him feel the sensations more. A struggle seemed to be going on inside him, as if he longed to ejaculate but could not quite yet. Perhaps the loss of control a release involved was at odds with his Yamish nature. Perhaps no demon could achieve climax easily. Whatever the cause, no one was complaining. Georgiana had a feeling everyone in the Lotus could have watched him strive for pleasure until the sun went down.

A woman could indulge herself with a man like this. With a man like this, a woman need never be let down.

As if he knew what she was wishing, his eyes flew open and sought hers.

His gaze was too intense to hold for long, threatening to bare more in her than it revealed of him. The sound of his hands working over his hard, oiled skin drew her gaze back down. She knew her cheeks were flaming. The pressure he was using distorted his shape. She wished those were her hands. She wished she were the one both punishing and pleasuring his flesh.

"Tell me you want to touch me," he demanded, his breathing at last humanly ragged. "Tell me you want to rub my penis, and I will come."

"I do," she gasped. "I do."

He made a sound she doubted anyone but she could hear, like someone muffling an outcry. His eyes did not simply close this time, they screwed shut. His hips thrust hard, and his ribs arched slightly in on themselves. He had covered the head of his organ with one fist, but she knew what was happening anyway. The tightening of his thigh muscles told her, the flush that stained his cheeks and chest. When his hand finally fell away, his cock was lax again and the floor between his thighs was wet.

The audience held its collective breath.

Their silence ended when his eyes opened. Amidst applause and whistles, coins began to rain onto the stage as if the monsoon had come. Realizing this added tribute must be expected, she reached embarrassedly for her reticule.

"No," said the demon, his gaze cool again. "You have given me enough."

She could not conceive of what to say. She was shaken beyond the use of words.

My old life is over, she thought without precisely knowing what she meant. *After this, I shall never be the Countess of Ware again.*

TWO

The coins were not Iyan's. Strictly speaking, aside from a small allowance to meet his daily needs, they belonged to the owner of his indenture. His employer would send a predetermined portion—undercounted, Iyan had no doubt—to the Yamish Ministry of Debts. As to that, the debt was not his own, either. It was his family's, which fact was enough to have led him, with relative docility, into his present servitude.

A son who would let his mother go to prison didn't deserve to be called a man.

Of course, a man who would take payment from a woman who had just given him such pleasure didn't deserve to be called Yama.

Iyan took a moment to regard the dumbstruck female staring up at him. She was pretty in the way human women rarely understood they were—warmly, wonderfully imperfect, with curly flaxen hair, bright blue eyes (the left of which was a fraction higher than the right), and a slightly too-long nose. Her figure was just as generous and made even more so by her pale corseted gown. Most appealing of all, however—at least from his perspective—was her energy.

She was a bright, brimming pot of sex, had she but known it, shooting rays of arousal everywhere she looked. Humans tended to believe demons could only feed from them when they touched, but this wasn't always the case. Some humans burned hotter, as did some emotions. As Iyan had stood on the stage waiting to begin, he'd felt this woman's rapt attention caress his body. He had not been surprised (though he had nearly betrayed himself by shivering with pleasure) when her energy poured into him through her gloves. In his year performing at the Lotus, Iyan had built up a tolerance to etheric-force and the emotions that went with it. This woman had penetrated every barrier he had. He hadn't released his seed that fully in the last twelve months, perhaps in his entire life.

That being so, he could not let her tip him, even if every coin brought him and his family nearer to freedom.

He bowed to her now, deeply enough to show respect, but not so deeply that the gesture could be considered an inappropriate public display. Her hand flew to her still-flushed throat. She was Ohramese by dress, which caught his interest as well. Her countrymen—though officially the occupiers of this city—didn't often venture into the "real" Bhamjran. The thought occurred to him that the company of a fellow outsider might be pleasant. He wished it were not a breach of good manners to suggest she attend a second performance.

It was, alas, and—no matter his present subjugated state—he would do her the honor of his best conduct. He turned, settled his somewhat upheaved emotions with a calming breath, and strode smoothly from the coin-strewn stage. The owner of his papers, a fat, bearded Jeruvian who had booked him into the Lotus, waited in the wings with his broom and pan.

Iyan donned the robe he'd left backstage and tied it. The Jeruvian did not have the civility to look away. From the way he stroked his beard in satisfaction, he might have been judging the condition of a favorite horse.

"Good show," he said. "Those women were ready to eat you up."

Not wishing to encourage him, Iyan nodded as brusquely as he could.

"Got enough get-up-and-go for tonight?"

Again, Iyan tipped his head. The worst part of his bondage was having to answer to this man. The best was letting him think he really was a demon who might lose control and kill him if pushed too hard. The Jeruvian did not treat the rest of his stable half so well.

He had begun to walk away when the man called him back.

"Letter came for you. Looks official."

Iyan retraced his steps and took the missive from the Jeruvian's meaty hand. The crumpling and smear marks spoke of failed attempts to break the government seal. Fortunately, the wafer was coded to open solely with Iyan's thumbprint. The paper itself was impossible to tear by human means.

"This is private," Iyan said. "I will open it in the alleyway."

"Go ahead," said the Jeruvian. "Just remember not to run off."

Iyan did his best to block his ears to the man's guffaws.

The Jeruvian would have split his corpulent sides if he'd read what the sheet contained. The second phase of the trial against Iyan's mother was complete, and the verdict was not favorable. She (or her family, since the court had also barred her from practicing her trade) had been ordered to pay an enormous sum in civil damages to the new Prince of Narikerr.

The previous prince, this one's brother, had died not long ago under questionable circumstances, and the current prince was determined to assert his authority by any means. The suit against Iyan's mother was one of the results. Without a shred of solid evidence, the similarly royal judge had ruled that not only was Iyan's mother responsible for the disappearance of the current prince's teenage daughter, but that said daughter was likely dead. Now Iyan's widowed mother—as the servant who had been responsible for the daughter's care when she went missing—must compensate for that loss as well.

Iyan's head began to throb. In a single stroke, the initial debt he'd agreed to pay was doubled. In another year, he would have been free. Now he could not see himself winning clear in less than three. If the money-grubbing, lying-bastard Jeruvian had his way, Iyan would be thirty before he could dream of living his own life.

He closed his eyes, struggling not to panic at his sense that the alley's sandstone walls were closing in. He could do this. He would work harder. He would perform three shows a day instead of two, maybe—Divinity help him—accept a private client or two. He'd had plenty of offers, and Bhamjrishi women did have a reputation for being kind. He might even enjoy himself if he could get past the affront to his pride.

His mother liked to say no job was dishonorable, as long as one did it well.

A sound caught in his throat, a choked laugh of irony. Shocked at himself, he bent and braced his hands on his knees. The sound stopped, but he could not straighten. This was not the ambition he had spun for himself as a boy, not even close. If he'd gone to university as he and his mother planned, he would have earned his degree this year—this summer, in fact. He would have been Iyan Ebefre, Doctor of Building Science. Instead, he was a step away from a whore.

If ever a Yama deserved to succumb to emotion, surely that time was now.

Georgiana had every intention of returning to her hotel. She followed the rest of the women from the Lotus and stepped into the blindingly sunny street. As the others chattered and strolled off in various directions, she looked toward the corner to see if she could spot one of the city's ubiquitous bicycle-rickshaws. The driver of a saffron-yellow affair with a matching fringed canopy glanced hopefully toward her.

She knew she ought to hail the conveyance. It was too hot to be out and too utterly ridiculous to linger in the area until the evening show. That had been obvious the moment the demon bowed politely and walked away.

Clearly, what had happened had not been important to him. Another day's work was all, as easily forgotten as it was performed. She would be an idiot if she tried to do anything except forget herself.

But he's perfect, she thought, the knuckle of one gloved finger pressed to her teeth. *He's absolutely, one hundred percent what I need.*

Ignoring the nonsense her brain seemed determined to churn out, she straightened her hat and turned her feet in the direction of her potential ride. As she did, a flash of peacock blue from the adjoining alley caught her eye a second too long.

The flash of blue was him, her ever-so-polite demon.

Wrapped in a robe, he leaned over his knees as if too weary to stand straight. Something about the pose made him appear no older than her own twenty-and-a-handful years, though a Yama's age could be hard for humans to judge. He still might be her senior. He had seemed so up on the stage. Vulnerability might make anyone look younger.

She saw he held something in one hand, an open letter that had—on the face of it—not conveyed good news.

I should go, she thought. He would not want her seeing him like this.

She did not move fast enough. His eyes turned and locked on hers just as they had earlier.

He can feel me looking at him, she thought, a shiver slipping down her spine.

He straightened to his full height, his face blank and proud once more. "Was there something you wanted?"

Here was her opening, whether she was ready for it or not. She forced herself to take one step through the alley's flowery cast-iron gate. "Forgive me for intruding, Mr. Sawai."

"Iyan," he said. "*Sawai* is not my name. Sawai means 'man and a quarter,' which is what the women of Bhamjran consider me."

"Oh," she said, aware that her cheeks were pink and in no doubt as to which part of him the extra quarter signified. "Mr. Iyan then. I hope it is not too presumptuous to inquire, but I was wondering if you might be available for hire."

He was silent for so long she had either offered him a deadly insult or his Ohramese was not as good as she'd assumed. Obliged to wait, she fought an urge to wring her hands.

"I take it," he said at last, "that you wish to hire me to do more than dance."

"I apologize profusely if I have offended you by inquiring."

He looked at her glove, at the ring she had not yet removed from her hand, the ring her mother-in-law fully expected her to wear until she died herself. "You are a married woman."

"I am widowed."

When he folded his arms across his chest, the blue silk robe did nothing to hide his physique. "You are seeking a forbidden thrill, a night of pleasure with a demon."

She began to shake her head, then stopped herself. The least she could do was be honest. "I do not deny your being different is a thrill, but it is the night of pleasure I want most. Because you are Yamish and I am not, there can be no attachment between us. We will both go our own way when the night is through."

"Surely you have other choices for partners."

She did not, *could* not. The demon's silver eyes bored into hers in search of what she was hiding, but she stubbornly said nothing. The why of this was her business. His was only to say yes or no.

*   *   *

Iyan was not as good as some Yama at reading the play of emotion through human auras, but he knew this woman concealed a secret. She might have been surprised to know he admired her for her silence. Discretion was, after all, more of a Yamish trait.

"You realize," he said, "that if we copulate—" He paused, oddly intrigued, as she flinched and colored at the same time. "If we make love, as humans put it, I will feed off your energy. Even if I wanted to, I could not avoid it. It is impossible for a human to experience an orgasm without radiating etheric-force, and if I agree to pleasure you, you will certainly experience more than one. Our night of pleasure may change your appearance, at least for a few days. I know many humans are sensitive about letting others see they have been intimate with my kind."

He watched her think this over, her gloved hands clutched unconsciously at her waist. It was all too easy to imagine those fingers bared and running over his naked skin, pouring that amazing sexual energy into him. If achieving release in front of her had been rewarding, how much more so would he find sexual congress? He might well experience more pleasure than he could stand. Too late, he wished he had not felt compelled to warn her. At this less-than-marvelous juncture of his life, more pleasure than he could stand sounded awfully appealing.

"I can make allowances for that," she finally said. "Perhaps stay in my hotel room until any traces fade."

His sense of insult was irrational considering he had brought up the matter, but it lashed through him all the same. Quite obviously, she did not think him good enough to have others know they'd been bed partners.

"My price is one thousand Ohramese pounds," he said, his manner icy even for him.

The woman's eyes widened. She might be inexperienced, but she knew this was an outrageous sum. The empress of all the Yama would not pay a lover that much. Iyan braced for her refusal, for her to laugh in the human way. Instead, she swallowed hard.

"Do I pay you or the man who swept up your coins?"

This time his anger surged too high for him to contain. The fact that he had invited this treatment by his demand only made it worse.

"I am an indentured servant," he clipped out, "not a slave. The man who swept up my coins is not empowered to arrange a transaction of this nature."

"I am sorry," she said, her hand coming out until it almost touched him. "I do not know how these things are done."

"And you think I do?"

His voice was sharp and raised. Human or not, she was not inured to people being furious with her. Her lip trembled in warning an instant before a tear slipped down her cheek. "Please forgive me," she said. "I will leave."

The tear performed an uncomfortable alchemy on his insides. He did not think he had seen anyone weep since he was a child. Certainly, he had never been the reason they had cried.

"Wait," he said, his voice no longer angry. "I will give you two nights. One for a thousand pounds and one for free."

Her eyes were wide and bright as stars. "Why would you give me one for free?"

"For my honor. Because I am not a whore."

He thought she was going to apologize again or even cry, but thankfully she controlled herself. She rubbed one knuckle beneath her full lower lip. "When would be convenient to . . . meet?"

"Tomorrow night. I shall request a leave from my duties at the Lotus."

He was beginning to grow addicted to her blush.

"Can you do that?" she asked.

"The terms of my servitude ensure it, and I have never asked for leave before. I am certain you will appreciate the edge a brief abstention gives my performance, though—naturally—I would be capable no matter what."

"Naturally," she repeated, the word flatteringly faint.

"You *will* be pleasured," he said with a hint of warning he wasn't sure he could explain. "You should rest before you come. We will meet at my rooms, unless you prefer to hire a place yourself."

Clearly speechless, she offered him a tiny notebook and a slim gold pencil from her reticule.

He scribbled his direction and looked up. "Where may I contact you if for some reason I am delayed?"

"I am staying at the Hotel Bhamjran." She hesitated and then put her shoulders back. "They know me as the Countess of Ware."

Her trust was a gift in any language. He bowed to her and, because they were alone, he bowed deeply. "I look forward to meeting my obligations."

When he rose again, she was smiling. It was the first time he had seen this supremely human expression on her face. To his surprise, it transformed her from simply pretty to beautiful.

Her eyes possessed a sparkle he thought he could grow to like.

"Oh," she said, her hand to her throat, "believe me, I look forward to it, too."

THREE

When the bicycle-cab brought Georgiana to Iyan's address, the area surprised her. He did not live near The Ladies' Lotus, but in a part of Bhamjran that, although not positively dangerous, had definitely seen better days. The old *haveli* that housed his rooms had also sunk from its prime as a rich town mansion. Its walls had been painted once but were now pitted by decades of wind-blown sand. Two ragged children, a boy and a slightly older girl, sat on the entry steps, bent studiously over a dented tin plate of the savory snacks called *farsaan*.

Georgiana recognized the treat because she had ordered it off the Hotel Bhamjran's menu the night before. Interestingly, the hotel's version had not smelled as good as the one these children were sharing.

"Sawai!" the children called as Georgiana alighted. "Your foreign devil guest is here!"

The girl then grabbed two batter-fried *pakora*—no doubt to prevent her companion from eating them while she was gone—and, without a word, escorted the aforesaid foreign devil across a once-grand lobby to a flight of stairs. The stairs' moth-eaten carpets muffled the only sound that accompanied their climb. The general disrepair made the place seem ancient, but the peeling Ohramese-style columns gave its age as closer to fifty years. As they ascended, they encountered evidence of others living in the house: embroidered slippers left outside an entrance, small wheeled toys fallen on their sides. Whoever these people were, they were either gone at present or very quiet. Finally, at the end of the fourth floor's hall, the girl rapped twice on a bright blue door, swallowed the last of her chili fritters, and abandoned Georgiana to her nerves.

The demon opened the door.

"Countess," he said in greeting.

He wore a black robe this evening, with silver piping that highlighted his alien eyes. Georgiana had forgotten how starkly beautiful he was.

"I'm afraid I'm early," she said, because she could not stand there calmly staring the way he did.

"It is no matter. With two shows a day, I have grown unaccustomed to self-denial. I have everything in readiness."

He stepped aside to admit her. She thought she had schooled herself to keep her composure, but at the mention of *readiness*, her mind flashed back to his performance and her body suddenly felt weak. A narrow passage led to his main room. Glancing down it, she saw two tall, onion-peaked windows and what appeared to be the foot of a low, wide bed. Wanting the matter of finances settled, she laid her net bag of coin on the small, carved table inside the door. She had withdrawn the money from the bank that morning, one thousand pounds in full.

Iyan looked at the coins and then at her. It might have been her imagination, but his face looked stiffer than usual.

If this was the case, the cause was destined to remain a mystery. "I appreciate your confidence," was all he said.

Unsure about his sense of humor, she didn't say even one of the dozen flirtatious things that flew through her mind. Instead, she followed him to his rooms, which were unexpectedly colorful and in surprisingly good shape.

Some effort had been exerted here to reverse the mansion's decline. The demon's sturdy bed sat in the center of a stretch of freshly polished floorboards, its head draped by a tent of gauzy orange and gold muslin. Like the curtain at the Lotus, the cloth was spangled with tiny mirrors. The ceiling from which it hung was high and airy, and on the walls were painted scenes from Bhamjrishi myth. A quick glance revealed an abundance of elephants, monkeys, and turbaned warriors with scimitars. To the right of the hall, a chest of drawers held a comb and brush, plus the letter she had seen him reading the day before. To the left, a doorway opened into a lavishly appointed bath.

That Iyan valued a nice bathing room did not surprise her; the one thing all humans knew about the Yama was that they were notoriously clean. Apparently, however, she had misjudged what being indentured meant to his kind. This flat was nicer than the chamber she had given her own maid.

The demon had been watching her look around. "It is comfortable," he said.

"It is lovely," she answered.

This observation seemed not to be out of place.

"You must remove your clothes," he said.

"Already?" she was startled into responding.

Something like a frown flickered across his face. "You wear your native garments. They do not make a woman feel as she should before sex."

Georgiana looked down at herself. She had dressed carefully with the aid of the hotel's maid, throwing off her lavender half-mourning for a bright-yellow cotton gown. Simple though it was, she knew it flattered her, and she felt rather cheery in it. She had even left off her wedding ring, thinking the reminder of her husband inappropriate for what she planned to do.

Evidently, these changes were not enough.

"I will give you a robe," the demon said, "but I will not let you undress in the bath."

He was either a mind reader or knew a good deal more about human women than she knew about Yamish males. "Why not?" she asked. "Since I am . . . since I am paying, should I not be allowed my preference?"

"It would be impractical to leave you in charge of our activities. You lack the experience to ask for what will give you the most pleasure. Watching you undress will arouse me, and the more aroused I become, the better service I shall provide."

She didn't understand how she could be titillated and embarrassed at the same time. She struggled to speak lucidly. "I thought you could become as aroused as you wished any time you liked. I thought *you* controlled your body."

"Perhaps compared to human males this is true, but even Yama are not machines. We must have inspiration, whether we provide it ourselves or receive it from others."

"So when you were onstage . . ." She could not bring herself to ask what fantasies played in his mind. His reserve forbade it, though her attack of doubts demanded another question be asked. Unable to bear being disappointed now, she turned her face from his steady gaze. "What if the sight of me naked isn't inspiration enough?"

He drew a breath before he spoke. "You want my assurance that I desire you."

She forced herself to nod and look at him again.

His face did not show expression so much as it relaxed. "Come here," he said, and she imagined she heard a hint of kindness in his low, soft voice. "Put your arms around my neck and lean up."

He was warm when she obeyed him, his skin hardly less silky than his thin black robe.

"Your hips are not close enough," he said, and pulled her to him until they were pressed together from breast to knee.

His sex was already half-risen, half-hard, yet still capable of being pushed down between them. At the feel of its generous size, Georgiana could not contain her sigh of pleasure—nor a restless squirm. The demon seemed not to mind. While one hand continued to secure her hips at his groin, the other slid up her back and into her hair. His fingers sent tingles along her scalp as they combed through her fair, tightly corkscrewed curls. The massage loosened far more than what he touched.

In truth, her entire body was about to melt.

"Kiss me," he said, "and feel me change."

She had perhaps six heartbeats of pressing her lips to his before he took control. First his tongue flicked her upper lip, then her lower, then slid deliciously between. With lips as smooth as satin, he drew on her, slowly, strongly. Suddenly energy rolled between them in a prickling wave. In the pleasure of his kiss, she had forgotten to pay attention to what was happening to his sex, but it reminded her of its existence in no uncertain terms, abruptly kicking up against her as its owner sucked in a startled breath.

"Sorry," she said when he broke away from her mouth. "I didn't mean to—"

"Shh." He took her by the shoulders and turned her around, his fingers moving deftly over her gown's back fastenings. "I'm getting you out of this now. This is going to be even better than I had hoped."

She did not want to wait to be disrobed; she wanted to kiss him again, but finally her gown, corset, petticoat, shift, and drawers lay in heaps around her on the floor.

"Such a lot of clothes," he said, standing slightly breathless before her, though he'd been patient enough up until then. "It is a marvel you did not faint."

"I left off the stockings."

Again came that little smilelike twitch beside the corner of his mouth. "I am sure that omission is all that stood between you and heat stroke."

"May I have a robe now?"

His hands were ghosting over the curves of her breasts, his eyes slitted with enjoyment, as if he could feel her energy from inches away. He returned his attention to her face with seeming reluctance. "No, Countess, you most certainly may not."

He grabbed her waist then, lifted her up, and slid her savoringly down his front until their faces reached the same level. Her naked breasts settled on his chest, but even more distracting was the way his erection prodded her through his robe.

Evidently, no exertion could diminish him. He was hot and firm and long, and she could not have been reminded more forcefully of his superior demon strength. Though her feet still dangled off the ground, he showed no strain as he tilted his head to kiss her.

He chose the perfect angle. At the first deep taste, her lips began to buzz.

She suspected her mouth would have been humming even without his gift for drawing energy—which she was happy to discover did not hurt. Though his kiss had a certain bridled savagery, it was sweet to her, his tongue too clever not to spur fantasies. It seemed able to move more quickly, more precisely than a human's, but also with more sheer strength. After a few heady minutes, she had to push back to catch her breath.

He was smiling then, just a bit. "Forgive me," he said. "You are more delicious than you know."

Forgive him for what, she wondered. For smiling? For kissing her with such passionate expertise?

She would never know. He was tumbling her back onto his traditional Bhamjrishi bed, its joints so expertly fitted they did not creak. Like some feline predator about to pounce, he crouched above her on hands and knees. The way his shiny hair waved down around his face made her long to pet him like a cat.

"Now," he said, almost purring it. "Let us discover how sensitive you are."

She had never been kissed as he kissed her then, had never been
studied and pleasured and caressed with no intent but to make her
writhe. He would not let her touch him, and soon she did not have
sufficient control of her limbs to dare. He was torturing her with
kisses, making her want him so badly she groaned aloud. When he
kissed the inside of her elbows, her knees jerked uncontrollably.
When he stroked her bottom, her breasts grew hot. The soles of her
feet seemed connected in some mysterious fashion to her deepest
sex. She grew wet as he brushed his lips across them and nearly
spasmed when he nipped one particular spot with his teeth.

None of her reactions, excessive though they were, put him off
in the least. Indeed, when she began to pant at his continued
fondling of her feet, he carefully set them down, tore off his robe,
and stretched his long body out beside her with what truly seemed
to be impatience.

"You are perfect," he said, his silver eyes so intense they burned.
"You possess every trait any man could want."

Any man but my husband, she thought, then shoved the memory ruthlessly away. Iyan was close enough to touch, and he was not
at that moment tormenting her. Not willing to miss her chance, she
reached for his cock.

She gasped at the same time he did. Here was silk beyond anything she'd felt: thick, pulsing hardness, living heat wrapped in
flesh. The branching vein that had fascinated her at the Lotus had a
twin running along his underside. Gently, and with a dawning sense
of enchantment, she explored his length up and down.

"Not yet," he said sharply when she reached his sac.

His fingers touched her wrist, but he wasn't pushing her away.
In fact, his eyelids threatened to slide shut. She took a chance and
pulled her firmest grip from the root of him to the tip. She caught
his foreskin in the process. As she'd seen him do during his per-

formance, she used the pliant covering to squeeze and caress his sensitive crest.

His strangled moan of reaction was as rewarding as anything he'd done to her.

"Countess," he rebuked. "Please."

"You said the more aroused you became the better you would serve me . . . unless that was a lie?"

His eyes focused on her again. From the lift of his straight black brows, he understood she was teasing. "Even a Yama has limits. But I see I must remind you who is in charge."

Abruptly enjoying herself in a different way, she lay back and threw wide her arms. "Would that be you?"

A flush moved into his face, and she worried for a moment that she had gone too far. But then he licked his lips as he had that afternoon in the Lotus, and his gaze settled on her breasts. She became aware of the tingling tightness at their tips. Her nipples pulsed like fire even as he looked.

"Be careful, human," he said, his voice gone slightly rough. "I know your body's secrets, *see* them as you cannot. The light of your energy tells me where you want to be kissed most now."

The claim was true. He leaned over her, his body heat like the sun, and fastened his mouth on her breast. He sucked her strongly enough that she felt the pull to her toes.

Then his tongue began to work.

Sensations jangled all through her body, but especially between her legs. Had he not secured her hip with his hand, she would have rolled to him, would have taken him inside her as quickly as she could. He was too powerful to overmaster, but she heaved and twisted anyway. When he shifted to her other nipple, she had to bury her hands in his hair.

She was on the verge of pleasure just from this, held an infuriating inch away from the culmination she had so often been denied. Frustration robbed her of her admittedly inferior human self-control. The sounds of longing that broke in her throat seemed twice as loud compared to his silence.

Her sole consolation was that he was breathing hard when his mouth lifted away at last. He held her gaze while his tongue, its forked marking clear, curled out to wet his now-reddened lips. His tongue *was* a little longer than a human's, moving with a sinuosity no man she knew possessed. Her involuntary shudder of response brought a flash of total blackness into his eyes. It was, she realized, his body's way of signaling a sudden increase in excitement.

"One more," he whispered. "One more part of you needs my kiss."

He moved too quickly for her to protest or even tense. With demon swiftness, he yanked apart her thighs, slung her calves over his shoulders, and sank his mouth to her sex. Here his sucking pressure, coupled with the agility and strength at his tongue's command, produced a spike of sensation so sharp she exclaimed at first in alarm. She thought she was coming, but then the feeling rose and rose until, with a flicker of his tongue that could in no way be reproduced by her kind, her pleasure broke in hard, throbbing waves.

She heard him make a sound and felt his fingers tighten painfully on her hips. She remembered what he'd said about being unable to avoid feeding from her energy when she came. She wondered just how deeply this affected him.

Very deeply, she thought as he set her down. The outlines of his body seemed to vibrate before her eyes. Color flushed his face and chest, outdone only by the rich russet of his cock. He bent toward her again, softly but insistently kissing a path up her body until he reached her mouth. There, despite what must have been a painful state of arousal, his kiss was deep and slow. Sensing how intensely he wanted her, imagining how hard holding back must be, the heat in her body changed, twisting from satiation back into need.

"Oh, God," she said. "I can't believe I want you again."

He splayed his hand across her belly, pressing gently in a manner that made her aware of how wet and tight she was. When he finished watching whatever evidence played through her aura, he met her gaze.

"I am glad you want me. As you can see, I want you as well. It is time I prepare myself for entry."

He looked prepared as he was. His sex was thrumming, so unremittingly upright his torso might have been a magnet and it an iron bar. But she did not have the nerve or the inclination to contradict him. If he wanted further preparation, who was she to stand in his way?

He opened a drawer she had not noticed in the side of the bed's platform. From this space he withdrew a dull silver bottle with a perfume atomizer's top. With a discernible wince, he pressed his raging erection out with one thumb. His other hand sprayed a cloud up and down its length. Fascinated, Georgiana sat up to watch. The cloud settled on his skin with a pearlescent glow, spreading until his organ was encased.

This seemed to cause him no discomfort. By the time he finished applying whatever the substance was, she could have sworn he'd swelled even more.

"It is a self-sealing prophylactic," he said with the merest hint of strain. "The technology is still prohibited to humans, but not, of course, to me. The sheath it forms is very thin and does not dull sensation, though it is a trifle cold."

"And you *enjoy* that?"

Her amazement brought a sheen of what simply had to be amusement into his eyes. "My arousal has . . . maximized because now I know I may be inside you with complete safety."

"Maximized," she repeated, completely enthralled by the part of him that warranted the term. "There's an appropriate word."

"Do not fondle me again," he warned, though her fingers had merely curled on her thigh. "My control is not what it should be tonight."

Though it was probably insensitive, Georgiana could not contain her grin. "I suppose a Yamish lady might complain, but allow me to assure you that whatever you manage will be better than I am used to."

"That is no secret. You, however, deserve the superlative." He studied her body as if considering his next move. "It would be best if you turned onto your front and allowed me to penetrate you from behind. You have more nerves at the anterior of your vagina and will thus receive the greatest benefit from my thrusts. Plus, you will not feel inhibited in your responses because of your concern that I am watching them."

"That—" She swallowed and tried again, a heat that really should not have been inspired by such clinical language running from her sex. "That is most considerate."

"I shall enjoy it," he said, ruining any hope she had of recovering control. "You need not worry about that."

He handed her an apple-green satin bolster on which to prop her hips. Even the little adjustments he made to her position were exciting. Her knees had to be wider, her bottom canted more dramatically, and each of these movements required an assortment of gentle touches from his hands.

She felt oddly protected, and just as oddly vulnerable. He knew what he was doing; that much was clear.

"Perfect," he announced at last. As if to test—or simply to appreciate—the truth of this claim, he drew his fingertips from her shoulders down either side of her spine and over the upraised curve of her bottom. There his thumbs stretched inward to brush the sticky softness of her labia. "Yes, you will take me admirably in this pose."

In the face of such satisfaction, she could not be embarrassed. Even if she were, she had no means to hide. By the time he shifted into place behind her, she was as needy as if she'd never had an orgasm in her life.

With her cheek pressed to the mattress, she watched him reach between their bodies to adjust himself.

She gasped as the sun-hot crown of him nudged her sex. Despite its sheathing, he felt perfectly naked—and perfectly huge.

"Do not be afraid," he said as he lifted his upper body on muscled arms. "My organ may be large, but I know how to wield it to enhance delight."

The pressure on her sex increased as his hips pushed forward, then subsided when he pulled them back. Again he did this, and again. Georgiana's fingers curled into his sheets. He was sliding the largest, silkiest part of him in and out just inside her gate, and the pleasure she received from this was cumulative.

Her pleasure had plenty of time to build up. His movements were as regular as a metronome. The tent that draped the head of his bed began to sway. Looking back, she saw his expression had undergone a subtle change. He looked, just a little, as if he were in pain. The hands that gripped her waist were hard.

"You are very wet," he observed somewhat tightly after a few minutes of this activity.

"I am . . . oh, Lord." She closed her eyes as an interesting motion of his hips sent the tip of his penis in a tight circle. "I have no experience with anything that feels this good."

"Ah," he said. Two more hip swivels filled a pause. "I am afraid that poses a challenge. I am unused to my partners being this easy to arouse. It is . . ." He trailed off and licked his lips, so she assumed he was not displeased with her responsiveness. "I am unable to judge your needs completely. Would you prefer to wait, or do you want full penetration now?"

"Now," she said with absolute decisiveness. "Oh, do it now!"

Iyan hesitated; he knew his judgment was not currently its sharpest. The surface of the human body was a conduit for energy, and he had been drinking from hers all night—most strongly when he brought her to her first pleasure. He knew there was little danger he would harm her. Especially at the instant of climax, humans drew from reservoirs outside themselves—universal energy, for lack of a better term.

Her effect on him, however, was definitely dangerous. He felt far too close to ejaculation—and far too disinclined to fend it off. He was used to having to urge himself to come, not struggling to hold it off.

Still, it was impossible to resist her demand, even had he not been honor bound to obey. Her voice was too husky, her body too obviously eager. At this particular moment, she wanted the very thing penetration was designed to give.

She wanted to be taken.

Braced for what was sure to be an unsafe heightening of sensation, he gathered himself to enter her lubricious heat. In his unusual eagerness to be inside her, he may have misjudged the force this would require. With one strong thrust, she surrounded nearly all of him.

Considering how incredible this felt on his thudding shaft, it took a moment to recover enough of his senses to realize why she'd cried out.

"No." He began to pull back in spite of his body's utter reluctance to be anywhere but where it was. "This cannot be."

She reached one arm back to grab his hip. "Don't stop."

"But I will hurt you. I have taken your maidenhead."

"I assure you I barely felt it. Can't you tell how much I want you inside me? Please, Iyan, I didn't pay you to stop now!"

This reminder might prick his pride, but the very fact that she was desperate enough to employ it was flattering. Too, she had not used his name before this. He had a sneaking suspicion he liked that more than he should.

"Very well," he said. "I shall be as careful as I can."

He pushed inside her again, and his elbows nearly collapsed. Oh, it was better the second time—hotter, smoother, her body admitting him all the way. She gripped him, sweet and tight, in the most intimate of clasps. The effect was actually comforting. Everything that had troubled him, about his life, about this night, was swept away. He bent down to kiss her neck, to nuzzle through her delightfully silly flaxen curls, letting his weight sink to his forearms.

"Oh, I like that," she murmured. "I like feeling how warm you are."

Whatever the cost to his control, he wanted her to like it, wanted her to moan and wriggle and fist her hands in his sheets. He moved faster, lengthening his strokes, aiming them precisely to slide along the nerves that would enjoy them most. The sighs and twitches this inspired satisfied him only for a while. Soon he felt compelled to tuck himself closer, until his chest curved along her back. A line of energy sprang up everywhere they touched.

With this to goad him forward, he cupped the softness of her mound.

To his amazement, she growled at him and arched her spine, driving her sex decisively to his root.

He did not need to be told to increase his pace.

His head began to spin with pleasure. He forgot himself. He knew only the ecstatic feel of her around him, the rising pressure, the need to thrust deep and hard. She was mewling beneath him, one hand reaching out blindly for his. Barely thinking what he did, he laced their fingers together, pulled both their hands upward, and braced them with something close to desperation against the firm headboard. He was shoving into her so hard nothing else could keep her from hitting it.

As he gripped her hand, he saw her wedding ring was gone. For some reason, this aroused him beyond bearing. He could not slow down. He could not go easy. With greater and greater force, his stomach slapped her lush bottom. It was not enough. He pressed his longest finger to the hot swell of her clitoris. She cried out as he began to rub. The noise should have alarmed him; no Yama would have made it. Instead, knowing it was a cry of pleasure destroyed his final hold on himself.

He came like one of those crude human freight trains, his breath huffing out violently, his seed shooting into the prophylactic like ecstasy turned to fire. The consideration he owed any woman was all that kept his own shout inside.

He might have prostituted himself this evening, but that last scrap of honor he could show his partner.

It was less of an honor, perhaps, when he bit his lip hard enough to bleed.

He collapsed on top of her, helpless to do otherwise. She was breathing hard beneath him, hot and sweaty and quite possibly the most wonderfully soft woman he'd ever felt.

"My," she sighed, astoundingly better able to speak than he. "That makes up for everything I've ever missed."

"I have just begun," he said with mild affront.

At the moment, though, he was too exhausted to prove his words.

four

Many hours later, Georgiana woke from a brief and dreamless sleep to sit up among the tangled sheets. It was dark outside Iyan's windows, but a silvery glow lit the bed. It came from the now-twisted bed hangings. Evidently, what she had thought were mirrors were really clever tiny Yamish lights.

She wondered if he stared at them at night and thought of home, if he pretended he was anywhere but in this human city. As she could not discern a single electric wire, she had no idea how the lighting worked. Of course, she was not inclined to wonder very hard. Her body was still warm, still relaxed from all the demon had done to her. Even more bemusing, the slightest inducement from him would have readied it again.

"Need to rest a little longer," he mumbled now.

He lay on his back beside her, his hands folded at his muscled waist. He seemed not to wish himself elsewhere at the moment. He looked calm: relaxed, in a formal sort of way. This was the first time

THE COUNTESS'S PLEASURE

she had seen his sex completely soft. She discovered she liked the look of it this way, too.

"I should go," she said, though she didn't want to. She felt easier sitting naked in the dark with him than she would have felt at tea with her closest friend.

That's because he is a stranger, she told herself, *and likely knows nothing of how a countess should behave. He cannot judge me the way friends do.*

Vaguely dissatisfied with this explanation, she began to swing from the bed. Her feet hit the floor, but before she could rise he caught her arm. True to his ability to isolate a single set of muscles, he did not move in any other way.

"Don't," he said. "A half an hour is all I need."

Georgiana experienced a wash of amusement as she turned halfway back to him. "I really must have pricked your pride when I suggested your job was done. Trust me, Mr. Iyan, you have shown me pleasure beyond my wildest imaginings. Moreover, I would think you'd want to conserve your strength for tomorrow night."

He actually frowned, though hopefully not because he was having second thoughts about his promise. He erased the expression quickly enough, rolling smoothly onto his side and propping his head on his hand.

"Why did you do it?" he asked.

"Why did I say your job was done?"

He shook his head. "In my culture, virginity is a gift. Not required, but appreciated."

"In mine as well."

"Then why give it to me, a perfect stranger?"

Georgiana pulled the sheet over her legs, suddenly uncomfortable with her nakedness. "If I gave it to someone I knew, they would realize my husband could not . . . that he was incapable."

"Your husband was ill?"

He asked so calmly it was difficult to mind answering. Georgiana sighed and plucked at the sheet. "I don't know what was wrong with him. Jonathan would never agree to see a doctor. He seemed healthy otherwise. He liked to ride and hunt with his friends. Sometimes I thought the problem was in his mind. His mother is enough to give anyone a complex." She turned her gaze to check Iyan's expression, despite expecting disgust and finding none. "I have read something of the new science of psychology."

"Yama know of this field of study, though we don't consider it a science." The demon pursed his lips. "You had no confidantes, no sister you could ask for advice?"

"Is a sister who a Yama would talk to?"

He blinked at the question being turned back on him. "Yes, as long as the sister was honorable. Secrets belong in the family."

"Well, my husband would have agreed with you on that, but I'm afraid I have no sister, only four older brothers who were so beastly to me as a child, I never learned to think of them as honorable. Whatever Jonathan's flaws, marrying him was a glimpse of heaven compared to them."

"You have my condolences. To distrust one's family is a tragedy."

"Once I was old enough, I was able to keep out of my brothers' way. And Jonathan's kindness made up for their cruelty. We knew each other from the time we were young."

"Humans marry for love more often than we do."

Georgiana thought she heard a question here, though the demon might not have realized he was asking it. "We were comfortable with each other. Not a perfect match perhaps, but a contented one. Whatever our separate disappointments, we managed to live with them."

She turned fully back to him, pulling her legs beneath the covers and folding them tailor-style. "What about you? Do you have brothers and sisters?"

He answered more easily than she expected. Perhaps he, too, liked having a stranger to talk to.

"I have one younger sister who lives at home. It is our law that Yama may only have as many children as our resources can support."

"How many children can a prince have?"

The demon shrugged. "Dozens if he likes, but *rohn*—those of us who belong to the lower class—rarely have more than two. It is a wise policy. Yama have never wished to overrun their lands."

"I wouldn't presume to claim differently, but Iyan—" She laid her hand on his warm shoulder, wanting to reach the feelings she sensed were hidden beneath his words. "I think *you* are the one who does not like this policy."

He pulled from her. "It doesn't matter if I like it. Anyone can see the results of uncontrolled population running hungry in Bhamjran's streets. If I were a Bhamjrishi citizen—" He cut himself short, twisting his head away.

The passion in his voice surprised her. "Go ahead," she prompted softly. "If you were a citizen . . . ?"

"I do not wish to speak of this," he said in crisp, cool tones. "This is a night for pleasure, not for pointless discussions."

"If you explained what you wished to say, you might find we're not arguing."

"Yama do not argue!"

She would have laughed if he had not abruptly blanched with horror at having raised his voice. He smoothed his face almost at once.

"Perhaps you should go," he said, clearly striving to sound calm. "I must not forget your greater human need for rest."

"As you . . . wish," she said unsurely.

"I will assist you with your clothes." He got up to gather her garments, then helped her dress every bit as efficiently as her maid would have. The current coolness of his manner underscored how much he had relaxed before.

"We do not have to meet tomorrow," she said when he was done. "You have given me all I asked."

She was trying to be considerate, but if possible, he grew stiffer.

"Yama keep their word," he said. "We will do as I have promised."

FIVE

"Georgiana!" hailed a distantly familiar voice just as she gained the shadowed lobby of the pink hotel. "Lady Ware!"

The voice came from behind her. Because she did not have time to hide behind a column, Georgiana faced the hearty Ohramese male who had now finished climbing the Hotel Bhamjran's broad exterior stairs.

It was Phineas James, a friend of her brothers from childhood—though hardly a friend of hers. He had on occasion joined her siblings in tormenting her, though he probably thought nothing of it. What else, after all, were younger sisters for? She had not seen him above twice since her marriage, nor had she mourned the loss. Today he wore the pressed tan khaki kit of the Empire's administrative branch, complete with jodhpurs, belted jacket, and mosquito-netted pith helmet. He looked better in this gear than some, being tall enough to carry it off. His big, dusty boots soon brought him close enough to speak.

"Imagine meeting you here at the crack of dawn!" he exclaimed, beaming down at her. "And me just off the train. The Empire is indeed a small world."

"I take it you've been posted to Bhamjran." She lowered her voice in the hope that he would lower his. Only staff were about at this hour, but she had no desire to draw attention to herself.

"Lord, yes." He wiped his perspiring forehead on the back of his sleeve. "Beastly hot this time of year, but a fellow's got to take something if he's ambitious. Sorry about your husband, by the by. Went grouse hunting with him once. He was a cracking shot."

"Thank you," she said, wondering if it was too soon to excuse herself politely. She shouldn't have cared. She owed this man no special consideration, but all her old dutiful habits had descended upon her like a noisome cloud.

"Say," he continued jovially, "once I'm officially settled, why don't I take you to a party at headquarters? I've been appointed to the Viceroy's personal staff. I know that crowd might not be what you're used to, but I'm told they throw walloping good balls."

"I don't know what my schedule will be," Georgiana said, "but I do thank you for asking."

James's face fell to an extent that took her aback. "Suppose you heard then. Suppose your brothers couldn't resist writing you."

Georgiana's brothers hadn't written her in her life, nor were their wives much better correspondents. Not knowing how or whether to explain this, her hesitation gave her companion all the conversational room he required.

"It was only my first cousin," he said with a defensive flush. "And it's not as though *I* approved of him marrying a demon. Yes, she's pretty, and, yes, she's a prince's daughter, but what good is that when you're a damn demon?" James's thumb jabbed his impressive, brass-buttoned chest. "I was one of the people who tried to stop him, so I don't see why I should be snubbed for his stupidity—begging your pardon, Lady Ware, if that's not what you meant to do."

"Not at all," Georgiana denied faintly, mentally cursing herself and him. "I assure you, I pay no attention to rumors."

Evasive as this assurance was, it was enough to restore her companion to good spirits. He shook himself, smiled knowingly, and laid one finger beside his nose. "Not in Bhamjran, you don't. Any rumor you hear in this city has to stay."

"So I'm told. And now, if you'll excuse me, I really must return to my room. Please accept my best wishes for your new posting."

"I say, that's decent of you!" James returned. "I always told your brothers you were a damn fine girl. I'll send 'round that invitation as soon as I can."

She nodded at this and left without further civilities, her stomach heavy with her awareness that Phineas James would not be put off easily. God knew what he thought of her coming in at daybreak. Nothing, if she was lucky, since he'd never been the sharpest knife in the box. Thankfully, it seemed one night with the demon had not changed her looks enough to discern.

Even if it had, it would not matter. She was leaving her old life behind her, or why come to Bhamjran at all?

Wearily, she climbed the long ornamental flights of stairs to the second floor, hoping with all her heart that she would sleep through the day. Never mind she and Iyan had not parted amicably, she had another night to look forward to. She would find a way to coax him into a happier state. She wanted to see him relaxed again, wanted—she realized, her hand pausing in the act of opening the door—to see him flash a genuine smile.

The longing startled her a bit. She liked the demon. The differences between them might be great—too great, chances were—but she liked him better than anyone she'd met in years.

You're intrigued, she told herself, impatiently stepping inside her suite. *You're intrigued* because *he's different.* That wasn't the same as liking at all.

Shutting the door behind her, she gazed past the sitting room to her high, Ohramese-style bed. She shouldn't have come to this hotel, not if she really wanted to leave her old life. All her countrymen stayed here, many of whom were just as obliviously idiotic as Phineas James.

She frowned and folded her arms, feeling stubborn for more reasons than she could sort out.

"I *do* like him," she declared aloud. "I'd be lying to my own face if I pretended that wasn't true."

The words lightened her mood—though the why of that was equally mysterious.

Iyan had finally figured out why the countess had slept with him. He'd known her explanation had only been half the truth, and all afternoon he'd been bedeviled by thoughts of the rest—until the very persistence of his preoccupation should have shamed him into leaving off. Now that the puzzle pieces were in place, he was sorrier for the knowledge than he could express.

To feel this badly, he must like her more than he should. Worse, he could not think the less of her for her ploy.

She was planning to take a lover when she went home, and she likely had the lucky human all picked out. Her virginity had been the only barrier standing in her way, the evidence of a secret she felt duty-bound to keep.

Giving it to him, a man who would never have the chance to betray it, was a gambit worthy of a *daimyo*.

His sole regret—or so he told himself—was that he had been a less-than-perfect pawn. He was feeling . . . possessive toward the countess, because she had chosen him to be her first true lover. The reaction was irrational, unworthy of both him and her. He had signed no agreement to be her spouse. The favor she had done him was of a different order entirely. She had not been saving herself for him; she had been trusting him to introduce her to pleasure. He had

no business growing sentimental, and certainly no business entertaining the smallest thought of falling in love.

That was inconceivable. In every way.

He would expunge this error from his mind. Tonight, he would
be what a Yama should.

The children who had been sitting on the steps the previous evening
were there again, this time dangling a ball of yarn before a fascinated seal-brown cat. On spotting Georgiana, the girl leapt up and
drew breath to yell.

"Wait," said Georgiana, before her arrival could be announced.
"I'm quite early. I do not wish to disturb . . . Mr. Sawai just yet."

The girl closed her mouth and waited, her impassivity probably
copied from her employer. She could not have been more than
twelve, old enough to marry in some provinces of Southland, but
she was still clinging to tomboyish ways. Her hair looked as if it had
not been near a comb in days.

Georgiana posed her query nonetheless.

"I am wondering if you know where I might purchase clothes
like yours."

The girl quoted a sum of money, which Georgiana concluded
was the price of her assistance. Getting into the spirit of the girl's en-
terprise, she handed over the coins without remark.

She was then led around the corner to a small basement shop,
where she was outfitted in a beautiful set of *salwar kameez*, or
ladies' pyjama trousers and tunic. The ivory and crimson cotton,
which was nearly as soft as silk, was embroidered with a net of bees
and flowers in golden thread.

"Very pretty," the shopkeeper approved as she stood Georgiana
in front of a crackled mirror. "You should go to the alley of the
goldsmiths and buy some jewelry for your neck and wrists. Then
you would look a proper woman."

"Could I impose on you to recommend a jeweler?" Georgiana asked, sensing this was the hoped-for response.

The shopkeeper did so while Georgiana's escort snorted and rolled her eyes, clearly of the mind that no sensible female wanted to look "proper."

Ignoring the girl's continued noises of disapproval, Georgiana took her time at the goldsmith's stall. To her amusement, the girl deigned to accept a shiny clip to contain her hair—though whether she would wear it or simply dangle it before the cat, only she could say.

In any event, Georgiana was rather grandly accoutered when she returned—only a little early now—to Iyan's residence.

"Sawai!" the girl shouted up, her manners unimproved by their collaboration. "The foreign devil is here, and she bought new clothes!"

This time, the girl let Georgiana walk up alone. The pyjama trousers made the process much easier, the freedom of movement they permitted pleasing in the extreme.

I could happily dress like this every day, she thought as she knocked on Iyan's door.

Iyan's silver eyes widened slightly at her appearance. It was hard to tell, but she thought he approved. She lifted the string-tied brown paper bundle that contained her discarded gown.

"I'll change back before I return to the hotel, but I thought you'd prefer me in local garb."

He stood aside to let her in. "You look . . . pretty. That is Sita's grandmother's work."

"The little girl who guards your door? I thought I saw a family resemblance. And the goldsmith definitely shared the grandmother's nose."

"I hope Sita did not force you to buy these things."

"Not at all. I was grateful for her guidance. And they are lovely." She jangled the bracelets appreciatively. "I never would have found them on my own."

She had reached the lofty center of his bright, light room, happier to be there than she had any right to be. Smiling, she turned back to Iyan. "I am glad you didn't change your mind about tonight."

"You do me honor," he said formally, a needed reminder to rein in her elation. "Permit me to put your parcel somewhere safe. You must, of course, be able to change back."

Was it her imagination, or did his voice hold a hint of censure? And if it did, for what?

"Is something wrong?" she asked him when he returned.

His answer was smooth as cream. "What could be wrong? A beautiful woman has come to share this night with me, and she is wearing beautiful clothes." He wrapped his arms behind her waist, pulling gently upward until she was lifted onto her toes. Her sense of being in his power was pleasantly arousing. His mouth descended to her ear. "I look forward to peeling you down to nothing but your jewelry."

He kissed her then, a kiss of perfect thoroughness and skill—and not a scrap of passion as far as she could tell. Though she tried to enjoy it, she soon pushed back.

"What is the matter?" he asked. "Is there something else you wish me to do on our final night?"

She felt an emotion from him then: a flash of anger and maybe hurt. The impression was fleeting, but not, she thought, in her mind. Her awareness that something troubled him, even if she did not know what, encouraged her to answer honestly.

As carefully as if he were glass, she laid her hand along his sculpted cheek. His tiny jerk of reaction was the demon version of a flinch. When she did not pull away, but continued to touch him, he covered her hand with his.

His eyes held hers intently and waited.

"I was hoping—" she began. "I do not know if it is fair to ask, but I was hoping I could persuade you to be more like you were last night."

"More like I was?"

"Easy with me. There's no one I could tell, you know, even if I wished."

"Just as I could tell no one your secret?"

She had a feeling she didn't fully understand this question. "Would you want to tell it?"

"No." He released his breath on a silent sigh, letting some inner resistance go. "You want me to be easy with you."

"Don't all lovers want that?" She let her hand slide from his cheek to his shoulder. His robe was a pale new-bud green. "How can one relish pleasure when one is busy guarding one's back?"

"My people are used to guarding their backs. We have a saying: a Yama's life is three-quarters plot, one-quarter subterfuge."

"Yes, but you are a man and a quarter, Sawai, so *you* have extra room to do what you want."

He turned his head toward his windows, but not before she spied the reluctant curve of his smile.

"Come with me," he said. "I have a surprise for you. Hopefully, you will like it better than my kiss."

He might have been teasing, and besides which he took her hand. Distracted by the gentle hold, she did not protest that she had meant no offense.

They climbed out his windows onto a balcony where an iron ladder led to the roof. Someone had recently scrubbed it. Not a single streak of rust stained her hands or clothes. At the top of the ladder was a little garden with symmetrically trimmed palms in pots and a huge wooden soaking tub. This *haveli* was taller than its neighbors, and set on a hill besides. The view it commanded was spectacular. All of Bhamjran spread out around them, its countless minarets turning pink and gold in the setting sun.

It was, Georgiana thought, like a scene from a fairytale.

"This garden is yours?" she asked, seeing his touch in the neat arrangements.

"The whole building is mine. It was given to me by a merchant whose offers to join her harem I refused. She meant it as an insult."

Georgiana managed to close her mouth. "All insults should be this nice!"

Her response clearly pleased him. He relaxed back against the parapet, his eyes gone warm as they crinkled at the corners. "The mansion is supposed to have a curse on it. The family who built it went bankrupt, down to the last niece and nephew. The woman I refused tried to restore it, but only succeeded in half bankrupting herself. Her bad luck was my good fortune. I do not have the time or resources to bring it wholly back myself, but I have made portions of it habitable, and I have my privacy—which I value."

"And the other people who live here?"

"A retired carpenter, a woman who runs a curry stand in the bazaar, and the mother of the children you met out front. All pay me with the work of their hands."

"A practical arrangement." *And a kind one,* she thought to herself.

"It has been convenient. No one would have bought the place if I tried to sell it. Bhamjrishi take their curses seriously. We hope to have two more apartments finished by summer's end."

Georgiana found herself unexpectedly close to tears. Here was better charity than any she had distributed on her estate, for this was help that left its recipients' pride intact.

"How did a man like you come to be indentured?" she asked because it suddenly seemed so wrong. "I cannot imagine you making the sort of mistake that would cause you to lose your freedom."

She saw at once that this was not a question she should have asked. Though he strove to respond politely, it was a visible effort.

"I thank you for your faith in my good sense," he said, "and I know you do not mean to intrude, but this is a private matter. A *family* matter."

This nearly silenced her, but not quite. "May I ask at least, does what I have paid you bring you closer to being free?"

He flushed as she had only seen him do at climax. "Yes, a great deal. But I owe you an apology. I was angry because you were suggesting I made a habit of selling myself, and as a result I asked more than I thought anyone would pay."

Georgiana covered her mouth, abruptly seeing the humor. "How annoyed you must have been when I agreed!"

"No," he assured her. "Or maybe a little, but mostly because I wanted you very much. Once you accepted, I could not honorably change the rather dishonorable terms I had demanded—at least not without losing my chance for a night with you."

"Poor Iyan!" she exclaimed, going to him to kiss his cheek. "Caught in an impossible dilemma."

"You did say I was worth it," he reminded her.

She laughed outright, the sound so infectious he could only hide his own reaction by kissing her. This time she responded as warmly as he wished, both their bodies heating so quickly they were soon holding each other a trifle tighter than was comfortable.

"Tell me your name," he murmured against the velvet softness of her cheek. "I cannot keep calling you Countess."

"Georgiana," she murmured back, her mouth moving hungrily toward his again. "Please call me Georgiana."

He did not get a chance. The hot welcome of her kiss silenced everything but sighs. He could not bring himself to release her, though somehow he did manage to divest her of her new clothes. Divinity bless Bhamjrishi costumes. They were infinitely easier to take off than what she'd worn before.

When she wore nothing but her gold coin necklace and wrist bangles, he scooped her off her feet and carried her up the steps to his soaking tub. The water was the same warm temperature as the air. She hummed as he lowered her into it, her neck falling back with a sensuality he suspected was more natural to her than her preposterous Northern corsets. This was the real Georgiana, not the proper and nervous woman who'd propositioned him in that alley, and certainly not the woman who'd tolerated an impotent husband.

He was glad then, fiercely glad, that she had not claimed to love her spouse. At least he need not be jealous of a dead man. That would be too humiliating to admit even to himself.

"I've never been naked outdoors," she said, her hands dabbling in the water, her eyes drowsy with admiration as he slipped from his robe. "It's rather nice."

He sat naked on the wooden rim, preparing to spray himself with the prophylactic that had fascinated her the night before. He was hard enough already to wonder at himself. She truly did push him to his limits.

"Wait," she said and touched his thigh.

The simple brush of her fingers made his organ jump.

"I'm not trying to rush things," he explained. "I need to apply this when my skin is dry."

She smiled, the expression miraculously suited to her face. "I wouldn't mind if you were rushing, but there's something I'd like to do first, while there's nothing between us but skin. Tonight, you see, my pleasure is pleasing you."

SIX

Her words were a powerful aphrodisiac. His stomach tightened with anticipation as she shifted through the water to stand before him. His knees parted even more as her hands moved slowly up his thighs. She was savoring the feel of his muscles even as she drained them of strength.

"A Yamish sheath does not dull sensation," he felt obliged to remind her.

She smiled, bending close enough to purse her lips and blow softly across the head of his sex. His foreskin had drawn back, and nothing blocked the tickling stream of air. The throbbing beneath his crown increased.

Her gaze slanted upward to check his expression. "It doesn't dull sensation even a little? Perhaps enough to lessen the transfer of energy?"

Transferring some energy then and there, she took his shaft in the crook between her thumb and fingers and tipped it closer to her mouth. Iyan could scarcely breathe. The sight of her wetting her lips mesmerized him. He had discovered from kissing her that human tongues were wonderfully soft.

"Maybe enough for that," he said, his voice gone low and hoarse.

"Then you can just as easily dry off when I'm done with you."

But she did not take him in her mouth as her words presaged. Instead, her hands surrounded his scrotum, tugging and massaging at the same time. The sensations were so pleasurable, Iyan could not completely restrain his moan.

"You like this," Georgiana said. "I watched you do it to yourself at the Lotus."

Iyan gasped for air. "It is important foreplay for Yamish males. Relaxing us there makes it easier for us to ejaculate later on. You may have noticed that release can be a challenge for my kind."

"I did notice," she said, her sultry tone implying that the discovery had excited her quite a bit.

When faced with such approval for what was in truth an inconvenient trait, Iyan's barriers to abandonment could not stand. His head fell back as the fingertips of her warm hand found the perineal ridge behind his sac. She rubbed him back and forth here in slow, firm strokes, hard enough that he felt the pressure deep inside. His buttocks tightened in reaction.

"I think you like that, too," she said.

"Yes," he admitted, a ragged whisper all that came out.

"It is helpful for ejaculation?"

He was having trouble thinking clearly enough to answer. His thighs had lolled completely at her ministrations, and now his hips tipped up to give her more access. When she took it, he had to grip the sides of the tub to keep from toppling back.

"Yes," he said, one sentence away from babbling. "Yes . . . extremely helpful."

He had no warning. She simply dragged the wet, warm flat of

her tongue up the rigid underside of his shaft. With her hands still
performing their magic between his thighs, she sucked the head of
him into her mouth. He groaned as her tongue swirled around him,
not even trying to hold in the sound. Ripples of pleasure rolled
strongly up and through him, wreaking havoc on his most sensitive
male nerves.

A heart-stopping moment later, she let him pop free.

"Will you come in my mouth?" she asked huskily.

Despite her lovely flush of arousal, he wasn't certain how she
wished him to answer. The truth was what he let out. "It will be too
soon for me to achieve release for some while yet—though I might
want to enough to cry."

She looked from the shuddering tower of his erection up to his
eyes. "Enough to cry? For a Yama, I gather that's a great deal."

"A *very* great deal."

The grin she flashed then was broad. "I confess I might enjoy
driving you to that point."

"Well," he conceded to his own surprise, "I confess I might
enjoy being driven."

He knew he was in for a challenge then. She gave him the full
benefit of her mouth and hands, inspiring equal measures of agony
and bliss. Her skill was greater than he'd expected, though its
chiefest charms were enthusiasm and generosity. She liked his reactions; she positively reveled in wringing muffled cries from him.
Within minutes, she had discovered every sensitive spot he had.

"Oh, *God,*" he finally moaned, the human expression coming
easily. "Oh, please, more pressure."

She gave it to him with hands and mouth, sending his arousal—
and his pleasure—soaring to the evening's first stars. The effect was
at once utterly overwhelming and not nearly strong enough. He
was, indeed, ready to weep with frustration.

She seemed to sense this, her motions easing, her hands sliding
down his legs to soothe the knotted muscles of his calves.

It was too late. He could not calm.

"I need to be inside you," he said. "Now."

At his grating words, she released him and looked up. Her lips were swollen, her cheeks stained rose. Her eyes seemed pure flame-blue within their fringe of gold. Human or not, she was the most beautiful woman he had ever seen.

He could not speak again. His voice would have been in shreds. He reached for his discarded robe to roughly dry himself, his excitement painful as he hurriedly sprayed the prophylactic up and down his shaft. The sheath flowed along his length like a ghostly hand.

He knew she was watching.

He knew she saw him grow that inevitable fraction bigger when he felt himself protected.

Nothing could check him now but his own sense of fairness.

"Turn around," he said, unwilling to slide into the water until she did. "Grip the edge tight with your hands."

Last night he had asked her to face away for her sake. This night, it was for his. He needed to take her, to *claim* her, with an intensity that stirred a strangely delicious terror. Never before had he felt this craving. Unless she turned away, he wouldn't dare to let his body's instinctive responses loose—or maybe he would. Maybe he wouldn't be able to avoid betraying the depth of his desire.

Almost afraid to begin, he kissed a path across her water-beaded shoulders, then tucked himself around her back. Her curves delighted him. He had to caress them—her breasts, her belly, the lovely vulnerability between her thighs. He pressed closer, his cock beating out a mute complaint that it was not yet where it wished to be. Her bottom wriggled against it. She had arched her spine to invite entry. She was ready for whatever he meant to do.

"I thought you were impatient," she said on a gasping laugh.

"I am." His knees bent even as he said it. "Oh, God, I am."

He parted her with careful fingers, sucked a breath at the first light touch of straining body parts, and then allowed his cock to take what it most longed for. Heaven could not compare to pushing inside her heat, and he simply had to draw out the process. She cursed his slowness, which made him want to laugh. Fighting the urge, he wrapped one hand around one of hers on the wooden rim and played the other up and down her front.

Her nipples were hard as jewels beneath the silky water. When he plucked and rolled them, she was not the only one who shuddered down to her toes.

"You're so big," she whispered. "You weren't this big before. Just how much can you Yama grow?"

He nuzzled her neck and struggled to speak. Her sex was so warm, so tight, it was difficult to order himself to pull his hips back again. "The extent of our . . . expansion depends on how much encouragement we are given. Your oral prowess was most effective. But if you are uncomfortable with my size . . ."

"No!" she said quickly, gasping with relief as he thrust forward again. "I like when you're deep inside me. I like when you fill me up."

He grunted. There was no other word for the involuntary, pleasured sound. To make up for it, he said—with more determination than steadiness—"I shall demonstrate the Empress's Thousand Strokes. The practice is composed of three short thrusts followed by one long one. Most women like the rhythm, which saves them from becoming overly tender while providing a lengthy stimulation period."

The back of her head rolled against his shoulder. The gesture was so sensual, so trusting, it tightened his throat.

"Yes," she sighed. "Whatever you wish. Just be sure the long stroke is really long."

He did make sure. He made sure and made sure until she dropped her forehead between her hands and rolled it from side to side. He was tempted to do the same. It was quite insane to have offered to exhibit this discipline tonight. He lost track at three hundred strokes. Her moans distracted him, as did the way she pulsed and twitched around his moving cock. Was he at three-fifty now, or four hundred? Had he just given her three short strokes, or only two? When she began to pant from the extremity of her excitement, he gave up.

"I cannot count anymore," he confessed above the sloshing water.

"Iyan," she said, laughing. "Let go. Let go with me."

She pulled his hand to her, guiding his longest finger to her clitoris, and suddenly it was as if Divinity itself had given him permission to drop his internal reins. All his strokes were deep then, deep and hard and fast, until waves of unbelievable pleasure built in his groin. His scrotum tightened, his body on the verge. If she had not moved his hand on her, he would have forgotten, but his dim awareness that she was about to climax gave his arousal the final kick it required.

He came just as her energy flared, and instincts too powerful to fight had him thrusting as if his life depended on taking every inch of her. Water surged from the tub. His peak found another peak, and yet another even higher. When his eyes squeezed shut with bliss, something that was not sweat rolled down his cheek. He did not have sufficient breath to cry out. He simply rode the contractions of his release until he was thoroughly, totally, devastatingly emptied.

For a moment, he wasn't sure where or even who he was. He had one arm braced, shaking, on the tub, while the other supported Georgiana around the waist. Carefully, he let her go and pulled free of her body's hold. Part of him expected the sheath to have burst, but it was whole when he peeled it off.

Georgiana had turned with wide and starry eyes to watch him remove it. Apparently, even this interested her. He felt naked before her, as he never had onstage, as he never had in his life. She seemed to know he did not wish her to speak. She stepped to him and slid her arms around his neck. Her face was solemn, but there was something in her gaze, or perhaps behind it, which spoke of joy.

It was, oddly enough, a very Yamish expression.

A peace fell over him as he stared into her human eyes. The moment felt sacred, like an enchantment that must never, ever be broken.

"I feel as if we should do something special," she whispered, "as if I should let you drink from my energy."

Without thinking, he brought his hand to rest lightly on her heart. The etheric-fire that whirled here was a human's deepest well—and the easiest to draw from.

"That would change you too much," he said, though her energy lapped at him temptingly. "Thus far, I have not taken enough to show, but you wouldn't be able to hide the effects of that."

"Would it be dangerous for you?"

He hesitated, then shook his head. "The emperor's medical ministry recently identified the genetic marker for a predisposition to addiction to etheric-force. My parents were not carriers."

"I have no idea what that means, but I'll take your word for it."

"Why do you ask this, Georgiana?"

"I thought it would be a nice way to thank you."

"To thank me?" Amazed that she could think he required it, he cupped her face in his hands. "The pleasure you have given me is the equal to any in the world. I do not have the slightest need to be thanked."

He had embarrassed her. "Well," she said, her eyes cutting away, "it was just a thought."

The enchantment was broken then, whether he meant it to be or not.

Luckily, Georgiana did not have to brave the ladder to Iyan's window a second time. An ordinary stairway returned them to the fourth-floor corridor.

If her legs hadn't been shaking so badly, she would have kicked herself for suggesting Iyan feed from her energy. The wonder of their lovemaking had obliterated her good sense. She had pushed for too much, too soon. She had tried to force a bond where none was meant to grow. Or maybe it was meant. Maybe she was simply too stupid, or too human, to know the right way to ask.

Georgiana knew a little about being married. She knew next to nothing about courting men.

Iyan led her back into his apartment through its front door. He helped her dress like the night before, with silent efficiency. Unlike the night before, however, she no longer had a second night to count on.

When the back of her bodice was completely fastened, he smoothed his hands across her shoulder blades. Without inflection, he spoke.

"Will you be leaving Bhamjran soon?"

She turned to him, her pride helpless against her urge to search his uninformative Yamish eyes. He watched her steadily, but that was all.

"I shall stay a little longer," she said. "A week or two."

"There is much to see. Bhamjran is a beautiful city."

"Yes." She bit her lip and stared at her feet. Surely this was his opportunity to ask to see her again. "Will you—" *return to the Lotus?* she almost asked.

"Will I—?" he prompted, but it was no longer her concern.

"Nothing," she said, and shook her head at herself. This was no way to say good-bye. Praying for a bit of dignity, she took his right hand in both of hers, in the manner of close Ohramese friends. If he thought this too forward, that was too bad. He was a friend. She would consider him one all her life. "You have treated me well, Iyan Sawai. I shall never forget these last two nights."

She seemed to have struck him speechless. He bowed to her and let her go.

*   *   *

He gave her the bow of lovers, the bow, in fact, of a husband to a beloved wife, reserved for those occasions when the mutual respect between spouses exceeded the ability of other methods to express. The gesture came to him so automatically he was embarrassed when he straightened. The emotion was misplaced. He could see she had not the slightest concept how presumptuous he had been.

In truth, she looked somewhat mournful as she walked out.

Stymied, Iyan pressed his hands to his aching head.

She had given him a week or two.

This was not time enough to court her, and certainly not time enough to cause her to forget the human lover she was returning to. Never mind she had offered Iyan her etheric-force, had offered to let him mark her, essentially. Iyan had cultural disadvantages to overcome. Divinity help him, she was a countess and he was still indentured! Yes, his was a noble race and always worthy, but in his present circumstances, it was practically an insult to pursue her. In all modesty, he didn't see how he could do what he needed in less than a month—and that might be giving himself too much credit.

He was mad to be considering wooing her at all. For a thousand and one reasons, he was mad.

"Then so be it," he said to the empty hallway. He loved her. His body had known it before he did. By the sacred ice of his homeland, he wasn't letting her go.

All of which meant he had better plan his next move without wasting time.

seven

Twenty four hours had passed without a word from Iyan. Georgiana had tossed and turned in bed for a few of them, gazed out her hotel window for too many more, and revisited their time together in her head at least a thousand times.

Her conclusions varied. One minute she'd be certain she was not alone in her affections. The next she'd be convinced he was just polite. She wanted to be *doing* something, but everything she thought of struck her as wrong—either too presumptuous or too insulting. Iyan was proud. And reserved. If there was to be a next move, she had to leave it to him.

At least, she thought she did. For all she knew, Yamish females took the lead in these things.

Finally, she rang for the hotel's maid to help her dress in her last fresh gown. It was a sky-blue silk with thin white pinstripes and a small bustle. The color did lovely things for her eyes, and this was her first time wearing it. Despite its being the height of Ohramese fashion, the gown made her feel like a new woman, a woman who could lead an interesting life even if the man she had been rash enough to fall in love with never returned her feelings.

Realizing she was famished, and now girded to face the world, she went down to the Hotel Bhamjran's terrace restaurant. The day promised, as usual, to be ungodly hot, but the terrace caught the morning breeze, and the view of the avenue below was splendid. Georgiana loved watching the Bhamjrishi go about their business, loved the date palms and sunshine, loved the occasional elephant with the fancy *howdah* seat on its back. Most of all, she loved her sense that the city would continue playing out scenes like these long after its latest conquerors were gone.

Georgiana's country and its people were not the center of the universe. They were simply some of its more privileged residents.

The native waiter, who recognized her from previous visits, seated her in her favorite spot near the terrace's balustrade. The table was small and pretty, with a fringed umbrella of bright pink silk. Georgiana retrieved the fan that had been considerately left by her plate and used it to cool her face. Contentment settled over her unexpectedly. A solution would occur to her, for if any city was built to heal star-crossed lovers, it was Bhamjran. Her lips curved with amusement. Perhaps the breeze would whisper the way out.

To her disappointment, the solution to her dilemma was not what came to her attention next.

"Lady Ware!" cried the last voice she wished to hear. "What a spot of luck that I should find you. It must be Fate."

Struggling to contain a groan, Georgiana shaded her eyes with the fan and watched as Phineas James—apparently believing he needed no invitation—pulled out and occupied her table's second chair. His good-natured, toothy grin did nothing to alleviate her dismay.

"What do you think," he said, his hands flat on the white tablecloth, "but the Viceroy's hosting a dinner tomorrow night! Some minister or other is touring the colonies, and they're pulling out all the stops. Do say you'll come with me and wear something just as pretty as what you've got on."

She couldn't deny his offer possessed a certain puppyish charm. The warmth in his eyes, however, which conveyed more than simple admiration for her gown, warned her she had better not lead him on.

"Regrettably," she said as a camel brayed in the street, "I am unavailable."

"Oh. Well. But there will be other events. I predict we'll be quite the pair, you and I. I can't thank you enough, you know. Being seen with you will work wonders to repair my stock."

This was less flattering than his appreciation of her looks.

"I'm afraid it won't," said Georgiana.

James squinted at her in confusion. It was early, but he had already sweated through his collar. Georgiana realized she must have begun to acclimate to the heat; that, or her companion was more nervous, and more desperate, than he let on.

"Won't?" he repeated, one thumb pressing a thick eyebrow.

"Can't," said Georgiana.

"Are you . . . Do you have an understanding with someone? Because I'm sure he'd see that accompanying me would merely be a friendly gesture on your part: a favor to help out an old acquaintance, to tell everyone *you* don't disapprove of me."

"I don't disapprove of you," Georgiana said. "At any rate, I only think your flaws are human. But the plain fact is, I don't disapprove of what your cousin did, and were the topic to arise—which it might—I could not pretend otherwise. Presumably, your cousin was in love with that Yamish woman, and she with him. I think they were very brave to marry, and I would have been much more likely to accept your invitation had you supported them."

As she said this, she felt the calm one can only feel when one has expressed a deep inner truth.

By contrast, James looked thunderstruck. "You think I should have supported them?"

"Assuming you felt some fondness for your cousin, yes, I do. I imagine they're a bit lonely now."

"*They're* lonely!" James exclaimed, rising to his feet in consternation. "Half my friends have cut me dead. The rest are whispering behind my back. I thought you cared, Georgiana. I thought you wanted to help."

"If you forgave your cousin for embarrassing you, which I'm sure was not his intent, if you were strong and showed no fear, you might find you had friends again—friends who were worth keeping."

He jerked as if she had struck him. "You don't know what you're talking about, and I can only pray you never have the misfortune to find out."

Whereas I can only pray I do. She couldn't help smiling as he bowed stiffly and stalked away. She felt absolutely wonderful, as if she had flung off three layers of petticoats. She had spoken her mind. She had not been angry or rude or unkind; she had simply been honest. *This* was the woman she wished to be: still well-mannered, still polite, but no slave to anyone's standards but her own.

It seemed as if choirs of angels ought to be breaking into song among the rustling palms. Instead, a second angry male took the seat Phineas James had just left.

Angry or not, this male was welcome.

To her surprise, Iyan wore an Ohramese suit of cream-colored linen, complete with pointed shirt collar and contrasting brown waistcoat. He looked wonderful in Northern garb but, ironically, even more exotic than he had in a Bhamjrishi robe. He was too handsome to dress like her countrymen. His raven's-wing hair was too long for fashion; his broad-shouldered physique too ideal. His jaunty straw boater hat was the perfect incongruous crowning touch.

As if he did not care what picture he made, he slammed a small silk-wrapped bundle on the table. A slight clinking sound ensued.

"Open it," he said.

Bemused, Georgiana undid the pretty blue kerchief's knot. Within the flower-embroidered cloth was an ankle bracelet that dangled coins to match the necklace she'd bought near Iyan's house. The gold was so pure she couldn't resist stroking her fingers over it. It occurred to her that the woman who wore this anklet would be belled like a temple cat. The fact that this appealed to her should have made her more uneasy than it did.

Feeling Iyan waiting, she looked up. "This is for me?"

"No, it's for that idiot who just left."

His anger made her heart beat faster—and not at all with fear. "Iyan, your gift is beautiful, but I cannot accept it. You have far better things to save your money for."

His jaw ticked when he clenched his teeth. "It is a gift of intention. If you refuse it, you are refusing me. If you accept it, you are signaling your willingness to entertain my suit, to allow me to court you *exclusively*."

A flush swept her body as if the sun had jumped ahead to noon. Accepting a gift of intention sounded very much like an engagement. Her sex went liquid, which—in this public place—still had the power to embarrass her. It was a moment before she could speak, and in the meantime Iyan positively glared at her.

"You thought that man and I—Oh, no, Iyan. Phineas James is not courting me, nor would I accept him if he were. He is hoping that being seen with a countess will restore his reputation, but I told him I couldn't help."

Iyan's answer was a growl that lifted her neck hair in a ruffling wave. "If his reputation is that bad, how dare he insult you with his company?"

"To be fair," Georgiana said, visions of fisticuffs prompting her to explain, "the problem was not of Mr. James's making. His cousin married a Yama, a prince's daughter, I believe. I'm afraid humans can be judgmental about such things."

Whatever effect she hoped her words would have, it was not that Iyan would go as white as the tablecloth. He was breathing raggedly as well, his chest going up and down silently. With a visible effort, he forced himself to relax.

"He married a prince's daughter? A tall, black-haired *daimyo* with slanting eyes?"

"I have no idea. I did hear she was pretty. The papers may have printed daguerreotypes of the wedding. Do you think she's someone you know?"

"I think she is the same spoiled . . . young person whose family is responsible for my being here, the same young person whose supposed death I have agreed to compensate them for. I can understand why she wouldn't notify her family; they are a ruthless clan, but princes have diplomatic responsibilities. They keep abreast of the foreign press. If the wedding was described in your country's papers, her father *must* know she is alive. For that matter, the judge may be aware as well. Ach. I should not be surprised. *Daimyo* are all too apt to stick together in these things."

His expression was so outraged that, even though Georgiana didn't really follow what he'd said, she curled her glove over his forearm. Iyan seemed not to notice the soothing gesture. The muscles beneath his linen coat sleeve were tight as cords.

"I cannot be certain they covered the wedding," she said, "though it would have been awfully good gossip to pass up."

Another thought seemed to be unfolding in Iyan's mind. This one was not angry.

"I could have the second verdict overturned," he said. "I'm sure the family would agree, if only to keep me from making their daughter's marriage general knowledge in Narikerr. Most *daimyo* would rather die than admit a child of theirs wed a human."

Considering what she thought he'd been proposing a minute ago, this stung a bit. She did, however, understand the most important consequence of what he said. "You mean you'd be free? Oh, Iyan, what wonderful news! You could go home."

She thought he had not noticed her touch, but now his hands turned and surrounded hers. "Forgive me," he said, his eyes once more seeing her. "I was distracted from our conversation."

"With good reason, I would say!"

"You misunderstand this change in my fortunes." He drew a lengthy, lung-filling breath. "I want to remain in Bhamjran. I want to form my own *daumark*."

"I'm unfamiliar with that term," she said, wondering where this was going.

Again, he hesitated before answering. "*Daumark* is the Yamish word for family, but it also means business concern. A *daumark* comprises one family or many who pool their resources. I know a number of skilled but poor Bhamjrishi who would be happy to profit along with me. We would purchase old buildings and restore them, beginning with the one I already own. We would run them as hotels and boarding houses."

"Why does this sound like a confession?"

"Because it is not done. Traditionally, Yama do not accept foreigners into *daumarks*. They only hire them as employees. But I cannot pay yet, and my associates will strive harder if they have a stake. I am sure this is a business strategy that will work."

Though his manner remained defensive, Georgiana did not doubt he was right. "Sometimes, to grow and be happy, a person must do what no one expects."

"I am glad to hear you say that, because I very much wish you to serve as my primary partner. You are warm and reassuring in the way human workers need. I would value having someone I trust by my side."

Georgiana's eyebrows rose. He wanted her to be his partner? In a business concern? Though it was highly pleasant to hear him speak of trusting her, this particular proposal took her aback.

"I would want you to marry me, of course," he went on with stunning casualness. "I am aware that, from your standpoint, marrying me could be considered a loss of rank. I have no title to share with you and will never be an aristocrat. I do assure you, though, that I have no intention of achieving anything less than the summit of my chosen field. Whatever privileges success affords in a town like Bhamjran, you shall enjoy. Moreover, we will have papers drawn up so your money remains your own. I would not like you to think I wish to profit from this match."

Without warning, a smile began to rise from Georgiana's center. She had just noticed the hands that held hers were icy cold. Iyan was not as collected as he appeared.

"That sounds very sensible," she said, keeping her amusement to herself for now. "And while I'm sure you'll achieve all you say, you do not know if I possess the skills to be an asset to your *daumark*."

"I presume you ran your husband's home."

Georgiana lowered her lashes. "Perhaps I ran it badly."

"I do not believe it. In any case, you are intelligent. I can teach you what you need to know. Business belongs in the family."

"I see. *That* is why you want to marry me: for the sake of business."

"I did not say that! Out of respect I am attempting to convince you I am rational. We are of different races, and we have known each other less than a week!"

The slight raising of his voice delighted her. "I believe I value rationality less than you."

"Very well," he huffed on a sigh. "I wish to marry you for no better reason than because I love you. What's more, I very much hope you come to love me in return. If you do not believe that can happen, please tell me now."

Georgiana let her smile show. "Luckily for you, I have excellent management skills."

"I do not care," he clipped out. A second later he opened his mouth on a silent O. "You are saying 'yes.' You are saying you could love me back."

"I believe I am saying more than that."

"You are saying you *do* love me? You are saying you will accept my suit?"

When she grinned and nodded, he actually laughed. The sound was soft but wonderful and very much worth the wait. It changed his entire face, perfecting what had been *too* perfect before. He did not stop when the waiter approached, but jumped up, lifted the startled man off his feet, and spun him in a circle.

"I'm getting married!" he chortled as he set him down. "This beautiful woman is marrying me!"

"Congratulations?" the waiter said, looking from him to her. With the laissez-faire of a true Bhamjrishi, he appeared more surprised by the embrace than by their pairing. His countrymen liked to say "Love had its own reasons."

Despite his lack of censure, the reaction recalled Iyan to himself. He sat again and straightened his lapels. "Please return for our order in a little while."

"You might have hugged *me*," Georgiana teased after the waiter was gone. "I'm the one who said 'yes.' "

Iyan took her hand and pressed its knuckles to his smiling mouth. He appeared to be struggling to control the expression but finally gave up and grinned. "If I hugged you, I really would forget myself. I would have to lay you out on this table and kiss you until you blushed."

"Oh," she said, her cheeks heating every bit as much as if he had.

He watched this with interest as his grin smoothed away. All that remained of it was a subtle softness in his silver eyes. She liked knowing she had put that softness there—maybe as much as he liked knowing he had caused her blush.

"I must leave you," he said, "for a few days. Until I am certain my legal status is sorted out. Perhaps it sounds foolish, considering I declared my intentions before I knew, but I will feel better if I return to you a free man."

"I understand. I would want the same in your shoes."

He regarded her thoughtfully. "I think I am just beginning to discover how wise my heart has been."

Calmly though the words were spoken, coming from him they were every bit as romantic as she could wish.

EIGHT

Iyan's nerves had plenty of time to strain during the three long days it took to wrangle the Yamish courts into reversing the decision they now had to admit they never should have made. No stranger to their foot-dragging, Iyan was patient but determined, sending telegram after telegram from the humans' bustling office until at last the judge did what he must.

Had he been any less persistent, he probably would have had to handle the matter in person in Narikerr. His willfulness saved him the trip. Sadly, that willfulness had less power against his other anxieties.

He had asked the woman he loved to marry him. He had an idea for a business, but not the business itself. His mother was going to turn to ice and crack when she learned his bride was human. Fortunately, she was not the sort of mother who would put a contract on Georgiana's life, but his thirteen-year-old sister—bless her little rebel soul—would probably beg to move in with them. These seemed larger challenges than the newly affianced should face, even taking into account that one of them was Yamish and, thus, not prone to panic.

Yamish or not, when a note arrived from Georgiana on the third afternoon, his emotions whirled so chaotically at what it might contain that he had to sit down.

"Dear Iyan," it began, which—despite being the way many human letters opened—encouraged his pulse to slow. He touched the *dear* with his finger before reading on.

> *I have discovered that the district surrounding your* haveli *has no free school. Am investigating the possibility of funding one so that you may always have an educated pool of workers from which to draw. Will consult local parents and administrators before proceeding.*
>
> *I trust this finds you well.*
>
> > *Love,*
> > *Georgiana*

The *love* was even better than the *dear*, but its impact paled beside what had come before. His eyes felt hot as he set down the letter. She was already thinking like his partner, and maybe like something more. How had she known a school for children like Sita was one of his dearest dreams? He had mentioned the importance of families being able to support their offspring, but not that he hoped one day to do this.

Paper crinkled, and he realized he had again picked up the letter and was crumpling it against his heart. He smoothed it but was less alarmed by his behavior than he might have been. Loving her was changing him, and he found he had no regrets. Indeed, at that moment, his strongest desire was to share the news of his success with her.

Still enough of a Yama to want to avoid the emotional pitfalls of too much privacy, he asked her to meet him in her hotel's restaurant. He felt oddly shy to see her, but her beaming smile of welcome eased it away. She listened to his story with interest, exclaiming in all the places he'd known she would. Hers were not Yamish reactions, but he liked them all the same. When the tale was finished, he felt for the first time that he had truly shed his burdens.

He didn't know what they ate after that, except that it was spicy and he was starved. Georgiana fed him with her fingers from the common plate and, to his astonishment, this was enjoyable. No one stared at them. No one seemed to notice they were different. The most attention they received was a smile or two.

"I love Bhamjran," she sighed, leaning lazily back once the food was gone. "They look at us and all they see are lovers."

"Foreign devil lovers."

"Well, yes," she laughed, understanding he meant her to. "There is that. But we are lovers first and foreign devils second. And you, dear Sawai, are a beloved celebrity." She leaned toward him over the table. "I wager you are looking forward to informing your employer of your freedom."

He leaned toward her as well. "I believe I am."

She smoothed her thumbs down his young smile lines. "When we are married, once a day I want to see you like this, with happiness shining in your face. The rest of the time you may appear as somber as you wish."

"Only if you agree that once a day I may hear you laugh."

"That is too easy!" she exclaimed, laughing then and there.

"I hope it will be." His face fell quiet, though joy and hope warmed him from within.

"I'm not afraid," she said softly. "I wanted an adventure when I came here, and now I have so much more."

Her look reached into him, stirring responses that were not for anyone but her to see. He had to swallow before he spoke. "How far is your room?"

She bit her lip as she smiled. "Two flights of stairs and a corridor."

"I believe I can manage that—though these last few days without you were very long."

"Endless," she agreed, which effectively finished the job her look had begun.

Georgiana knew exactly why Iyan buttoned his coat as he rose. Her memory of just how aroused he could get was vivid. Distracted by her reaction, it was no wonder she didn't spot their unwelcome observer until it was too late.

Phineas James stood in the archway that connected the terrace restaurant to the hotel. Perhaps he had come to try his luck with her again. Perhaps he simply liked the food. Whatever the reason, they noticed each other at the same time.

Georgiana and Iyan had not been touching, but when James saw them, Iyan put his hand lightly on her arm. James's gaze had been cool already. It sharpened on seeing that—and more as he registered the signs of who and what her companion was.

"Lady Ware," James said, but the greeting was thin-lipped and not polite. His gaze raked Iyan up and down. "I must say, *this* explains a few things."

She had no chance to answer. Iyan moved between her and the other man. He was James's equal in height, but his muscles were leaner and, in his current garb, not obvious. Georgiana could see wheels turning in James's mind. He was deciding whether he could take his rival and, if so, whether it was worth a scene.

"Do you wish to clarify that remark?" Iyan asked in a tone so quiet it sounded mild. "You have a right to express your opinion, of course, but in fairness I should warn you that, as a demon, and possessed of more than human strength, it would be all too easy for me to crush you like a bug."

"Er," said James, his mental gears abruptly clunking the other way. Georgiana could hardly blame him. Iyan's absolute confidence intimidated all by itself. "No. Thank you. I'll . . . just give the Viceroy Lady Ware's regards."

He stepped aside then, enabling Iyan and Georgiana to pass into the lobby.

Iyan did not speak until they were beneath the tinkling shadow of the chandelier.

"Forgive me," he said. "That was childish, and I know I enjoyed it too much."

"I truly never intended to accompany him anywhere."

"I am gratified to hear it."

Georgiana glanced at his austere profile. "You wouldn't really have crushed him like a bug."

"No, no," he assured her, gently taking her elbow as they reached the grand stairway. "Most likely not. I am only . . . irritated that he is going to gossip about you—even if this is Bhamjran."

"Oh, that doesn't matter," Georgiana said.

Iyan stopped on the landing to gaze at her. "You really mean that?"

"Yes, I do." Then, because it was true, she grinned. She didn't care what James said or to whom he said it. She would take her own advice. To hell with what rank demanded. From now on, she would only have friends who were worth keeping.

Iyan looked away—overcome, she suspected, because a flush tinged the tops of his high cheekbones. Without meeting her gaze, he took her hand. His fingers warmed her through her gloves.

"Please walk faster if you are able," he said. "I am extremely eager to reach your rooms."

Considering what *extremely eager* meant to a Yama, Georgiana picked up her skirts.

He gasped another six steps up. "You are wearing your anklet."

"Yes," she said. "I haven't taken it off in three days. My petticoat muffled the jingling."

She was certain no eyes in history had ever burned like his, nor any man's breath come so labored. Ignoring the other guests coming down the stairs, he scooped her off her feet and carried her the rest of the way. Since he had a Yama's native speed, their pace was swift enough to draw second glances. He cursed in his own language as she worked the lock, then scarcely waited until the door was closed to fall upon her mouth. In truth, he forced the door shut by setting her down and thrusting her back against its hard surface.

The strength of his hips pinned her off the floor.

Georgiana clung to him eagerly. His kiss was hungry, his arousal a steel-hard ridge between her legs. He rocked it against her as if they could make love with their clothes still on. Because this was not true, he groaned impatiently.

"I love you," he said, releasing her mouth long enough to speak. "I need your hands on me. Take off your gloves."

She was happy to do so, but mere bare hands were not enough to satisfy him for long. Moments later, he yanked up her skirts, tugged down her drawers, and then fumbled with his own buttons.

"Iyan," she breathed at the awe-inspiring sight of him springing free.

He knew what he wanted. He pulled her hand to him, squeezing it hard around his throbbing girth. Her palm tingled strongly everywhere they touched. He must have felt it, too. The pulsing of the blood in his shaft increased.

"Divinity help me," he said, his voice actually shaking. "I want you naked, but I can't wait."

She found his mouth and kissed him hard, urging him to respond just as greedily.

"Don't wait," she murmured when he gasped for air. "Take me now."

"I'm going to pay for this," he muttered cryptically.

In spite of the warning, he hiked her hips higher. One long stroke was all it took to claim her. She was ready for him, hot and dripping wet. He moaned at the feel of her, holding as deep inside her as he could go. When her body tightened, his eyes flared black. They were face to face, their gazes locked. He seemed to realize this just as she did. Their hearts beat with matching wildness against their ribs.

This was what she had been craving the last three days—longer, to tell the truth. She had been wanting to watch his eyes as he took her ever since they met.

"All right?" he whispered, sparing just enough breath. "I could change position if you prefer the way we were before."

Rather than answer, she nipped his ear.

What happened then was like riding heat lightning. His blood was up in the most literal sense of the words. He growled as he had when he mistook James for her lover, the sound feral and primitive.

This, she sensed, was what all Yama were beneath their control.

Then his hips exploded into motion.

She came in heartbeats, but he did not slow. She came again, and he slid to his knees with her on his lap. His teeth worried her bodice and ripped a tear.

"I want to see your breasts," he rasped, gripping her hips to move her forcefully on his shaft. "I want to touch them. Pull this down."

She bared herself and sighed at his immediate sucking kiss. She had to help then, or he would have lost his rhythm; he was bent too awkwardly to thrust as strongly as before. His choked sounds of pleasure were worth the effort. Wanting more, she freed the buttons of his waistcoat and thrust her arms beneath his shirt. Energy tingled from her touch to the rippling muscles of his back. Loving the effect, she ran her hands up and down.

"Georgiana," he sighed. He tipped her back and pressed her into the floor. "I'm sorry. I can't slow down."

She didn't want him to. She wanted him to lose himself as she had. She dug her heels into the carpet, gripped his buttocks, and pushed up to meet his thrusts.

His face twisted, and for a moment she feared she was hurting him.

"No," he said, pulling her hips up when she would have stopped. "More. *More.*"

She knew where he was then. He had pursued his desires too quickly and now was longing to come but could not. His head fell back with his mouth agape, pulling breath after breath into his lungs. He changed the angle of his strokes, then again, seeking friction on the magic spot to trigger his release.

"Can I help?" she whispered as she squeezed the rounds of his bottom.

"You are," he groaned. "You are."

"Does it hurt?"

She couldn't help how aroused she sounded when she asked. His eyes flashed black again.

"It hurts like heaven," he said, his voice as dark as his eyes. "Like fucking heaven itself."

She came at his words, and he laughed in pain. He rolled without warning onto his back, neatly bringing her atop him. "You ride me, Georgiana. You take me home."

She took him. With kisses. With sighs. With love bites to his chest that made them both shudder. She stroked all the parts of him she had wanted to touch before: his shoulders and his neck, his upper arms, and his belly. Every part of him responded. He grew so hard and long, she had to be careful not to hurt them both, but every time she feared he couldn't stand more stimulation he urged her on, sometimes with no more than incoherent cries. Finally, she thought to reach behind herself to massage his now drawn-up balls.

His cry then was of sheer relief. His orgasm seized him as if it had been waiting only for this. He thrust up forcefully inside her, pouring out his release in long, hard spasms that tightened his spine like a bow.

He relaxed with a gasp beneath her, both their skins dripping sweat.

Georgiana smiled. "My goodness, if I'd known that was all it took to bring you to climax . . ."

He tried to speak, then sucked another ragged breath. "Hah," he managed. "If you'd known that was all it took, you wouldn't have changed a thing."

He was right, of course, and knew it better than she did. He was smiling as she snuggled down against him, but before she could relax, he rose and lifted her with him.

"No more clothes," he said. "And no more floor."

He stripped them both with more strength and coordination than she expected him to muster. She was half-asleep as he carried her to the bed, sighing with pleasure as their bodies settled naturally together. Her anklet jingled as she slung her leg over his.

"I'll wager you couldn't sleep these last nights without me," he said with a hint of purely male satisfaction.

She hummed in answer and gave in to her need to rest.

She woke to the feel of his fingertips drawing a gentle circle across her breasts. Sensation trailed behind his touch, as if he stirred some part of her that wasn't flesh. She knew at once what he was thinking of.

"I shouldn't have pushed you that night," she said. "I should have remembered it wouldn't be just energy you took from me, but emotion, too. I know you aren't comfortable with that."

He'd been watching his hand, but now his black lashes rose. His expression was calmer than she had ever seen it, somehow deepening her own sense of peace. "I wanted to do it. I wanted to bind us. I simply didn't want you to think I needed any more gifts than you'd given me."

"And tonight?"

He kissed her forehead, soft as thistledown. "Lie back," he said. "I'll show you what I want tonight."

*   *   *

Her aura was so bright she always glowed a bit to him, but now, as she lay back against the pillows, Iyan opened himself to see beyond the physical.

As he did, her energy field pulsed with color—aurora borealis in human form. The largest whorl was above her heart, sparkling green like an emerald. It turned slowly, grandly, its center funneling down to infinity. Yama were aware of each other's auras but could not draw from them as they could from humans'. Iyan held his hand above her sternum, unsure if the touch of fear he felt was his or hers. He had never done this before. He wasn't certain what to expect. Then he pressed his palm to her skin.

Her energy crept up his arm like thick, warm water. His pulse beat faster. His chest tightened. Georgiana touched his ribs with her hand.

"Are you all right?" she asked, her voice seeming at once to come from inside him and far away.

He felt her worry, but it was soft. He felt her love with a startling sense of recognition. It was very like the love he felt for her: tender and amused, curious and passionate. Amazement colored it, and gratitude. With all their seeming differences, who could have predicted that they, in all the world, would fit so well?

Whatever other Yama found in the act of feeding, it wasn't what Iyan wished. He took his hand away. He had seen all he needed.

Surprised, Georgiana's fair gold brows arched in inquiry.

"They were the same," he said, unconsciously forming a loose fist over his own heart. "Your emotions. I couldn't tell the difference between them and mine."

"Hmm," she said with a little smile. "So . . . nothing to be afraid of then."

"No." He smoothed her curls back from her face. "And you? You don't feel drained?"

"No. I don't think you drew much off. I'm not even sleepy, though you look more alert than you were."

She was dragging her fingers up the inside of his thigh, and he became aware that he was indeed energized. His skin was humming with unusual sensitivity, no doubt the aftereffect of what they'd just done. By the time her wandering fingertips reached the end of his sex, it was stiff.

Despite her claim that she wasn't tired, he knew he was the better candidate to exert himself. Far from minding, he eased her hand back and rolled his weight between her legs. His erection settled naturally into her softest folds, as if it knew her body was its home. Her squirm of welcome was as sweet as her sigh.

The northern-style bed rocked like a ship.

"Is this your pleasure, Countess?" he asked as he teased his swollen crown up and down. "To be taken yet again by your fiancé?"

"Oh, yes, Sawai," she said, her hands doing magic things to his spine. "Most definitely!"

THE
BREED NEXT DOOR

LORA LEIGH

PROLOGUE

 "You were created. Created to give your lives to the Genetics Council at any time deemed appropriate. You are animals. Nothing more. You have no sire. You have no bitch mother. You have only us. And we will decide if you are strong enough to live or die."

The dream was merciless, stark in the memory of who and what he was as he watched the scientist point out the procedure that had created him.

The genetic enhancement of an unknown sperm and ova. The fertilization, the development before it was ever placed within a human womb. And finally, the death of the vessels that had carried each Feline Breed babe to term.

Nothing was hidden from the immature creatures. They sat on the floor of their cells and watched the graphic video daily. They saw it nightly in their dreams.

"You are not human. No matter your appearance. You are an

animal. A creation. A tool. A tool for our use. Never imagine you will ever be anything different . . ."

Tarek tossed within the nightmare, years of blood and death passing by him. The lashes of the whip biting into his back, his chest. Hours of torture because he had not killed savagely enough or because he had shown mercy. The pain of knowing that the dream of freedom might be no more than a fantasy, quickly lost to death.

He came awake in a rush, the blood pounding through his veins, sweat dampening his flesh as the horrors he had fought so long to distance himself from returned.

Breathing roughly, he rose from the bed, pulling on a pair of boxer briefs before leaving the bedroom.

He inhaled deeply as he left the room, his brain automatically processing the scents of the house, sifting through them, searching for anomalies. There were none. His territory was uncorrupted, as secure now as it had been when he settled into his bed.

He rubbed his hand over the ache in his chest, the almost ever-present remembrance of that last beating, and the whip running with a current of electricity that sent agony resonating through his body.

He was created, not born.

Those words echoed through his mind as he opened the back door and stepped onto the porch. *Created to kill. Not human . . .*

He stared into the bleak emptiness of the late-fall Arkansas night as he let the memories wash over him. Fighting them only made it worse, only made the nightmares worse.

You will never know love. Animals do not love, so before you ever imagine this is a benefit due you, forget it!

The trainers had been quick to destroy any flicker of hope before it drew breath, took form, or hinted at an end to their tortured suffering. The psychological training had been brutal.

You are nothing. You are a four-legged beast walking on two. Never forget that . . .

Your ability to speak does not mean you have permission to do so . . .

He stared into the star-studded night.

God does not exist for you. God creates His children. He does not adopt animals . . .

The final destruction. A silent snarl curved his lips as he glared into the brilliance of a sky he had never been meant to see.

"Who does adopt us then?" he snarled to the God he had been taught had no time for him or for his kind. "Who does?"

one

Wasn't there some kind of law that said a man wasn't allowed to look that damned good? Especially the tight, hard bodies who persisted in mangling a perfectly good lawn at the wrong time of the year.

Lyra Mason was certain there had to be such a law. Especially when said male, Tarek Jordan, committed the unpardonable sin of whacking down her prized Irish roses.

"Are you crazy?" She ran out the front door, yelling at the top of her lungs, waving him away from the beautiful hedge that was finally managing to achieve reasonable height.

That was, before he attacked it with the weed-eater he was wielding like a sword.

"Stop it. Dammit. Those are my roses," she wailed as she sprinted across her front lawn, skidded around the front of her car, and nearly slipped and broke her neck on the strip of lush green grass in front of him.

At least he paused.

He lowered the weed-eater, tipped his dark glasses down that arrogant nose of his, and stared back at her as though she was the one committing some heinous act.

"Turn it off," she screamed, making a slicing motion across her throat. "Now. Turn it off."

Irritation and excitement simmered in her blood, heated her face, and left her trembling before him. He might be bigger than she was, but she had been maneuvering big, brawny men all her life. He would be child's play next to her brothers. Maybe.

He cut the motor, lifted a brow, and flashed all that bare, glorious muscle across his chest and shoulders. As though that was going to save him. She didn't think so.

The man had lived next door to her for almost six months and never failed to totally infuriate her at least once a week. And she wasn't even going to admit exactly how much she enjoyed razzing his ass every chance she got.

"Those are my roses!" She felt like crying as she rushed to the broken, ravaged branches of the four-foot-high hedge. "Do you have any idea how long it took me to get them to grow? Have you lost your mind? Why are you attacking my roses?"

He lifted one hand from the steel shaft of the weed-eater and scratched his chin thoughtfully.

"Roses, huh?"

Oh God, his voice had that husky little edge. Dark. Deep. The kind of voice a woman longed to hear in the darkness of the night. The voice that tempted her in dreams so damned sexual she flushed just thinking about them.

Damn him.

He tilted his head to the side, staring at her roses for long moments behind the lenses of his dark glasses.

"I can't believe you did this." She flicked him a disgusted glance as she hunched in front of the prize bush and began inspecting the damage. "You've lived here six months, Tarek. Surely it occurred to you that if I wanted them cut down I would have done it myself."

Some men just needed a leash. This was obviously one of them. But he was fun—even if he was unaware of it. It just wouldn't do for him to know how often she went out of her way to come down on him.

"Sorry, Lyra. I thought perhaps the job was too large for you. It looked like a mess to me."

She stared up at him in shocked surprise as he said the blasphemous words. Only a man would consider roses a mess. It was a damned good thing she liked that helpless male look he gave her each time he messed up.

She could only shake her head. How long did the man have to live beside her before he learned to leave her side of the yard alone? He needed a keeper. She considered volunteering for the job. "You should have to have a license to use one of those. I bet you would have failed the test if you did."

A grin quirked his lips. She loved that little crooked grin, almost shy, with just a hint of wickedness. It made her wet. And she didn't like that, either.

Her eyes narrowed as she ignored the chill in the early winter air, her lips thinning in true irritation this time.

He was obviously ignoring the chill. He didn't even have on a shirt. It was barely forty degrees, and he was using a weed-eater like it was June and the weeds were striking a campaign to take over. That or he just didn't like her roses.

"Look, just take your little power tool to the other side of your property. There are no neighbors there. No roses to mangle." She gave him a shooing motion with her hand. "Go on. You're grounded from this side of the yard. I don't want you here."

A frown edged between his golden-brown brows as they lowered ominously and his eyelids narrowed. What made men think that look actually worked on her? She almost laughed at the thought.

Fine, he was dangerous. He was getting ticked. He was bigger and stronger than she was. Who gave a damn?

"Don't you give me that look," she snorted in disgust. "You should know by now it doesn't work on me. It will only piss me off worse. Now go away."

He glanced around, appearing to measure some invisible line between where he was to his own house several yards away.

"I believe I'm on my own property," he informed her coolly.

"Oh, are you?" She stood carefully to her feet, staring over the edge of her pitifully cropped rose bush to where his feet were planted. Boy, he really should have known better than that. "Go read your deed, Einstein. I read mine. My roses are planted exactly six feet from the property line. From oak to oak." She point out the oak tree at the front of the street, then the one at the edge of the forest beyond. "Oak to oak. My brothers ran a line and marked it real carefully just for dumb little ol' me," she mocked him sweetly. "That puts you on my property. Get back on your own side."

She would have chuckled if it weren't so important to maintain the appearance of ire. If she was going to survive living next to a walking, talking advertisement for sex, then some boundaries would have to be established.

He cocked his hip, crossing his arms over his chest as the heavy weed-eater dangled from the harness that crossed over his back.

He was wearing boots. Scarred, well-worn leather boots. She noticed that instantly, just as she noticed the long, powerful legs above them. And a bulge . . . Nope, not going there.

"Your side of the property is as much a mess as your bush is," he grunted. "When do you cut your grass?"

"When it's time," she snapped, pulling herself to her full height of five feet, three and three-quarters inches. "And it's not time in the middle of winter when it's not even *growing*."

Okay, so she barely topped his chest. So what?

"I would get in the mood if I were you." He used that superior male tone that never failed to grate on her nerves. "I have a nice ride-on lawnmower. I could cut it for you."

Her eyes widened in horror. He was staring back at her now with a crooked grin, a hopeful look on his face. She sneaked a look around his shoulder, stared at his grass, then shuddered in dismay.

"No." She shook her head fervently. This could be getting out of hand. "No, thank you. You hacked at yours just fine. Leave mine alone."

"I beg your pardon." He threw his shoulders back and drew up in offended male pride as he propped his hands on his hips.

He did it so well, too. Every time he messed up something he pulled that arrogance crap on her. He should have known it wasn't going to work.

"And so you should," she retorted, propping her hands on her hips as she glared back at him. "You hacked your grass. Worse, you hacked it in the winter. There's no symmetry in the cut, and you set your blade too low. You'll be lucky to have grass come summer. You just killed it all."

He turned and stared back at his lawn. When he turned back to her, cool arrogance marked his features.

"The lawn is perfect."

He had to be kidding.

"Look," she breathed out roughly. "Just stick to mangling your own property, okay? Leave mine alone. Remember the line—oak to oak—and stay on your side of it."

He propped his hands on his hips again. The move drew her eyes back to the sweat-dampened perfection of that golden male chest.

It should be illegal.

"You are not being neighborly," he announced coolly, almost ruining her self-control and bringing a smile of pure fun to her lips. "I was told when I bought the house that everyone on this block was friendly, but you have been consistently rude. I believe I was lied to."

He sounded shocked. Actually, he was mocking her, and she really didn't like it. Well, maybe she did a little bit, but she wasn't going to let him know it.

She refused to allow her lips to twitch at the sight of the laughter in his gaze. He very rarely smiled, but sometimes, every now and then, she could make his eyes smile.

"That realtor would have told you the sun rose in the west and the moon was made of cheese if it would assure him a sale." She smiled mockingly. "He sold to me first, so he knew I wasn't nice. I guess he neglected to inform you of that fact."

Actually, she had gotten along quite well with the real estate agent. He was a very nice gentleman who had assured her that the homes on this block would only be sold to a specific type of person. So, evidently, he had lied to her, too, because the man standing across from her was not respectable, nor was he family-oriented. He was a sex god, and she was within a second of worshipping at his strong, male feet. She was so weak.

He was a rose assassin, she reminded herself firmly, and she was going to kick his ass if he attacked any more of her precious plants. Better yet, she would call her brothers and cry. Then they would kick his ass.

No, that wouldn't do, she hastily amended. They would run him off. That wasn't what she wanted at all.

"Perhaps I should discuss this with him." He tipped his glasses down his nose once again, staring at her over the rim. "At least he was right about the view."

His gaze roved over her from her heels to the tip of her head as his golden-brown eyes twinkled with laughter—at her expense, of course. As though she didn't know she was too homey. A little too normal-looking. She wasn't the sexy, siren type, and she had no desire to be. That didn't mean he had to make fun of her.

It was perfectly acceptable for her to toy with him. Having him turn the tables did not amuse her in the least.

"That was not amusing," she informed him coldly, wishing she could hide behind something now.

The ratty jeans she wore hung low on her hips, not because of fashion, but more because they were a bit too loose. The T-shirt she wore fit a bit better, but it was almost too snug. But she was cleaning house, not auditioning for Fashions R Us.

"I wasn't trying to be amusing." His grin was wicked, sensual. "I was being honest."

He was trying to get out of trouble. She knew that look for what it was. It wasn't the first time he had pulled it on her.

"I have three older brothers," she informed him coolly. "I know all the tricks, mister . . ."

"Jordan. Tarek Jordan," he reminded smoothly.

As though she didn't already know his name. She had known his name from the first day he had moved in to his house with the honkin' Harley he had ridden across her front lawn.

Damn, that Harley had really looked good, but he had looked even better sitting on it.

"Mister," she repeated, "you are not putting anything over on me, so don't think you are. Now keep your damned machines away from my property and away from me, or I might have to show you how they are used and hurt all that male pride you seem to have so much of." She shooed him again. "Go on. On your own property now. And leave my roses alone."

His eyes narrowed on her again. This time, his expression changed as well. It became . . . predatory. Not dangerous. Not threatening. But it wasn't a comfortable expression, either. It was an expression that assured her that an abundance of male testosterone was getting ready to kick in. And he did male testosterone really well. He got all snarky and snarly and downright ill-tempered as he glared at her, his voice edging into dangerously rough as he growled at her and attempted to berate her.

She refused to back down.

"Don't look at me like that, either. I told you. I have three brothers. You do not intimidate me."

His brow arched. Slowly.

"It was very nice to see you today, Lyra." He finally nodded cordially. "Perhaps next time, you won't be in such a bad mood."

"Yeah. Sometime when you're not mangling the looks of the block would be nice," she snorted as she turned away from him. "Geez, only I could get stuck with a neighbor with absolutely no landscaping grace. How the hell do I manage it?"

She stomped away, certain now that she should never have let her father talk her into this particular house.

"It's close to the family," she mocked, rolling her eyes. "The price is perfect," she mocked her eldest brother. "Yeah. Right. And the neighbors suck . . ."

Tarek watched her go, hearing her mocking little voice all the way to the porch as she stomped up the sidewalk. Finally, the front door slammed with an edge of violence that would have caused any other man to flinch. Breeds didn't flinch.

He glanced down at the weed-eater hanging from his shoulders and breathed in deeply before turning to glance back at the lawn.

The cut of the grass was fine, he assured himself, barely managing not to wince. Fine, it might not look so great, but he had fun cutting it. Hell, he even had fun using the weed-eater. At least, until Ms. Don't-Attack-My-Roses came storming out from her house.

As though he wasn't well aware that all the female fury was more feigned than true anger. He could smell her heat, her arousal, and her excitement. She wasn't hiding nearly as much as she thought she was.

He chuckled and glanced back at the two-story brick-and-glass home. It suited her. Nice and regal on the outside, but with depth. Lots and lots of depth. He could see it in her wide blue eyes, in the pouty softness of her lips.

LORA LEIGH

She was a wildcat, though. Well, she was as fiery as a wildcat anyway. He cleared his throat, scratched at his chest thoughtfully, then hefted the weed-eater off his shoulders and headed back to the little metal shed behind his own house.

He liked his house better, he told himself. The rough wood two-story with the wraparound porch was . . . comfortable. It was roomy and natural, with open rooms and a sense of freedom. There was something about the house that soothed him, that eased the nightmares that often haunted him.

He hadn't been looking for a home when he gave in to the real-tor's suggestion to check out the house. He had been looking for a rental, nothing more. But as they pulled into the driveway, the fresh scent of a summer rainfall still lingering in the air, blending with the smell of fresh-baked bread wafting from the neighboring house, he had known, in that moment, this was his.

This house, too large for him alone, the yard begging for shel-tering trees and bushes and the laughter of children echoing with it, called to him. Six months later, this home he hadn't known he wanted still soothed the rough edges of his soul.

He pulled open the door to the shed, pausing before stepping into the close confines of the little building to store the weed-eater. He was going to have to replace the shed with a larger one. Each time he stepped into the darkness, he felt as though it was closing in on him, trapping him. Caging him in.

There was something different, though. He paused as he stepped from it, staring back into the interior as he considered it thought-fully.

He hadn't smelled the usual mustiness of the building. For once, the smell of damp earth hadn't sent his stomach roiling with mem-ories. It was because his senses were still filled with the soft scent of coffee, fresh-baked bread, and a warm, sweet female.

Lyra Mason.

He turned and stared back at her house, rubbing at his chest, barely feeling the almost imperceptible scars that criss-crossed his flesh there.

Coffee and fresh-baked bread.

He had never eaten fresh-baked bread. He had only smelled it drifting from her house in the past months. It had taken him forever to figure out what that smell was. And coffee was, unfortunately, a weakness of his. And she had both.

He wondered if she could make better coffee than he did.

Hell, of course she could, he grunted as he turned away and stalked to his back door. Jerking it open, he stepped into the house, stopping to pull off his boots before padding across the smooth, cream-colored tiles.

The kitchen was made for someone other than him.

He still hadn't managed to figure out the stove. Thankfully, there was a microwave or he would have starved to death.

He moved to the coffeepot with every intention of fixing some before he paused and grimaced. He could still smell the scent of Lyra's coffee.

His lip lifted in a snarl as a growl rumbled from his throat. He wanted some of her coffee. It smelled much better than his. And he wanted some of that fresh-baked bread.

Not that she was likely to give him any. He had cut her precious bush, so she would, of course, have to punish him. This was the way the world worked. He had learned that at the labs from an early age.

Well, he had known it. The scars that marred his chest and back were proof that it was a lesson he had never really fully learned.

He propped his hands on his hips and glared at Lyra's house. He was a Lion Breed. A fully grown male trained to kill in a hundred different ways. His specialty was with the rifle. He could pick off a man a half-mile away with some of the weapons he had hidden in his bedroom.

He had excelled in his training, learned all the labs had to teach him, then fought daily to escape. His chance had finally come with the attacks mounted on the Breed labs seven years before.

Since then, he had been attempting to learn how to live in a world that still didn't fully trust the animal DNA that was a part of him.

Not that anyone in the little city of Fayetteville, Arkansas, knew who or what he was. Only those at Sanctuary, the main Breed compound, knew the truth about him. They were his family and his employers.

He dropped his arms from his chest and propped his hands on his hips.

He couldn't get the smell of that coffee or that bread out of his mind. That woman would drive him crazy—she was too sensual, too completely earthy. But the smell of that coffee . . . He sighed at the thought.

He shook his head, ignoring the feel of his overly long hair against his shoulders. It was time to cut it, but damned if he could find the time. The job he had been sent here to do was taking almost every waking moment. Except for the time he had taken to cut the grass.

And the time he was going to take now to see if he could repair the crime of cutting that dumb bush and getting a cup of Lyra's coffee.

A taste of the woman would come soon enough.

TWO

Bread lined the counter of Lyra's perfect, beautiful kitchen. Fresh white bread, banana nut bread, and her father's favorite cinnamon rolls. A fresh cup of coffee sat at her elbow, and a recipe book spread out on the table in front of her as she attempted to find the directions for the étouffée she wanted to try.

The cookbook was no more than several hundred pages, some handwritten, some typewritten, and others printed from the computer and bound haphazardly over the years. Her mother had started it, and now Lyra added her own recipes to it as well as using those already present.

The soft tunes of a new country band were playing on the stereo in the living room, and her foot was swaying in a cheerful rhythm along with the music.

"Do you actually like that music?"

A shocked squeak of fear erupted from her throat as she jumped from her chair, sending it flying against the wall as she nearly threw the coffee cup across the room.

And there he stood.

Her nemesis.

The man had to have been placed here just to torment and torture her. There was no other answer for it.

"What did you do?" She turned and jerked the chair from where it had fallen against the wall, snapping it back in place before turning and propping her hands on her hips.

He was here. And acting just a little bit too awkward to suit her. He had to have messed up something again.

He stood just inside the doorway, freshly showered and looking too damned roughly male for any woman's peace of mind. If he were conventionally good-looking, she could have ignored him. But he wasn't. His face was roughly hewn, with sharp angles, high cheekbones, and sensual, eatable lips.

A man shouldn't have eatable lips. It was too distracting to those women who didn't have a hope in hell of getting a taste.

"I didn't do anything." He ran his hand along the back of his neck, turning to look outside the door as though in confusion before returning his gaze to her. "I came to apologize."

He didn't look apologetic.

He looked like he wanted something.

He rubbed at his neck again, his hand moving beneath the fall of overly long, light-brown hair, the cut defining and emphasizing the harsh planes and angles of his face.

Of course he wanted something. All men did. And she doubted very seriously it had anything to do with her body. Which was really just too bad. She could think of a lot of things that tough male body of his would be good for.

Unfortunately, men like him—tough, buff, and bad—generally never looked her way.

"To apologize?" She caught the half-hidden, longing look he cast to the counter and the cooling bread there.

"Yes. To apologize." He nodded ever so slightly, his expression just a shade more calculating than she would have liked.

She firmed her lips, very damned well aware that he was not there to apologize. He was wasting her time, as well as his, by lying to her.

He wanted her bread. She could see it in his eyes.

"Fine." She shrugged dismissively. What else could she do. "Stay the hell away from my plants, and I'll forgive you. You can go now."

He shifted, drawing attention to his wide chest and the crisp white shirt he wore. He had changed clothes as well as showering. He wore form-hugging jeans with the white shirt tucked in neatly. A leather belt circled his lean hips, and the ever-present boots were on his feet, though these looked a little better than the previous pair.

His gaze drifted to the bread once again.

It figured. And the hungry, desperate gleam in his eyes was just about her undoing. Just about. She was not going to let him sweet-talk her out of it, she assured herself.

She stared back at him coolly as her hand clenched on the back of the chair. He was not going to eat her bread. That bread was gold where her father and brothers were concerned, and she desperately needed the points it would earn her. It was the only way she was going to get her pretty wooden shed built, and she knew it.

He glanced back at her, this time not even bothering to hide the cool calculation in his gaze.

"We could make a deal, you and I," he finally suggested, his voice firm, almost bargaining.

Uh-huh. She just bet they could.

"Really?" She let go of the chair and leaned against the counter as she watched him with a skeptical look. "How so?"

Oh boy, she just couldn't wait to hear this one. It was going to have to be good. She knew men, and she knew he had obviously been preparing the coming speech carefully.

But she was intrigued. Few men bothered to be straightforward or even partially honest when they wanted something. At least he wasn't pulling out the charm and pretending to be overcome with attraction for her to get what he wanted.

"However you wish," he finally stated firmly. "Tell me what I would have to do to get a loaf of that bread and a cup of coffee."

She stared back at him in shock.

She wasn't used to such straightforward, fully mercenary tactics from anyone. Let alone a man.

She watched him thoughtfully.

He wanted the bread; she wanted a shed. Okay, maybe they could trade. Not what she had expected, but she was willing to roll with the opportunity being presented.

"Can you use a hammer any better than you can a weed-eater?" She needed that shed.

His lips thinned. He glanced at the bread again with a faint expression of regret.

"I could lie to you and say yes." He tilted his head and offered her a tentative smile. "I'm very tempted to do so."

Great. He couldn't use a hammer, either.

She stared back at the muscular condition of his finely honed body. A man didn't look like that as a result of the gym. It was natural muscle and grace, not the heavy, packed-on appearance guys got from the gym. But if he couldn't cut his own lawn or swing a hammer, how the hell did he manage it?

She shook her head. Obviously nature really, really liked him, because Tarek Jordan was so not an outdoor sort of person.

"Let me guess. You're really good on the computer?" She sighed at the thought. Why did she attract the techies instead of the real men?

"Well, I am actually." He offered her a hopeful smile. "Does yours need work?"

At least he was honest—in some things. She guessed that deserved some compensation, though she fully admitted she was just too nice sometimes.

"Look, promise to keep your machines away from my property line, and I'll give you some coffee and a slice of bread," she offered.

"Just a slice?" His expression fell, rather like a child whose favorite treat had been jerked from his hands.

Men.

She looked over at the counter. Hell, she had baked too much anyway.

"Fine. A loaf."

"Of each kind?" Hope sprang in those golden eyes, and for a moment it made her wonder . . . No, of course he had eaten fresh-baked bread. Hadn't everyone? But there was a curious glimmer of vulnerability there. One she hadn't expected.

She glanced at the counter again. She had four loaves of each kind and plenty of the cinnamon rolls. It wasn't like she didn't have enough.

"Come on in." She turned to get an extra coffee cup when she stopped and stared at him in surprise.

He was taking his boots off? He did it naturally, toeing at the heels until the leather slid from his feet, and then pulling them off to sit them neatly at the door.

His socks were white. A pure, pretty white against the dark maroon of her ceramic tiles as he walked to the table.

He waited expectantly.

What the hell was he? An alien? No man she knew had white socks. And they sure as hell didn't care if they took their shoes off at the door, no matter how grimy or muddy they often were. Her brothers were the worst.

She poured the coffee and set it in front of him before turning to get the sugar and creamer from the counter. As she turned back, she frowned as she watched him take a long sip of the dark liquid.

Ecstasy transformed his face.

The expression on his face made her thighs clench as her sex spasmed in interest. Which only pissed her off. She was not going to get any more turned on by this man than she already was. She was doing perfectly fine without a man in her life right now. She did not, repeat, *did not* need the complication.

But if that was how the man looked when he had sex, then her virginity could be in serious danger. Strangely predatory, savage, filled with pleasure, his face carried a primal, intense look of satisfaction and growing hunger.

For a moment, her chest tightened in surprising disappointment. She wanted him to look at her like that, not at her bread.

Just her luck. Someone else to harass her for her bread instead of for her body. Not that she wanted him to harass her for her body, but it would be nice if someone would.

Taking out a bread knife, she sliced into a loaf of the banana nut bread and then into the white bread. The white bread was still warm enough to melt the fresh, creamy butter she spread atop it.

Fine. Maybe she could bribe him into hiring someone to cut and trim his lawn so he would leave hers alone. Stranger things had happened.

The coffee was rich, dark, and exquisite. The bread fairly melted in his mouth. But that wasn't what was keeping his dick painfully engorged as he savored the treats. It was the smell of this woman, hot and sweet and aroused.

That arousal was killing him. It wasn't intense and overwhelming, but curious and warm. Almost tentative. He savored the smell of it more than he savored the bread and coffee he was trying to stay focused on.

"So what do you do on the computer?" She was cleaning the

loaf pans she had used to bake the bread, carefully washing and drying them at the sink.

He glanced at the slender line of her back, the taut curves of her rear, and shifted restlessly in his chair. His hard-on was killing him.

He hadn't meant to give her the impression he worked mainly on the computer, but he guessed it was better than telling the truth.

"Mostly investigations and research." He shrugged, telling as much of the truth as possible. He hated the thought of lying to her. Which was strange. He was living a lie, and he knew it. He had been since his creation. So why should it bother him now?

"Criminal or financial?" She picked up the coffeepot and walked to the table, filling his cup with the last of the heated liquid.

He frowned at the question as he watched the way the soft, midnight silk of her hair fell forward, tempting his fingers. It looked soft, warm. Like everything he had believed a woman should be.

She wasn't hard, trained to kill, or living her own nightmares, as many of the Feline Breed women were. She was feisty and independent but also soft, exquisite.

"More along the lines of missing persons," he finally answered. "A little bit of everything, though."

He nearly choked on that one. He was, quite simply, a bounty hunter and an assassin. His present assignment was the search for one of the escaped Trainers who had murdered countless Feline Breeds while they were held in captivity.

The assignment was starting to take second place to the woman in front of him, though.

Damn that coffee was good, but if she didn't get the scent of that soft, heated warmth simmering in her pussy across the room and away from him, then they were going to have problems.

He could feel the growing sexual need tightening his abdomen and pounding in his brain. He wanted to shake his head, push the scent away from him in an attempt to make sense of it. He had never known a reaction so intense, so immediate to any woman.

From his first glimpse of her outraged expression when he committed the supreme sin of riding his Harley over her lawn, she had captivated him.

She wasn't frightened of him or intimidated by him. She didn't watch him like a piece of meat or an animal that could attack at any moment. She watched him with equal parts frustration, innocence, and hunger.

And if he didn't get the hell away from her, he was going to commit another sin. He was going to show her just how damned bad he did want that curvy little body of hers.

"I guess I should be going." He rose to his feet quickly, finishing off his coffee before taking the cup and his empty saucer to the sink where she was working.

She stared up at him in astonishment as he rinsed them quickly before sitting them in the warm, sudsy water in front of her.

He stared down at her, caught for a moment in the depths of her incredible sapphire eyes. They gleamed. Little pinpoints of brilliant light seemed to fill the dark color, like stars on a blue velvet background. Incredible.

"Thank you." He finally forced the words past his lips. "For the coffee and the bread."

She swallowed tightly. The scent of her wrapped around him—a nervous, uncertain smell of arousal that had his chest filling with a sudden, animalistic growl.

He throttled the sound firmly, clenching his teeth as he backed away from her.

"You're welcome." She cleared her throat after the words came out with a husky, sexy tone of nervousness.

Dammit, he didn't have time for such complications. He had a job to do. One that didn't include a woman he knew would run screaming from him if she had any idea of who and what he was.

She had wrapped the loaves and set them out on the counter by the door for him. He jerked his boots on quickly and picked up the bread, opening the door before turning back to her.

"If you need any help." He shrugged fatalistically. "If there's anything I can do for you . . ." He let the words trail off.

What could he do for her besides complicate her life and make her regret ever meeting him? There was little.

"Just stay away from my yard with your gadgets." Her eyes glowed with humor. "At least until you learn how to use them."

The woman evidently had no respect for a man's pride. A grin tilted his lips.

"I promise."

He turned and left the house, regretfully, hating it. There was a warmth within the walls of her home that didn't exist within his own, and it left him feeling unaccountably saddened to leave. What was it about her, about her house, that his suddenly seemed so lacking?

He shook his head, pushed his free hand into his jeans pocket, and made his way across her neatly trimmed backyard to his own less-than-pristine lawn. And his less-than-content life.

THree

A cold winter rain fell, not quite ice, but close enough to chill Tarek's flesh as he stood in the shadows of his porch late that night.

He wasn't certain what had awakened him. But something had. He had come instantly alert, his senses rioting, the tiny, almost imperceptible hairs raising along his body as he slid from the bed and dressed quietly.

Now he stood within the concealing darkness, staring around the backyard, his eyes probing the night as his unique vision aided him in seeing through the moonless night.

In his hand he carried a powerful ultralight submachine pistol. It rested at the side of his leg as his opposite thigh held the weight of the lethal knife tucked securely in the scabbard he had strapped there.

The hairs along the back of his neck prickled, warning him that he wasn't alone in the darkness. His eyes scanned his yard and then turned to Lyra's.

Her upstairs lights were on; every few minutes he could see her pace past her bedroom window. She needed heavier curtains. Something hardened in his chest, became heavy at the thought that whatever stalked the darkness could be a threat to her.

His jaw tightened as he lifted his head, drawing in the scents surrounding him, and quickly, automatically separating them.

Something was out there; he knew it, and he should be able to smell it. It made no sense that the answers he sought weren't on the air around him.

He could smell the scent of Lyra's brothers. They had shown up that evening, carrying bread when they left. Damn their hides. He had considered mugging them for one insane minute.

He could smell the lumber they brought, sitting in her backyard, and the smell of charcoal on the air from the steaks they had grilled for dinner. But there was no scent of an intruder.

He flexed his shoulders, knowing the rain could be distilling the smell, knowing he was going to have to venture into it and hating the thought.

He moved silently from the porch, careful to stay in the shadow of the small trees he had taken the time to have planted before he moved in. Most were firs of some type, evergreens that never lost their concealing foliage. They were spaced at just the right distance to provide the concealment he needed as he made his way along the perimeters of his property.

There.

He stopped at the far corner, lifting his head to breathe in roughly, feeling the rain against his face, the ice forming in the sodden length of his hair. But there was the scent he was searching for, and it was on Lyra's property.

He turned his head, and his eyes narrowed, searching for movement that wasn't there, yet the scent of it was nearly overpowering.

Where are you, bastard? he growled silently as he made his way to the stack of lumber, using it to conceal himself from the back of the house, allowing him a clear view of her back porch as he thumbed the safety off on the powerful weapon he carried.

Icy rain ran in rivulets down his hair, his arms, soaking the flannel shirt and jeans he wore. He pushed the chill and the feel of wet fabric out of his mind. He had trained in worse conditions than this for years.

He breathed in again, sifting through the scents until he could determine where this one was coming from. The wind was blowing in from the west, moving across the house and through the small valley the housing development was situated in.

The scent was definitely at the back of the house. It was too clear, too thick with menace to have been diluted by the shrubbery in the front yard.

The moonless night left the yard nearly pitch-black, but the DNA that made him an abomination also made him capable of seeing much more clearly than the enemy stalking the night with him.

It wasn't a Breed. He could smell a Breed a mile away. But neither was it a harmless threat. He could feel the menace in the air, growing thicker by the moment.

Moving from the concealment of the stack of lumber, he edged his way closer to the house. Even more important than locating the threat was keeping Lyra in the house and safe. She was so damned feisty, if she even thought anyone was in her backyard she would be out there demanding answers and ignoring the danger.

He moved around the little wooden arch that held the bench swing, carefully sidestepped the beginnings of a flowerbed he had seen her working in days before, and slid along the fence that separated her property from her neighbor on the other side.

He could feel the intruder. The itch along the back of his neck was growing more insistent by the moment. He paused, bending low beside an evergreen bush as he scanned the area again.

And there he was. Crouched at the side of the house and working his way to the porch. Dressed entirely in black, the bastard might have escaped notice if Tarek hadn't caught the movement of the whites of his eyes.

He was good.

Tarek watched as he made his way to the electrical box at the side of the house. Too damned good. Tarek watched as a penlight focused a minute sliver of light as the intruder worked.

When he was finished, Tarek bet his incisors the security system had somehow been canceled. The lights were still on, and not even a flicker of power had been interrupted. But there was an edge of satisfaction in the way the black-clad figure now made his way to the back door.

It wasn't happening.

Tarek moved quickly, raising his gun, aiming, only to curse virulently as the figure turned, jerked, and raised his own weapon.

Tarek rolled as he heard the whistle of the silenced weapon. Expecting, foolishly perhaps, for the assailant to turn and run, he came to his knees, aiming again, only to be slammed back to the wet grass as the gun was kicked from his hand.

He rolled to the side and jumped to his feet. His leg flew out to connect with a jaw, and he heard the grunt of pain as the other man went backward, flailing for balance.

Tarek whipped his knife from its sheath, prepared now as the other man came at him. He kicked the gun from his hand, turned, and delivered a power kick to his solar plexus, snarling as he flipped around to see the bastard coming for him again, armed with a knife as well.

At the same time, the back porch light flared, blinding him for one precious second as the assailant made his move. Pain seared his shoulder as the knife found its mark before he could jump back.

A gunshot blasted through the night. The sound of the powerful shotgun made both men pause, breathing roughly before the assailant turned and ran.

"Like hell," Tarek snarled as he rushed after him, his feet sliding in the muck beneath his feet before he found traction and sprinted behind him.

He almost had him, dammit. He was within inches of throwing himself against the other man and bringing him down when another silent shot whistled past his head, causing him to duck and throw himself to the side instead.

The sound of a vehicle roaring down the street shattered the night. Tires screamed as the car slammed to a stop, voices raised demandingly, then it peeled from the front of the house as Tarek raced to get a glimpse of it.

"Fuck! Fuck!" His curse filled the night as the black sedan, no plates of course, roared away.

The assailant was well trained and obviously came with backup. The suspicion that it was the Trainer he was searching for filled his mind. But why go after Lyra? The man was smart enough, well trained enough that he could never have mistaken which house to attack.

On the heels of that suspicion came the knowledge that he, the hunter, could very well become the hunted. And it looked as though Lyra had been drawn into the middle of the war playing out between the Council and their now-free creations.

"The police are on their way," Lyra screamed from the back door. "Tarek, are you okay?"

At least she was still in the house.

A growl vibrated through his chest as he turned and ran back to the yard, locating the knife and illegal machine gun from the now-muddy yard.

The back door was open, and there she stood, dressed in a long gown and matching robe, holding that fucking shotgun like it could protect her.

He snapped his teeth together as he heard the sirens roaring in the distance and stomped to the house.

"Do not mention me, do you understand?" he ordered as he

stopped in front of her, staring into her wide, shocked eyes as she blinked up at him.

"Do you understand me, Lyra?" he hissed impatiently. "Do not mention me. After they leave, I'll come back. Do you understand?"

He reached out to grip her arm, pulling back at the sight of the blood trickling to his hand. Fuck, his shoulder burned.

"You're hurt." She swallowed tightly.

The sirens were getting closer.

"Lyra." He bent close, breathing in her scent, her fear. "Did you hear me?"

"Yes. Why?" Her breasts were rising and falling roughly, her pale features emphasizing her large, dark eyes.

"I'll explain later. I promise." He grimaced painfully. "As soon as they leave, I'll be back. I swear, Lyra. But don't tell them what happened."

His cover was shot to hell if she even hinted at him. The police would converge on his house, and he would be forced to tell them exactly who he was. Good-bye assignment, good-bye Trainer.

She nodded slowly, glancing back into the house as the sound of the sirens echoed around them.

He nodded fiercely before turning and disappearing into the night. The cut to his shoulder wasn't life-threatening, but it was deep. He was going to have to take care of that first.

He disappeared into his house as the police units whipped onto the street and skidded to a stop outside Lyra's house. He locked the door quickly, taking precious seconds to pull off his boots before moving through the dark house.

What the hell was going on?

He stripped off his clothes in the laundry room, dropping the cold, soggy clothing into the washer before taking a clean towel from the cabinet and wrapping it around his arm. Damned blood was going to stain everything.

He strode quickly upstairs, moving through his bedroom to the bathroom where he could take care of the wound to his shoulder.

As he cleaned and carefully stitched the wound, he sifted through the earlier events, trying to make sense of them.

Why had someone attempted to break in to Lyra's house when it was clear she was home? Burglars waited until their victims were in bed, most likely asleep, or gone. They didn't break in while lights blazed through the house, and they sure as hell didn't hang around after they were clearly caught.

And they weren't as well trained as Lyra's burglar had obviously been. That wasn't an attempted robbery. It was a hit. Why would anyone want to kill Lyra, unless it was to get to him? A warning? And if it was that damned Trainer, how the hell had he learned Tarek was tracking him?

He smeared gauze with a powerful antiseptic before laying it over the stitched wound and taping it securely in place.

Then he dressed and waited. He stood at his bedroom window, watching, waiting, as the police talked to Lyra, wondering how well she would heed his earlier warning. Praying she would. Knowing it might be better for both of them if she didn't.

four

He was a Breed.

Lyra answered the questions the police asked, filled out and signed a report, and waited impatiently for them to leave.

Thank God she hadn't called her brothers before jerking that shotgun up and racing to the back door. She hadn't even thought of it. She had watched through her bedroom window as the moon broke past a cloud, shining clearly on the figures struggling in her backyard. She had recognized Tarek immediately.

Tarek Jordan was a Breed.

She had seen it in the fierce glow of his amber eyes as the light had shined into them, in the overly long incisors when he had snarled his furious orders on the back porch.

It made sense.

She should have suspected it from the beginning.

He had lived in the house beside her for months. His obvious discomfort in doing things most people did every day of their lives should have clued her in. The haunted shadows in his eyes.

His inability to cut grass should have told her something immediately. All men knew at least the rudiments of cutting grass.

The joy he found in a freshly made cup of coffee and homemade bread. As though he had never known it.

She had thought him a computer geek. That wasn't a computer geek fighting in her backyard. That had reminded her of her brothers, practicing the tae kwon do they had learned in the military. He had reminded her of an animal, snarling, his growl echoing through the yard as he fought with the attempted burglar.

She should have known.

She had followed every news story, every report of the Breeds, just as her brothers had joined in several of the missions years before to rescue them. They had told her the tales of the ragged, savage men and women they had transferred from the labs to the Feline Breed home base, Sanctuary.

Men near death, tortured, scarred, but with the eyes of killers. Men who were slowly being fashioned into animals—killing machines and nothing more.

"There's nothing else we can do, Ms. Mason," the officer taking her statement announced as she signed the appropriate line. "We've called your security company, and they'll be out here tomorrow to repair the system."

"Thank you, Officer Roberts." She smiled politely as she handed the papers back to him, wishing they would just leave.

"We'll be going now." He nodded respectfully.

It was about time.

She escorted them to the door, closing and locking it before pushing her feet into a pair of sneakers and waiting impatiently for them to pull from the drive.

The minute their taillights headed down the street, she grabbed

THE BREED NEXT DOOR

her keys, threw open the door, and slipped onto the porch. Closing it quickly, she sprinted through the rain toward Tarek's.

She wanted answers *now*. Not whenever he decided to show.

A frightened scream tore from her lips as she passed one of the thick evergreen trees in his yard and was caught from behind as another hand clamped over her mouth.

A hard arm wrapped around her waist, heated, muscular, nearly picking her from her feet as he began to move quickly to the house.

"How did I know you would do something so stupid?" His voice was a hard, dangerous growl in her ear as he pushed her through the living room door and slammed it shut. "I told you to stay put, Lyra."

He released her quickly, throwing the bolts closed on the door before punching in the code to the security pad beside it.

"You were too slow," she snapped. "What the hell was going on tonight?"

She turned on him fiercely, with every intention of blasting him over the previous hours' events. Her eyes widened, though, as she caught sight of his pale face and the bloodstained bandage.

"Are you okay?" She reached out, her fingers touching the hard, sun-bronzed flesh just beneath the bandage.

"I'll live," he grunted. "And stop trying to distract me. I told you to stay put."

His eyes glittered a menacing gold in the dim light of the heavily curtained living room.

"I don't obey orders so well." She licked her dry lips nervously. "And I was tired of waiting."

"The police had barely left, Lyra." He pushed his fingers through his damp hair with rough impatience. "I was on my way."

His voice gentled, though not by much as he stared down at her. For a moment, his expression softened and then turned fierce once again.

"You would drive a grown man to drink," he finally growled before turning to stalk through the house. "Come on, I need coffee."

"Do you know how to fix it?" She followed him quickly, the question falling from her lips before she could stop it.

"Hell no. But I'm fucking desperate," he snarled impatiently, his voice rough.

"Then don't touch that coffeepot, because I want some, too."

She moved quickly in front of him before coming to a dead stop in the middle of the immaculate kitchen.

"Fine, go for it." He moved past her to the door where the tiles shone damply, the smell of disinfectant heavy in the air.

"What are you doing?" She was almost afraid to touch anything. It was almost sterile-clean.

"Blood." He grunted. "I don't want it staining the tiles."

He knelt on the floor, a heavy towel in his hands as he mopped at the puddle of cleaner he had poured on the floor.

Her brothers, bless their hearts, would have waited for her to try to clean it. She doubted they cleaned anything besides their weapons, at any time. The slobs.

"Do you ever cook in this kitchen?" she questioned him nervously as she moved to the cabinet and the coffeemaker sitting there.

"I'd need to know how to first," he grunted, working at the floor with single-minded intensity. "I'll figure it out eventually."

She searched the cabinets until she found the bag of pre-ground coffee and two mugs.

The term *bare cupboards* definitely applied to this man.

"What do you eat?" The silence was stifling as he rose to his feet to watch her measure the coffee into a filter with narrowed eyes.

"I eat," he finally growled as he moved through the kitchen into a short hall.

Seconds later she heard water running in the sink and then a heavier flow, as though into a washer.

He moved back into the kitchen a minute later as she was checking the refrigerator.

Cheese. Baloney. Ham. Yuck.

"Not all of us are gourmets," he grunted, moving to the cabinet over the stove and pulling down the bread she had given him that afternoon.

There was no sign of the cinnamon rolls. Half a loaf of white bread was left and perhaps a third of the banana nut bread.

She checked the freezer and then sighed. He had to be starving. A body that big took energy.

"What happened tonight?" she asked as she moved back to the coffeemaker and poured two mugs of the dark brew.

"Someone tried to break in to your house, and I caught him." He shrugged, his voice cool as he took his mug from her.

"Yeah." She believed that one. "Fine. I'll just go home then and call my daddy and my three ex–Special Forces brothers and let them know what happened. Shouldn't hurt, if that was all it was."

He paused, his gaze slicing back to her for a long moment before he lowered the mug.

She didn't think anything could take his mind off that coffee.

"Ex–SF, huh?" He breathed out roughly, shaking his head with weary acceptance.

"Yes, they are." She nodded mockingly. "They retired about five years ago. They were even part of the Breed rescues that took place just after the main Pride announced their existence."

His expression stilled and grew cold and distant.

"I know you're a Breed, Tarek." She wasn't playing games with him. She hated it when they were played with her. "Tell me what's going on."

He grimaced tightly before picking up his mug and moving to the kitchen table as though putting distance between them. She followed him.

He turned his head, watching as she leaned against the counter across from him and waited. Other than appliances, the kitchen was bare. No disorder. No clutter or decoration. The living room had been the same as she remembered. As though he had yet to decide who he was enough to mark his home with those things that defined him. Unless . . .

"Did you buy the house?" she asked him then.

Surprise crossed his features. "It's mine." He nodded before sipping at his coffee. "What does that have to do with anything?"

Nothing, except the thought of him leaving bothered her. Fine, he had no interest in her outside of her bread and her coffee, but she liked him. At least he wasn't boring.

"Nothing." She finally shrugged. Thankfully, she was wearing her thick flannel robe rather than one of her thinner ones, the ones that would have shown her hard nipples clearly and made it impossible to hide her response from him.

That was what pissed her off so bad about him. He was the one man in years who had actually interested her, and he seemed totally oblivious to her as a woman.

It sucked.

"You haven't told me what happened tonight yet," she finally reminded him. "I've been pretty patient, Tarek."

He grunted at that statement. "Yeah, I saw that while you were running through the rain."

He inhaled deeply, grimaced, and shifted restlessly in his chair. His hand rubbed at his arm, just below the bandage, as though to rub away the ache.

She ached for him, for that wound. The sight of his blood earlier had weakened her knees and filled her with a fear she hadn't expected. He had been hurt. While she dealt with the police and filing that stupid report, all she could think about was how severely he could have been wounded.

"I don't know," he finally answered, staring at her directly. "I knew someone was out there. I followed him. I caught him messing with the electric box and attempting to get to the back door when I tried to stop him." He pushed his fingers through his hair again, feathering the dark gold strands back from his face. "I don't believe he was after your TV set, though."

She didn't like the sound of that.

"The security company said the alarm couldn't be dismantled in the electrical box. That it has a backup . . ."

"It can be done." He shrugged heavily. "Your system is residential. It has its drawbacks. I'll get you a new one tomorrow."

"I didn't ask you to do anything." She was growing sick of this cat-and-mouse game of his. "I want to know what the hell was going on. Any burglar worth his salt would have run when he was noticed. This guy didn't run. Why?"

"I don't know. I was hoping you would." That wasn't a lie.

He stared at her, his unusual eyes darker, heavy-lidded . . . She swallowed tightly. That was not lust glittering in the golden depths. Men like him didn't get turned on for frumpy little accountants.

She drew in a deep, uneven breath, flickering her tongue over her dry lips nervously. He followed the movement, his gaze heating.

Okay. This was odd enough. She could understand being hotter than hell herself, but now he was? Why? Did he have a flannel fetish or something?

"Fine. It was no big deal then." She crossed her arms over her breasts just to be certain he couldn't see her nipples pushing against the cloth. "I'll just go home . . ."

"Not tonight." His voice was darker, deeper. "It's not safe as long as your system is down. You can stay here or call your brothers. It's up to you."

"I can take care of myself." She drew herself up stiffly as she faced him.

He rose from the table, suddenly appearing stronger, broader, fiercer as he scowled down at her.

"I said, you could stay here or call your brothers. I did not give you any other choices." A growl echoed in his voice as his eyes seemed to glow with arrogant intent.

"I didn't ask you for choices, Tarek." She wasn't about to bow down submissively to him, either. "I don't need a keeper."

His jaw tightened furiously, his lips thinning as he glared at her.

And that really shouldn't have turned her on further. But it did. She could feel the moisture gathering, pooling, spilling along the sensitive folds between her thighs. Her breasts felt heavier, swollen, too sensitive.

And he wasn't exactly uninterested anymore.

Her gaze flickered down, her face flushing heatedly before she jerked it back up. He was filling out those jeans like it was nobody's business.

And he hadn't missed the direction of her look, either.

"Don't tempt me, Lyra," he suddenly warned her, his voice rasping over her sensitive nerve endings. "My control is shot for the night. Either call your brothers or march your sweet ass upstairs to my spare room, or you're going to find yourself flat on your back in my bed. Your choice. The only ones left. Make it."

FIVE

He was nearly shaking with the need to touch her. Tarek stared down at her pixie features, the blood pumping so hard and so fast through his veins it was nearly painful. His cock was a torturous ache between his legs, the glands at the side of his tongue swollen and throbbing.

His hard-on made sense. The rush of blood was explainable. The tongue was an enigma, and the taste of spice in his mouth confusing. The only thing that did make sense was the need to kiss Lyra.

She had tormented him for months. Tempted him. Laughed at him and mocked him with a gentle, feminine warmth that shouldn't have touched him as deeply as it had.

The smell of her arousal was killing him. It was hot, liquid sweet, and he was dying to lap at the soft cream he knew was spilling from her pussy. It would be hot, frothy with her growing need, and as rich as sunrise.

"Hell of a choice." Her arms tightened over her breasts.

He knew what she was hiding. The lush curves of her breasts, her swollen nipples.

"Make it fast if you don't mind," he growled. The erection was killing him. "Because the scent of your arousal is making me insane, Lyra. Pretty soon, I'm going to make the choice for you."

A whimper escaped her lips as her eyes widened in horror. In shame? He frowned as she paled and then flushed furiously, her eyes brightening as though with tears.

"What?" He caught her shoulders as she moved to turn from him, turning her back to face him, knowing that touching her was the biggest mistake he could make.

"You smell me?" She trembled, embarrassment bringing tears to her eyes as she struggled against him.

He sighed wearily. Dammit, he was too tired, too hungry for the taste of her to watch every damn word he said and every move he made. He wasn't exactly the social sort, and the "rules of polite society" wasn't a class he had found the time to take.

"Lyra." He breathed out roughly, his hand lifting to her cheek, marveling at the silken texture of her flesh. "I'm an animal," he whispered softly. "My sense of smell is so highly advanced that I can detect any scent. Especially the sweet, soft heat coming from you. It's like forcing a starving man to stand before a banquet and not taste the riches."

She blinked up at him, swallowing tightly, her gaze suspicious, softening only slightly as his thumb smoothed over her lips.

He wanted to say more, but the silken curves held his attention, mesmerized him.

His tongue throbbed as the glands spilled more of the spicy taste into his mouth. The blood pumped harder through his veins as his control slipped further.

He lifted his hands from her shoulders carefully.

"The bedroom is upstairs, third door on the landing. Get away from me, Lyra. Now. Before I lose all control."

She frowned back at him.

"I don't like the way you make decisions for me, Tarek," she snapped furiously. But, thank God, she began to back carefully away from him. "It's annoying."

"I'm certain it is." The smell of her still wrapped around him, tormented him. "We can discuss it tomorrow over coffee. Now go to bed."

She sniffed in disdain, glaring back at him as she reached the doorway.

"This tendency to boss me around best not become a habit," she warned him again. "Otherwise, I might disabuse you of the idea that you can get away with it. Count yourself lucky I'm letting you off the hook and escaping. Otherwise, you'd be one molested kitty, Jordan."

He could do nothing but stare at her disappearing back in shock as she muttered the heated words. Molested kitty? He groaned at the phrase. Good Lord, the woman was going to make him completely insane.

He sighed in relief, forcing himself to let her go before pulling the cell phone from its holder at his side and pressing the calling pad impatiently.

"Jonas." Jonas Wyatt, head of Feline Enforcer Affairs at Sanctuary, answered on the first ring.

"We have a problem," Tarek said quietly. "I think I encountered our Trainer tonight. Unfortunately, it wasn't me he was after."

He couldn't get the scent of the assailant out of his mind. It was too damned close to the smell of the clothing, admittedly from years before, that the bastard had worn. Not exact, but damned close.

"Explain." Jonas was a man of few words, which was one of the reasons Tarek liked working for him.

"He was breaking into the neighbor's house. Lyra Mason, she's the sister to three . . ."

"Special Forces agents." Jonas finished for him. "Grant, Mar-

shal, and Tyree Mason. They headed the force that took down some
of the main Breed labs."

Tarek closed his eyes, pinching the bridge of his nose in irritation. "Did you know she lived here when I bought this house?" he
questioned him.

"I knew *of* her. I hadn't run a full investigation because I saw no
reason to." He could almost see Jonas shrug with the words.
"Twenty-four, accountant, lives modestly, a nice little nest egg but
nothing substantial. Medical records show a virgin, with all the normal childhood ailments and no police record. I didn't have time to
go deeper and had no reason to. Why?"

Tarek shook his head. "No reason. I might need to come in soon,
though; I think I need a checkup or something." He ran the sides of
his tongue over his teeth, feeling a soft warmth spill into his mouth.

"What's wrong?" Jonas was sounding concerned now. About
damned time.

"I don't know." He moved to the small foyer that led to the
stairs. "Those damned glands at the side of my tongue. They're inflamed and doing funky shit. I swear I taste cinnamon."

Silence filled the line.

"Where's the girl?" Jonas asked then. "The Mason girl."

Tarek frowned at the question.

"My guest room. Her security system was breached."

"Hell!" Jonas breathed roughly. "Have you fucked her?"

A growl rose in his throat. "That's none of your damned business now is it, Jonas?" he asked silkily, dangerously. "Don't over-
step your place, buddy."

"Can it, Tarek," he snorted. "And listen close. This is straight
from the old scientist who treats the main Pride members. The
swollen glands contain a special hormone. That spice filling your
mouth, buddy, is an aphrodisiac. Lyra Mason is your mate."

Tarek laughed. Damn, he hadn't taken Jonas for a comedian.

"Fine. Whatever." He grunted. "Now tell me the truth."

He was going to kill Jonas for playing fucking games with him. He wasn't in the mood.

"No shit, Tarek." Jonas sounded much too serious. "It's kept very quiet. A complete ban on the information unless a couple appears to be mating. One of the best-kept secrets in the world."

Heat rushed to his head, and then to his dick.

"What do you mean, 'She's my mate'?" Could that account for the almost obsessive lust that had developed in the past months? The patience with her that he would never have had with anyone else? The growing, clawing hunger that kept his cock hard, his senses inflamed?

"Biological, chemical, whatever you want to call it," Jonas snorted. "If you kiss her, it causes the hormone to affect her even more than you. Mating Heat. Complete sexual abandon from now until forever. You poor bastard." There was an edge of envy in his voice, though.

Complete sexual abandon? From now until forever? His mate?

"She's mine," he whispered.

"Yep. That's what the doc says. Somehow, nature picked your perfect woman for you. Have fun."

"Have fun?"

Jonas chuckled. "Tarek, you sound dazed, buddy."

He gazed up at the stairs before closing his eyes and shaking his head miserably. He had a feeling Lyra was really going to have a reason to be pissed now.

"Shit," he breathed out roughly. "This is not a good time for this, Jonas. I don't have time for sexual abandon or some kind of fucked-up aphrodisiac. Get the cure out here."

Jonas laughed at that.

"I'll bring the latest attempt at contraception instead," he informed him. "Tell her what the hell is going on, and before you take her, be sure she takes the little pink pill. It's worked so far. Their best guess is that the Mating Heat is nature's way of ensuring the success of the species. Because without this pill, conception of the first child occurs quickly. They sure do make some pretty babies, though."

Babies? Tarek swallowed hard. The thought of Lyra carrying his baby did things to him he couldn't explain.

"Just get me some help out here," he snapped, attempting to cover the emotional response suddenly surging through him. "I'm telling you, Jonas, it's getting dangerous here."

"That goes without saying," Jonas agreed. "I'll head out there myself with Braden and cover you. Let me know how she takes it."

Tarek grunted at that one.

"The information. Not that." He laughed, entirely too amused to suit Tarek. Then his voice sobered. "She's a good woman from what I learned, Tarek. You could have done worse."

"She could have done much better," he said. "You say it's permanent?"

"Like a drug," Jonas said, his voice quieter now. "There are only a few mated couples so far. They're still doing tests, trying to find answers. But so far, it's permanent."

He was fucked. He would have to tell her the truth. If she had a brain in her head, she would run as fast and as far from him as possible. And he would be stuck, obsessed—hell, in love with a woman he knew he had no right to, and no chance of touching.

SIX

The next morning dawned cold, the rain still falling in a listless, icy drizzle along the windowpanes. Every curtain in the house—thick, heavy, rubber-backed curtains—was closed tightly, and the atmosphere between Lyra and Tarek was decidedly tense.

Breakfast consisted of rich, strong coffee and the mound of sausage biscuits Tarek had nuked in the microwave. She had managed to choke down two. God, how did he stand that stuff? Then she sat, finishing her coffee, watching as he consumed the rest.

He was too quiet. Brooding. His expression savagely relentless as the silence became thick enough to cut with a knife. She could almost see it distorting the air around them.

"I have to go home," she announced as she rose to her feet and took her cup over to the sink. "The security company should be around soon . . ."

"I canceled the call." His response had her turning back to him slowly. "My people will be here in a few hours to replace the system entirely."

She stared back at him silently for long moments. This wasn't the lazy, often-cautious man she had come to know. He was still, prepared, his body tense. Still sexy as hell, but the caution had been replaced by a dangerous sense of expectation.

"Really?" she finally answered, crossing her arms over her breasts. "And I gave permission for this, when?"

When he raised his eyes to hers, she shivered, a tremor racing up her spine at the intense lust, the pure, driving hunger she saw in those eyes.

She could feel her vagina weeping. The juices were fairly dripping from the hidden flesh. And he could smell it. She watched him inhale slowly, as though savoring the scent of her.

"Pervert," she snapped, frowning as sensuality fully marked his expression. "Fine, you make me hot. You can smell it. Now it's time for me to go home. Thanks for saving the night and all that."

She turned for the door.

"Touch that doorknob, and you'll regret it."

Her hand was within an inch of gripping it when she drew back slowly at the sound of his voice. She turned, swallowing tightly at the savage expression on his face as he lifted his cup and finished his coffee slowly.

"Tarek, you're going to piss me off," she warned him, suddenly wary. "The silent He-Man crap doesn't get it with me."

He leaned back in his chair, watching her with predatory interest. She had seen glimpses of this side of him, but it had never been focused entirely on her. It had her body tightening, adrenaline and excitement rushing through her.

She was sick. That was all there was to it.

He scratched at his chest slowly.

"Amazing things, genetics," he finally stated with a forced calm that made her think of the eye of a hurricane. This was not going to be good.

"Really?" She lifted a brow, standing close to the door as she arched her brow mockingly.

"Really." He nodded. "All kinds of little things start cropping up, surprising the hell out of you, reminding you that Fate does get the final laugh on all our asses."

Oh, this just wasn't going to be good at all.

She moved closer. The bleak, haunted shadows in his eyes had her chest tightening in fear.

"What's wrong?"

He stared back at her silently for long, tense moments.

"I'm debating something," he finally growled, his voice deepening, roughening as his gaze pinned hers. "I've debated all night."

Why did she have this bad feeling he was debating something that she really wasn't going to be pleased with?

"Yeah?" She inserted mild curiosity into her tone when every bone and muscle of her body was trained on what was coming next.

"Yeah." He nodded slowly, his gaze drifting over her body with lustful intent. "You've made me crazy for months. I'll be damned if I haven't stood by, amused, curious, letting you razz on me every chance you've had."

Yeah, that one had bothered her, too. He never got pissed. Surely he wasn't getting pissed now?

"What, you want an apology?" she asked him, incredulous. "A little late, Tarek."

"I couldn't figure out why." He shook his head slowly. "Then, the strangest thing happened. The more I smelled the sweet heat flowing from your pussy, the more I denied myself a taste of it, the more I started noticing a few changes."

She flushed heatedly at the explicit language, furiously chiding herself silently over her breathless reaction to it.

He rose from the chair as she watched him warily.

"Changes?" She swallowed tightly as she glimpsed the more-than-healthy bulge between his thighs.

"These little glands along my tongue swelling. The taste of spice filling my mouth. The hunger for you growing by the day until I could almost taste your kiss. And I wanted your kiss bad, Lyra. So bad it was killing me. I wanted to push my tongue in your mouth and make you taste it, too. Make you as crazy for me as I was for you."

He stepped closer.

Lyra was breathing roughly, her hands knotted in the front of her robe as she watched him advance on her.

"Are you sick or something?" She had to force the words from her mouth.

A mocking, bitter smile twisted his lips.

"Or something," he agreed as he towered over her and then stepped slowly behind her.

She was not going to run from him, no matter how weird he acted.

"Would you like to know what's wrong with me, Lyra?" He bent close, his breath whispering over her ear as he spoke.

A shiver raced up her spine as her nipples tightened further, rasping against her gown, almost making her moan at the pleasure of the action.

"No." She had a feeling she was certain she didn't want to know.

"There's this nasty little hormone filling my mouth." That growl was deeper now, more animalistic. "It's an aphrodisiac, Lyra. Caused only when a male Feline Breed hungers for his mate. Do you know what's going to happen if I kiss you?"

Her knees weakened. A hormonal aphrodisiac? Something to make her hornier? She didn't think so.

"What?" She couldn't hold back the gasping whisper.

"If I kiss you, it goes into Mating Heat. Complete sexual abandon until you've passed ovulation. Do you know you're preparing to ovulate? That my body is reacting to it? That my cock is so damned hard, my balls so tight with the need to fuck you that it's like an open wound in my gut? All because you're ovulating. My mate. My woman."

Her eyes widened in horror at the words he whispered at her ear.

"You're crazy." She jerked away from him, turning on him furiously. "That's not possible."

The curve of his lips was bleak.

"You would think, wouldn't you?" He moved to the counter, picking up a small oval disc that he slapped on the kitchen island. "This will stop conception. Nothing can stop the heat. Now, my problem is, I'm ready to rip that gown off your body and throw you to the damn floor where I can fuck you until we're both screaming. Until you're as wild for me, as crazy for me, as I am for you. Or you can run out of that door right now, as fast as you can run, and find someplace, any place, to hide until I can find enough control to keep from hunting you down and taking you like the animal I am. Make your choice now, baby, and make it fast. Because this kitty is all out of patience."

seven

Make a choice? He wanted her to make a choice?

She stared back at him, eyes wide, trying to force her brain past the shock to actually make a decision as to whether or not she was still sleeping. Because this had to be some kind of screwed-up nightmare. That was all there was to it.

"Let me get this straight." She edged farther back from him, simply because she was becoming so wet her panties felt damp and his eyes were getting darker. "Your tongue has glands. That have a hormonal aphrodisiac in them?"

He nodded as he advanced on her. He didn't say a word, just nodded his head as he inhaled deeply. She trembled at the knowledge that he was actually smelling her.

"If you kiss me, we go into heat?"

"You go into heat." He smiled, a tight, hard curve of his lips that denoted way more male intent than she was comfortable with.

She cleared her throat. "What do you do?"

"I put out the flames."

She moved back.

Okay. She was retreating. So fucking what? He was stalking her across the room like the damned Lion he was. And the closer he got, the hotter she got.

"Tarek . . ." She jerked in surprise as her back came up against the wall, staring up at him in shock as he stopped, only inches from her, his hand lifting.

He touched her. The backs of his fingers brushed against her throat before trailing down to her collarbone, his eyes tracking each movement his hand made as her breasts began to swell and throb.

"You're running out of time." His guttural whisper had her womb clenching furiously, the breath locking in her chest.

This was a side of Tarek she wasn't accustomed to. A side she knew should not be turning her on as it was. He had barely touched her. In nearly six months of confrontations, arguments, and snapping debates, he had never touched her, never kissed her, and she was going up in flames for him.

She could feel it in every cell of her body, every hard pulse of blood through her veins.

"How long does it last?" she finally asked. "The heat stuff?"

His eyes narrowed as his head lowered. He was going to kiss her, she knew he was. But he didn't. His lips moved to her neck, burning a heated caress to the sensitive flesh where her shoulder and neck met. There, his lips opened, his tongue stroking her skin a second before the incisors scraped against it.

Her hands flew to his arms, her hands gripping his wrists as her knees weakened.

"It lasts forever." Bleak, bitter pain filled his voice. "From now until forever, Lyra. Always mine."

He bit her. Not hard enough to break the skin or to cause her undue pain. But he bit, his teeth clenching in the tender muscle as she arched on her tiptoes, a sizzling bolt of electric pleasure pulling a strangled cry from her lips.

Her clit pulsed, her vagina wept, her nipples became so hard, so tight, they were a near violent ache as a lethargic weakness left her gasping rather than fighting for freedom.

"Always?" She should have been alarmed. Always was not supposed to be in her vocabulary. She had no desire to be under a man's thumb, just under this man's body.

His lips moved back up her neck, his tongue licking at her flesh as a rumbling growl broke from his chest.

"Just a taste," he whispered as he reached her lips, his arms lowering from the braced position against the wall beside her head. "Stay very still, baby. I just need a taste."

His lips ghosted over hers as she stared back at him, her gaze locked with his, seeing the hunger, the aching, soul-deep need he had kept hidden beneath lowered lashes or behind mocking humor.

But now it was laid bare to her, as clear, as desperate as the aching hunger for him that pulsed low in her stomach.

She trembled as she felt his hands at the front of her robe, his lips, nipping at hers, parting them, retreating, only to come back for more as she held on to his wrists with a death grip.

The buttons on her robe gave way, the edges falling apart as they both breathed harshly, the silence of the kitchen broken only by their gasps of pleasure.

"You're so wet. I can smell how wet you are. How sweet," he whispered as he stared back at her, his fingers working on the buttons of her gown. "Like the fragrance of summer, heating me, reminding me of life, of living."

His words shook her to her core.

"Do you know what the smell of your sweet pussy does to me?" He smoothed her gown apart, the cool air brushing against her naked breasts as she whimpered in an arousal so sharp, so desperate, she wondered if she would survive it. "It makes me hungry,

Lyra. Hungry to take you, to hear you screaming beneath me as I bury every inch of my cock as deep inside you as possible."

She cried out sharply, unable to contain the sound. Could a woman orgasm from words alone? His explicit language was driving her over the edge, earthy and lustful, filled with a desire no man had ever shown her before.

He grimaced, showing the incisors at the side of his mouth as his gaze moved to the rapid rise and fall of her breasts.

"Look how pretty." He took her hand from his wrist, spread her fingers, and then wrapped it around the lush mound.

She stared back at him in shock, her eyes flickering to where she cupped her own flesh, her hand surrounded by his.

"Feed it to me," he whispered then, his voice wicked, filled with lust. "I want to taste it."

She shuddered, a whimper escaping her throat at the pure eroticism of what he was doing to her.

His hand moved back hers. "Give it to me, Lyra. Press that pretty, hard nipple into my mouth."

She couldn't believe she was doing it. That she was lifting her breast, leaning forward as he bent his knees, lowering himself to allow the straining nub to pass his lips.

He licked it first.

"Oh God, Tarek." She was shaking like a leaf, pinpoints of explosive pleasure detonating through her body.

He licked it again, his tongue, rasping roughly, like wet velvet gliding over the sensitive tip.

Then he growled. A hard, savage sound as his lips opened, parted, to envelope the hard point into the wild, wet heat of his mouth.

She climaxed.

Lyra's hands shot to his head, her fingers tangling in the rough strands of his hair as something exploded deep within her womb. Pleasure rushed through her sex, drenching her, spilling to her thighs as she lost her breath.

He hadn't even kissed her yet.

His head rose from her nipple, his hands lifting, pulling hers from his hair as he settled them against her sides.

He laid his against her shoulders, smoothing the unbuttoned gown and robe slowly from her arms as she shook before him.

Lyra swallowed tightly, small whimpers passing her lips as she stood naked before him. Naked—she never wore underwear beneath her gowns—while he was fully clothed, watching her with glowing gold eyes, his expression predatory, savage.

"Sweet little virgin," he whispered, his gaze moving down her body, finally coming to rest on the bare, slick folds between her thighs. "Naughty little baby." His eyes moved back to hers. "Imagine how my tongue is going to feel there. Sliding through all that hot, sweet syrup. Will you come for me again, Lyra? Will you cry for me again?"

He took her hand, moving it to the snap of his jeans as he watched her with savage eyes.

"Make your choice now, Lyra. Accept me."

Good Lord, what was she supposed to do about him? She was standing there naked in front of him, and he still could not reason out that she had already accepted him? Even with all the weird Breed mating stuff, she couldn't imagine not accepting him.

"Kiss me," she demanded roughly, her fingers moving to the metal snaps of his jeans, releasing them slowly, the hard heat of his erection beneath making the task difficult.

"God." He snarled the prayer as he shuddered against her, his hands gripping her hips as his eyes clenched shut for long seconds.

"Kiss me, Tarek," she whispered, reaching for him, her lips brushing his as his head lowered, his eyes blazing with hunger, pain, and need as he watched her. "Make me crazier."

The front of his jeans parted beneath her trembling fingers, the hard, generous width of his erection rising from the material, flushed and desperate as she glanced down nervously.

She licked her lips.

"I hope you know what to do with it." She finally swallowed tightly. "Because I don't have a clue."

And he didn't bother with explanations.

In that second his head lowered, his lips slanting over hers as his tongue licked and then pressed demandingly between her lips.

Immediately the taste of spice exploded in her mouth. Heat surrounded her, whipped through her mind, then cell by cell began to invade her body.

She thought the clawing, driving hunger for his touch, his kiss, couldn't get worse.

She was wrong.

Exploding fingers of sensation began to tear through her nerve endings. Her womb clenched, knotted. The already aching flesh between her thighs began to burn with a spasming, violent need.

She screamed into his kiss, rising on her tiptoes for more, pressing against him, trying to sink into the heat emanating from beneath his clothing.

He tore his lips from hers, his breathing rough, harsh as she tried to claw up his body and capture his lips again.

"That fucking pill." His voice was animalistic, rough, hungry.

"No. Kiss me again." She pulled his hair, dragging his head back down until his lips covered hers again, a groan tearing from his throat as her tongue pushed between his lips.

It was wildfire. It was destructive. She could feel the flames licking over her body, pinpoints of electricity sensitizing her flesh. And pleasure—the pleasure was overwhelming.

She felt him pick her up. Lifting her from her feet as she lifted her legs, bending them to clasp his hips as the fiery hot length of his erection suddenly seared the folds of her cunt.

He was moving. Walking. Sweet heaven, how was he walking?

He pulled his lips back again, his movements jerky as he braced her rear on the kitchen island and jerked open the small plastic container.

He pushed the pill between her lips.

"Swallow it," he growled. "Now, Lyra."

He was moving against her, his cock sliding in the juices of her sex as he stared down at her fiercely, raking the tender bud of her clit, sending spasms of sensation ripping through her belly.

She swallowed the pill before her gaze dropped to her thighs.

She whimpered.

"Do it," she whispered, watching the bloated head of his cock part her and then slide up, raking against her clit.

"Damn," his voice was filled with lust, with a strengthening demand as his fingers caught in her hair, pulling her head back to force her gaze to his. "I told you. I'm eating that sweet pussy first."

"I can't wait, Tarek," she whimpered, her hands pulling at his shirt, amazed as the buttons tore free, revealing his golden chest. "Now. I need it now."

"You can wait."

But he wasn't about to.

Her eyes widened as he pushed her back, spreading her thighs as he lifted her legs and buried his head between them.

The first swipe of his tongue through the sensitive slit of her cunt had her screaming. He licked at her, lapping at the juices spilling from her vagina as he groaned against her flesh.

She had never imagined such agonizing pleasure. She writhed beneath him, twisting, bucking against his mouth as he circled her clit, only to move lower to lap at her again.

He nibbled at the sensitive lips, parted her, and then suddenly, astonishingly, drove his tongue inside her. She exploded in a firestorm of blazing pleasure as his tongue fucked inside her with hard, blistering strokes. Her muscles clenched, shuddered, and more heated liquid spilled to his greedy lips.

And still, it wasn't enough.

She was gasping, tears dampening her face as she shuddered a final time, staring up at him as he straightened between her thighs.

"Tarek?" She sobbed his name beseechingly. "I need more."

She was exhausted, but the fire burning in her womb was never-ending.

"Shh, baby." He lifted her quickly in his arms. "I refuse to take you on the kitchen counter, Lyra. I won't do it."

He stumbled as her legs wrapped around him, clasping his hips tight, her clit rubbing against the shaft of his cock as he began to carry her to the stairs.

"I won't make it upstairs." She was riding the thick wedge, the agonizing pleasure ripping through her mind.

If she could just get the right position. Just a little higher . . .

She felt the thickly crested head part her, lodge against the tender opening before his first step onto the stairs forced it inside her.

He stumbled, growling, one arm locked around her as he braced his hand to the wall, breathing harshly.

"Not like this," he breathed roughly. "Oh God, Lyra. Not like this. Not your first time . . ."

Regret, remorse. She saw it in his expression, heard it in his voice. But stretching her entrance wide, teasing her, tempting her, was the head of the instrument she needed to relieve the agonizing lust clawing at her pussy.

She shifted in his embrace, feeling him slip farther inside her before coming to a halt against the proof of her virginity.

"Baby . . ." He whispered the endearment against her ear as he struggled up another step.

Each move pulled his cock back, pushed it in, and stroked her no more than inches inside the gripping muscles of her cunt, sending shudders wracking through her body at the exquisite pleasure.

He was killing her.

"I'm sorry." He stopped, bending, placing her rear at the edge of the step as he knelt in front of her. "God, Lyra. I'm sorry."

She had no more than a second's warning before his hips flexed and then pushed forward, driving his thick, hot erection to the very depths of her hungry, gripping pussy.

Shocking, blistering. The sudden penetration had her arching as the pleasure/pain of his abrupt entrance sizzled across her nerve endings. Overfilled, stretched tight, she could feel his cock throbbing inside her, setting flames to her ultra-sensitive depths.

Lyra's head fell back against an upper step, her legs lifting, clasping his back tightly as he began to drive inside her.

It was unlike anything she could have imagined. She could feel him pushing the tender muscles apart, stroking delicate tissue, and sending almost unbearable pleasure whipping through her system.

She held on to him, feeling his lips at her neck, his incisors scraping over her flesh as the pressure began to build inside her womb, the pleasure coalescing, tightening with each desperate lunge of his cock inside the snug depths of her cunt.

She could barely feel the hard wood of the step beneath her. All she felt was Tarek, heavy, hot, wide, overfilling her, making her take more, thrusting inside in an ever-increasing tempo until she felt the world dissolve around her.

Then she felt more.

Her eyes widened, staring in dazed shock at the ceiling above her as, simultaneously, his teeth bit into her shoulder, holding her still for something so incredibly unreal, she was certain she had to be imagining it.

He slammed in deep, his body tightening as she felt an additional erection, an extension swelling from beneath the hood of his cock, locking him inside her, caressing a bundle of nerves high inside her pussy, and sending her rushing past ecstasy into rapture. The heat of his semen filled her, pulse after violent pulse echoing in the flexing depths as he growled harshly at her neck.

He was locked inside her. The extension holding him in place sent cataclysms of sensation exploding through her over and over again.

When it finally eased, when the hard pulsing jets of his release and the violent shudders of her own eased, her eyes closed in exhaustion.

She had thought no arousal could be worse than what she had known before his kiss. She was rapidly learning just how wrong she was.

EIGHT

You are not human . . . You may look in the mirror and de-clare your humanity. You may tell yourself that looks are all that matter. They do not. You are animals. Created in a lab, a man-made creation, and you will serve the men who made you. You are animal. Our tools. Nothing more . . .

Tarek stared at the ceiling as he held Lyra in his arms, her head on his chest, her body draped over his. She was like a kitten, determined to get as close as possible in her sleep, curling around him with a sigh before she had relaxed into exhaustion several hours before.

He wasn't human. That had been driven irrevocably home on the stairs, his body covering hers, as it betrayed his sense of humanity. His belief in himself as a man, not an animal.

A barb.

He closed his eyes as bitterness swamped him.

He pushed back the shudder of pure lust at the memory of the sensations.

Dear God, the pleasure. It had been unlike anything he could have anticipated. The extension had been highly sensitive, pulsing, throbbing in orgasmic delight as he poured his semen into her.

He breathed in roughly, grimacing at the erection he still sported. He had a feeling he would never get enough of the feel of her silken cunt, with or without the Mating Heat.

His hand smoothed over her hair, his fingers tangling in the soft strands as he relished the feel of her lying against him.

She was warm. Precious. She was a gift he had never imagined he would ever have.

And she liked him. He knew she felt at least some affection for him, though perhaps not as much as he felt for her. Hell, he had fallen in love with her during the first few months he had known her. He had known it was love. Known the possessiveness, the joy, the sheer delight he found in her could be nothing else.

He wanted to clutch her to him, tighten his arms around her and hold the world at bay forever. But he knew, realistically, it wasn't possible. He could only hold her for now and see how she reacted when she awakened.

And that part terrified him.

Would she be disgusted?

Hell, of course she would. What sane, reasonable woman could so easily accept something so animalistic? So outside the bounds of what she knew was human?

He felt her shift against him and restrained his growl of impatient lust as her leg slid over his thigh, her knee nearly touching the taut flesh of his scrotum.

Sweet Lord, she made him hot. And he wasn't blaming it on the Mating Heat. He had known what she would do to him from his first confrontation with her.

She sighed against his chest, a soft little sound that clenched his heart as her hand smoothed over his chest and then back again.

He stilled, his breath nearly suspending as she repeated the action, her body tensing.

"What happened to you?" Her fingers picked up the nearly invisible line of scars that criss-crossed his chest.

"Training." He hoped she would leave it alone. Prayed she would let it go.

"What kind of training?" She leaned up enough to open drowsy eyes, though her gaze was as sharp as ever.

He was willing to bet she drove her father insane. She was too curious, too independent, and too set on having the answers she demanded.

"Simply training, Lyra," he finally answered her. "At times, I was not the perfect little soldier I should have been."

He heard the bitterness that laced his voice, wincing at the sound of it.

Her fingers moved over the abrasive scars once again as her gaze flickered to his. A gaze filling with anger. Making her angry had not been his intention. He wanted only to shelter her from what he had known during those years. There was no reason for her to know the brutality, the mercilessness of those who created him.

"I hope they're dead." Her snarl surprised him, as did the blood-thirsty fury in those beautiful eyes as she stared back at him. "Whoever did this, I hope you killed him."

He had. But it wasn't something he was proud of.

He was proud of this small sign of protectiveness from her, though. She was angry on his behalf, not with him.

"It's over. That's all that matters." He touched her cheek, amazed at her, just as he had been from the first moment he had seen her.

She snorted at that, a completely unladylike sound that didn't really surprise him as her expression conveyed her disagreement with him.

"I need a shower." She finally shifted from him, her moves hesitant.

THE BREED NEXT DOOR

"I'll show you the shower and get you one of my shirts to wear." He moved from the bed before turning back and lifting her into his arms.

She gripped his shoulders, staring up at him in surprise.

"You're tender." And she was as light as a feather. "Perhaps try a bath to relieve the soreness. I have some Epsom Salts in the cabinet that will make you feel better."

Jonas had suggested hot baths rather than showers to help ease the soreness as well as the building heat for a small respite.

He knew the scent of her and could detect the change as she moved farther through the ovulation process. The pill she had taken would do nothing to stop the heat, only the end result of the ovulation process. There would be no egg, no conception. He ignored the small flare of regret at the thought of it.

"I'm hungry, too," she informed him. "And I don't want any of those nasty biscuits, either. I want some real food."

He set her down in the bathroom, staring down at her in confusion. "Such as?"

"I'll call Liu's. She'll have one of her boys deliver." She stared around the large bathroom before looking back at him pointedly.

An invitation to leave. That one was hard not to miss. But not yet.

"Let me know what you want, I'll have a friend pick it up for us," he suggested instead. "For the time being, I would prefer not to let anyone I don't know into the house."

A small tremor raced through her body as she glanced away from him for a moment and breathed in heavily.

"Fine. I can understand that. As long as I get my Chinese fix."

He listened carefully to the dishes she wanted ordered, restraining his smile. It was enough to feed an army. It was a damned good thing he had a near-perfect memory.

"Bathe. I'll call Jonas and have the food picked up. By the time you're finished, it should be here."

He could smell the heat building in her and wanted her to have the time to enjoy the food.

"Thanks. Now go away." She waved him away with a delicate gesture of her fingers. "I don't need you in here right now."

His lips quirked at her irritated expression, but he did as she asked. And he prayed. Prayed she had forgiven him for the animal he was, rather than the man he knew she needed.

"I need to go to the house for some clothes and stuff." Lyra found her gown and robe in the washroom, folded neatly on the top of the dryer after they had consumed the delivered Chinese food.

Her hunger was sated, but that was all. The steadily rising lust building in her body was about to make her crazy.

It tingled in her breasts and spasmed in her vagina. And she ached for his kiss—literally. She was certain no drug could be as addictive as his kiss was.

"You can't leave the house yet, Lyra." His voice brooked no refusal.

Okay, a man could be really sexy when he was being dominant, especially this man. But she just wasn't in the mood for it. She wanted to be fucked, but she would be damned if she was going to ask him for it. And because she knew he could smell her arousal, she knew he was very well aware of the hunger building within her.

She turned carefully, clutching the folded material to her breasts. "Too bad. I need clean clothes and time to think . . ."

A bitter smile twisted his lips as a raging pain reflected in his gaze.

"The time for thinking was before you decided to take my kiss."

She shook her head against the anger in his voice.

"Not about this," she informed him fiercely. "I have to decide things, Tarek. This has changed my life, you know it and I know it. There are other things involved than just you and I and this Mating Heat, or whatever you call it."

Heat? Try inferno. It was killing her.

"Then take care of it on the phone." There was no give in him.

Good Lord, why hadn't she heeded the warnings of his complete male stubbornness that she had glimpsed over the months? He looked about as immovable as a boulder.

"I need clothes. My laptop . . ."

"You won't have time to wear clothes, or to work . . ." He advanced on her, his eyes lowering over the lust gleaming in his gaze. "You'll be lucky to have time to eat."

Her stomach clenched at the growl in his voice as he reached out, taking the gown and robe from her before setting them back on the washer.

"I want to take you in the bed this time." His fingers tangled in her hair as he dragged her head back, his head lowering as though for a kiss.

As though she were that easy.

She didn't care how hot she was or how much the arousal was becoming painful. She was not just going to bow down and accept whatever. She might not be a Breed with a clear appreciation of this Mating Heat stuff, but she still had a mind of her own.

Before he could stop her, she twisted away from him, moving through the doorway and stalking through the kitchen to the foyer. She wasn't going to attempt the back door. But she might have a chance of getting to her own house before he stopped her through the front yard. Icy rain and all.

"Lyra. Where the hell do you think you're going?"

He moved ahead of her before she could reach the door, staring back at her broodingly as she restrained the urge to kick him.

"To my own house," she reminded him. "Remember? Clothes? Laptop?"

"No." The rough growl sent shivers up her spine and spasms attacking her vagina. Damn him. A man should never have a voice so inherently sexy.

"Tarek, you are under the impression this Mating Heat of yours somehow gives you rights you do not have." She pointed her finger into his chest, pushing back at the stubborn male muscle that wouldn't budge an inch.

Savage intensity tightened his expression, giving him a dangerous, predatory look.

"You are my mate. It's my place to protect you." He fairly snarled the words, lifting his lip to display those wickedly white incisors.

"It's daylight, Tarek," she pointed out as though speaking to a young child. Sometimes, men responded to nothing else. "I'm safe, sweetheart. I'm just gonna walk across the lawn."

"You will not." He stepped toward her.

And of course, she retreated.

The look on his face assured her that he was done ignoring her arousal and now ready to do something about it. Of course, the erection straining beneath the loose fit of his sweatpants pretty much assured her of that on its own.

"Tarek, these strongman tactics are going to piss me off," she bit out, irritation surging through her. "I don't like it."

"So?" His lips tilting in a mocking smile. "Tell me, *mate*, how will you stop it?"

Cool male confidence marked his features.

"I'm really going to hurt you," she muttered, frustration surging through her because she knew there wasn't really a damned thing she could do.

She could call her brothers.

But that wouldn't really be fair. Would it?

No, she decided, this one she had to handle on her own.

She backed up again as he moved closer, her eyes narrowing on him.

"I am not ready to have sex with you yet," she stated imperiously as she tried to escape into the living room.

He smiled. A wicked, sensual smile that had her pussy weeping. Damn him.

"Aren't you?" He stalked her through the large room, her gaze moving around the heavy furniture, taking in the clean masculine lines and nearly clinical sterility of the room. There wasn't even a picture.

"No. I'm not."

Oh but she was. It was beating through her veins and pounding in her chest. Her breasts were tight with the need for it, her pussy clenching in hunger.

He stopped as she edged around the heavy cherry wood coffee table, watching him warily.

"You make me want to smile," he whispered then, his eyes filled with warmth, with longing. "Even as stubborn as you can be, you make me want to smile."

Her heart melted. Now, dammit, how was she supposed to stand her ground when he said things like that?

"Now is not the time to be nice, Tarek," she snapped, infuriated at him.

"But I want to be nice to you." He used that whiskey-rough voice like a caress, and it was much too effective for Lyra's peace of mind. "I want to be very nice to you, Lyra. I want to lay you down on that couch, spread your pretty legs, and show you just how nice I can be to you. Wouldn't you like that, baby?"

The heat in the room jumped a hundred degrees. She could feel perspiration gathering between her breasts and along her forehead, and hunger tearing her apart.

She didn't run as he made his way around the table. She watched him, wondering what the hell had happened to her willpower, her strength, her determination to not let this man get around her so easily.

But he did. Not with his words. Or his intent. It was the longing in his eyes, the vulnerability, the joy that sparkled there as she faced him.

"I'm really going to get mad at you one of these days," she warned him as he stepped closer, surrounding her, his hand moving beneath her hair to cup her neck. "And don't bite me again, either. That's just too freaky."

She could feel the wound pulsing, achingly sensitive.

"You complain about the bite, but not the barb?" The casual tone of his voice was not reflected in the tenseness of his body.

"Yeah, well." She cleared her throat nervously. "The barb I can forgive you for. That bite is going to get your ass kicked if my brothers see it, though. I'd prefer to keep you in one piece."

He stared down at her thoughtfully.

"I think you enjoyed the barb." He lowered his head, his tongue rasping over the small wound from his bite. "And I think you liked the bite, too, Lyra."

She shivered as his tongue rasped over it, sending currents of pleasure whipping through her.

"Maybe," she gasped in pleasure, standing still, her hands at her sides, curled into fists to keep from touching him, to keep from disturbing the emotion she could feel weaving around her.

"Come here, baby." He pulled her into his arms, leaving her no other choice but to lift her own, her hands moving to his neck, to his glorious mane of hair. "Let's see how much you like both."

His head lowered, his lips covered hers, and she was lost. She knew she was lost. Taken in a firestorm of sensual heat as the delicately flavored hormone began to surge through her already prepared senses.

She moaned into his kiss, her lips parting, accepting his tongue, drawing on it as a savage growl vibrated in his throat.

Her nails bit into his shoulders, scraped the flesh, caressing him in turn as his hands gripped her buttocks and lifted her against his thighs.

She was aware of him moving her, laying her back on the cushions of the overstuffed couch as he moved over her.

He pushed the shirt over her breasts, but neither of them could break the kiss long enough to tear it off. But somehow he had removed his sweats.

She could feel his cock, hard and heavy against her thigh as his hands roved over her sensitized body. They moaned, the sounds of their pleasure mixing, merging as he lifted her to him, the broad crest of his erection pressing against the slick, readied entrance to her spasming pussy.

"Lyra . . ." His harsh, graveled voice pierced her heart as he tore his lips from hers, raising his head to stare down at her with eyes that seemed to melt with emotion.

Oh God, she loved him. Everything about him. Every portion of him.

"Now," she whispered as he paused. "Love me, Tarek . . . Please . . ."

He grimaced, his lips pulling back from his teeth in a savage snarl as he stared down at her in surprise.

"Don't you know, Lyra?" His smile was bittersweet. "Don't you know just how much I do love you?"

She would have smacked him, or at least yelled at him for saying it with such hopeless pain. But he chose that moment to begin pushing into her, stretching her snug muscles as he worked his cock inside her.

Fiery, agonizing heat filled her. The pleasure was lightning fast, flaring through every portion of her body as he rocked against her.

She felt him, inch by inch, sinking into her, just as he had taken her heart. Bit by bit, forcing her wide, searing her with not just the pleasure, but the sheer gentleness he used.

"I would die for you," he whispered against her ear, hiding his expression against her neck as she convulsed around him, her hands locking in his hair. "Don't you know, Lyra, I live for you now. For now and for always."

He surged through the final depths of her aching sex, pushing in fiercely before retreating with the same agonizing pace he had used to enter her.

"Tarek." She bit his ear. He was making her wild, setting her heart aflame, sending her body into quaking shudders of pleasure. "Just live for me," she gasped. "Oh God." He thrust into her quickly, retreated slowly, stealing her breath, her thoughts.

"Oh baby, I'm not nearly finished with you." His voice was so dark, so velvet-rough it nearly sent her into climax. Her womb convulsed; her breath caught in her throat as her clit swelled in nearing ecstasy.

He leaned back, his knees pressing into the couch as he draped her legs over his thighs. His hands free, he lifted her against him, holding her to his chest as he stared into her shocked face.

"Take off the shirt."

His cock throbbed inside her. Her pussy was sucking at him with rapturous greed, and he was worried about her shirt?

"Now." His voice hardened, his gaze turning stubborn. "I won't give you what you need, Lyra, until you do."

Her hands lowered from his neck, gripping the shirt and struggling to jerk it over her head as one hand gripped her buttock and lifted her several inches from the thick wedge of his cock. Then he released her, thrusting hard and deep inside her again as she whimpered in delirious need.

The shirt cleared her head, though she struggled to force it from her arms. Finally it was gone, her hands moving to his shoulders again, her legs tightening around his hips as she fought to force him to move inside her.

"Tarek, I'm going to skin you alive if you keep torturing me." She knew the pitiful whimper in her voice didn't exactly carry the threat well. But he should know her well enough to know she would keep her word. Maybe.

He chuckled.

"Hold on. We're going to the bed."

"The bed?" Her eyes widened in horror as he moved easily from the couch.

She shuddered as his cock shifted with each movement.

"I heard that last time," her strangled gasp nearly became a mewl of rapture as his cock began to fuck in and out of her with each step. "Those steps . . ." She moaned at the sensation of his movements inside her. "Aren't so comfortable."

"We'll make it." He sounded too confident. Too determined.

Sweet Lord, he was going to kill her.

She swore he would. She knew he would.

"Oh God. Tarek. Tarek, I can't stand it," she was screaming his name as he began to take the steps with a heavy, quick stride.

His cock slammed inside her, taking her breath before retreating, rocking in, thrusting forcibly, then rocking inside her again.

Her nails dug into his shoulders, gasping, desperate cries fell from her lips as she tightened her legs around his hips and fought to hang on.

The first orgasm ripped through her on the sixth step. On the twelfth she was shuddering, jerking in his arms as the second stole her breath and her mind.

She was only barely aware of him actually making it to the bed, laying her back, and gripping her hips as he began to fuck her into a third, destructive climax.

She arched, her breath leaving her body in a rush as she felt his release tear through him then. The barb swelled forcibly from beneath the head of his cock, pressing into the delicate bundle of nerves that no man would have reached otherwise. It throbbed, caressed, and sent her flying into an orgasm that had no beginning and no end. It only had Tarek, holding her, his teeth scraping the wound he had left earlier before his teeth locked on it once again and dark oblivion overtook her.

"I love you. Oh God, Tarek, I love you . . ." Velvet darkness enclosed her as the words whispered free, her heart expanding as her soul seemed to lift, shudder, and open to accept a part of him that she knew even death could never steal.

NINE

"... I'm just tired, Dad. I had dinner out with a friend last night, and I have all this work backed up. I just think it would be best if you and the boys come over after all this rain lets up. You know how they mess up my kitchen when it's wet outside . . ."

Tarek listened to Lyra spin a song and dance to her father later the next evening that even he wouldn't have believed from her.

His sensual, sexual little mate was giving her father excuses that even he, who had no experience with parents, would never have tried.

What was it that made her think that delicate, sweet little voice was fooling anyone?

You're crazy! he mouthed slowly, ignoring her as she waved him away with a graceful little flip of her hand.

After two days of sex that should have killed him, in positions he hadn't tried in all his sexual lifetime, he was even prone to be fairly prejudiced in her favor. But the sweet, candy-coated innocent tone had him rolling his eyes at her before giving her a fierce frown.

What? she mouthed back, shooting him an irritated glance before turning her attention back to the call she had made to her family.

Considering the fact her brothers were Special Forces, he doubted their father was dimwitted. Yet here was his independent, feisty mate, reclining naked in his bed with nothing but a sheet to cover her, weaving an excuse that had him wincing painfully.

Her silken hair was tangled around her flushed face, her blue eyes gleaming with irritation, and she had the nerve to sit there and attempt to put her father off in such a way.

She was tired. She didn't feel like cooking. Her brothers made messes . . .

Give him a break. Hell, give him strength because he had a feeling the full fury of a father plus his sons would arrive on her doorstep, fouling the careful setup Braden had there to catch the Trainer.

"Yes, Dad, I know how irked they get when they have to wait to do things, but my yard looks like a swamp right now, and they couldn't do anything even if they wanted to. They just want a free meal, and I'm busy."

She was pouting. Seriously pouting. What happened to the independent "do it my way or no way" woman he knew? He shook his head, pushing his fingers through his hair as he tried to think of ways to fix this before her family became his headache.

There was no stopping her. He sliced his hand across his throat, frowning at her warningly. To no effect. All he got was a glare in return.

That glare effectively hardened his cock. All she had to do was think about opposing him, and that stubborn flesh rose to rigid life. Dammit. She was wearing him out.

But what a way to go.

He would have grinned at the thought if she hadn't chosen that moment to tell *daddy*, in that sweet innocent tone, that she was going to work all evening.

It was enough to make him groan silently.

"Yes, Dad, I promise I'm being careful and locking the doors and windows at night." The promise was made in an almost automatic tone. "I promise, the only wild animals I'll let in are the four-legged variety. Not that I've seen any lately." She grinned cheekily at her words as she winked at Tarek.

Insane woman! He snarled silently, mouthing the words to her as she rolled her eyes at him. Who did she think was believing this?

"This isn't bread-baking day," she yawned after the muted sound of her father's deep voice stopped speaking. "Besides, I'm busy. They can wait another day or two." She nestled deeper in the pillows, frowning as he watched her with almost morbid fascination.

She was actually convinced she was pulling this off. He could see it in her face. In her father's tone of voice, he heard another story. Not that he could hear the words, just the alert tone, the almost military crispness.

She was going to get him killed. His training was excellent, but three Special Forces of the caliber that had helped free the Breeds from the Council Trainers and soldiers wouldn't be in any way easy to defeat. Especially considering he couldn't exactly kill his mate's family.

"Yes, Dad, I promise to rest, and I'll call you tomorrow," she answered in a placating tone that was so sickeningly sweet, it had him wondering if his dinner was going to stay down.

He made a note to never be taken in by that tone of voice himself.

When she finally hung up the phone, he glared at her sternly.

"I hope you are not convinced that you pulled that off," he growled furiously. "We will now have your entire family ripping the neighborhood apart looking for you."

"Don't be silly." She laughed at his prediction. "They'll come here first. I don't think they entirely trust you. Something about not being able to find enough background information." She wiggled her finely arched brows suggestively. "Have you been a bad boy, Tarek? Hiding records and such?"

She shimmied beneath the sheet, bracing her hands on the mattress as she leaned closer to him, her eyes dancing with shimmering lights of amusement as she gave him a suggestive little smile.

"Should I spank you for being bad now?"

His brows snapped into a frown. He was ignoring the ache in his cock. He needed a shower and food or he was going to collapse in exhaustion.

"You, I will spank later." He pointed his finger at her with determined emphasis. "Someone needs to teach you better than to play such obvious games with men who know you much too well."

"Yeah. Right." She had the nerve to laugh at him. "I didn't lie to him. He can see straight through my lies. Everything I said was the truth . . ."

"In a roundabout way," he grunted.

"How do you think I managed to get out of his house?" She plopped back against the pillow, the sheet falling away from her breasts and their hard, tempting nipples. "But you can punish me now if you want to."

She was becoming much too confident in her ability to drive him completely insane.

Finally he just threw up his hands as he rose from the bed and stalked to the bathroom door. If he was going to have to fight her brothers, he didn't want to smell of sex when that happened.

"I am taking a shower," he snapped. "I have a feeling I might want to be prepared for the visit I will have to endure by your family. And you are a troublemaker, Lyra. This will come back and smack you on the ass one of these days."

"Really?" Interest lit her laughter-filled gaze. "I bet it makes me wet."

He snorted. "I have no doubt, you little hellion."

And before his body could overrule his mind, he forced himself into the bathroom, closing the door behind him before he joined her in the bed again instead.

As he stepped beneath the steaming water, he made a note to contact Braden and warn him to be expecting trouble. He had a bad feeling that plenty of it was now heading his way.

Lyra laughed as the bathroom door closed behind Tarek and let the warmth that teasing him brought her fill her heart. She loved the look on his face. For once, the shadows that normally lingered there were gone. In their place may have been irritation or incredulity, but she had seen the happiness there as well.

She made him happy.

She sighed at the thought, an odd satisfaction filling her. Making him happy shouldn't make her feel as though she were glowing from the inside out, but it did.

And it made her want to cook. Something really incredible. Something that would make that bit of confused happiness fill his eyes once again.

She had food. Finally. It had taken her hours last night to convince him to have someone deliver the basic kitchen products as well as some real meat, rather than that stuff he nuked every day.

Yuck. That was nasty stuff.

She shook her head, rising from the bed and pulling on her gown and robe as she ignored the tenderness between her thighs. That and the pulse of desire. She had a feeling that Mating Heat or not, she could forget her response to him ever dimming. He had made her wet the first time she laid eyes on him, and she had a feeling she would be wet for him on her deathbed.

She left the bedroom, padding quickly down the stairs to the wide foyer and turning into the kitchen.

She stopped abruptly. Her eyes widened, terror rushing through her system as her knees weakened.

"Well, it looks like Tarek took a little mate," the intruder sneered, his weapon aimed at her heart. "I bet the Council will have a lot of fun with this one. After we take her Lion out, of course. The only good Feline is a dead one."

Lyra turned to run only to slam into the hard body blocking her way. The contact sent pain streaking across her nerve endings, causing her to gasp in shock as she jerked away from the other intruder.

What now? Breathing roughly, she fought to hold back her fear, her eyes wide, as hard hands pushed her into a kitchen chair.

"He'll kill you." She clenched her fingers at her side, trying to think, to find a way to escape, to warn Tarek.

"He might try. He'll fail. We were very careful this time. He won't even be able to smell us." Evil, malicious. The taller of the two men stared down at her curiously as he held the weapon on her. "So tell me, what's it like to fuck an animal?"

Lyra swallowed tightly. "Ask your wife."

He grunted at that, smiling mockingly. "Doesn't matter." He shrugged. "The scientists will get the answer."

She had to warn Tarek.

Her gaze flicked to the entrance of the kitchen. He would be finished soon, coming down the stairs, unaware of the danger awaiting him. Unable to smell the threat.

She swallowed tightly.

The Council had tortured him for most of his life, treated him like an animal, refused him even the most basic human considerations.

He had never eaten homemade bread. Had never drunk real coffee. He didn't know how to cook, but from what her brothers had said, many of the Breed labs had been dens of filth and neglect. Yet he kept his home sparkling, free of dust, and took off his shoes at the door. He was a man desperate to live, to be free. A man who knew how to love despite the horrors he had known.

And now these two thought they were going to use her to kill him? She couldn't, she wouldn't allow it.

He belonged to her now. He was her heart, her soul, and she couldn't imagine life without him. She would die without him.

Think Lyra. Her eyes darted around her as the two watched her closely. *Warn him. How could you warn him . . .*

Smell. He could smell arousal. He could smell fear.

Rather than tamping back the horror racing through her, the terror clogging her mind, she gave it free rein instead. She had to warn him . . .

Tarek stepped out of the shower, drying quickly before jerking clean sweatpants on and moving to the door to let Lyra know the shower was now free.

He stepped into the bedroom, frowning at the empty bed for a long second before his head raised slowly, a new, intrusive scent reaching his nostrils.

Fear.

He could smell it, sharp, warning, riding the soft trail of Lyra's unique scent. But there was nothing else. No other smell drifting through the bedroom door to give him an idea of what awaited him downstairs.

She was his mate, and he could feel the danger surrounding her pulsing in the air.

He jerked the cell phone from beside the bed and keyed in the alert for trouble before tossing the device to the mattress and striding to the chest of drawers.

He pulled one of the smaller weapons from the drawer before stripping the adhesive backing from the light, skin-adhering holster. Smacking it to the side of the gun, he anchored the weapon in the small of his back before pulling on his shirt.

He grabbed the spare gun from the top of the chest and checked the ammo before moving for the doorway.

Pausing, he listened carefully. There were no lights on, but he didn't need any. And he didn't know who or what was downstairs, but it wasn't a Breed. There wasn't a chance in hell a Breed could disguise his scent so effectively. But sometimes, rarely, certain humans could.

Trainers knew how. It was hard, at times nearly impossible, but it could be done.

As he moved to the stairs he inhaled carefully. He smelled no Breed or human scent other than Lyra's and her fear. It was overwhelming, imperative. But alongside it was a curiously hollow sterile scent. As though something had been cleaned. And another, not quite as crisp, as though something were bleeding away whatever had been used to disguise the evil that filled it.

A cold snarl shaped his lips.

There were two, and one of them was nervous, wary. Perhaps not quite as certain as the other. That one was weak. He would make a mistake.

As Tarek started down the stairs, he laid the extra weapon on a step, close enough to jump and retrieve if he needed it. If he went in armed, they would know he had been aware of them, and they would search him, using Lyra to keep him in place while they took the hidden weapon.

"Lyra, you left the lights out," he called out as he stepped into the foyer. "No more of your games now. Where are you?"

He kept his voice teasing, taunting as he moved to the kitchen where her scent was strongest. He stopped at the entrance, placing his hands on his hips as he surveyed the scene.

Everything inside him clenched with fear as he fought to present a casual attitude. He could feel the growl growing in his chest, his jaw clenching with the need to taste blood.

The two men stood on each side of her, one with his weapon

lying threateningly against her temple. She didn't make a sound, but he could see the tears shimmering on her face, her lips moving.

I'm so sorry . . .

"Well, I admit, Tarek, I hadn't thought it really possible." Anton Creighton shook his head as he made a clucking sound. "And to find you so careless. Your Trainers were sloppier than I had thought them to be during your stay at the labs."

Cold, steel-gray eyes stared out of a pale face. A black cap covered his blond hair, but Tarek remembered the color well. His broad, heavily muscled body appeared relaxed, but Tarek could see the tension in it. The other man wasn't nearly as confident as he appeared to be.

And his partner was terrified.

"The stink of your man is starting to bleed through whatever you used to cover him," he informed Creighton coolly. "He's scared."

Creighton's eyes narrowed as Tarek refused to rise to his prodding. His gaze flickered to the other man.

"Good help is so hard to come by." He smiled coldly. "But he did well enough to keep you from detecting us until the time was right."

Tarek nodded with all signs of absent attention as he glanced at Lyra.

"So what do you boys want tonight?" he asked, keeping his voice measured, nonthreatening.

He knew Creighton better than the other man thought he did. He was easy to play with, maneuverable to a small degree, and living on a prayer as he fought to escape both Breeds and Council soldiers.

Creighton was basically a coward. When the labs were attacked by government and independent forces to rescue the Breeds held there, he had deserted the fight rather than risking capture. He was considered a criminal to both sides now.

"Just the girl." Creighton shrugged dismissively. "As soon as I dispose of you, I can use her for a little trade. You should have stayed off my ass, Tarek. But because you're so persistent, I'll take care of you now and ensure my return to the Council ranks with your pretty little mate."

"The Council is disbanded, Creighton." Tarek watched him pityingly. "There's no one to trade with."

A rich chuckle filled the air.

"You really believe that, Tarek?" he asked, shaking his head. "No need to worry, Lion-boy. They're still there. Tucked away nice and safe, but there all the same."

"Shut up, Creighton," his partner hissed. "Kill him and be done with it."

Lyra flinched, her gaze turning wild at the demand.

Damn. She was the wild card, not these two bastards. And there wasn't a damn thing he could do but pray her common sense won out.

"Your boy is a little impatient, Creighton." Tarek mocked as he leaned against the doorframe, crossing his arms over his chest as he watched them. "A little bossy, too, isn't he?"

Creighton's ego was legendary.

"Shut up, Tim," he snapped. "I have him under control."

"You sure he's not a Coyote?" Tarek nodded to good old Tim, with his washed out hazel eyes filled with fear and lanky dark brown hair. "He shakes like one."

Creighton's chuckle was mocking, grating on Tarek's nerves as the barrel of his gun slid against Lyra's temple in a cold caress.

"He'll do," Creighton assured him as he stared back coldly. "Unfortunately, there's no bounty on your head. But I guess I'm going to have to kill you anyway. If you had just let me be, boy, I would have done the same." He shook his head in mock regret. "Some Breeds never learn though."

Just a little more. Just a few more seconds.

He could smell Braden and another Breed at the back door. But he could also smell the overwhelming scent of fury at the front door. Human fury. A father's fury.

Shit.

"This was really a bad time to come calling, Creighton." Tarek shook his head, almost feeling sorry for the other man now. "It's bread night, you know."

He glanced at Lyra, praying she would get the message. She blinked, amazement and a surge of renewed fear glittering in her eyes.

"Bread night?" Creighton stared at him in confusion. "What does bread have to do with anything? Has freedom rotted your brain?"

"Sadly, for you, I believe it may have."

The back door splintered as the house alarm began blaring. Lyra, bless her sweet heart, was no one's fool. Before Creighton could stop her, she threw herself to the floor, rolling beneath the table as her feet kicked out at Tim's knees as Tarek dropped, whipped the gun from his back, and fired back at the Trainer.

The front door exploded as Creighton went down and Tarek threw himself beneath the kitchen table, his body covering Lyra's as he left the other man for Braden and whoever the hell was screaming bloody-assed murder to take care of.

"I told you it wasn't going to work. You can't play with men who know you so well, Lyra," he growled, reminding her of his warning as she spoke to her father earlier. He pulled her deeper beneath the table, forcing her behind him, sheltering her between his body and the wall as she struggled to push him away.

Braden and Jonas were on the floor, weapons raised ready, as three well-trained Navy SEALs burst into the room, weapons drawn, murder glowing in their eyes.

"Dammit, Tarek, let me go before they destroy the house," Lyra yelled at his ear. "They'll tear it apart."

"Better the house than me," he grunted, holding her in place as the black-clad figures halted at the table, followed by a set of legs clad in jeans.

The father.

Hell.

"Look, I like this house better than mine." She smacked his shoulder before putting her knees into his back and pushing. "And they're going to ruin it."

"Dammit, stay in place, woman," he snarled. "I can rebuild the house, and as I can't kill the bastards because of you, I'd really prefer to stay out of harm's way. If it's all the same to you," he snarled mockingly.

"Moron."

"Brat."

"Well, at least she's alive," a mocking voice drawled as three Navy SEALs hunkered down to stare beneath the table.

Eyes amazingly similar to Lyra's stared back at him. They quickly took in the fact that he wasn't about to let her move just yet, and she was fairly content to be where she was, insults notwithstanding.

"You can't shoot my future husband." She finally managed to wiggle past him.

Heaving a sigh, Tarek glanced across the floor as Braden came slowly to his feet.

"Are those assholes bleeding on my kitchen floor?" Lyra was out from under the table just ahead of him, facing her brothers, hands on her hips. "Why are they bleeding on my floor?"

"Blame your boyfriend under there." The broadest of the four men faced her squarely, his black head lowered to snarl back at her, anger lighting his eyes. "He shot them. We didn't. And since when the hell is this your house?"

"Since *I* said it was." Tarek pulled her back, his instincts flaring at the other man's fury toward his mate. This was not acceptable.

"And who the hell are you?" Violence raged in the brother's expression. A violence he could damned well direct somewhere other than toward Lyra.

"Her mate . . ." His cold smile didn't go over any better than his announcement.

Pandemonium ensued.

ten

"I can't believe you actually got into a fist fight with my brother." Lyra's expression was none too pleased later that night as she stood before him, inspecting the black eye and split lip he had gained from the effort.

"Neither can I," he grunted, wincing as she pressed the alcohol pad she held to the abrasion on his cheek. "It was wasted effort. You, Lyra, are a troublemaker. I've seen this tonight."

"Me?" She drew back, her eyes innocently wide as she stared back at him in surprise. "What did I do?"

"You antagonize your brothers." He caught her hips as she attempted to move from the bed where he sat. "You deliberately challenge their authority and continually keep them in a state of combat-readiness. That fight was your fault. Had you been a bit more forthcoming, as I encouraged you to be on the phone, they would not have charged in, determined to protect your honor."

Her lips twitched. The little hellion.

"If you had stayed out of it, there wouldn't have been a fight." She braced her hands on his shoulders to hold him back from licking once again at the scratch she had somehow gained from the night's adventures.

The red mark extended from her shoulder, past her collarbone, and although the sting was irritating, it was nothing compared to the fires burning in the rest of her body.

"No man gives you orders but me," he grunted at being denied access to her sweet flesh. He deserved something in reward for the aches and pains echoing beneath his flesh.

"You don't give me orders, either," she informed him imperiously. "What is it with you guys that you think you can?"

He sighed wearily, seeing his life stretching out ahead of him, constantly amazed or exasperated at one small woman. Not that he wasn't looking forward to it. But Lyra had a habit of antagonizing her brothers where perhaps she should be less confrontational.

He was definitely going to have to talk to them alone in regards to this. She seemed to enjoy keeping them upset.

"The fact that you can so easily get into trouble?" He arched his brow mockingly. "Lyra, sweetheart, after discussing this with your brothers, I'm certain you are a trouble magnet."

The fight had been a damned good one. Clean, brutal, fists flying, and curses raging as he and Grant, her oldest brother, proceeded to destroy the kitchen.

When they finished, Lyra had stomped to the bedroom to pout while they agreed to a beer and a heated argument on whether or not Lyra would stay with him.

Not that there was a question of it as far as he was concerned, but in the eyes of her family, he had seen their love for her, and their fears. He wasn't exactly the boy next door. He was a Breed, and he had just nearly gotten her killed. It would be enough to terrify a brother who had accepted responsibility for his headstrong sibling.

And they seemed to accept him and his ability to protect her.

Most men would have been hesitant. Thankfully, the prejudices against the Breeds were absent in the Mason family, due to the fact that her three brothers had been instrumental in the rescues of many of the Breed captives.

He pulled her to him then, his chest tightening at the memory of Creighton's gun caressing her temple, the bullet much too close to extinguishing the fire that warmed everyone she touched. How could he endure life without her now?

"You didn't have to fight them." She leaned against him, her slender body flowing easily against him as he lifted her to straddle his lap, his arms wrapping tight around her back as his lips lowered to the mark he had left on her shoulder. "I had them under control."

"You had them in cardiac arrest," he sighed. "Your poor father will never be the same."

Lyle Mason, the father in question, had been most determined to take his daughter home, to wrap her in the protection he felt only he could provide. He had been a man tormented with thoughts of losing the daughter he so obviously adored.

Not that Tarek understood the family dynamics, but he understood the need to protect, the need to love the tiny woman he held in his arms. She was his light. His world. She could be nothing less to anyone who loved her.

He pressed her tighter against him, feeling her rock against the erection straining beneath his soft pants, dampening the material with the damp heat of her pussy.

She wasn't wearing panties beneath her gown. His hands smoothed down the material until he caught the hem and lifted it, his hands gripping her smooth, bare ass.

A moan locked in his throat at the feel of her sliding against him, her breathing deepening, the scent of her heat filling the room.

"Don't leave me, Lyra." He couldn't stop the words from slipping past his lips as he held on to her, lifting her, laying her back to the bed as he rose above her.

"I have no intention of leaving you, Tarek." Her eyes were glowing with emotion, with hunger. "I told you, I love you. And I don't say that lightly. Not to anyone."

He touched her cheek, his throat tightening as he fought past the confusion, the disbelief that this woman could love him. That God, in all his bountiful mercy, had finally adopted him and given him this gift he never thought he could have. Something, someone, to always call his own.

"The next time you start a fight with your brothers, I will spank you, though," he growled as her head raised, her lips finding the hardened nub of his nipple as she nipped at it playfully.

"Sounds like fun. How many fights are we talking about before I get my just desserts?"

He moaned as her fingernails raked down his abdomen before her fingers hooked in the waistband of his sweatpants and began to lower them slowly.

"You are a hellion," he breathed out roughly as he moved from the bed and stripped quickly.

Her gown went flying past him as he shucked his pants. When he straightened, there she was, on her hands and knees, her tongue reaching out to lick the bulging head of his cock.

Her black hair fanned around her face, her blue eyes glowing with emotion and hunger. They were as brilliant as the brightest, purest sapphire, and more precious than gold to him.

Her pink little tongue flickered over the crest of his erection again, leaving a trail of fire around the sensitive hood as he tensed at the pleasure shooting from his cock to every other nerve ending in his body. He didn't think pleasure could get any better—until her lips parted, her heated mouth opening to accept the head of his cock into the damp depths.

Tarek watched as the flushed, straining crest of his erection disappeared between her lips, her tongue stroking the underside with such incredible pleasure he wondered if he could bear it.

His hands tangled in her hair, clenching tight as a strangled growl filled his chest, escaping his lips as she began to suck him with hungry abandon.

Her movements were hesitant, innocent.

She was killing him.

She stared up at him, laughter and arousal gleaming in her gaze as her tongue stroked, her mouth drawing on him, her wicked hand moving slowly up his thigh until she cupped his balls with silken fingers and destructive pleasure.

"Brat," he groaned, fighting for breath. For control.

His tongue was throbbing like a toothache, the need to spill the excess hormone into her mouth making him wild. He could taste the spice, feel its effect on him, feel his cock tightening further, the need to release becoming a near-agonizing pleasure.

And still her mouth moved on him. Slow, delicate licks, deep, drawing caresses until a purely animalistic growl erupted from him.

Tarek tightened his hands in her hair, pulling her back as he felt the pulse of the barb just beneath the hood of his cock.

"Enough."

"Hmm. I'm hungry." She licked her lips sensually, full, swollen lips. "Maybe I want more."

She laughed, a low, sweet sound, as he pushed her back to the bed, spreading her thighs as he lowered his shoulders between them.

There was no time for preliminaries. He had to taste her. Sample the delicate liquid silk of her pussy before he went insane. Or kissed her.

If he kissed her, there would be no waiting. He was riding too close to the edge, her own hunger rising so quickly the scent of it was going to his head.

"I'm going to eat you up," he groaned a second before licking through the bare, syrup-laden silk of her intimate folds. "Every inch of you, Lyra. Until the taste of you permeates every fiber of my senses."

She breathed in roughly, the flesh of her tummy convulsing as he watched it with narrowed eyes. He could see so much there. Each ripple of creamy flesh corresponding with the level of her arousal.

His tongue circled her clit before he drew it between his lips, watching as her stomach seemed to convulse. As he suckled at her, he moved his fingers to the drenched folds of her pussy, opening her farther until he could work a finger inside the hot depths.

She jerked against him, her hips writhing, pressing closer to the penetration as her creamy juices began to flow.

"Oh God, Tarek, you're making me crazy," she cried out desperately, her vagina rippling around his finger. "Stop torturing me like this."

He hummed his pleasure of her taste. Sweet. Addictive. He pushed her closer to the edge of her release, his finger thrusting deeply inside her, caressing the responsive depths as she lifted to him.

"Tease." Her rough accusation was thick with her pleasure. "Fuck me, Tarek. Don't make me have to kill you."

He would have smiled if he weren't so consumed by the hunger for her.

"Tarek . . ." Her half-scream was followed by the tightening of her pussy around his finger, her tummy tightening. "You'll pay for this." Her knees bent, her feet pressing into the mattress as she lifted closer. "I swear I'll make you pay . . ."

He gave her what she needed. Adding another finger to the snug depths of her cunt, he began to pump them inside her using his lips, his tongue, the suction of his mouth to drive her higher, to send her into fragmented explosions of ecstasy.

She arched to him, crying out his name as he quickly rose above her, lifting her, pressing his cock into the convulsing tissue of her pussy as he gritted his teeth against the pleasure.

She was so tight. So hot.

Liquid silk. Lava-hot cream.

He gripped her hip with one hand, lowering his weight to the elbow of his opposite arm as he felt her legs wrap around him.

Her pussy flexed around him, tiny flutters of sensation, tight, rippling caresses washing over his erection as he worked it into her, first short, desperate thrusts and then hard lunges as he began to fuck her with all the strength and desperation of the hunger surging inside him.

His lips lowered to hers, his tongue spearing into her mouth as she moved beneath him, opening for him, taking him with strangled screams and ever-tightening ripples of her responsive pussy.

She was ecstasy. She was life.

The tempo of his thrusts increased as the hormone surged from his tongue to her system, heating them both further, sending them rushing headlong into orgasm.

As he felt his release tightening his balls, the extension beneath the hood of his cock began to engorge, becoming firmly, heatedly erect and locking him tight inside.

Violent shudders shook her as her arms tightened around his neck, her head turning as his lips unerringly found the mark that branded her as his mate as he began to flood her with his semen.

Shocking, violent pleasure. A bonding unlike anything he could have known. And Lyra. Always Lyra. The center of his life.

"Oh God. Tell me that barb thing does not go away with the heat," she gasped when they found the sanity to breathe. "I wouldn't be pleased."

"I guess you'd have to hurt me?" He chuckled weakly as he rolled to his side, pulling her against his chest as he sighed in contentment.

"I'd have to hurt you bad." She sighed.

"But you'd still love me." She'd better.

"I'll always love you." She nipped at his chest before leaning her head back to smile up at him mistily. "Always, Tarek. You might not be the boy next door, but the Breed next door works much better."

Their laughter was soft, content. His soul was fulfilled.

He wasn't completely human. But neither was he an animal. He was a Breed, a Breed who had found his mate, and his life.

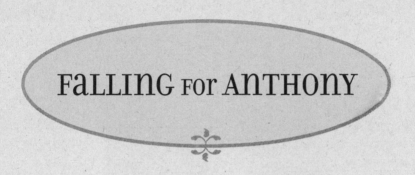

FALLING FOR ANTHONY

MELJEAN BROOK

one

Appearances are almost always deceiving.
—*The Doyen Scrolls*

A single glimpse at the disarray in Colin's bedchamber and the valet's harried expression was all Anthony Ramsdell needed to determine that his best course of action would be to exit, and quickly. Colin Ames-Beaumont, the younger son of the Earl of Norbridge, could not be hurried in his dress—neither the most pleasurable entertainment nor the most beautiful woman could ever induce him to leave the house before every fold of his cravat lay perfectly in place—and anyone who happened to be in his vicinity at that time could be subject to his valet's attentions, should Colin judge that person unfashionable in any way.

Anthony had made that mistake more than once, and though his green waistcoat, black coat, and tan breeches might pass Colin's inspection, his linen lacked the proper amount of starch and was no longer blindingly white. His evening shoes, though he'd done his best to shine them, were scuffed from regular use. His chestnut hair had grown too long in the front; Colin had chided him the week before for letting it fall into his eyes like a schoolboy—a look, Colin had observed, that ruined his own sartorial perfection by association. As Colin had only been half-joking, Anthony was certain if he stepped into the room the valet would have scissors out in a trice.

Self-preservation sent him retreating downstairs, smiling. He couldn't be annoyed by his friend's vanity; he understood Colin too well for that. He was only glad that the other man had recently changed his style from brightly colored silks and cosmetics to the simple elegance of a dandy—even if that elegance took him almost two hours to achieve and, by all appearances, was now only beginning the second hour.

Knowing from experience how that time could drag on, Anthony headed for the earl's study. He'd been a frequent guest in the house for years, spending as much time with the Ames-Beaumonts as with his own family, and the study had always been one of his favorite rooms. Though much smaller than the library at the earl's ancestral home in Derbyshire, it held a significant selection of volumes, with enough variety to satisfy Norbridge's mercurial taste and Anthony's predictable one.

He knocked once on the door out of habit—when he'd been a boy, the earl had always required him to announce his presence in that manner—and chuckled self-consciously. Norbridge wasn't inside and would not issue an authoritative command to enter; Anthony had met with him that morning and, their business completed, Norbridge had left for Derbyshire shortly thereafter.

Thinking of the agreement they'd reached, hollow resignation settled in Anthony's stomach. In two days, he would join Norbridge's good friend, Major-General Cole, on the Peninsula to serve as his personal physician for as long as the campaign against Napoleon persisted. Norbridge had shaped the proposal as a request, but Anthony had recognized it for what it was: a demand for repayment of a debt.

A debt Anthony readily acknowledged, but would have preferred to settle another way.

Any other way.

He sighed, closing the door behind him and walking along the bookshelves lining the adjacent wall. Furnished with dark, heavy wood and rich fabrics, the room was an impoverished scholar's luxurious dream; Anthony took little notice of or pleasure in his surroundings. He hadn't indulged in a bout of self-pity since childhood, but as he stared blankly at a leather-bound volume of *Paradise Lost*, he thought spending the next hour privately whining to himself might be just the thing.

The sudden clang of metal against stone drew his attention to the opposite end of the library, and the invectives Anthony had been planning to hurl against God silently expired on his tongue. Colin's twin sister, Lady Emily, stood with her back to him, hair unbound, swinging a sword wildly at the marble fireplace; the blade skidded across the mantle, knocking books and a small statue to the floor. A deep scar in the stone revealed where she'd struck the first blow.

"Emily?" Surprise gave his query a sharp edge, and he briefly wondered if she'd been sent by some higher power to purposely torment him on this day of all days. Another reminder of everything he could never have and shouldn't want to have.

Emily had constantly been at his and Colin's sides until they had begun attending public school. Anthony had suffered a childish infatuation with her, and his teenage years had been fraught with frustrated longing. But her head had been filled with romantic dreams and noblemen, and she'd never looked twice at her brother's poor, untitled playmate.

Eventually, he had outgrown his feelings for her, and they had become friends. Their meetings had been brief and infrequent of late years, however, due to his medical studies and her social schedule.

Having recently passed his exams, he'd thought to enjoy her bright and humorous company more often, and to renew their friendship—but Spain and his duty to her father would make that impossible.

His certainty that he was the butt of a cosmic joke faded when she stiffened, and the sword froze mid-swing. She turned to glare at him and spoke through clenched teeth. Firelight glinted against trails of moisture on her cheeks. "Get out, Anthony. I don't want to hurt you."

He eyed the sword warily but didn't move. If she'd simply been weeping over some feminine dilemma, he would have been the gentleman and left, but concern for her safety prevented him from leaving her alone to act out her rage and violence.

He had thought he'd witnessed all of her moods, but the pinch of her elegant brow and the angry, bitter slant to her mouth was new. Emily possessed a perpetually sunny, dreamy disposition; over their long acquaintance, he'd seen her upset only a few times. It would not be too difficult to help her regain her natural good humor. He would stay until she did, and until he was certain she would cause no harm to herself.

And despite her warning, he did not feel he would be in danger. He had no fear that Emily would turn on him.

He attempted a smile and said, "Hurt *me*? And what have I done? Inadvertently criticized a new hair ribbon?" Though he strove for a light tone, it came out stiffly, as if he meant to insult her.

She stared at him for a long moment before presenting her back to him.

Anthony bit back a sigh, a flush crawling up his neck. He'd forgotten that around Emily, his humor seemed to twist, and he invariably sounded like an idiot or a prig. Perhaps it would be better to fetch Colin; Anthony might not be up to the task.

That would mean leaving her alone, however, and he was loath to do that, even for a few moments. To cover his embarrassed silence, he crossed the room and chose a seat on the green velvet sofa angled between the desk and the hearth. From that vantage point, she stood in profile to him, and he studied her features as best he could. The firelight danced across the gold of her hair but left her expression shadowed. Her shoulders were squared, and she kept a tight grip on the handle of the sword. The tumble of hair down her back and the long column of her dress should have softened the impression of rigidity in her posture; instead it lent a tight, brittle cast to her form, like a porcelain figurine on the verge of shattering.

Discarding any further attempts at humor, he said quietly, "Has something happened, Emily?"

She gave a hard, short laugh. "How astute you are, doctor! Are you so observant with all of your patients? Obviously, *something* has happened."

His color rose again, but this time his embarrassment was tinged with anger that she would mock his concern. He tamped down both feelings; at least she was responding to him.

He hesitated and then ventured, "Has yet another suitor disappointed you, then?" In the five years since her debut she'd had scores of admirers and nearly as many proposals—none of which had been to her satisfaction.

"*Yet another?*" she repeated, her voice rising with each syllable. She whirled to face him. Her cheeks were pale, her eyes large. He knew they appeared hazel in the sunlight, striated with green and blue; now, they were dark with fury. "I detect disapproval, Anthony—"

He shook his head. "No, I only meant—"

"And who do you think you are to disapprove of *me*?" She threw her hands up, and he instinctively drew back from the swipe of the blade. It hadn't come near him, but he kept a cautious eye on it as she continued her tirade, hacking the air to punctuate each question. "Do you think my dreams of love are not worth pursuing? Do you think them so worthless, so impossible? Is it so ridiculous to believe that love can be all-consuming and true, and to *wait* for that before pledging myself for eternity to a man who can't be what I want him to be? Am I a fool to think I can have that? Are my expectations too great, my requirements too exacting?"

Her voice broke on the last, and for just a moment, she seemed to withdraw into herself before gathering and refocusing her anger. Her wild jabs at the air ceased, and she pointed the tip of the sword at Anthony with cold deliberation.

"And what of your dreams, Anthony?"

He looked away from the blade, startled by the sudden change in her demeanor. Where she had been heat and fury, now she was ice and mockery. "What of them?" he said carefully, hoping she would not mention his youthful infatuation.

He'd never thought to see one of her smiles contain the cruelty of the one that now curved her lips. "Come now, Anthony—don't tell me you *wanted* to be a doctor. It was the most painless way for you to get a title other than 'Mister.' My father's suggestion, and you went along with it, allowed him to pay for your education, because you thought he'd make you *his* personal physician, and you and Colin could carry on as you always have, here in London."

A hot, dull flash crawled up Anthony's cheeks. He hadn't realized she knew the particulars of his debt to her father. And he couldn't refute her other charges—he hadn't been hungry for a title, but he had wanted to advance his position in society so he wouldn't be bound by circumstances of his birth.

His gaze dropped to the scar on his palm, a lingering reminder of the blood-brother pact he and Colin had performed years before. They had used the earl's sword—the one Emily now wielded so casually—and, afterward, his hand had become swollen and he feverish. His mother had said the infection was to remind him of his place, to remind him of his duty to help raise the family from their straightened circumstances.

Anthony had never asked if the earl had found similar meaning in Colin's sickness.

"And you'd never have to return to the family that rejected you for lowering yourself. The family that would rather have you remain a starving, indebted gentleman than work in a profession, even as their house falls into disrepair around them." She paused for a breath. "But perhaps your jaunt on the Peninsula will make you a hero, and you will restore the family name and fortune."

He'd thought Emily couldn't hurt him, but she didn't need the sword to do that. He regarded her silently, pain and resentment thrumming under his skin. Everything about her declared her station in life: the pale peach walking dress skimming over her curves was of the finest cut and cloth; the way she held herself erect, the sweep of her neck, the high planes of her cheeks, the softness of her hands all confirmed the ease and luxury that permeated her existence. She would never understand his dismay at her father's suggestion that he join Cole in Spain. She could never conceive of the shame that came from being reminded of his place by the very man who had offered him hope of something better.

He didn't know what had come over her to speak to him as she had, but if he stayed in this room much longer, he was going to say something he would regret. With stiff lips, he said, "My lady, I must beg leave—"

But her thoughts must have also strayed to her father, for her gaze turned inward and she continued as if he hadn't spoken, "What you have failed to learn is that we—Colin, you, and I—are nothing to my father. Only Henry and my nephew matter to him, because Henry is the heir, and Robert is Henry's heir. My father is on his way to Derbyshire now, to fawn over the boy as his twelfth birthday approaches. He expected me to join them in their adoration—but children cannot interest me." Her mouth trembled and she looked away from Anthony, and her tone softened. "But I can hardly fault you for your stupidity; I myself have only just realized this today."

Compassion warred with his embarrassment and anger. The

Countess of Norbridge had died in childbed after delivering Emily and Colin; the earl, deeply in love with his wife and stricken with grief, barely acknowledged their existence for the first years of their life, and only took a passing interest in them as they aged. He saved his attentions for Henry, who was ten years older. Emily had never seemed to mind her father's indifference—but perhaps that had not been the case, and she had suffered from it.

But his own wounds were too fresh to completely forgive her for exposing them, and his tone mocking as he replied, "And what other astounding revelations have you had today?"

Emily slanted him a cynical glance, hefting the sword. "That he cares more for this than he does for us." He followed her gaze as she examined the length of it, turning the short bronze blade from side to side. "It's been in my family for so long, the story of its origin can barely be credited: my ancestor, a knight, finding it during the Crusades and bringing it back from the Holy Lands. It never needs to be sharpened; it's never corrupted by age. I suspect my father cleans it at night, to keep its legend alive for my family. He usually keeps it in Derbyshire—except he's been spending so much time in London, he brought it to have it near him here." She tilted her head, her eyes glinting with dark curiosity. The hard edge to her voice returned. "I wonder what will happen if I smash it against stone a few more times?"

Anthony frowned and forgot about his intention to leave. "You won't be able to reverse the damage you do to it, Emily. Are you certain your anger—whatever the cause—is worth this?"

"Oh, yes," she breathed, and in a smooth, quick movement, she whipped around and slammed the tip of the sword straight into the marble. He shook his head in exasperation.

Then her cry of surprise sent him surging to his feet, crossing the short distance to her side. Astonishment furrowed his brow.

She'd embedded the sword halfway into the stone.

Her hands fell away from the hilt, and she covered her mouth with shaking fingers. Her eyes were wide, and her voice trembled with light, genuine laughter—familiar laughter. "He apparently sharpened it *very* well."

This was the Emily he knew. Anthony grinned. "Apparently."

She continued to stare at the sword. "Have you ever seen anything like this? It is extraordinary, don't you agree?" She lowered her hands from her face, and Anthony saw the bright streak of crimson on her cheek.

He caught her wrist; turning it, he saw the thin line of blood welling from a shallow slice in her thumb.

"Oh!" Emily stared at the cut. "I didn't even feel it. When the sword stopped moving, it jarred my hand over the hilt, but I didn't realize I'd touched the blade."

"I have this," Anthony said, digging a clean handkerchief from his pocket.

Her fingers were long and delicate; the scent of lavender rose from her hair. The warmth of her skin against his seemed to gather and spiral directly to his loins. He ignored the sensation and forced another grin. "Aren't you fortunate I'm a physician? You could have bled to death from such a wound." His jest sounded strained to his own ears, and he hoped she wouldn't notice.

She lifted her gaze to his. Her humor had fled, and though he did not detect her previous bitterness in her expression, he could not determine her mood. His own anger had cooled, leaving behind embarrassment and a growing arousal—and her proximity made him doubly aware of both.

With the barest of smiles, she said, "You have the most amazing countenance—I can read every thought you have."

His hands stilled, the handkerchief half-wound around her thumb.

Absently raising the fingers of her uninjured hand to his brow, she smoothed back the forelock that had fallen into his eyes and murmured, "The lift of your eyebrow, the crinkle of your eyes, the corner of your mouth: they all give you away." She touched each feature as she spoke; admiration filled her expression, surprise—as if this was the first time she had *looked* at him. "It is so rare for a man to have such finely drawn features as you, and yet there is no doubt of your masculinity."

The tilt of her head was assessing; dumbstruck, he could not reply.

"You are truly beautiful; it is no wonder Colin has always kept you close to his side. You are a magnificent accessory, the perfect complement to him." Though her words stung, he knew she intended no insult; and, taken aback by her compliments, he could find no reply. He finished tying off the makeshift bandage in silence.

She looked past him, her eyes soft and unfocused. "When we were younger, I used to wish that you weren't so unsuitable, that one day you would discover you were the long-lost son of a duke or—"

He drew a sharp breath, and the sudden heavy weight in his chest made his voice harsh. "Don't be ridiculous."

Her tiny smile froze in place and became brittle again. "Yes, it was ridiculous. All of my dreams were." Pulling away from him, she grabbed the sword and yanked it from the stone. It slid out easily, as if from liquid.

Anthony turned away from her, collapsing onto the sofa before his legs gave out beneath him. *Even worse than not being noticed,* he decided, *was being noticed and found wanting.*

Some masochistic impulse made him watch the sway of her hips as she walked toward the earl's mahogany desk and placed the sword on its display stand. She paused for a moment, cast him a calculating glance, and slid her forefinger along the flat side of the blade. He followed its progress, and the image of that simple touch on his skin rose, unbidden.

When had her movements become so sensual? Was it deliberate?

Do not be a fool, he admonished himself. He was unsuitable. Considering the hopelessness of a match between them, only a witless idiot would think there was a possibility of his having her.

And the proof, he supposed, was that the most brainless part of his body liked the idea of having her very much.

"Are you upset with my father?" she asked softly—too softly. As if she were planning something.

He answered her carefully, uncertain of the motive behind her question. "No," he said finally. "I'm disappointed in myself for expecting too much."

She nodded, and her cool smile did not fade. "I did, too. We make quite a pair." She tapped the sword with her fingernail and then stepped away from the desk. "Perhaps I should find a way to let him know how disappointed I am."

Anthony nodded absently, disliking the direction the conversation was taking and searching wildly for a topic that would ease the icy tension that lingered in the room, that would leave them on a better footing before he left.

Before he could speak, Emily said, "I did have one other *astounding revelation* today. A rumor came to my attention, and I had to ascertain its truth for myself. I have just come from Cranborne Street, off Leicester Square."

Grateful that he would not have to come up with a subject, and relieved that she had shifted her attention to gossip, Anthony grinned slightly and prepared to laugh at some entertaining *on dit*.

Her color high, she added, "While I was there, I learned that if a woman takes a man's organ into her mouth, she can make him do anything she wishes."

He blinked, his smile paralyzed on his face, his mind unable to comprehend that the statement had come from *her*; his body, however, understood perfectly. The sudden, superb ache of his erection broke through the numbing hold shock had placed on his other emotions: jealousy, concern, and desire fought to place words on his tongue.

Emily stole them away by lifting her skirts, straddling him, and capturing his lips with hers.

TWO

There is not always a choice;
alternatives are not always to be had;
there is not always a decision to make.
—*The Doyen Scrolls*

Surprise held Anthony's mouth immobile and closed under hers, and she slid her tongue along his bottom lip, demanding entry. The practiced caress brought Anthony to his senses; Emily shouldn't know how to kiss like that, and she certainly shouldn't be on his lap with her hemline bunched around her thighs.

He grasped her wrists tightly and pushed her upper body away from his. Her weight shifted against his rigid sex, and her name was a hoarse groan instead of a stern warning. "Emily!"

She stared at him, her face set. Her lips glistened from the kiss, but her expression was determined rather than passionate.

Deliberately, she rocked against him.

His breath hissed out from between clenched teeth as he fought for control. He should have tumbled her onto the floor, removed her from his person, and stopped this madness. He couldn't; she was a lady, a friend, and should be treated as such—even when she behaved as shockingly as this. Instead, he gave her a shake. "Do you wish to bring ruin to your family? Who taught you this?"

"A little bird," she replied; he shook her again for her flippancy and had to grit his teeth. Each movement of her body ground against his erection. "A bird of paradise," she added, her eyes flashing as if she dared him to reprimand her. "I had questions; she answered them."

"You went to a courtesan?" He couldn't begin to fathom it. He recalled her mention of a visit to Cranborne Street; though no longer a fashionable part of London, it had some claim to respectability. A courtesan—a very discreet one—could possibly pose as a widow and live among the gentry there. "Why?"

Her mouth pressed into a firm line. She turned her head and pulled against his grip.

Torn between relief and regret that she'd apparently abandoned her attempt at seduction, Anthony released her wrists. Her hands fell to her sides, drawing his gaze down; a strangled sound caught in his throat.

An ivory stripe of bare thigh peeked out above a garter of white ribbon. Pink silk stockings embraced her slim legs and trim ankles. As he watched, Emily's fingers curled around her hem, and she raised the dress higher, fine muslin sliding over satin skin.

Realizing that her seduction hadn't ceased and his resistance would soon fail, he wrapped his hands around her waist and began lifting her away from him. She countered by slipping her hand between them, firmly stroking his length, up and down.

Even with two layers of clothing between her palm and his shaft, he felt every inch of the scandalous caress burning into him. His hips jerked, nearly unseating her; he steadied her automatically, his hands trembling against her waist.

"Good God, Emily," he said desperately. "Stop this."

Her fingers plunged beneath the placket at the front of his breeches; without his being aware of it, she'd unfastened the buttons. She pulled at the front of his drawers as she nimbly untied the tapes.

"Stop!" he repeated—and then his erection was in her hand and his voice failed him. With quick fingers, she worked his arching sex from its confines. It rose up against the tousled folds of their clothing. She held it carefully, though with the strength of his arousal, it needed no support. At the sight of her pale hand surrounding the base of his shaft, his defiance fled.

And in the back of his mind, where his self-pity and disappointment lingered, a desire long suppressed emerged: *She'll have to marry you. She'll be yours.*

Possession—an emotion unfamiliar and heady—ripped through him, left him breathless, and mingled with self-disgust that he would ever use such a method, that he was participating in this calculated ruin.

Emily rose higher on her knees, her eyes cold with purpose. She guided his tip to her entrance; he immediately recognized that she wasn't ready, but she began to sink onto him before he could implore her to wait.

The pleasure of being enveloped by her heated depths overwhelmed the discomfort of his entry until she whimpered softly in distress. He realized that despite her practiced kiss and her knowledgeable fingers, she didn't know more than the mechanics of intercourse.

With clinical detachment, he heard himself say, "Lift yourself up, then push back down. Slowly."

Her face blazed with color, but she followed his instruction. Considering that she had been bold enough to instigate this, Anthony had a moment to wonder at her embarrassment—was it caused by their actions, his frank instruction . . . or because it was *him*?—before the leisurely drag of her inner muscles up his length captured every bit of his attention.

She took him in again, more easily than before; her body had begun producing moisture. With a small, relieved sigh, she began riding him in slow, shallow strokes.

It was torture, but he dared not force her all the way onto him for fear of hurting her. To keep himself from thrusting deep, he leaned forward and buried his face between her breasts, biting the bodice of her dress. He inhaled sharply, letting the dark, warm scent of her fill his senses.

She suddenly paused with his shaft halfway inside her, and his teeth threatened to tear through lace trim. "Anthony?"

He hoped she would take his choked grunt as an answer; at that moment, nothing he could have said would have been sensible.

After a brief hesitation, she said, "Do not spill your seed inside me."

That brought his head up. Uncertainty and fear pinched her mouth.

"I won't," he promised.

"Will you spill it soon?" she said, with a fleeting, pained expression.

"Not immediately." Chagrin flushed his cheeks. When he had become a willing participant, he should have seen to her pleasure. "Have you exhausted yourself? Do you want to stop?"

She shook her head. "I will finish this," she said, rising up with determined vigor. She dropped, carried down by her weight.

She cried out in surprise at his full penetration; Anthony, unable to help himself, held her locked against him with his hands on her hips. His boot heels dug into the carpet. Fire licked at his spine, drawing his muscles taut.

After a long, shaky sigh, she began to move again, and he drew her hands to his shoulders so she could brace herself against him. Slipping his fingers between them, he sought the tiny organ at the apex of her sex. His thumb stroked; she gasped and tried to pull away; he followed, briefly triumphing in the soft sounds of pleasure she began to make low in her throat.

Not immediately, he had told her, but the slick glide of his fingers against her, of his shaft skimming against his hand with every thrust into her, undid him. His body tightened, trembled. He fought it, trying to wait for her, ringing the base of his cock and squeezing in a hopeless attempt to slow his orgasm. The urge to find his release inside her, to make his possession complete, almost overwhelmed the memory of his promise—but at the last moment he withdrew.

Grabbing for the first piece of cloth at hand—her chemise—he wrapped it over his glans as his orgasm tore through him, clenching his teeth against a shout.

And when the last shudder faded, the enormity of what they'd done hit him.

He stared down at the semen-soaked linen in his hand. *Oh, God.* Had he really been stupid enough to imagine that Norbridge would allow him to marry Emily? That he would be a match for an earl's daughter, just because he'd compromised her? More likely, if he discovered Anthony had made love to his daughter, Norbridge would ruin him, make it impossible for Anthony to live or work amongst polite society.

Had he only believed it for that moment so he could allow himself to yield to her? *If I had been a man, instead of a boy searching for ease and pleasure, wouldn't I have kept us both from ruination?*

Shame stiffened his tongue, but he knew he had to apologize. He lifted his gaze; she was staring at him, her expression arrested on his face.

"Don't . . . blame yourself," she said. Her voice trembled, and she closed her eyes. "I told you I would hurt you."

Unsure how to respond, he gestured to their clothing and said the first thing that came to his mind. "I've not been hurt—only mussed." He attempted a smile. "Colin will be severely displeased by my state of dishevelment tonight; I hardly think he'll let me accompany him to his gentleman's club now."

To his horror, tears started in her eyes. As if she hadn't heard his jest, she said brokenly, "I have been an idiot to think love means anything. It is a fraud, isn't it?"

Without waiting for his answer, she buried her face in his shoulder and sobbed. His concerned queries yielded no answer. At a loss, he could only hold her, stroking her hair in a vain attempt to soothe her unrelenting despair.

Self-recrimination tore at him—why had he allowed her to do this? The answers that came to his mind were not pleasant, and in the end, he could only murmur against her temple his apologies, and his promise to return from the Peninsula and make reparations for the wrong he'd done her, to take away the troubles that plagued her.

He repeated the vow again and again as she cried, and he felt the weight of it settle over him. His life had never had a purpose, but one sat before him now. It would not be a grand purpose, but it would be *his*.

He would return and make it right—and she would be happy again.

"I promise," he said.

ALBUERA, SPAIN
MAY 1811

A soft breeze had swept away the haze of burnt gunpowder enveloping the fields, but the acrid odor lingered. The moonlight made formless lumps and shadows of the soldiers lying on the ground; its dim glow erased their identities, the blue and green and red of their uniforms showing gray and black.

Anthony raised his lantern high, trying to peer past the circle of light it cast, silently urging the dead men around him to moan or call out for help. None would—he'd checked each still form in the field, bending hundreds of times to feel for a pulse that was almost never there. Earlier, he'd seen medical personnel and soldiers from both sides scouring the battlefields for survivors and collecting weapons. Now, as it neared midnight, the search for survivors had waned until the only living beings in that wretched place were him, the two hospital mates he'd accompanied, and the handful of soldiers they'd found and treated and who now waited in a medical cart for transport back to the hospital.

Across the ridge that ran the length of the Albuera River, the wagons carrying the dead back for burial were still at work, slowly taking the course the battle had followed and collecting its casualties. It would be early morning before they reached this field.

"Doctor?"

With a resigned sigh, Anthony lowered his lantern. A few paces away, Assistant Surgeon Dilby stood wiping his hands with a blood-streaked cloth. The skin around the young surgeon's face looked as if it had been stretched and released, hanging tiredly under his eyes and chin.

Suddenly feeling his own exhaustion, Anthony looked past him. On the edge of the field, the cart was visible only as a dim outline, the lanterns hanging from its bench seat two feeble spots of light. "Is the last one settled?"

Dilby nodded and tucked the end of his rag into his leather apron. "Phillips is still with him. He's stabilized; he might make it to the hospital. I don't know if the major will. He woke up that once, but . . ." He shrugged. "I'm surprised he lasted this long, what with his guts on the outside."

Anthony smiled faintly as they began their trek back to the cart. In only two months of war, he'd seen men live through worse and die from less. "He hasn't cocked up his toes yet, Dilby—perhaps he'll survive to let Surgeon Guthrie perform his magic."

"Skill and instinct, not magic," Dilby retorted quickly, and Anthony grinned. The young mate's adoration of the Principal Medical Officer had been clear since they'd met. Glancing sidelong at Anthony from narrowed, baggy eyes, he added, "But a personal physician wouldn't know that."

Anthony didn't take offense at the deliberate insult; he knew his service in the war was not a heroic effort but simply a way of repaying a debt. He'd rather have done anything but practice medicine and amateur surgery on the battlefield, and would rather have been anywhere but the Peninsula. Dilby deserved some reply, however, so he forced humor into his tone and said, "Convince Cole of my uselessness on a day when his gout is particularly painful, and I'll apprentice myself in the surgery tomorrow."

Chuckling, Dilby veered away from Anthony to avoid the corpse of one of Napoleon's soldiers. His tone became wistful. "I suppose when the war is over, you won't be his personal physician any longer. You'll set up a practice in London, join society, and treat ladies' nerves."

With only the slightest break in his stride, Anthony stooped and felt for a pulse. Half of the soldier's face had been torn away, probably victim to English shrapnel. "Hardly appropriate work for a gentleman," he said softly. They were familiar words; Anthony's mother and sisters never failed to remind him of it in the letters he received.

When Anthony caught up to him a moment later, Dilby continued, "At least when you marry, you will be able to present your wife at court. My Sarah would have liked that." The folds on his face creased into the tender smile that appeared whenever he mentioned his wife or their young daughter.

Anthony tried to return the smile and to keep the doubts that had plagued him for two months from squeezing at him, but the words made his chest tighten nonetheless. *When you marry.* His promise to Emily hadn't been an understanding, and yet he could not help but hope that his vow had touched her, that she would consider his unspoken offer of marriage.

Would she wait for him? Likely not.

But as Colin's brief letters never contained information about her entering into an engagement, he saw no reason to give up that hope. There was little other pleasure to be had on the Peninsula.

With his gaze focused on the ground and his thoughts far from

a bloodstained battlefield in Spain, it took Anthony a moment to realize that Dilby had stopped abruptly and was staring ahead, his
eyes wide.

Anthony's question died on his lips as the light from the cart's
two lanterns winked out, followed by the sound of crumpling metal.
Surprise kept him rooted briefly to the spot—the medical cart was
clearly marked to let medical personnel work unmolested, even in
the heat of battle—until Phillips's sharp, terrified cry spurred him
forward.

He broke into a run, the racing of his heart echoed by his pounding feet. Behind him, Dilby shouted, "We are medics! *Docteur!*"

The lantern swung wildly in his hand. Its erratic illumination
prevented him from clearly seeing the cart, but the half moon
limned the shape of a man—too big to be Phillips—scrambling
atop the cart and bending over until he was hidden by its wooden
sides.

Suddenly cautious, Anthony slowed his pace to a jog, forcing
himself to take deep breaths, and to think instead of blindly react.
He hadn't heard a firearm, but the man could be armed—and Anthony was not. He had to assume that the only rifle the medical
team carried with them, which had been in the cart with Phillips,
was under their assailant's control. He was uncertain if the man had
been wearing a uniform; perhaps a soldier needed help but was
crazed from the battle and acting irrationally?

Fifteen feet from the cart, he stopped and steadied the lamp, staring at the scene and trying to make sense of it: the brown, gory lump
at the front of the cart, the smaller one beside it. His stomach
clenched as he realized the mule's head had been torn from its body,
the ragged cavity at the top of its shoulders still steaming.

Fear shivered over his skin, slick and cold.

Dilby came up beside him, panting from exertion. Metal glinted
in his hand. "I found this . . . oh, God Almighty save us!"

Anthony silently repeated the prayer. Even amidst the terrible carnage of the battlefield, this violence struck him as unnatural, a malevolent perversion. A man, even a madman, couldn't have done that to the mule.

Every instinct told him to flee; he gripped the handle of the lantern tightly, as if its small weight could anchor him, and called out, "Phillips?"

A choking, gurgling noise answered. Dilby whimpered, backing up a step.

Anthony glanced at the younger man and met the horrified gaze that mirrored his own. He said hoarsely, "I should try to help him."

Dilby shook his head violently and took another step back. "I don't think—" He broke off with a shudder, the final words hanging unspoken but palpable between them.

I don't think he's still alive.

Anthony looked back at the cart. "I have to try."

As if seeing Anthony's determination bolstered his courage, Dilby squared his shoulders and nodded. His face was pale, the loose skin stretched tight with tension. His voice trembled, but he managed to say, "*We* have to try."

Anthony nodded gratefully; he didn't consider himself a coward, but he certainly did not want to face alone whatever waited for them—and if Phillips had been seriously hurt, Anthony would need Dilby's medical assistance.

He glanced at the sword bayonet the other man had found, and now held in a white-knuckled grip. Though the sturdy blade had a smooth brass handle, it was too short and awkward for effective hand-to-hand combat, but at least it offered them some protection. "Can you use that if you need to?"

"For Sarah and little Nellie's sake, I will," Dilby said.

Anthony's expression hardened, anger burning through the fear that had overtaken him. Dilby and he weren't soldiers; whoever hid in the cart had attacked unarmed and injured men.

He swept the lantern in a circle, looking for a weapon of his own. He found nothing, and delaying any longer wouldn't help Phillips—if Phillips could be helped at all.

In silent agreement, they rounded the cart, careful to keep a significant distance from it. They couldn't hide their presence; Anthony's lamp made them a target, as did Dilby's ragged breathing.

War hadn't prepared him for what Anthony saw; it wasn't the death or the mutilation that made the vomit rise in his throat, but the gleeful expression of the creature who waited for them. Naked, completely hairless, it lay on top of the bodies of the soldiers, their blood splattered across its pale skin. Its penis was engorged, as if murder had been an erotic pleasure. Its elbow was propped against Phillips's leg, and it rested its chin in its hand. It watched them, grinning, blood smeared around its mouth. Casually, almost like Caesar plucking grapes from a platter, it reached down and tore Phillips's thumb from his hand and began sucking the blood from it.

"Oh, God," Anthony whispered, and the creature laughed sharply.

"No," it said, and Anthony recoiled, his horror magnified that the thing could speak. Despite its shape, it had seemed more animal than man. "Not Him. But imagine how grateful I am that His humans decided to kill each other and leave this feast for me." It rose to a sitting position and tossed the thumb over the cart's side. As one, Anthony and Dilby stumbled backward. "And how fortunate that I should also find living prey."

Vampire. Anthony recalled reading about such folk tales with Colin when they'd been children and trying to frighten Emily with them. What could kill a vampire? Fire? Beheading? His mind reeled, trying to remember.

He must have spoken the word aloud; the creature shook its head, still smiling, and corrected, "Nosferatu. Unlike vampires, we originate from Heaven itself." Pride swelled its voice.

"From Hell, more like!" Dilby shouted, holding the bayonet in front of him; Anthony was suddenly struck by the absurdity of it. They needed to run—there was nothing here to save, only evil.

Long teeth gleamed in the lamplight. "They didn't want us there, either." Gracefully, the nosferatu stepped down from the cart.

It was playing with them, Anthony realized. It enjoyed their fear as it slowly stalked them, and if he and Dilby fled, it would catch them.

Unless only one of them went and one stayed behind to fight it. He could keep it busy, distracted, while Dilby escaped.

A leaden weight seemed to fill Anthony's chest. He thought of his family, of Colin and Emily, and swallowed past the constriction in his throat. "Run, Dilby."

Dilby turned toward him; Anthony saw he was preparing to argue.

"Don't be stupid," he said sharply, fearful that if the other man hesitated, his own courage would fail. He added softly, before Dilby could speak, "For Sarah and little Nellie's sake."

The creature began laughing.

An indecisive, stricken expression slipped into the other man's eyes—then he flipped the bayonet around, its handle toward Anthony.

Anthony took the weapon; with a choked "Godspeed—and thank you," Dilby fled into the night.

The nosferatu chuckled. "I will be done with you in minutes and then I will track him down. Perhaps I'll keep you alive long enough to hear him screaming, so you'll know how worthless your sacrifice was."

Anthony didn't bother to reply; he simply waited. He knew he probably had only one chance to defend himself and that it wouldn't come until the creature moved much closer.

As moments passed, and Anthony failed to respond or move, the nosferatu frowned. "Run or fight," it commanded, its voice as petulant as a child with a disappointing toy.

Anthony silently stood his ground.

"I can smell your fear: so weak, so human." The nosferatu sneered, apparently hoping it would prick Anthony's pride.

They stared at each other for a long moment; finally, with a cry of rage, it attacked.

Even though he'd expected it to be strong, Anthony hadn't known it would be so fast. One instant it had been standing at the cart, the next it was on him, knocking the bayonet from his hand and grabbing him up into a crushing embrace.

Pain screamed through him but remained unvoiced as his ribs snapped under the pressure. Something tore inside him. *I wonder if Guthrie can fix this,* he thought wildly, and would have laughed if he'd had the breath. Desperately, he swung the lantern against the creature's back, his one gambit for survival.

Instead of spilling oil and igniting its skin, the metal thunked solidly against muscle and fell from Anthony's hand.

The creature laughed again and dipped its head, fangs bared. Anthony closed his eyes, waiting for the nosferatu to rip at him, but as they pierced his neck the teeth were almost gentle.

The nosferatu pulled back, yelping in surprise and releasing him; Anthony collapsed on the ground. His ribs shrieked, and his lungs felt pinched by a vise, but he turned and tried to crawl away.

The creature caught him and rolled him onto his back. Its eyes glowed amber as it stared down at him. "Tell me where it is—I can feel its power; I can taste it in your blood," it said, crouching over him.

Anthony shook his head, not knowing what he was denying. He couldn't have spoken in any case; he couldn't catch his breath. A metallic, salty fluid flooded his mouth, but though his body convulsed, he couldn't cough it away. *Lungs collapsed,* he realized.

As if coming to the same conclusion, the nosferatu smiled, its eyes boring into his. "Show me, then," it commanded. Almost immediately, Anthony felt an insidious touch in his mind, a darkness that dug painfully at him, and tried to close his eyes against it.

He failed.

"Show me," it repeated.

In the library of Beaumont Court, he and Colin with the earl's sword between them, slicing shallow cuts into their palms and pressing them together. Blood brothers.

The creature frowned. "That is why I taste it, but you have more recent knowledge of it in a different location. Show me."

Anthony resisted when the first images of the memory flashed in front of him, unable to stand the thought of it—that abomination—seeing Emily as he'd seen her: her romantic idealism shattered, the devastation that had driven her to seduction.

The nosferatu simply pushed harder, tearing through his amateur defenses.

Anthony tumbled headlong into Emily's arms once more. Then darkness crawled in, obscuring her face, her touch; all that remained was the echo of his vow.

And even that faded.

"Anthony," a voice said, and the darkness skittered away. The bright light that replaced it should have been blinding; Anthony automatically tried to squint against it but found his lids already closed.

Memory of the nosferatu rushed back.

It took a Herculean effort, but Anthony opened his eyes. He found himself lying on his side on the ground, the battlefield stretched out around him. The light surrounding him had washed its colors pale—and it originated, he realized, from the man who had spoken.

"Dilby?"

"He lives; your sacrifice succeeded—and it allows me to offer you a choice." The voice resonated through Anthony's body like music, painful in its exquisite beauty.

Anthony rolled over and looked up. He moved easily, as if the nosferatu had never crushed the life from him.

Except in his nakedness, the speaker was nothing like the creature that had attacked him. His bronzed skin seemed to glow with its own luminescence. His black hair had been cut brutally short; his face could have been sculpted from amber. Obsidian eyes stared down at him, and Anthony had to look down again, away from that penetrating gaze.

"Who are you?"

"They call me Michael," he replied. He spoke the name as if it was an explanation in itself.

Understanding dawned as Anthony took in the rest of the figure before him: black feathered wings spread elegantly out from bronzed shoulders.

His eyes flew back to Michael's, and the denial sprang from Anthony's mouth, "I made a promise that I have to keep."

Michael shook his head and held out his palm to assist Anthony to his feet. "I cannot give you that. You must be thought dead to everyone you knew before. I can only offer another choice: become as I am—a Guardian, an immortal protector, or accept your death and all that comes after."

Dead to everyone you knew. Grief touched him, but it could not grab hold. This could not be death. This could not be an end.

Anthony took the proffered hand, feeling absurdly small and weak next to the Guardian. *He offers me a choice to become like him?* "It appears a simple decision," he said.

The reply could have been carved from stone, along with the grim smile that accompanied it. "Appearances are almost always deceiving," Michael said.

THREE

A demon wields despair like a sword,
cutting deep into the afflicted human.
—*The Doyen Scrolls*

It was odd, Emily thought, that she could so calmly receive the news of her twin brother's impending death; her hands did not shake, her lips did not tremble. She remained still, at once proud and saddened the physician's prognosis had not evoked in her an overwhelming, incapacitating grief. Surely Colin deserved such a reaction, but it would do him no good right now.

"Are you absolutely certain? Nothing you can do will cure him?" And yes, those were her words, spoken without the hint of a sob—her voice, serene and composed, as if she were discussing the weather instead of the death of her sibling. When the fire had taken half her family, she had wept for days. But now, despite her bond with her twin, despite a lifelong tendency to be swept away by her emotions, she could not summon a tear.

Fear, she imagined, did that to a person.

Dr. Johnson folded his hands, shifting uncomfortably in his chair. The whiskers along his cheeks and jowls undulated as he seemed to search for words; Emily supposed he was torn between his need to reassure a member of the fairer sex and his professional duty. All the physicians who had examined Colin had been similarly conflicted, particularly upon realizing the extent of the manor's— and Emily's—isolation.

The lack of servants had apparently escaped Dr. Johnson's notice, however, and as Emily was the only family member with whom he could consult, duty prevailed. "Regretfully, I do not believe any other outcome is possible," he said. "His condition worsens daily, and the poison within him has not seemed to decrease, despite the bloodlettings. And the leeches . . ." He trailed off, shaking his head in puzzlement. "I have never read of a sickness having that effect."

Emily smoothed her fingers over her bombazine skirt, willing away the memory of the leeches lying, pale and withered, against Colin's skin—as if *his* body had sucked the lifeblood from *them*. "How much time does he have?"

"As always, these matters are difficult to judge, but I would predict no more than a week. Days, perhaps."

"Days," she repeated softly and shivered. She could survive the days—surviving the nights was less certain.

She had not told the doctor everything she knew of Colin's condition: his sharp, frightening hunger after the sun had set, the unbelievable strength his emaciated form possessed, and the speed at which his injuries had healed. Nor had she told him—or anyone else—the truth about the assault leading to Colin's sickness, nor the method of their escape; it had not been a dog that had bitten him, but something far worse.

Something that, try as she might, Emily still couldn't quite believe—but she knew if she shared her memories of the attack, they'd be dismissed as grief-induced hallucinations—or worse, considered a sign of madness.

No, trusting the doctor with complete information was impossible; if she had only herself to think of, she might have told him, but she couldn't risk Robert's future by exposing herself. She was fortunate her reputation in society had remained as unscathed as it was, considering her romantic . . . indiscretions.

Sorrow and regret rushed through her. She could have confided in Anthony; he might have thought her fanciful and silly at times, but he had never doubted her word. If a treatment for Colin could be found, Anthony would have braved Hell itself to locate it.

But Anthony had been dead these eight months, and soon Colin would join him.

Unaware of her thoughts, Dr. Johnson rose. Clutching his bag, his expression sorrowful, he said, "I shall return next week, my lady, after I consult with my colleagues in London."

She nodded agreement and walked with him to the foyer, but she knew there was nothing he would find, nothing that could be done. Colin would likely be dead before he returned.

Emily pushed the heavy door closed behind him and then turned to lean against the wood with a sigh. Dr. Johnson had been the fourth physician from London to examine Colin in as many weeks, and his conclusions had been no different from the others'. She'd hoped one of the doctors would have recognized Colin's illness for what it was, instead of what she'd told them—but it was either too rare for them to have seen or heard of it before, or as horrifying and as unnatural as Emily feared.

If it was the latter, then God help Colin—and her.

Deliberately delaying her return to Colin's room, Emily returned to the front parlor and began clearing the tea service. The pale green walls and the peach damask upholstery on the sofa and chairs were bright and fresh; ten years had passed since Catherine, Henry's wife, had decorated the room, but the fabric showed little sign of wear, as if untouched by visitors or family.

If I had come, alleviated her loneliness instead of playing the whore, perhaps they would not have been in London when the fire struck. I should have roasted with them.

The thought rose unbidden, and Emily determinedly shook it away. She'd had similar macabre ideas over the last several weeks, brought on, she assumed, by the fatigue and stress of caring for her brother under such unusual circumstances. Her tired and frightened mind had been giving truth ghastly twists: Colin and Emily *had* been infrequent visitors to the manor, each preferring the excitement of London to the dullness of country life—but Henry and Catherine had been in town for the end of the season, not because of loneliness, and certainly not because they'd discovered that Emily had taken lovers.

Though she had once wanted her father to discover her indiscretions, to feel the same bitter disappointment in her that she once had in him—to feel *anything* for her—now she was grateful that her family had not died amidst a scandal. Except for Colin, her family had never known what she'd done. Emily had thought she would never forgive herself for being in the arms of a man when the house had caught fire. Nor had she thought she could live up to the trust Robert had bestowed upon her when she and Colin had found him, saved by his nurse taking the rear stairs to the exit.

Yet she had.

After the fire, for Robert's sake, Colin and Emily had remained in the country for the summer; except for the brief trip to London that had ended in attack and catastrophe, they hadn't intended to return to the city until the next season.

"To find a wife for me, and a mother for Robert," Colin had laughed. Emily had been amused then; but now, looking around the room that should have been comforting instead of sterile, its springtime motif an ineffective respite from the dreary Derbyshire winter, she wondered if any wife of Colin's choosing could have made this a true home for Robert.

Or now that he would never marry, if she could provide the support Robert needed. She had never imagined herself a mother, yet circumstances were forcing her to become one.

The delicate teacups rang sharply against silver as she set them down. She lifted the heavy tray—then nearly dropped it when her housekeeper appeared silently beside her.

"Mrs. Kemble!" Emily gasped, laughing at the startled jump of her heart. The silver tray wobbled but then steadied under the older woman's sturdy hands. Emily gratefully passed it to the housekeeper. "I thought you, Sally, and Mr. Davison had already left for Hartington for the evening."

"No, ma'am," Mrs. Kemble said. Emily felt the other woman's concerned—and slightly disapproving—gaze upon her face. The servants had accepted Emily's order that they leave the manor at night and to return only after dawn, but they felt the sting of her demand—particularly Mrs. Kemble and the other servants who usually lived in the house. Emily paid their lodging expenses at a Hartington inn, but they were not pleased at being forced from their home, even temporarily. "Mr. Davison was delayed in the north field, and he has only just returned. We are leaving now, unless your ladyship would prefer we stay?"

Emily hardened herself against the hopeful note in the housekeeper's voice. "No, thank you, Mrs. Kemble. If Sally has left supper in the larder, Colin and I can make do by ourselves for the remainder of the evening."

The housekeeper nodded stiffly but hesitated before turning.

"Was there anything else, Mrs. Kemble?"

"Well, ma'am, I had intended to visit my daughter in Kent—"

"Oh!" Emily's hand flew to her mouth in dismay. She had forgotten that the housekeeper had requested leave for the birth of her grandchild. The servant must have felt obligated to stay during Colin's sickness; she had been scheduled to leave two days before. "Mrs. Kemble, I am sorry—you must of course depart immediately! Have you received word about the baby?"

The housekeeper shook her head. "I'm afraid it was stillborn, ma'am. I was meaning to let you know that I wouldn't be taking the time away after all, so you could depend on me to remain here while Master Colin is ill."

"Thank you, Mrs. Kemble," Emily said. "But wouldn't you prefer to be with your daughter?"

The housekeeper shrugged. "Babes die, ma'am. And my daughter is a strong lass."

Perhaps it was her own recent loss that made Mrs. Kemble's statement seem so coldhearted, Emily thought minutes later as she slowly climbed the stairs to Colin's room. It was true that childbirth was frequently accompanied by death; one should be prepared for an unhappy outcome.

But Emily hoped that, no matter how much death surrounded her, she would never be as prepared as Mrs. Kemble.

She winced as the key scraped in the bedchamber's lock, but upon opening the door she saw the noise had not disturbed Colin's unnatural sleep. He lay on the bed in his nightgown, his arms still tucked neatly at his sides in the position she had arranged them following the physician's examination. She had pulled layers of blankets over him, but despite his clammy temperature and the chill in the room, he'd kicked them off. His thin ankles and calves stood out in sharp relief against the pillowy mattress, his white skin almost the same color as the sheets.

Aside from her lamp, the soft blaze in the fireplace provided the only light in the room; in the early days of Colin's sickness, when he'd been awake during a portion of the daylight hours, he'd been too sensitive to sunlight to allow it to shine through the windows. Though he was no longer conscious enough to object, Emily continued to draw the drapes every morning. Now, the orange glow of sunset peeked between them, settling in stripes on the rugs.

Cursing herself for allowing it to become so late, Emily ran to the bed, falling to her knees and reaching beneath the bedframe.

Her fingers sought and brushed cold metal, and with a clatter, she dragged out the heavy chains and manacles she'd hidden from the physician and the servants.

She lifted Colin's left arm. It hung cold and limp as she snapped the iron cuff around his wrist and twisted the key. Her heart no longer ached as it had the first few days she had performed this procedure. Initially, it had been at Colin's insistence—after she found him one night eating raw meat in the kitchen, he'd begged her to chain him. She had done it the first time to humor him, and to erase the haunted look from his eyes; now, she did it out of fear and self-preservation.

Her fingers were gentle as she slipped his right wrist into the iron. His bones looked fragile beneath his skin, the ligaments clearly delineated. The frailty was deceptive, she knew—he was preternaturally strong—but she could not bring herself to treat him carelessly, no matter what he'd become.

She wrapped the chains around the bedposts. The metal links jangled rhythmically as she pulled on their length; Colin's arms slid bonelessly toward the headboard. When there was only a little slack in the chain, she wound them around the posts once more and locked them together.

Clutching the key in her hand, she glanced at his face and was relieved to see his eyes still closed. His blond hair, only a few shades darker than hers, curled disheveled over his forehead. Knowing that he'd have hated its disarray, she quickly smoothed it into some semblance of order, watching him carefully for movement.

The illness had not been kind to him—the face Emily had often considered a masculine version of her own had withered and shrunk, erasing his angular beauty. Dark hollows around his eyes and in his sunken cheeks had left him skeletal; she was glad Colin couldn't see himself as he was now. If he'd been aware of the physical decline that accompanied the mental one, he'd have been devastated.

His eyelashes fluttered. Her heart leaping into her throat, Emily yanked her hand away and took three hasty steps back. She watched him in frozen trepidation. He did not move again; after a moment, she pressed her lips together against the absurd urge to laugh, to lose herself in hysteria.

There had been times in the last few weeks when she'd feared madness was not far from her—she'd managed to counter the feeling, doggedly hanging on to normalcy through sheer will.

She turned on her heel, striding determinedly to Colin's writing desk and opening the curtains adjacent to it. The sun had disappeared over the horizon, and the deepening twilight cast the garden below into shadow. She looked out for just a few moments, letting the vastness outside fill her, give her a brief sense of freedom—from the house's locked rooms and her own secrets—before turning and sitting at the desk. Setting down the lamp, she pulled paper and pens from a drawer.

Letters were normal—about normal events, to normal people. Performing such an everyday task would anchor her, remind her of her sanity.

After dashing off a few short letters to personal friends, she faced the daunting task of writing to her nephew, Robert.

How much of the truth should she relate to him? How much should a twelve-year-old boy know? After losing his father, mother, and grandfather in so short of a time, now must he face the prospect of losing his uncle?

Not that Colin had been a significant part of Robert's life before that summer, she thought sadly. Nor had she. She remembered the words she'd once spoken to Anthony Ramsdell: *Children cannot interest me.* She closed her eyes briefly against the pain the memory of that night brought and brushed her forefinger over the thin, raised scar on the fleshy pad of her thumb.

She had been wrong—she could not have known how wrong she had been until she had spent the summer becoming acquainted with her young nephew. And had she known, would she have acted differently that night? Would she have called Anthony unsuitable, used him in her childish scheme for revenge?

For the briefest moment, she allowed herself to recall his offer, to imagine the course her life might have taken if she'd accepted it. *If I had not been so focused on my own needs and dreams, would he be alive? Would I be with him now?* But a marriage between them could not have prevented the fire, nor could it change what had happened to Colin.

Thinking of Anthony helped remind her that neither life nor death could be taken for granted; determined not to lose another moment caught in bitter reflection, she wrote:

Robert,

I hope this letter finds you comfortably settled and applying yourself to your studies. As you have recently come into your title, your new friends might give you a nickname; please do not allow them Nobby or Norby. Though it sounds quite stuffy now, insist on Norbridge. You will thank me for it in the future.

Your Uncle Colin's condition is very ill, but do not fret—I am certain he will soon be himself again and his cravat as tightly knotted as ever before. He should be recovered at the end of the half, and we will enjoy the holiday together.

Perhaps in the summer months we should visit the Lake District and try to muss his clothes during our travels. You might also enjoy Brighton, or a few weeks in London (although not too far into the summer, I hope). Or perhaps you would like to remain in Derbyshire? Our previous summer passed so pleasantly here, I should not mind another. But I shall accede to your wishes on this matter, my young lord.

Your loving aunt,
Emily

A smile hovered over her mouth as she folded the letter and sealed it. Robert might consider her an eccentric guardian, but he would have little doubt of her affection. Would that she'd had the same from her father . . .

A gleam in the darkness caught her attention and she turned. Colin lay on the bed watching her hungrily, his eyes reflecting the lamplight. His lips were pulled back in a ghastly smile, revealing long, pointed canines. He turned his head and sank his teeth through his sleeve and into his bicep.

I should let him kill me, she thought.

Emily buried her face in her hands and wept.

four

A Guardian may choose to Ascend at any time; however, after one
hundred years have passed, they may also choose to Fall—the
alternative added as a reward for service.
—*The Doyen Scrolls*

Anthony landed neatly atop the city's tallest spire. Around
him, Caelum spread out in a circle of coruscating buildings
and temples. Its shining marble columns and towers speared into the
cerulean sky, piercing a blue that had never been darkened by
clouds.

Anthony no longer raised his face to capture the sun's warmth,
as he often had in England; without the cold and rain for contrast,
its rays did nothing more than bring light. And now that he could
see clearly on the darkest of nights, he did not even need that.

But he could fly, and for that he loved the unchanging sky.

The tip of the spire was not wide enough for perching; balanced
on one foot, he waited, currents of air drifting across his wings.

The city's edge shimmered in the distance; it pulled his gaze, as
it always did. A dark line marked the abrupt cessation of ivory
stone—beyond it, a waveless ocean stretched to the horizon. He had
explored its endless breadth and depths, but both the sky and the

deep had been empty, and his splashless dives had disturbed nothing.

But Caelum thrummed and pulsed with life. Behind silent marble walls, thousands of Guardians watched, waited, and protected. They passed through the Gates and came back with Earth's odors clinging to them.

Anthony had learned to avoid those who were newly returned.

Like all new Guardians, he had to wait nearly one hundred years before he would be allowed to traverse those Gates: one hundred years of studying his new abilities and training to fight their enemies; one hundred years for everyone he'd known to die; one hundred years to forget the immediacy of being human. Until then, reminders of his past were as painful as they were alluring, and he preferred not to torture himself with them. It served no purpose.

Suddenly restless, he glanced away from the edge of the city, his eyes searching the ground below. Though hundreds of yards in the air, he could see the individual veins of color within the courtyard tiles, but he was not interested in the stone. Movement near one of the archways opening into the courtyard caught his attention—two Guardians held each other in an intimate embrace.

Two males, he realized. They kissed, and though Anthony was struck by the gentleness with which they touched each other, he had to look away. It was not unusual in Caelum to come across lovers in the public areas, but even after eight months, he had not grown accustomed to witnessing sexual acts performed between couples of the same gender. Over time, his shock and disgust had faded into mild discomfort, but he reasoned that he was, and maybe always would be, a product of his upbringing.

After all, he had not become accustomed to the idea of a male and female publicly displaying themselves, either. If a member of the *ton* had ever been so bold, he would have been expelled from society. Even if it took place behind closed doors, public knowledge of a liaison between unmarried lovers could have ruined the couple.

Emily had known that risk, but she had still pressed her lips against his.

Before that night, he'd dreamed of her touch countless times. Afterward, he could only look back with shame that his one opportunity with her ended in a mechanical coupling that had brought pleasure to neither of them. He still didn't know why she'd chosen him, but no matter her reason, their joining had likely failed her idealistic expectations. The image of her, eyes red-rimmed and her chemise stained with his semen, declaring that her faith in love had vanished, had been pinned like an insect into his memory.

No. He shook himself, forcing thoughts of Emily, of London, from his mind. Dwelling on what had been could only lead to unhappiness, could only bring frustration and regret. Here in Caelum, there were no titles or possessions, and value was not determined by birth or profession. He had a multitude of lifetimes ahead of him, and he would not spend them aching for a past that had rejected him at every turn.

With a deliberate shrug, he unrolled his wings and focused on the weight of them—they were heavy, but no more a burden than one of his legs or his arms. He tested the breeze against his skin and breathed the sterile air deep into his lungs.

Then he folded the white feathers tight against his body and plummeted.

He kept his eyes open as he rushed toward the ground. The wind created by his descent whipped his hair behind him and tore his shirttails from the waist of his breeches. The wildly fluttering hem cracked against his buttocks, startling a laugh from him before the torrent of air made him swallow it.

At the last possible moment, he snapped his wings wide. They caught air, and his trajectory changed sharply, vertical to horizontal. The effort wrenched his muscles, and he strained to hold himself aloft as he skimmed a foot above the courtyard tiles. His knees scraped; he cried out in surprise and tumbled over, skidding to a halt against sturdy, robe-covered legs. The brown wool smelled faintly of smoke.

Hugh's legs, Anthony realized with dismay as he lay on his back, stunned. *This stunt will likely earn me a stiff lecture.* He smiled in amused anticipation of it, particularly as the lecture would come from someone who looked a very young eighteen. Hugh's face, surrounded by boyish curls, could have been any youth's in a Botticelli painting, and yet his eyes bespoke his real age—they were too patient to have belonged to even the most mature boy.

Appearances, Anthony reminded himself, *are almost always deceiving.* It had been one of the first lessons he'd been taught upon entering Caelum, and one of the hardest for him to absorb. As a physician, he'd been trained to trust what he observed and to act accordingly. As a Guardian, he had to learn to distrust it, along with many other things he'd taken for granted when he was human.

Instead of lecturing, his mentor only looked down at him thoughtfully and said, "Perhaps we should move on to the lessons for tactical aerial combat."

The unexpected response to his reckless dive, combined with the thrill of his relatively successful landing, had Anthony shaking with laughter.

Hugh's expression didn't change; if anything, it became more sober. He watched as Anthony picked himself up and waited until his laughter had passed.

"Michael has summoned us."

Anthony paused in his attempt to tuck in his shirt. Michael had transformed him, brought him to Caelum, and then left him in the care of his mentors. Anthony hadn't expected to see Michael again until his hundred years had passed and Anthony received his first assignment.

"Why?"

The faint disapproval that thinned Hugh's lips was the strongest emotion Anthony had ever seen him display. "He's sending you on a mission."

Anthony's brow creased into a frown and unease skittered down his spine. "To Earth?"

Hugh didn't reply, turning stiffly in the direction of the Hall. Anthony was forced to follow him on foot—Hugh preferred walking to flying, as if the journey to every destination was a pilgrimage— and the trek gave him too much time to remember all the reasons he'd want to return to Earth, and too little time to forget them again.

Michael's residence, like much of Caelum, bore the unmistakable influence of the ancient Greeks. Columns topped with intricately carved scrollwork stood like sentinels around the building; on the doors, an enormous marble frieze depicted Michael's battle against the dragon.

Anthony had studied the sculpted scene during his exploration of the city and had been astounded that the artist's skill had so perfectly replicated the visage of the man in stone. Michael—naked, wingless, and armed with a single sword—stood alone against the dragon. Behind him, an army of angels lay beaten; riding the dragon, a horde of demons eagerly awaited victory. It captured the moment just before Michael had thrust the sword into the dragon's heart— his muscles bunched with effort, his expression desperate but determined.

Michael had been human then, but it had been his triumph that led to the formation of the Guardian corps. The first Guardian, he was the Doyen and the acknowledged leader. Although every Guardian had an equal voice in Caelum, if Michael did intend to break tradition and send Anthony to Earth before his training had been completed, there would likely be little opposition.

Unless that opposition came from Anthony.

Guardians prized free will above all other things. Though choices were sometimes limited, Michael would never force Anthony to do anything he resisted.

Anthony could—and would, he determined—decline the mission when it was offered. The decision quieted the unease that had plagued him and allowed him to enter Michael's sanctum with confidence.

The interior was as palatial as Anthony had expected, but except in scale it differed little from his own residence. Archways and columns divided the single large, open room. A seating area in the front held an elegant array of sofas, chairs, and ottomans. Their styles varied widely, a testament to Michael's age and the extent of his travel, and came togther in an arrangement too soft to accurately reflect the owner.

Anthony did not relish the prospect of talking to Michael while lounging on sofas and cushions, and was relieved when Hugh led him into the armory at the back of the room. Weapons lined the walls: ancient axes and bludgeons; swords and spears; newer firearms. The floor had been left empty—in his apartment, Anthony used the similar space to practice his fencing skills with Hugh. His mentor, despite his monkish appearance, was a formidable opponent; Anthony imagined Michael was invincible.

The Doyen waited for them beside a display of Japanese katanas and aboriginal slings. He wore a white linen tunic and loose, flowing trousers, and he'd chosen to vanish his black wings. The effect should have been less daunting than Anthony's last encounter with him, when Michael had been winged and naked, the glowing angel of death, but somehow his muted appearance seemed more impressive simply for its deception.

Anthony wondered if the effect was deliberate. Did Michael think to intimidate him into returning?

"Six months ago, the nosferatu you encountered in Spain killed three members of the Ames-Beaumont family," Michael said without preamble. "Several weeks ago, he attacked the remaining family but did not succeed in his attempt to kill them. You will go with Hugh and assist him in destroying the creature, before he finds another opportunity to strike at them."

If Michael had hit Anthony with his full strength, the blow would have been less painful than his words. Anthony staggered under their impact and spoke through numb lips, "Who?"

Hugh said quietly, "The earl, Henry, and Catherine."

Anthony sucked in a sharp breath, his relief that Colin and Emily had survived immediately accompanied by guilt—and, as the full import of Michael's announcement sank in, rage. His voice shook with it. "Six months? It killed them *six months ago,* and you are only now sending someone to destroy it?"

Michael didn't respond to Anthony's anger, his expression as hard and unyielding as ever. Realizing that the Doyen did not feel he had to explain himself, Anthony stepped forward, his fists clenching. If he had to, he would beat the answers out of Michael, and damn the consequences.

"We weren't certain he had targeted the family until the latest attack," Hugh said. His mentor's rational tones slipped under Anthony's anger and made him pause mid-step and listen. "The three died when he set fire to their London townhouse; although we had heard reports of a nosferatu in London at the time, the two events did not seem connected until three weeks ago. I've since been to the townhouse and verified he'd been there—his scent lingered in every room, from before and after the fire."

The fire. Sudden tears blurred Anthony's vision. If the nosferatu had killed them himself, their terror and pain would not have been less. The rage that had been focused on Michael shifted to its proper object and burned cold under his skin.

He recalled the pleasure in the creature's eyes when it had drank his blood, its insistence on delving into his memories. *Its scent lingered in every room of the house.* "What is it searching for?"

Approval flashed across Michael's face at the question, but Anthony did not care what the Doyen thought. If it had been something in his mind that had brought tragedy upon the family, he would be the one to stop it—and for that, he had to know what the nosferatu sought. He had to think ahead of it.

What had been particular to the memories it had pulled from him?

"My sword," Michael said suddenly. "Blood had been spilled from it on both occasions."

Anthony started in surprise. "The sword from the Second Battle?" At Michael's nod, Anthony gave a short, humorless laugh. Norbridge's prized relic was far more valuable than the earl had known.

Beside Anthony, Hugh's body went rigid and he leveled an accusing stare at the Doyen. Michael returned the stare, unapologetic.

Though he noted the exchange, Anthony didn't stop to wonder what had caused the sudden tension between the men. He had his answer, and he didn't want to waste any time going over details. There would be time enough later, after the nosferatu was dead.

He pivoted and stalked toward the exit. "I will collect my weapon and meet Hugh at the Central Gate in ten minutes," he said. Without waiting for an answer, he swept through the doors and took to the sky.

Hugh was silent until he was certain Anthony could not hear him, but Michael anticipated his objection.

"He wanted to know; I found the answer. You disapprove?"

"You entered his mind without his permission—that makes you no better than a demon. Or the nosferatu who started this." Hugh shook his head. "We don't do that."

"*You* don't." Michael's expression hardened. "The world has changed, Hugh, and the forces Above and Below are changing with it. Finding the sword is an omen."

"An omen—and yet you send a novice?" Hugh folded his hands together beneath the sleeves of his robe. His tranquil posture would not deceive Michael, yet he refused to betray his anger by word or expression. "You can have no reason to include Anthony. His familiarity with the family might be an asset to the search, but it will bring insurmountable complications. He learned quickly, but his lack of training, his ignorance of demons and nosferatu—he has not yet discovered his Gift. He cannot disguise himself from those he knows and who think him dead."

"You think he cannot shift his form because he cleaves too strongly to his memories," Michel said. "I am sending him because he cannot shift; he must face the people he has left behind without disguise, without lies."

"It is an irresponsible decision. You will expose us—"

"Transforming him was a mistake," Michael said. "And if I do not send him to Earth now, the damage will be irreversible. He cannot be a Guardian."

Hugh could not hide his shock. "Do you send him to his death, then?"

"I did not realize you thought so little of your own skills and your mentorship. If he has not learned enough to keep himself alive . . ." Michael's smile chilled the room. "Do you wish to have another go in your place, then? Do you refuse your part in this?"

"No," Hugh said, regarding the other man intently. "What has happened between his transformation and now? What have you learned?"

To his surprise, Michael looked away. "Your Gift may force me to answer truthfully," he said. "But if I do not answer, there is neither truth nor lie."

Hugh withdrew his hands from his sleeves. "If Anthony dies—"

"You will Fall?" Michael anticipated him again and laughed with genuine humor. "No. You'd not leave the corps for this. I'm disappointed in you, Hugh; whether he lives or dies, you should have more faith that everything will be as it should." He waved his hand in a dismissive gesture, turned toward the display of weapons, and selected a long, curving Saracen blade. "Now, go. If Anthony's impatience and anger still burns as hotly as when he left, he might not wait for you and go through the Gate alone."

Hugh couldn't take the time to respond; though it annoyed him, Michael was right: Anthony was completely unprepared to experience Earth as a Guardian.

FIVE

A Guardian's Gift will come to him when he is ready for it;
the Gift is a reflection of a Guardian's human life, but not always
a welcome one.
—*The Doyen Scrolls*

"*We have never spoken of that night.*"

Colin flicked Emily a meaningful glance so she could not mistake which *night he spoke of*, then turned his attention back to the horses. The steady clip-clop tempo of their hooves increased after a murmur from him. Emily tucked her lap blanket tighter around her hips, thankful that the pink in her cheeks could be blamed on the cold—if Colin could see the color at all. Night had fallen quickly, and they had only just turned into the long drive leading to the house.

"*Why would you wish to speak of it now?*" She folded her hands in her lap and stared at the lines of buttons at the wrists of her gloves. "*I can hardly think you would want to relive the experience. Going home to find our father, our brother, and his wife have perished in a fire does not make for easy conversation.*"

"*No. Earlier that night at the hotel, Emily. Where, by the slimmest chance, I happened to see you with a—*"

The phaeton lurched forward as one of the horses shied, break-ing its smooth gait. Colin's fingers tightened on the reins, and he spoke a few soothing words before looking back at Emily.

"What could have possessed you to behave so recklessly?" Guilt shadowed his eyes, as if he blamed himself for her actions, and that shamed her more than his disappointment or censure could have.

She was saved from an immediate reply as the horses whinnied and tossed their heads, the metal in the harness jingling discor-dantly. Colin frowned, his gaze skimming along the trees lining the drive.

A shiver of uneasiness ran up Emily's spine, but it wasn't caused by the darkness. Her recklessness had not brought ruin to her fam-ily, but it may have had just as damaging an effect.

"I told Anthony he was unsuitable," she admitted.

"Anthony?" Colin pulled on the reins, bringing the team to a vi-cious halt. He turned in his seat to stare at her, anger lining his mouth with white. A muscle in his jaw flexed. "You rejected Rams-dell and then went to a whore?"

"No." She swallowed past the constriction in her throat. "He was first, and then I sent him to his death thinking that I considered him unworthy of further attention."

The horses shifted restlessly. Colin turned away from her, clicked his tongue, and they practically leapt forward in their eagerness to go. Emily watched his profile, wondering if she could ever repair her status in his eyes, if he could ever forgive her for courting ruin and insulting their friend.

She started in surprise as a laugh broke from him, and he gath-ered the reins in one hand and wrapped his other arm around her shoulders and hugged her close. "Em," he said with a wry smile. "Ramsdell was likely the happiest man in the world when he died. If you had to ruin yourself, I suppose I should be glad you gave my friend the one thing he'd dreamed of in the process."

She tilted her face into his chest and couldn't stop the giggle that

rose in her throat. "That is a shocking and inappropriate response
for a brother to have."

"You're my sister," he said, as if it were that simple. "Your rep-
utation has remained intact, so the only person to whom you will
have to explain yourself will be the husband you select. You have
obviously tortured yourself over the past—I would never add to it.
I would as soon remove my arm as hurt you." He glanced down.
"Are you weeping all over my new greatcoat? I should really hate
to see it ruined with tears."

Emily grinned. "No, I—"

The horses screamed, and then Emily was screaming as the
white, naked creature lifted Colin up, and then the blood was spurt-
ing from her brother's neck. And then it came for her, and she felt
its teeth rending, ripping—

Emily woke, her hand automatically flying to her throat, but
smooth skin met her fingers instead of torn flesh and blood.

Nightmare, she realized, but her relief did little to ease the racing of her heart. The dreams had come frequently in the last month,
but she'd rarely been able to wake from them. She wasn't certain if
that was a blessing or not; the sudden awareness was almost as ter-
rifying as being trapped within them until the end.

In the grate, coals shifted and tumbled. She rolled onto her side,
pillowing her head against the arm of the chaise, and watched the
shadows cast by the embers' glow. Exhaustion settled over her like a
blanket, but she didn't want to sleep again. She wanted to rise from
the makeshift bed, turn around, and find Colin whole and healthy.

Because that hope faded day by day, she let her eyes drift closed.
Some nightmares were preferable to reality, and it had been a long
time since she'd believed in fairy-tale endings or miracles.

But maybe . . .

Even as she scolded herself for her silliness, she sat up, made a
wish, and looked over at Colin's bed.

Colin's *empty* bed.

Oh, God. The chains lay serpentine across the sheets, the manacles gaping. She blinked, but nothing changed, and she didn't wake up.

How had he unlocked the chains? Had he escaped the room, or was he hiding in the dark? Should she call for him, or try to run? Would running attract his attention?

Her heartbeat drummed slow and thick in her ears, and she fought the panic that darkened the edges of her vision. She resisted the urge to look behind her, toward the fireplace and dressing room. He hadn't been there moments ago, and he wasn't there now, waiting for her to turn around before he grabbed her.

Her room was only four doors down the hall, and it had a sturdy lock. She was light on her feet; it would only take seconds to—

A scraping, sliding noise interrupted her frantic preparations. She caught her breath on a sob, her body tensing as her brother grasped the leg of the bed and dragged himself into view. His face was pressed against the floor; she didn't think he had noticed her. He slowly crawled around the edge of the bed on his elbows and stomach, digging his fingers into the rug with each forward pull. His legs slid behind him, and he gave a kittenish mew when his knee bumped the footboard.

The pathetic scene wavered through her tears. She wanted to help him, but the risk was too great, his weakness deceptive. Better to leave the room and lock the door behind her—in the morning she would repair him to his bed and try to discover how he'd loosed himself.

Though the rational decision heartened her, it took a few moments to screw her courage. Then she gathered up her skirts and sprinted to the door.

She knew the moment he saw her; she heard a growl, but she was already pushing at the handle.

It wouldn't open.

She cried out in dismay, certain it had not been locked when she'd fallen asleep. But she took no time to ponder the mystery of it, spinning around and fleeing to the dressing room. It wouldn't lock, but she could prop a chair against the door.

She didn't make it. Halfway across the room, Colin crashed into her and sent her sprawling against the coal bin next to the grate. It spilled over with a clang and an explosion of black dust. She reached out blindly for the iron poker that flanked the hearth.

He caught her wildly grasping arm, yanking her against him. Pain, excruciating and hot, ripped through her shoulder, and she screamed.

His fingers tore at her neckline, his nails scoring her skin in long furrows. She flailed at him with her free arm, numbly recognizing that her death was upon her. She stilled and let it come.

His head bent, his breath cold against her skin. She closed her eyes against the bite, praying that it would be quick—praying that it would be complete. She did not want to become what he was.

"Colin." Whether she spoke the word as a plea or to bestow forgiveness on this thing with her brother's face but the mind of an animal, she didn't know. But her voice must have touched some last bit of humanity in him; his weight shifted, lessened—and though she waited in agony, the bite didn't come. Hopeful and afraid, she opened her eyes.

And looked into the face of a dead man.

Anthony Ramsdell had wrapped his hands over Colin's jaw and was holding those sharp teeth away from her neck. Beside him, a youth in a monk's robe pried Colin's fingers from her dress.

Anthony gave her a lopsided grin. "You two are a little old to be wrestling, aren't you?" A pair of white, feathery wings waved gently behind him.

When did I die? Emily wondered, and then Colin attempted to struggle against his captors, jolting her shoulder. She shrieked, and merciful darkness flooded the pain anyway.

*　　*　　*

Colin fought wildly, but after they'd extricated him from Emily, Anthony and Hugh no longer had to be gentle with him. Hugh lifted and tossed Colin back onto the bed and had a manacle around his wrist before the vampire could move. Colin screeched in fury, pulling against the chains.

Anthony left Colin to Hugh; the older Guardian could certainly handle a vampire, particularly a half-starved one. Scooping Emily from the floor, he carried her down the hall to the room he remembered as hers.

It still was, apparently; although Anthony had never entered Emily's bedchamber, the romantic cream and rose perfectly suited the girl he'd known.

Except she was no longer that girl, he reminded himself.

With a sigh, he set her on the bed, glancing cursorily down her form to determine the worst of her injuries. The claw marks on her collarbone were bloody and raw; coal dust had settled into them, and they needed cleaning. The lump above her shoulder demanded his immediate attention, however, and it would be far better to reset the dislocation while she was unconscious.

He rolled up his sleeves, smiling grimly. For years, he had resented the necessity of his medical training and, when he'd been sent to the Peninsula, the circumstances under which he'd learned combat medicine. Emily's injuries weren't as serious as those he'd seen during the war, but he'd never been so pleased that he had the knowledge to help someone.

It took only moments to tear the dress away from her, revealing her white chemise. His hands were sure and steady on her shoulder, aided by his increased sensitivity and strength. She whimpered when he pushed the joint into place, but she didn't regain consciousness. He found a pitcher of water and a wash basin on her nightstand; he used it and a cloth to clean out the scratches and one of her nightgowns to make a crude dressing.

More of the black dust covered the left side of her face, and he gently wiped it away, leaving a clean trail of damp, porcelain skin. He traced the curve of her lips; they were softer than he remembered, and he suddenly wanted to wake her up, to see her smile. He wanted to capture every expression her mobile features could produce, find her flaws and pronounce them endearing, worship her scent and her touch and her voice.

Hugh had warned him before they'd entered the Gate that some Guardians became enthralled upon returning to Earth—Caelum's sterility could not prepare them for the sensorial onslaught. It could overwhelm or captivate their heightened senses, rendering them helpless until they learned to adjust.

Anthony's determination to reach Beaumont Court had prevented him from noticing much of his surroundings; once he had entered the house, he'd finally understood why Hugh's warning had been necessary. His senses had been immediately attuned to Emily's every movement, her every breath. When she had wept, it had taken every bit of his strength to stay away from her. When she had screamed, he'd used every bit of it to reach her.

He brushed her eyelashes with his thumb; they were long and thick, tipped with pale gold. No tears streaked her cheeks now, though the flesh around her eyes was tender and swollen.

They were the only marks of strain that he could see; despite her loss, despite the burden that had been placed upon her, she'd remained steadfast. He'd never imagined that the girl full of dreams would be a woman with a core of steel. Since learning of the nosferatu's attack on Colin, he'd berated himself for failing to fulfill his vow to return, for leaving her alone—but she had not needed him.

Except, of course, when her brother attempted to rip out her throat.

His gaze returned to the dressing above her breasts. Blood had already seeped through the thin material. Frustration made him clench his teeth; he needed better supplies—and a few servants to help find clean cloths and renew the water. As he had neither of those things, he ripped a length of bedsheet to replace the nightgown and exposed the scratches. He frowned at their ragged edges and their depth. They would scar, leaving a physical reminder of her terror.

Instinctively, he willed her flesh to knit itself, imagined the skin closing and repairing in the same manner he willed his clothes and his wings to appear, and pressed his hand to her injury.

He pulled it back as his palm burned against her skin. Pain shot through his arm, but it was the smooth, undamaged skin at her neck that made him curse aloud in surprise.

His exclamation brought Hugh instantly to the door, and Anthony had the absurd desire to know whether his mentor had actually run from the other room or just walked very quickly.

He repressed the question with a grin. "I believe I have discovered the nature of my Gift."

Hugh looked at Anthony's hand, then at Emily lying on the bed. "Waking unconscious women?"

"No, healing—" Anthony paused and glanced at Emily. Her eyes were still closed. "You just made a joke," he said in disbelief.

Hugh regarded him steadily. "Hardly. I was expressing hope: we need her awake. This situation is more complicated than we had realized. Colin's behavior is not just the result of starvation; he has not been completely turned."

Anthony's heart sank. "We can't kill the nosferatu then. We'll need him to finish it."

"Yes."

"Can we trust him to do it?"

Hugh cast him a reproving glance and walked slowly over to the bed to look down at Emily. "Of course not. Nosferatu are even more treacherous than demons. And though demons are bound by law not to kill humans, nosferatu are not. He'd not hesitate in murdering Colin." Almost absently, he touched Emily's perfectly healed skin. "Which leads me to our other problem."

Anthony tore his eyes away from the other man's fingers and fought the possessive urge to remove the Guardian's hand from Emily's chest. "Which problem is that?" he asked tightly.

"Lilith." A long-suffering sigh escaped him, and he folded his hands into his robe. "A demon."

SIX

Human motives are rarely as simple as they appear, their actions
driven by myriad emotions and thoughts. Demons name them—
greed, lust, envy—but these shallow words cannot do the human
heart justice; Guardians must learn to read its complexities.
—*The Doyen Scrolls*

Emily tried to remain asleep, snuggling deeper into the
warmth surrounding her. It had been so long since she'd felt
secure, and the arms holding her were strong, the voice crooning in
her ear familiar.

But the insistent ache in her shoulder would not let her rest, nor
would the lingering sense of horror that crept around the edges of
her sleep. Something had gone dreadfully wrong.

She slowly surfaced; the crooning that had lulled her stopped,
the arms holding her tensed as if in expectation of her waking and
then slipped from around her.

Anthony's arms. Anthony Ramsdell had saved her.

Perhaps she had stopped believing in miracles too soon.

When she opened her eyes, she was lying on her bed, a blanket
draped over her. Pillows propped her shoulders and head, and she
had to turn only slightly to see him.

Anthony leaned back against the headboard, his long legs

stretched out in front of him. She felt the pressure of his thigh against her hip, as if he'd withdrawn his embrace out of propriety but couldn't completely give up all physical contact.

His wings were gone, and the hesitancy on his face made her want to cry.

She smiled instead. "I suppose it was too much to hope that I'd actually make it to Heaven."

He pressed his lips together as if holding back a laugh. He'd always done that, she remembered—particularly when he was around her. He'd always taken his time answering, always paused before laughing, as if he didn't trust himself to speak or react spontaneously.

She had taken advantage of that once, and the memory made her flush with shame. She forced herself to add, "After all, women who compromise innocent men are hardly candidates for sainthood."

As an apology for a wrong, it wasn't a very good one—but judging by the way the corners of his eyes crinkled in amusement, one he appreciated.

"And I am sorry I died and couldn't return to make a reformed hoyden of you as I'd promised," he replied solemnly.

She gasped in mock outrage and then burst into laughter. It felt good to let her worries go, even for a moment—but that moment passed all too soon, and her laughter expired on a sigh.

She sat up, holding the blanket to her chest with her uninjured arm. He must have already seen her in dishabille, but it seemed important to maintain at least some semblance of modesty in front of him, particularly if he had become what she suspected.

Thinking of the wings she'd seen, she pulled the covering higher.

The pain in her other shoulder flared, and she winced. Noting his concerned look, she asked, "Is it broken?"

"No. It was dislocated; it will be sore for some time. Unless I can heal it," he added.

Something about his tone made her narrow her eyes. That summer, Robert had used that same tone when he'd promised to show her a trick he'd taught his pony; he'd been bursting with pride at his own cleverness. She had ended up with mud in her hair and down the back of her favorite riding habit. "Unless you can heal it?" she echoed suspiciously.

He nodded, and his hair fell into his eyes. She had to resist the urge to smooth it back. She clenched her fingers more tightly on the blanket to give her uninjured arm something to do besides touching him, besides assuring herself that he was real.

He watched her carefully. "Do you need to lie down again? I know this is a lot to absorb, but—"

She pinned him with a disbelieving stare and didn't wait for him to finish. "Half of my family died six months ago. Since then, my brother and I were attacked by a monster, and that monster was chased away by a red-skinned flying woman with a sword. I've had to send my staff away for their own safety, because my brother has become another monster. *That* is a lot to absorb. Discovering that my dead friend has become an angel is nothing."

His lips pressed together again, but he managed, "I'm not an angel."

She paused and examined him closely for the first time. His hair was as untidy and overlong as always, and it was still a deep chestnut brown. He'd rolled up his shirtsleeves, revealing strong, tanned forearms with a light dusting of hair. Though his shirt was of a fine cloth and blindingly white, he didn't wear a coat to cover it, or a cravat. She should have realized that his exposed, masculine throat was too immodest for Heaven—and the cling of his breeches against his lean, muscular thighs would be positively indecent.

Why had she never before noted how lovely his eyes were? They seemed to glow with blue fire, and his grin made her heart skip.

"You are beautiful enough to be one," she said boldly, and enjoyed the blush that crept over his cheeks, "but your clothing probably left too much to be desired."

"Colin always professed that sartorial excellence was next to godliness," he said.

At the mention of her brother, Emily could not keep the sadness from her smile; she didn't try. "Can you heal him?" she said, and was sorry that her question made his good humor fade.

"No."

She sighed. "What are we to do with him?"

He raised his hand and cupped her cheek. She turned her face into his palm, afraid to see the answer in his eyes. "Hugh is watching over him right now. I'm not certain we can help him, but we will do everything we can." He tipped her chin so she had to look at him. "If we do find the creature that did this, Colin will live—but he will never be human again."

"What will he be? Like you?" She couldn't stop the hopeful note from entering her voice. Whatever Anthony was, it had to be better than the thing Colin had become.

"No. He'll be a vampire," he replied, and when her lip trembled at his answer he smoothed his thumb over it. He held her gaze with his and addressed her darkest fear. "He'll be himself, for the most part. He won't be evil, Emily—he won't be like the nosferatu who attacked you."

She released a deep, shuddering breath; she had been so afraid Colin would die, would *have* to die, that she'd never allowed herself to consider an alternative.

And yet an alternative was possible—perhaps not a perfect one, but one she could accept.

She had thought happiness had deserted her, but it suddenly bubbled through her like water and washed away the grief and shame that had held her soul numb. On impulse, she kissed his thumb, then dipped her chin and pressed another to his palm.

When he looked at her in surprise, she bounced up onto her knees and kissed him heartily on the mouth. Her shoulder protested the movement, but her face was all smiles when she pulled back and said, "I could kiss you forever for what you've just given me."

He lifted an eyebrow rakishly, but ruined the effect of it with his crooked grin. "Please do."

His answer widened her smile, even as it left her nonplussed. Aside from his hesitation upon her first seeing him, his bearing was more self-assured than she remembered. It wasn't arrogance, but a quiet confidence that left her uncertain, shaken.

Amidst her confusion, she tried to think of some witty reply; her gaze lowered to his mouth, and heat unfurled in her belly so quickly her thoughts deserted her and left her speechless.

Her sudden silence must have alarmed him. "Emily? Is it your shoulder? Do you want me to try to heal it?"

She nodded dumbly, grateful that he had given her an excuse. It wouldn't do to admit that she'd just had the most delicious inclination to trail kisses from his mouth to that gorgeous, shockingly bare throat. She wanted to taste him there, run her tongue down the cords on either side of his neck.

Perhaps there wasn't much difference between vampire and sister after all.

She turned to hide her disconcertment, presenting him with her back. She let go of the blanket and it dropped to her lap, allowing him better access to her shoulder.

Her chemise was a plain, sturdy one; beneath its wide shoulders she could see the dull bruise that had already formed below her skin. There were several more down the length of her arms, and she suddenly felt embarrassed, exposed—not by her underclothing, but by the fear that he would see her failure in those marks. Anthony had apparently been strong enough to defy death, and she . . .

"For a moment, I stopped fighting him," she admitted quietly. "I almost gave up."

The dip of the mattress signaled his movement as he kneeled behind her. His body seemed to radiate warmth; remembering the comfort she had felt when she'd awakened, she wanted to lean back against him, let him support her with his steady strength.

"You did, though." His voice was low, his fingers gentle as he probed lightly at her shoulder.

Her breath hissed out between clenched teeth, and he murmured an apology and removed his hand.

Despite the pain, she had to smile at his long, disappointed sigh. "It didn't work?"

"No. I will try again in a moment—I've only just discovered this gift."

Shifting around, she looked at him curiously. "What do you mean?"

His gaze fell to her chest. "When I healed the claw marks Colin left on you, that was the first time."

With a sense of wonder, she touched her clavicle. She had forgotten about the scratches. She glanced down, looking for any sign of them—but aside from a small tear and a stain of blood on the neckline of her chemise, there was none. "Thank you," she said belatedly.

She felt his gaze linger on the rise of her breasts, and the heat in his expression made her nipples peak beneath the soft linen. He glanced up, a small smile playing at the corners of his mouth, and she was once again reminded of the difference in his mien.

He would never have looked at her with such blatant interest, nor been so openly pleased by her reaction.

Whatever he had become, it was definitely not an angel.

She clung to that thought and tried to shift her focus from his sensually sculpted mouth to something less . . . unnerving. Something secure. Something that had nothing to do with heat and craving and the bewildering sense that everything she'd thought she'd known about desire had recently tumbled into pieces around her.

"Tell me about angels," she blurted.

His eyes narrowed, as if he sensed she was running from him.

But his tone was even when he said, "I don't know any. Hugh and I are Guardians."

She waited a beat and then blinked. "Oh," she said. "Of course. Guardians."

He stared at her in surprise and then grinned. "I was going to make it difficult for you, make you drag each bit of information out of me. I can tell you've caught on."

"I have a nephew," she said dryly.

At her comparison of him to a twelve-year-old, his lips pursed as if he'd eaten something sour.

She wanted to lick that expression from his very adult mouth. With a deep sigh, she prompted, "Guardians?"

He regarded her intensely for a moment, and she nervously wetted her lips. Following the movement with his eyes, he said, "Guardians are men and women who have been chosen to protect humans from demons and creatures such as the nosferatu. We aren't angels, though I'm told we have similar abilities and powers as them."

"Such as?"

"I'm strong, fast." He met her gaze; the outline of his thick, dark lashes emphasized the startling blue of his irises. "I can materialize wings and fly." This, with a wistful tone.

She tried to imagine him soaring through the air and felt a dig of envy and disbelief. But she had seen his wings; she could not doubt him.

"And you can heal," she said.

He reached out, his hand hovering over her shoulder. A focused expression came over his face—then frustration as he pulled his hand away. "Not always." His lashes swept down as he looked at his fists, and he continued softly, "Not every Guardian can heal— we each have particular gifts. My mentor's, for example, is Truth. It is very difficult, if not impossible, to lie to him. Unfortunately." He added the last with a rueful grin.

She remembered the youth who had been with him and his strange attire. "Your mentor—is he a priest? He's so young!"

Anthony's shoulders shook with laughter. "I've heard from other Guardians that Hugh was either a novice or a scribe during King John's reign. I do not know for certain, however—he has never related his history to me."

As she could easily imagine Hugh bent over a parchment or an illuminated manuscript, she nodded. "You do not age, then?"

"No. Our powers develop and increase over time, though. Most Guardians can not only create wings and clothes, as I can, but also shift their shape completely."

She eyed his breeches, leather riding boots, and loose shirt. "Your clothes are an illusion?" A blush heated her cheeks at the thought of him sitting next to her, naked but for a trick. Her fingers itched to reach out and test.

"They're real," he said, grinning as if he'd read her thoughts. "Things that are familiar to me are easy to create; also, things that I want very badly, like the wings. But shifting is much more difficult—Hugh claims I am holding on to my human life too strongly to let my form change."

Remembering all the people in her life she had recently had to let go, and the grief it had brought, she said quietly, "That is not such a bad thing, is it?"

He touched the corner of her lips, smoothing away her frown. "No." His eyes became troubled. "Emily, there is something I need to tell you."

Her gut tightened in immediate refusal—she didn't want to know what had brought that tortured expression to his face.

He took a deep breath. "The nosferatu attacked you and Colin and set fire to the house in London because of memories he found in me."

"The nosferatu set fire to—" Her voice broke. She closed her eyes, blinking back tears. "Why?"

"He wants your father's sword. We believe the fire was intended to divert attention from its loss afterward; but, he must not have found it—and that is why you and Colin were targeted next."

"The sword?" She shook her head in wordless denial. Pain ripped at her heart, grief all the worse for her certainty that she deserved it, that her childish desire to hurt her father had caused it.

Numbly, she whispered, "I killed them." She raised dull eyes to his face. "I destroyed my family."

seven

It is not the Guardian's duty to seek justice, only to protect. Judgment is a function for those Above; Morningstar and his cohorts were thrown out because of their ambition to punish, and to take on roles that were not theirs. A Guardian does not follow in a demon's footsteps.
—*The Doyen Scrolls*

Anthony's relief that she hadn't turned accusing eyes on him after his admission immediately disappeared. Confronted with her tormented expression, he'd much rather have had her blame him.

"No, Emily—whatever you are thinking, stop." If not for her shoulder, he would have shaken her to break the stricken hold that his information had taken on her. "Listen to me: if anyone is at fault, it is the nosferatu. The Guardians who failed to track him after my death. Me, for being unable to resist him." He leaned forward and made her look at him when she would have bowed her head. "Not you. This course was set in Spain, when he drank my blood. There is nothing you could, or could not, have done."

She broke away from his gaze and shuddered, as if his words had torn something dark and heavy from every cell of her being. When she looked at him again, he saw the resignation that had replaced the agonized self-recrimination. "Then tell me how it started," she said quietly.

Though he related the story of his death as unemotionally as possible, tears coursed down her cheeks and her body drew tight in horror. When he had finished, silence hung between them, broken only by her low, hiccupping sobs. Finally, she used the heel of her hand to wipe away the moisture from her face; her voice distant with memory, she said, "When he came after us, Colin and I had just returned from London—we'd taken Robert to Eton, then met with the solicitors. The house seemed so dreary without Robert, we decided to take Colin's new phaeton out for a drive. It was a beautiful day, even for November."

Anthony smiled; how impractical, and how like Colin, to keep a fashionable high-perch phaeton not just in London, but in Derbyshire.

When she saw his expression, Emily returned his faint smile—but their shared amusement quickly faded as she continued, "We went too far; it was dark as we came up the drive to the manor, and that was when it attacked Colin." Her lids lowered briefly, as if she wanted to shut away the memory. "Took him right off the seat. By the time I got hold of the reins and stopped the horses, it was already feeding from him."

He clenched his hands to keep from pulling her to him. "What did you do?"

Her eyes flashed. "I got the whip—but before I could hit it even once, *she* was there."

"The red-skinned flying woman you mentioned before?"

Emily nodded. "She had a sword—she nearly severed its head from its neck while it was feeding from Colin, but it still managed to get up and fight her. Then they both disappeared. And I went to get help. The staff assumed that he'd been attacked by an animal— I let them think that. Until I saw the changes in him, I thought my wits had deserted me."

"They didn't," Anthony said. "Although witnessing such a thing might have driven anyone mad, you took care of your brother and stayed strong for him."

"I do not know if I could have been for much longer," she replied with simple gratitude. "I am glad you are here."

I am, too. The thought surprised him—he had originally made the decision not to return, but upon hearing of the nosferatu, he couldn't *not* return. It had not given him joy—it was an obligation he had to fulfill. Now, seeing her, talking to her, he was grateful he'd had this opportunity.

She was watching him expectantly; wondering how much she had read in his expression, his gaze fell. The bruises on her shoulder were becoming livid, and a quiet frustration ran through him. His Gift had manifested itself so easily before—why couldn't he heal her now? What had he done differently? He *felt* the ability in him, but how had he made it work?

The answer hovered, just at the edge of his mind, and he grasped for it.

"Anthony?"

"Just a moment," he said, distracted, and raked his fingers through his hair. He saw her look up at the mess he'd left behind and turn her face to hide a smile. The unmarked sweep of her neck pulled at him: how had he done it? He'd held his hand over the wound and willed her to heal—but when he'd done the same to her shoulder, thought *Heal,* nothing.

And then he knew.

He hadn't willed *her* to heal, he had willed the *process* of healing—had imagined and guided the reparation of her skin, the recovery of her flesh.

And when he looked at her shoulder, he knew the muscles that needed their fibers repaired, the broken vessels that needed mending. He knew how to erase the bruising, ease the tender joints and ligaments—even knew the names for each.

It wasn't a matter of wishing it; one had to know how to do it.

When he placed his hand on her shoulder and willed it, it flowed through him in an explosion of heat and pain. He gritted his teeth, forced himself to hang on until the last bruise faded from her skin. His arm was numb when he pulled it away, but the look of astonished wonder on her face made up for it.

Triumph rushed through him, and he grinned. "Apparently, those endless hours of studying anatomy were actually worth something."

And—because the thrill of success roared through him, because she was laughing up at him with those beautiful eyes and mouth, because he could not help himself—he grabbed her waist, pulled her from the bed, and kissed her.

She held on tight to his neck as he swung her in a circle, giggling against his lips.

Emily slipped her arm painlessly through the sleeve of her robe and shook her head in amazement.

He'd healed her, then kissed her—and when the kiss had become something else, had become charged with heat and tension, she'd bolted. She'd run off to the dressing room—ostensibly to change, but primarily to regain her composure.

Anthony's arrival had certainly given her reason to be giddy, but she was not a lovestruck girl in her first season. She had been that girl once, her head filled with romantic notions. She'd been a silly girl—a girl who would have tortured herself with the past, would have been overwhelmed by melancholy because she thought such suffering romantic and noble.

And when those romantic ideals actually had been shattered, she'd allowed herself to be overwhelmed by bitterness instead and tried to hurt those she loved most.

She'd been a silly, *stupid* girl.

She sighed as she emerged from the dressing room. Her bedchamber was empty; she wandered slowly down the hall toward Colin's room. She couldn't fathom why she was thinking about love when her brother still lay dying. Did Anthony's presence give her that much hope, make that much of a difference?

Yes, her heart sighed when she found him. He'd pulled a chair next to Colin's bed, his hands spread over Colin's chest. His focused expression told her that despite his declaration that he couldn't heal her brother, he was trying.

"It should not cause him pain," a voice said quietly from behind her.

Although she hadn't heard Hugh approach, his words had been so calmly uttered she hadn't been startled. Or maybe she'd already experienced a lifetime of fear, and nothing would surprise her again.

The idea was oddly depressing.

She didn't glance away from Anthony and her brother as she replied, "I know—the healing isn't at all uncomfortable." *It's even pleasurable,* she thought, remembering the warmth that had stolen through her, easing the soreness and pain. But she couldn't say that to the young, monkish man standing next to her.

She felt the long, measuring look Hugh gave her. "I was not speaking of your brother," he said finally.

She frowned, walking into the room and pausing at Anthony's side. This close, she could see the strain that held his features taut, the slight shaking of his hands. She could feel the heat emanating from him.

"Anthony," she said softly, and laid her hand on his shoulder. "We'll find another way."

He stiffened, and she felt a final burst of heat come from him before he relaxed and turned to press his face against her belly. His arms came up to circle her hips.

"He's so thin," Anthony murmured, and Emily thought of how they'd been inseparable growing up, the improbable pair of youngest sons from impoverished gentry and wealthy nobility. She remembered how he'd always slipped into her thoughts, even when she'd been determined to only dream of dukes and princes.

Her lips parted on a sigh, and she threaded her fingers through his hair and held him against her.

And let those foolish dreams go.

EIGHT

During the First Battle, the three new orders of beings were determined: the angels, who fought for those Above; the demons, who sided with Morningstar; and the nosferatu, who abstained from the battle until the victor became clear. The demons were thrown down from Heaven, and they made their corrupt mirror in Hell. The nosferatu were not welcomed Above or Below; they are forever denied rest, hunted by angels and demons alike—and now, Guardians.
—*The Doyen Scrolls*

Anthony stood at the window as the fingers of dawn slowly began peeling back the night, piercing the overhanging clouds with gold and blue.

Colin had been restless in the waning hours but had finally fallen into the daysleep. As the three of them had watched over him, Anthony had told Emily the history of the Guardians. Despite her earlier declaration, she *had* found his explanation a lot to absorb.

He glanced at Hugh, who had said nothing during the account, except to nod once or twice when Anthony had looked to him for clarification. His mentor was staring out the other window, ever alert. Though the nosferatu could not attack during the day, the demon Hugh had sensed could.

The chains jangled, and Anthony turned as Emily began unlocking Colin in expectation of the servants' return. She leaned over the bed for Colin's left wrist, and the hem of the nightgown lifted, revealing the delicate line of her ankles. His eyes skimmed up her form, allowing himself to linger for a moment where the robe pulled tight over the enticing curve of her bottom, and then he moved to her side to help her.

Wordlessly, she handed him the key and began unwinding the chains from around the bedposts. He looked over at her, and a smile tugged at his mouth. "My story has shocked you into silence."

"No," she said. "I am merely trying to comprehend it all and think of what should be done next." She dropped the chains to the floor with a sharp clatter, and Anthony pushed the pile under the bed with his foot. She slanted him a wry glance. "And perhaps I am overwhelmed."

"When one is inundated with information," Hugh said without moving from his post by the window, "that is usually the end result. My pupil has yet to learn that short summaries are easier to deliver, and easier for the listener to take in, than epic narration."

How typical of Hugh to want the details framed in the most boring, succinct manner possible. Anthony's lips quirked. Perhaps he had embellished too much, but Emily had been a captivating audience. Her eyes had been wide, her skin flushed with excitement, and he had enjoyed being the object of her rapt attention.

He was absurdly pleased that her expression betrayed no similar excitement when Hugh recited, "Quite simply: after the First Battle, a group of angels descended from Above to reside in Caelum, to protect humans from the manipulations of those Below. But the humans began to think of the angels as gods; the demons, out of jealousy, decided to wage another war, the Second Battle. They managed to create a dragon, which defeated the angels—but a human was able to stop it."

"Michael," Emily said with a trace of awe, and Anthony grinned. Michael's battle had been one part of the narrative he'd lingered over. "And the sword he used somehow came into my family's possession, and the dragon's blood imbued the metal with the power to defeat the original angelic orders."

"Correct. After Michael's victory, those Above decided to create the Guardians, a corps of men who would protect against demons and nosferatu in the angels' stead. The Guardians' humanity would allow them to move among the humans as the angels never could. Michael took up residence in Caelum and began selecting those who would be in the corps."

Emily was silent for a moment and then she looked at Anthony. Her dark eyes sparkled with repressed mirth, and he felt her glance spear through him and settle heavy in his loins.

"Thank you, Hugh," she said. "That was *much* less epic."

Hugh bowed his head in acknowledgment, and Emily's gaze became thoughtful. "Why hasn't the nosferatu tried to kill us since that first assault?"

"You spoke to me of a female demon who interfered that night," Anthony said, with a quick glance at Hugh. If it had been a demon, the nosferatu might be dead.

She raised her eyes to Anthony's face. "If it was a demon, why would she have saved us?"

"If it is Lilith, as I suspect, do not suppose a rational motive," Hugh replied. "She'll reveal herself soon—she can't tolerate anonymity, and last night's mischief suggests that she is tired of waiting in the background—and then we'll discover whether she has killed the nosferatu."

"And the sword?" Anthony asked. "If the nosferatu lives and was able to delve into Colin's memories as he did mine, he might have already discovered its location."

Emily was shaking her head. "Colin doesn't know where it is." A blush crept up her cheeks, and she looked away from Anthony. "I had it sent—"

"Don't say it!" Hugh broke in sharply. Anthony and Emily stared at him in surprise, and Hugh added in his normal, staid tone, "Their hearing is as good as ours. Perhaps better."

Anthony felt Emily's sudden tension, and her hand clenched

tightly on his. He realized, "If they are listening, then they will know she has the information they want."

Hugh nodded, and Anthony wondered if his mentor had counted on something like this to flush out the nosferatu. To use Emily as bait.

Unease flitted across Emily's features. If the nosferatu came for her, it would tear her apart in its quest for the sword.

"It would be best if you did not leave her side," Hugh said.

His voice tight, Anthony promised, "I won't."

Emily slowly brushed her hair, studying the line of Anthony's back in the mirror as he paced the length of her room. He moved differently than he used to, with new confidence; before, he had walked as if he didn't care to be noticed, entering a room and sitting as quickly as possible in an unobtrusive location. Now, he seemed to fill her bedchamber with his presence, each long stride marking off territory and claiming it as his.

Claiming Emily as his.

He turned and met her gaze in the mirror. Her cheeks reddened at being caught in a stare, but she refused to look away. A faint smile curved his mouth, and he resumed his pacing.

Emily set down the brush and pressed her cool palms to her burning face—but her hands could not soothe the heat that coiled low in her belly.

But his hands could.

The image of his fingers on her breasts, in the dark hollow between her thighs deepened her blush. Anthony caught her gaze again and, as if arrested by her heightened color, paused a few feet from her chair. His eyes darkened as they skimmed over her slim form.

Though her lips parted in expectation, he abruptly walked away.

Disappointment surged through her, but she could not find the courage to issue an invitation. She stared at her reflection, wondering when she had become a coward—and why she found it difficult to clearly state her desires now. In the past, it had seemed so simple to convince a man—including Anthony. A kiss or a coin and their objections fell away.

I don't want to have to kiss his objections away, she realized.

For the second time, he tested the lock at the door, and she sighed. "The servants won't come in; I've left instructions for them to let me sleep undisturbed."

He jiggled the handle again. "It would be unfortunate should one come in here and see me; I'm supposed to be dead, and most of your staff knows me well," he reminded her. "And I do not have Hugh's ability to go about undetected."

She rose from her chair, crossing the room and pulling back her bedding. "I wonder that I was allowed to see you," she said, and climbed into her bed. She sat, her arms curled around her knees.

"I'm not supposed to return while you, or anyone else I knew, still lives," he admitted. As if finally convinced that her room was as secure as it could be, he joined her at the bed and sat down on the edge. His hip was only inches from her feet, and she fought the urge to wriggle her toes beneath warm, firm muscle. "I have barely begun my training; I shouldn't have come back to Earth until another century had passed."

Her eyes widened. "Did you break the rules? Will you be tossed out like the demons, or a fallen angel?" The thought that he would be punished for helping her made her chest ache.

He grinned and dipped his head, and she could tell he was trying not to laugh. "No, Michael bade me to come. In any case, there is no punishment for a Guardian. Falling is simply making the choice to reverse the transformation. If a Guardian chooses to leave the corps before the first one hundred years, then he Ascends and waits for judgment. After the hundred years, he can either return to Earth and live out the remainder of his life or Ascend."

As a reward for service, it left much to be desired. "If you chose to come back, everyone you knew would be gone," she said sadly.

FALLING FOR ANTHONY 257

He gave a short nod. "From what I understand, most who choose to Fall decide not to return." He glanced up at her face, sucked in a breath as if she'd hit him. "Don't look like that—it's not worth your tears. I'm fortunate to be alive at all, and becoming a Guardian is an opportunity I never could have dreamed of," he said gently.

She buried her face in the cradle of her knees and waited until the burning behind her eyelids stopped. Finally, she raised her head and propped her chin on her fist. "You might like to know that your sister Elizabeth was married six months ago to Lord Ashcom."

"Oh?" He lifted an eyebrow, his tone bland. "My mother must have been pleased with such an advantageous match. They did not even wait to come out of mourning for me."

Death had apparently not softened his feelings toward his family. "I believe she will have a first advantageous grandchild *very* soon," Emily said with an arch smile and was rewarded as he feigned a scandalized expression.

"Hardly appropriate behavior for a lady!" he replied, and his sarcasm was not lost on Emily. His family had always insisted on respectability, had disapproved of Anthony for his profession, and yet it had likely been his sister's impropriety that had netted her a viscount. His family would never see the hypocrisy; Elizabeth's actions had gained a peer and access to a modest fortune. It mattered little to them that a physician was a respectable position in society; Anthony would have been paid for his services. His attempts to secure himself a comfortable living had relegated him to *trade* in their lofty view, no better than a merchant.

But it hardly signified now.

She opened her mouth to tell him so and was surprised to find his countenance overspread with a deep blush.

As if embarrassment had congealed on his tongue, he said stiffly, "Allow me to apologize, Lady Emily. I do not mean to suggest that *your* behavior has ever been less than appropriate, nor lowered your status in my eyes."

She stared at him, puzzled, until she recalled what he had just said of his sister. Then she burst into laughter.

"Oh, Anthony!" she said when she could manage the words. She wiped tears from her lashes with shaking fingers. "You of all people—" A giggle erupted, and she clapped her hand over her mouth to stifle the girlish laugh.

He watched her, his blush fading, replaced by the confident teasing of a long-time friend. "You were rather shameless."

Her giggles ceased as mortification struck, sobering and cold. She sighed. "You don't know the extent of my shamelessness, Anthony." She pleated the hem of her nightgown with nervous fingers, studying the wrinkles the folds left in the linen. She couldn't bear to look at him, to see the censure in his blue eyes as she admitted, "I didn't wait to mourn for you, either. I didn't even wait until I'd heard news of your death—within two weeks of your leaving for Spain I was in another man's bed."

She felt his stillness, his tension. She dared a glance at his face. He was looking blindly at his hands; a muscle in his jaw flexed, his chiseled lips held firmly together, as if he didn't trust himself to immediately speak. A flurry of emotions passed over his features, and those that she recognized twisted in her belly and made her regret her admission: hurt, jealousy, surprise.

His voice was hoarse. "Are you looking to me for absolution?"

"No." She took a deep, shuddering breath. "I'm at peace with the past; I don't know why I told you." But she did—he had always looked at her as if she was an untouchable romantic heroine with no faults, even after she had used him. She wanted him to know the woman, the whole woman, she'd become—blemishes and all.

He didn't reply. Silence stretched between them, and she was desperate to fill it. "Anthony." His name was a plea.

He finally turned to her. Her throat tightened with relief when she saw his lopsided grin, but the self-deprecation lurking in his gaze ripped at her heart.

"And all this time, I thought you'd fallen prey to my masculine charms and were wasting away in my absence," he said. "Who was this paragon for whom I was a substitute, and why isn't he married to you now?"

If her nightgown had been paper, it would have shredded beneath her anxiously working fingers. "They weren't—" She took a deep breath, tried to find a way to explain. "After that night—after you left—I was sick. A fever and infection. And when I recovered, I went out and sought the most unsuitable lovers I could find. I paid for their services and then their silence," she said in a low voice. She met his shocked gaze with her own, and added with force, "And you were not a substitute for anyone. They were . . . convenient."

"As I was?" The question was ripe with anger, but he quickly suppressed it. Though she wished she could deny it, he had the truth of it: he *had* been convenient.

He fell back against the mattress, staring at the ceiling. After a moment, he raked his hands through his hair and propped himself up on his elbow to look at her. She tore her gaze away from the collar of his shirt, the broad expanse of skin and muscle his new position afforded her.

His concern was as intense as his anger had been. "Whatever could have possessed you to risk your reputation, your future—your family? What happened that you would be so reckless? Were you in love with any of them?" The last seemed dragged out of him.

She shook her head, and a miserable smile pulled at her mouth. "I wanted that risk—with men with whom my father would not approve an alliance, so he might be as disillusioned as I was," she admitted.

"Why not tup the footman then?" he asked carelessly.

She could not keep the reproof from her voice. "Anthony."

He sighed. "I'm doing my best to reconcile the idealistic creature I knew with the woman who tells me that she not only used me out of convenience, but also a collection of prostitutes—in some plot against her father?" He reached forward and placed his hand over hers, stilling the agitated crumpling at her hem. "I knew you were not yourself that night—but frankly, whatever the cause, your reaction was ridiculous."

Her mouth fell open, and she laughed. In retrospect, it had been easy enough to call herself silly, yet she had always recalled the violent bitterness that had motivated her and justified herself with memory of that emotion. Put in Anthony's blunt manner, her motives *did* seem absurd.

"You will laugh," she said. "But it was because I found out my father loved a courtesan. His mistress, Mrs. Newland."

Anthony didn't laugh; instead, he looked at her as if she'd grown a third eye. "Emily," he said gently, like a mother imparting an obvious fact to a stupid child, "many men take mistresses before and after marriage; some even love them. Surely you didn't expect your father to mourn your mother forever?"

"Yes," she said simply. She tried to give a nonchalant shrug, to remind herself that it no longer mattered, but she couldn't keep the thickness from creeping into her voice. "Theirs was a romance that the *ton* still speaks of: the dashing earl and the beautiful daughter of a duke. He grieved for my mother so much that he could not love us; it gave him a reason to ignore Colin and me. It was a reason that was beautiful, tragic. I wanted love like that for myself." She paused, glancing down at their clasped hands. His thumb softly stroked the back of her fingers as he listened. "But if he loved his mistress, then his indifference toward us could not stem from his undying love for my mother. It simply meant that he never found us worthy of his love."

"Emily . . ." Anthony shook his head, a smile tilting the corners of his mouth. "You are an idiot. Colin loves you. The *ton* adores you," he said, and added with an uneven grin, "Even I love you."

"I used you horribly," she reminded him, but the heaviness in her chest eased, and Emily found herself smiling back. "You can't love me."

"Since I was fourteen years old," he said.

"Don't be absurd," she admonished, and her smile faded. "I *was* an idiot," she admitted with a sigh. "But I was young."

"It was only ten months ago."

"Many things can happen in ten months."

"Yes," he agreed quietly.

They sat in companionable silence for a few moments, until the absent stroke of his thumb abruptly stopped.

"Did you meet this courtesan? Was she the rumor in Leicester Square, where you learned—"

He broke off, and his gaze dropped to her lips. She suddenly recalled the words she had spoken to him.

I learned that if a woman takes a man's organ into her mouth, she can make him do anything she wishes.

His hand clenched on hers, and she knew he was imagining it as well. A restless ache swept through her, tightening the peaks of her breasts, settling warm and taut beneath her womb.

She slowly nodded; his expression intensified, his jaw clenched. She leaned forward, a liquid movement, and brushed his hair from where it had fallen into his eyes.

"This would not be wise," he said, a raw edge to his voice.

Desire thrummed through her; she could feel the answering tension in him and didn't need to question what he thought *this* was.

"We've already decided I have a tendency toward idiocy," she said, and then paused when Anthony pressed his lips together. She touched his mouth softly with her fingertips. "Why do you do that?"

He caught her hand in his and tugged her toward him almost playfully. "What?"

She rocked forward until her knees were against his thigh and sat back on her heels. An unladylike position, perhaps, but a comfortable one. "You don't allow yourself to laugh when you are with me. Am I so formidable?" She tried asking the question lightly, but she knew he would hear the anxiety that ran beneath her teasing tone.

"Yes." He turned her hand and kissed the inside of her wrist. An innocent kiss, but tongues of flame licked the length of her arm. Her body tightened, trembled. His gaze locked on hers, warm, rich blue. "Your every smile, your every word leaves me breathless and delighted. If I laughed as often as I wished, there would be no other sound in the room."

His words pierced her like arrows. She drew in a deep breath, her eyes searching his face. "You aren't laughing now," she whispered.

He sat up and rested his forehead against hers. "A nosferatu is stalking you. He would kill you and your brother."

"He sleeps, as does my brother," she said, and threaded her fingers through the hair at his nape. It was soft, and his skin was like silk beneath her hands.

"A demon waits."

"Hugh watches for her." Her palms smoothed down his shoulders and felt the strength of him beneath his shirt. He shuddered under her touch, his lashes swept down as he closed his eyes.

"When I leave, I will not return for a century."

"When you leave, every day I will stare up at the sky and thank Heaven and you for looking after a silly, stupid girl and her vain brother."

A laugh rumbled through him but did not escape. He sealed her lips with his, and she rose up against him, winding her slim arms around his neck. She immediately sought to deepen the kiss, opening her mouth, a soft moan of anticipation sounding low in her throat.

He yielded to her quiet demand, his lips parting. His tongue gently traced the sharp line of her teeth before dipping inside, tasting.

His leisurely exploration sent delicious shivers along her spine. She arched closer, but he pulled away with a long, unraveling sigh.

"You undo me, Emily," he said.

She wanted him to become undone. She raised her fingers to her lips and felt the lingering moisture. His impassioned gaze followed the movement and then with a low growl of frustration, pushed away from the bed.

He strode toward the window, but not before Emily saw the taut stretch of his breeches across his loins and the outline of his shaft.

Tempted to lure him back, she got as far as uncurling her legs from beneath her before he turned around and pinned her to the bed with a heated stare.

"They will hear," he said, his voice thick. "Hugh, the nosferatu, the demon—if they are listening, they will hear us. Every sigh, every word, every movement of my body against yours."

The images his words conjured sent pleasure coursing through her, even as she recoiled at the thought of being on display—particularly for creatures such as those.

"I will be silent," she said.

"I fear I will not."

She tucked in a grin and flicked a glance at his straining erection. "You were last time."

He chuckled, a rich, deep sound that filled the room. She hugged a pillow to her chest, smiling with pleasure. It wasn't an outright laugh, but it would do.

Shaking his head, he said, "*Last time* was possibly the least-fulfilling sexual encounter—outside the marriage bed—in the history of England."

Her face went scarlet, and she hurled the pillow at his head. He caught it easily, and his renewed humor was payment enough for her embarrassment. "Go to sleep, Emily," he said. "We'll discuss your ineffective courtesan-learned technique later."

"I've learned many techniques since then," she muttered, but lay down, curling around her remaining pillow. She felt the warmth of his gaze on her and was certain that her roiling emotions and lingering arousal would never let her rest.

And then she slipped into dreams.

*   *   *

Anthony knew the moment she fell asleep. He heard it in the cadence of her breathing and the subtle relaxing of her form.

He still held her pillow in his hands, and he deliberately un-clenched the fists he had sunk deep into its softness, grateful that it had not exploded into a shower of feathers under the pressure of his grip.

He should not feel the jealousy that swept through him, nor the anger directed at those lovers she'd taken—he had her once, and his motives had not been pure. Yet he still wanted to tear apart every man who'd touched her, erase from her every memory of them: nameless men who had likely brought her more pleasure than Anthony ever had.

His erection rose taut against his lower abdomen, hot and insistent. Even now, with her back to him and sound asleep, the curve of her shoulders and hips, the nip of her waist, the spread of her hair behind her was an overpowering lure, the urge to bury himself within her silky depths irresistible.

God, he would have done anything to bring her pleasure now. But it was not the right time—there would likely never be the right time.

"Anthony."

Though several walls separated them, he had no trouble discerning his mentor's voice. His reply was quiet, to avoid disturbing Emily's sleep. "I'm here."

"Are you enthralled?" Hugh asked bluntly.

Anthony bit back the angry response that rose to his tongue; of course his mentor had heard Emily's and his exchange. And he knew that Hugh's real question was: *Given your feelings, can you effectively protect her?*

Emily sighed in her sleep, and he walked over to stand next to the bed. Her lips were gently parted, her lashed fanned against her cheek. Lavender and her unique, feminine fragrance filled his senses.

He could easily lose himself in her, but he would never permit himself that luxury if it endangered her. He would die before he allowed that to happen.

Again.

"No," he finally murmured. "Being near her has always affected me thus." A lifelong enthrallment.

There was a long pause and then Hugh said, "I will not listen anymore."

Anthony glanced in the direction of Hugh's voice, his eyebrows arching in amusement. Had the Guardian just given him leave to make love to Emily if he wished—and had he really thought Anthony needed that approval from him?

But he was not insensible to the tacit compliment accompanying the approval—if Hugh thought Anthony incapable, he would never have offered privacy.

"Have you sensed the demon?"

"Everywhere," Hugh said cryptically and then was silent. The short answer was a signal that Hugh either knew where the demon was but was biding his time before confronting her—or conversely, that he had no idea but did not want to alert the demon to her advantage.

Anthony tilted his head and tried to open his senses to locate the demon, as Hugh had once instructed him.

Nothing.

He sighed at the failure, but it did not dishearten him. He would have years to learn, and he was no stranger to study.

Emily turned over with a rustle of linen. Her nightgown climbed over her knee, revealing sleek muscles and satin skin. How simple it would be to draw his palm over the length of her limbs, to seek the dark secrets between them.

If he had eons to study them, it would not be enough.

He'd thought the taste of her he'd had long ago would be— though he had been aroused, there had been little passion; it had been swept away by his surprise and her bitterness. When he'd returned, he thought he could resist her sensuality, could keep his craving for her under control; the kiss they'd just shared had banished that notion. He knew she made him happy; he'd forgotten how she made him ache.

And with every move, every laugh, every word she reminded him, until it seemed as if there had never been anything else.

nine

Those who have been transformed yet cannot release their former lives should Ascend. For those, the hundred years of tutelage is an eternity, and their pain upon return to Earth—where nothing is as it was—excruciating. Guardians do not wish pain upon their own; those unfortunates should be encouraged to Ascend and not made to feel an obligation to serve.
—*The Doyen Scrolls*

Emily looked in on Colin when she woke; he was as still as ever, but it did not make her ache as it once had. "It will not be much longer," she promised him. She straightened his bedding and smoothed the hair that had become tangled on his forehead. Although she knew Hugh was in the room, watching, she could not see him. His silence and invisibility unnerved her, and she left the bedchamber as quickly as she could.

Anthony waited in the hallway, his eyes hooded and dark. "Where will you be?"

She paused at the top of the stairs. He could not be with her always. Only a fool would reject the protection he offered her, and yet they could not risk the servants seeing him. "Because I have minimal staff, we have not kept many rooms cleaned and heated. In the library," she decided. "Should Mrs. Kemble need to speak with me, you could wait in the adjoining parlor until she has left." A door connected the two rooms; he would be able to exit the library without going into the hallway, and he would still be close enough to help her should anything occur.

He nodded. By the time she took the first step, he had disappeared in a blur of movement.

She smiled to herself as she descended the stairs. He took such pleasure in his new abilities. She imagined him, a thousand years in the future, grinning as he healed those he protected.

It was an image that made her as happy as it made her want to cry.

She found him waiting for her in the library, turning the pages of a slim volume of poetry. He glanced up at her, a charming, slightly petulant look in his eyes. "I thought I might be able to read more quickly, but I can't."

Byron would likely have been gratified. "Not everything should be done quickly," she said dryly. "He titled it *Hours of Idleness,* after all."

A lazy, carnal smile spread across his face. "There are many things to spend hours on; poetry is not one of them."

She blushed, her nipples tightening as his gaze slid down her form. Wanton need slipped through her; she had the sudden urge to lock the door, push him onto the sofa, and replay the scene that had gone so wrong before, in London. Only this time, make it right.

But his gaze shifted from her, and he tilted his head, listening. "Someone comes," he said. "By the jingling of keys, I'd wager it is Mrs. Kemble."

Emily straightened, a flush coursing through her as if she were a child about to be discovered in some naughty act. Anthony grinned and strode to the parlor door. The flex and roll of his buttock muscles made her mouth water.

She looked up and found him watching her. He winked salaciously and closed the door on her gasp of embarrassment.

Composing herself took effort, but she managed to smooth her countenance before the housekeeper's brisk knock sounded at the door.

"Good morning, Mrs. Kemble," Emily said as the older woman swept into the room. "I think I shall take my luncheon in here today. I have some correspondence to complete in my brother's stead, and we are behind in tallying the accounts." Color rose in her cheeks as her effort to appear as if everything was normal brought forth a garrulous spill of words; she did not need to explain herself to the housekeeper.

Mrs. Kemble sniffed. "Very well, milady." She looked Emily up and down. "Have you come out of mourning, milady? We will need to air your wardrobe."

Emily nodded. Anthony had ripped her best mourning dress; though she had others, when she had faced the selection of blacks and grays, she had not been able to make herself wear them. She had chosen a fine woolen dress in pale blue instead and then topped it with a sunny yellow shawl as a ward against the chill in the house.

As Emily had only just entered her period of half-mourning, the disapproval on Mrs. Kemble's face deepened. But she only said, "I will send Mr. Davison to Hartington to collect one of the upstairs maids."

Though she wondered at the housekeeper's boldness at showing her displeasure, she didn't comment. Mrs. Kemble was not the softest of women, but she had served the family faithfully for years. It was likely the peculiar arrangements had strained the other woman's temper. "Aggie White is staying with her family only half a mile away," Emly reminded her.

The housekeeper's eyes lit with an almost gleeful malice. "No, milady—have you not heard? Aggie got herself with child and took her own life." With a harrumph, she added pointedly, "A fitting end for a woman who guards her virtue lightly."

Emily's face paled with anger. "Mrs. Kemble—" she began coldly, but was interrupted by the crash of the library door as Hugh forced it open.

He filled the entrance, shaking his head. "Lilith." His voice was tinged with amusement, but the sword in his hand glinted with serious intent. "That was unsubtle, even for you."

Emily stumbled backward, shocked. Mrs. Kemble said, "Fuck."

Then Anthony was in front of Emily, his sword raised protectively. The housekeeper glanced at him and rolled her eyes.

Emily stood on her toes to look over Anthony's shoulder and then blinked in disbelief as Mrs. Kemble rippled, changed, and became the demon who had saved Colin's and Emily's lives. Black hair fell sharply back from a widow's peak, and pointed teeth gleamed against crimson lips—all of her skin was crimson, Emily realized as *all* of it came into view. A moment later, the demon dressed herself in an indecent combination of tight, black leather breeches and corset. Membranous, batlike wings sprouted from her back. She grinned at Emily, and a forked tongue snaked out to swipe over her red, red lips. "Like what you see?" Her eyes glowed with scarlet light.

Emily drew back in horror, and Lilith laughed and turned toward Hugh. "I had despaired you'd never figure it out, and I was ready to expire from *ennui*. Keeping humans entrenched in nightmares and trying to convince them to kill themselves becomes trying after a day—a month of it is torturous. It's so much more entertaining to play with *you*."

Hugh's youthful face took on an expression of deep resignation. "Oh, joy," he said.

Lilith hopped onto the back of a sofa, perched there as if weightless. Despite her easy, grinning demeanor, Anthony sensed that her mood would shift quickly and did not lower his guard. He clasped Emily's hand in his and pulled her behind the desk to put its solid mass between them and the demon.

Hugh flicked a glance at them and nodded in approval. Lilith's strange, glowing gaze fixed on Anthony. "I see you've found a pigeon to teach." Her eyes narrowed, and she stilled. "A very young pigeon—now what in the world would induce Michael to send a fledgling?"

"Tell us about the nosferatu, Lilith." Hugh's voice took on a commanding tone that Anthony had never heard from him. A wave of power surged through the room, and Anthony had the desperate urge to spill every secret he'd ever had.

Emily's grip on his hand tightened, and he squeezed back in gentle reassurance.

Lilith hissed, and her claws ripped holes in the silk upholstery. "*Free will*, Hugh," she spat the words. "You think to force answers from me with your Gift?"

"Your free will does not matter. You were never human." Another wave emanated from him, and Lilith growled in anger. "Tell us about the nosferatu."

Emily suddenly took a step forward, drawing all attention; her hand shook in Anthony's, but her voice was steady as she said with gentle entreaty, "Please. You saved our lives once when you drove that creature away—now my brother's life hangs in the balance. Please."

Lilith's eyes widened and then she broke into gales of laughter. Just as quickly, her laughter stopped, and she said with quiet menace, "I like to kill—and because rules forbid me from slitting your throat, I have to satisfy myself with the likes of the nosferatu."

"You could have killed him *after* he had finished with both Colin and me," Emily persevered. "And yet you stopped him."

"Did you kill him, Lilith?" Hugh asked calmly. This time, his question was not accompanied by the thrust of his Gift.

Palpable relief filled the room as Lilith admitted, "No." A slow, mischievous smile crept across her lips. "But if you want to know more, there'll be a price."

They remained silent, waiting.

She turned to Hugh and licked her lips. "Just one little kiss."

He could not help it; as a desperate, trapped expression settled over his mentor's sober features, Anthony laughed out loud.

*   *   *

Emily jabbed Anthony in the ribs with her elbow when Hugh finally emerged from the library. He obediently wiped the grin from his face, and she was relieved when he chose not to comment on the slight flush lingering over his mentor's cheeks.

"You heard?"

Anthony nodded. "You'll be leaving tomorrow?"

"At first light." Hugh glanced at Emily. "The nosferatu escaped to the south; Lilith tracked him as far as London, where she lost him. Nosferatu do not usually remain in populated areas for long, and she wondered what had interested him in this house, so she returned out of curiosity."

Remembering the nightmares, the sense of desolation that had claimed her over the last month, Emily said, "Where she decided to stay and torment us."

Hugh smiled ironically. "Her presence likely kept the nosferatu from trying again. As much as Lilith likes to wreak havoc, she likes hunting nosferatu more, and it would not have attempted an attack with her nearby."

Strange that she had so much to thank the demon for, Emily thought. That she and Colin had been saved as a result of Lilith's malevolent games.

"As long as we are here, he won't risk betraying his presence," Anthony added. "We're going to force his hand."

"How?"

Hugh regarded her steadily. "I'm going to go get the sword. In the morning, I'll come to you for the location, retrieve it, and return before sunset."

Anthony frowned. "And Lilith?"

"I'll take her with me," Hugh said.

It would be a risk, Emily thought, but Hugh did not seem concerned about his ability to handle her. And Anthony could not protect both Colin and Emily against Lilith, if she decided to stay and cause trouble. "Keep your enemies close," she whispered.

Hugh nodded grimly.

Anthony stood at the window as the sun rose over the horizon. He and Emily had spent the night watching over Colin; Hugh had waited until Colin fell into his daysleep, then Emily had written a name and address on a slip of paper. Hugh had read and promptly eaten it.

Then she'd pushed a folded letter into Hugh's hand, asked him to leave it where he found the sword.

Two figures slipped through the garden and then took to the air—two pairs of wings, one of white feathers, the other black and leathery. Anthony envied them for just a moment, before he turned toward the bed.

Emily had already fallen asleep; the lines of exhaustion on her face had faded, replaced by serenity. All night, she'd kept him company as they'd watched Colin. They had talked to him, reminiscing their childhood. Each reminder of the past only seemed to make the present slip away more quickly, and Anthony felt the oncoming rush of the future bearing down on him with the inevitability of death.

In Spain, his death had seemed unreal; the transformation into a Guardian had made loss an illusion. Now he knew what waited for him when he left: a future without Emily. There was only the present, and each mile Hugh flew toward the sword brought the end of his time with her closer.

Later, he could not recall if pain or hope prompted him to make the decision, only that the kiss he pressed against the back of her knee sent a thrill through him that a plummet from the greatest height could not equal. And that when she turned to him with heavy eyes and a question on her lips, he fell willingly, completely.

The early morning sunlight played over her features, flushed with sleep. He shook his head, placed his forefinger against his mouth: a warning to be quiet, a notice of his intention. "I do not know if they've gone out of hearing range yet," he said softly.

Her eyes widened briefly and then she gave a small nod.

That permission to proceed overwhelmed him for a single moment; he wanted to dive in, devour her in one fell swoop. He forced himself to move slowly as he slipped his hands under the bend of her knees and pulled her toward him, her back sliding over the mattress. Her nightgown rode high on her thighs as he set her feet on the edge of the bed; she pressed her knees together, as if in an instinctive attempt to prevent exposure.

A rueful smile curved her lips, and he felt the weight of their self-imposed silence. What message was she trying to convey with that smile? Did she think it funny that modesty should assert itself at such a time? Did uncertainty linger despite her bold acceptance?

His fingers skimmed over her calves and the firm length of her thighs. He watched her, looking for sudden reluctance, a change of mind.

Her eyes darkened; she lifted an elegant brow, her expression one of gentle exasperation. "Even now, you hold yourself back, waiting—and for what?" she whispered. A shift of her weight, a twist of her legs, and she was kneeling before him, the height of the bed bringing her to eye level. "Do I have to *say* how much I desire you?" She cupped her breasts and then slid a palm down her torso to dip in the linen between her thighs. His gaze followed her hand's journey, envied it. "When my body aches for you, weeps for you—you pause and wonder if my passion is in earnest?"

It was his turn to smile ruefully. A lifetime spent certain of her disinterest had left its mark on him; a mark that he barely recognized in himself, yet she had deciphered perfectly. He had let the past overwrite the evidence of her desire; he had been a convenience then, but he was no longer.

He wanted to laugh, he wanted to shout; he grinned instead, and said, "I thought you promised to be quiet?"—and decided that after ten long years of yearning for her, devouring would be exactly the right thing.

He tasted her mouth first, slanting his lips over hers and delving deep. She met his ardor with a joy that was almost tangible in its fervor. The flavor of her laugh melted on his tongue, but it could not satisfy his hunger.

And then her laughter faded, replaced by a passion that burned. She gripped his shoulders tightly and arched into his kiss. Fisting his hand in her long, sun-tipped hair, he pulled her firm against his torso and felt the soft press of her breasts against his chest, her hardened nipples. He suckled lightly on her tongue, wringing a moan from her throat. He softly bit her lower lip as a reminder and then licked its sweet fullness when she stifled the sound.

A rock of her hips, and the delicious pressure of her sex against his rigid length made him inhale sharply against a groan of pleasure. She smiled in wicked delight beneath his lips.

In answer, he cupped her bottom and lifted her, her weight nothing to his preternatural strength. As he climbed into the bed, the ease with which he held her against him reminded him to be careful, but could not dispel the urgency of his body as he lay her in the center of the mattress, could not stop the need coursing through him nor the pounding of his heart.

And he could hear hers, he realized in awe: the quick beat of blood and muscle and arousal. His eyes closed in sudden, grateful prayer. Then when she shimmied and pulled the nightgown over her head, he could not look away.

He took in her beauty with a single, ravenous glance, to hold and savor later. Her small breasts, peaked with desire, her nipples dusky rose. The soft swell of her belly, the curve of her waist. The golden curls at the apex of her thighs, the hint of clinging moisture, the glimpse of the pink cleft hidden beneath. She lay before him, a banquet of silken skin and moist desire, and he knew he would never have his fill.

Emily. He breathed her name silently against her abdomen and glanced up. She leaned back on her elbows as she watched him, her eyes bright with anticipation and fierce heat.

He slowly dragged his fingertips up the insides of her thighs and felt her tremble. Her words ran through his mind: *if a woman takes a man's organ into her mouth, she can make him do anything she wishes.*

When he placed his mouth on her, could he make her love him?

Part of him rejected the thought, calling such a wish unfair, selfish. He would be forced to leave once his mission was completed. Her life would continue without him—far better that she thought him a pleasurable interlude in a time of grief and fear than love him.

But the other part of him, the part that had kissed her knee and awakened her, could not regret it.

And the whole of him rejoiced at her blissful sigh as his fingers slid into the heat and wet of her.

He parted her slick folds, ran his thumb softly over her clitoris, and then circled with gentle pressure. Her head fell back as a shudder of ecstasy raced through her. Unable to content himself with touch, he eased back, lifting her leg over his shoulder; pressing forward, he revealed her to his starving gaze.

Moisture glistened, her femininity swollen with her arousal. He licked, sampled; her hips rose in a wordless appeal.

He bent his head and feasted.

Emily clutched at Anthony's shoulders, dimly aware that at some point he had made his clothing vanish—one moment she had been scratching at his shirt, the next his skin had been beneath her fingers, warm and firm—but she wasn't certain of anything else. She had been pleasured this way before and thought she'd known what to expect.

But she hadn't realized she would be consumed by fire, that every point of her body would burn from inside out—only to be reborn with each devastating lick, every exquisite bite.

His tongue flicked roughly against her clit and then he covered her with his lips and soothed with a gentle, suckling lick. His mouth never stopped, his fingers never ceased their thick thrusts; he only slowed when she shuddered, the frantic coil of orgasm unwinding brightly within her. And then, though she pulled at his hair and tried to draw him over her, he began again—easily at first, sipping to relieve painfully sensitive flesh, then with skill and fervor as pleasure mounted, as she sought his mouth and lifted herself to him.

But such intensity could not last, and when she came yet again her hands fell from his shoulders, her body replete, exhausted.

He moved up to lie beside her, and the rigid arch of his sex drew her gaze. It swayed with his movement, thick and heavy, the head shining and wet with his arousal. But when she reached for it he caught her wrist and pulled her over him so she lay against his broad chest, her thighs on either side of his hips. She felt his erection against her mons, probing at her slick heat, and she rubbed lightly against it.

He caught her mouth in a leisurely kiss that warmed her through, circled her waist with his hands, and held her still. Then, with a flex of his buttocks, he began his slow entry.

She broke away from his mouth and buried her face against his neck as he pushed in and in. She was tender, sensitive, and the delicious stretch of her muscles around him bordered on painful, his hard length intrusive. It was possession as she'd never experienced it: unyielding in its gentleness, inflexible as it claimed.

Tears burned in her eyes—not from pain, but from something deeper, more elusive.

And still he pushed endlessly inside her, until she thought she might scream of it. He was no larger than before and yet he filled her as she'd never been and left her gasping and biting his shoulder.

Her fingers clenched on his biceps, and still he held her hips motionless against his penetration until he'd seated himself fully.

He remained locked against her, as if he couldn't bear to withdraw. She raised her head to urge him into motion. His face was stark, his skin taut across his cheekbones, and she saw the sheen in his eyes that he tried to blink away.

And understood that she had possessed him as unexpectedly—and as certainly—as he had her.

Oh, God. It wasn't supposed to have been like this. He was Anthony, her friend, and she loved him dearly for it—but it wasn't supposed to be *this*. She would not mourn for him when he left again—this would shatter her.

She'd been a silly girl who'd dreamed of love, and a stupid girl who'd declared love a fraud; but she'd never imagined that when she found it, it would be richer, more powerful than dreams, and the impossibility of keeping it more painful than the worst betrayal.

"No, Emily." The words seemed ripped from him, hoarse and broken. He sat up, shifting deep within her, and rolled her onto her back. He pulled and thrust, the strength of it chasing the wind from her lungs. "Just feel. Don't think of what can't be." Her back bowed as he drove into her again. "Just this."

And she allowed herself that fantasy; she rose to meet his heavy thrusts and let him withdraw each time as if she could hold him to her forever. He pressed into her, over and over, and each deep plunge seemed to push that inevitable parting a little farther away.

He braced his hands beside her head and never took his eyes from her face. She felt him watch as she gave herself over and writhed beneath him. She felt him memorize her as she clenched and arched, as he wrung the last bit of pleasure from her exhausted body.

A moment later, when he drove into her a final time and pulsed deep within her, she watched him.

ten

Battles must be fought: demons and nosferatu would destroy human souls and lives; Guardians must thwart the creatures before irreparable harm is done.
—*The Doyen Scrolls*

Anthony poured the final pail of steaming water into the copper bath and gave Emily a dubious look. "Are you certain you wish to do this?"

She finished tying her apron and nodded. "If all goes well, he'll be better by the end of the night. I won't have him waking up looking like he does now."

Anthony walked over to Colin's bed. Coal dust had darkened his blond hair, which was matted and stringy. Other than his hair, however, he was clean.

He turned back to Emily, ready to protest, but she silenced him with a frown.

Undaunted, Anthony suggested, "Why don't you and I take a bath instead?"

Her severe expression faded, replaced by a warm, feminine smile. "Later."

That sultry promise rolled through him, and he fairly leapt

across the room to kiss her before she recalled that there would probably not be a *later* for them. "I'm only doing this because of this—and earlier," he said when he lifted his lips from hers.

"Kisses as payment?" she said breathlessly. "Lilith would be proud."

He laughed, and her eyes darkened with pleasure. With regret, he released her and strode back to the bed, reached down, and tugged Colin's nightshirt over his head with one quick movement. He lifted his friend's naked body, mumbling as he crossed over to the bath, and set him gently in the water.

"What did you say?" Emily asked as she propped Colin's neck away from the rim with a cushion of folded towels.

Anthony blushed. "I said it isn't natural to see a friend naked, let alone carry him around that way."

Grinning, Emily began soaping Colin's chest. "I'll never tell him."

"Good." He watched her efficient movements and then helped hold Colin out of the water when she pushed him forward to wash his back. "You are good at this," he said with admiration.

Pink tinged her cheeks. "I don't make a habit of washing grown men, if that is what you are thinking."

Surprised, he met her gaze. "No," he said. "I wasn't thinking that at all. Just that you have a talent for caring for people."

"So says the poor doctor who resented having to become one," she said. She glanced up, her eyes wide. "I didn't mean that like it sounded."

He smiled. "I am glad I'm not the only one; around you, nothing I say seems to come out as I want it to." A hint of a smile curved her lips. He added, "And you are correct, I didn't want to be one. But now that I have this Gift, I am grateful I studied."

Nodding, she began lathering Colin's hair. "The unexpected pleasures are often the sweetest," she said softly. Her eyes took on a faraway cast, a mixture of sadness and love in their warm depths. "I did not know how much joy Robert would bring to me. He brought me out of it—that resentment I nearly let destroy me, my family. I was searching for someone to love me, a way to humiliate my father, and what I really needed was to think of someone other than myself."

"Surely it wasn't that simple," Anthony said. He dipped one of the buckets into the bathwater and poured it over Colin's head at her signal.

"No, it's not that simple," she agreed with a shake of her head. "But it feels that way now. Being with Robert made me remember how good it felt to believe in love, to regain that optimism and innocence—hope without *naïveté*. I was able to let go most of that bitterness I'd let consume me."

She looked up at him. "I blamed my father—but he was not a bad man for ignoring me, was he? Nor was he really a good man." She wrapped a dry towel around Colin's head and rubbed. "He was just a man who fell in love twice."

Her words made his chest ache. "Yes," he agreed, his voice hoarse. "You will, too."

"I hope that is true," she said. Tears dripped from her lashes and landed with a splash in the bathwater. "Help me lift him out, then hold him up while I dry him."

He did as she bade, watching as she pressed a towel to her face before turning toward him, briskly wiping the water from Colin's body. "In the letter, I apologized to Mrs. Newland," she said. "When I visited her that day, I was horrible. I called her terrible names."

"How did she react?" Anthony said quietly, unsurprised. He'd seen the name she'd written on the paper for Hugh.

Emily smiled in reluctant admiration. "She held her own. When I accused her of using her courtesan tricks to entrap my father, she told me exactly what those tricks were." Her smile faded. "And then I found you in the library, and took out my disappointment on you."

Anthony lay Colin on the bed. "Did your father ever mention the sword after you sent it to her?"

"No—I meant to make him ashamed, to let him know that I knew about her—but I don't think he ever was. And that made me angry." She worked Colin's arms into the sleeves of a clean nightshirt.

"Hence the other men." He tucked the blankets under Colin's still form.

"Yes. I thought if he could buy love, then I could, too." There was no shame in her eyes, no regret. "I am just human. Just a woman."

His woman. For a short, short time.

She met his kiss halfway. With a growl of need and hunger, he scooped her into his arms and strode from the room. Her hands roamed everywhere. His face, his chest, his back all felt the branding heat of her touch—a heat he feared and hoped he'd never forget. Her fingers slipped down, measured the rigid length of his cock, and he did not have the strength to make it to her bedchamber.

He entered the first room he found, turned, and pressed her up against the door, using her weight to push it closed. She gasped against his neck as he palmed her breasts and rubbed his thumbs over their hardened peaks through her bodice.

Desperate to feel her skin, he ripped her dress and chemise lengthwise from neckline to hips, muttering an apology. Her shuddering laugh ended on a moan as his lips closed over her nipple, suckling, biting.

Her hands fisted in his hair. "Tell me, Anthony," she demanded. "There is no one to hear."

The words pierced through him, but he could not speak.

She tugged, insistent. "I need to hear it."

She deserves to hear it. He laved his tongue along the underside of her breast and found his voice. "I love you," he said, and her breath caught. "I love the softness of your breasts, and the way you shiver against me when I worship them with my mouth, my tongue."

As if in answer, she trembled and watched with dark eyes as he circled her nipple with his tongue and drew the peak deep. Her hips rocked back against the door; her gaze never left his as he released her nipple and trailed kisses over her belly. "I love your navel, the little dip and shadow," he said, and flicked his tongue inside. The smooth muscles of her stomach quivered.

He reached lower, found the edge of her torn clothing, ripped it all the way to the hem. Tilting her hips forward, he dragged his tongue down her sex and held her up when her knees would have given out. "I love the taste of you, hot, drenched, the way you watch me unashamed." He grasped her behind her knees, lifted, and stood.

She reached between them and guided him to her. The head of his cock slid along her damp folds, notched against her entrance. "I love the way your muscles clasp around me as you take me inside, as if you want to keep me out but can't bear to." Her back arched, and she pressed down hard, filling herself when he would have gone slowly.

His throat closed as her warm sheath completely surrounded him. "Emily," he said, his voice rough with tension. "I can't keep telling you. I am coming undone."

Her thighs clenched as she lifted herself and then slipped back down over him. "Let me help you," she said. Her arms slid around his neck, and she rose and fell again. "You love it when I ride you, like this." A swivel of her hips stole his voice and his control, and he pushed her against the door and thrust hard. The sweet cling and drag of her inner muscles made him shake. He held her up with one forearm and slid his other hand between them.

"You love that I am tight—oh God, Anthony." He strummed her clit and felt the taut bud slick under his fingers. His hand moved lower, felt the stretch of her around his shaft, fisted himself, and pressed against her in sharp rhythm.

Her breath came in pants. "You love it when I spend," she said, "when I come apart in your arms." Her back bowed, and her nails raked along his back. Unclenching his hand, he allowed himself to sink deep, deep. The tremors that quaked through her small frame echoed the clasp and pull along the length of his cock, the vibrations of the door behind them as he stroked hard, as he took a few last greedy gulps of her before he buried himself completely.

She whispered the words against his lips as he came, gave back to him what he'd given to her. "You were never unsuitable, Anthony. I was." And silenced his protest with a kiss.

She rocked him to climax again as the base of the sun flattened against the horizon. He helped her as she dressed, his fingers lingering over skin soon covered. Together, they chained Colin for what she prayed would be the last time.

Her dinner of cold meat, cheese, and bread felt heavy in her stomach, and the wait for Hugh's return interminable. Anthony paced at the library window as twilight faded, watching as darkness fell.

She could not bear to look into it.

"Do you think something has gone wrong?"

Anthony raked his hand through his hair. "I don't know." His voice filled with frustration. "Why did Michael send me? I know nothing of demons or nosferatu, or protecting those I love."

"Stop," she said mildly, though anxiety coiled tighter inside her.

He glanced at her and grinned crookedly. "Thank you."

Rising from the sofa, she walked over to stand next to him at the window. He dropped a quick kiss to her lips and held her against his chest as he peered out into the night. "There they are," he said finally.

Emily turned, but she could only see her wavering reflection in the glass. "Where?"

Anthony stiffened against her, leaning forward as if to confirm something he was seeing. "He's carrying Lilith," he said. Grabbing her hand, he pulled her out into the hallway and ran with her to the front door.

Her heart pounded in her chest as he paused. When she looked at him, he said, "Appearances are almost always deceiving—I'm not opening this door until I'm certain it is them."

"Why do they need a door?" Emily said breathlessly.

He blinked, and a moment later a crash came from the front parlor. "Perhaps the rules are forfeit," he said with a grim smile, and they ran to the parlor.

Hugh and Lilith lay in a shatter of glass; a cold breeze fluttered in through the smashed window. Hugh raised feral eyes to Anthony.

"Heal her," he commanded and leapt to his feet.

Anthony didn't hesitate, kneeling beside the demon. Emily moved to his side, gasping when she saw the hole torn in Lilith's neck, the blood spreading across the peach and green rug.

"What happened? Did the nosferatu do this?" Anthony said. He pressed his hands to her throat, and his body wrenched as he began the healing.

Hugh met Emily's wide-eyed gaze. "He has your nephew."

"Robert?" Her lips trembled, and a sick, numbing pain swept through her. Anthony's hands jerked away from Lilith's body, and he caught Emily when she would have slipped to her knees on the shards of glass. He carried her to the sofa.

"Heal Lilith first," Hugh said, his voice almost gentle. "We may need her to fight."

Emily nodded slightly, and Anthony returned to the supine demon. "Is he alive?" she asked dully.

"Unharmed, when I last saw him—the nosferatu will likely use him to bargain for the sword. He knows he could never defeat all three of us."

Emily closed her eyes in relief, in dread. "But it is not so difficult to defeat the heart of an aunt?"

"No." Hugh's gaze was sympathetic. "I will not resist should you decide to make the trade."

"If he takes the sword, he will kill us all," Lilith said, her voice raspy. Anthony pulled the demon to her feet and then dropped her hand. "Better one die than five. Six, including your brother."

"Quiet, Lilith," Hugh said sharply. "You do not truly believe that."

Lilith shrugged carelessly.

Emily bent forward, covered her ears with her hands, and fought the urge to scream. She felt Anthony's fingers against her shoulder, gentle and reassuring, and wanted to push them away. She wanted to hold her grief close and alone.

She slid her palm into his and felt her numbness ease. When she finally looked up again, her anger was hot and bright. "Where is he?"

As if in morbid answer, Robert's voice rang weakly through the room. "Aunt Emily!" The words were laced with sobs and pain, and she started to her feet with a cry.

Anthony steadied her with a hand on her forearm and shook his head. "That's not him," he said. "He's trying to draw you out."

"Are you certain?"

His eyes never left her face. "Yes."

She noted that his sword was in his hand now—Hugh and Lilith had armed themselves as well and stood shoulder to shoulder facing the hallway.

Her heart slowed to a deep, rolling beat within her as she heard the swing of the front door, and then the bump and slide of a body dragged across the parquet in the entrance hall.

The nosferatu hulked in the doorway, but she could only stare at the slim, lanky form of the boy who lay on the floor, his eyes closed. Robert's small hand and wrist were enclosed by the creature's huge fist, and the nosferatu pulled the boy farther into the room, coming to a halt fifteen feet from the small group by the sofa.

"I can hear his heartbeat," Anthony whispered. "It is strong."

The nosferatu smiled, his lips thick cuts of liver against his pale skin. "Unless I tear his arm off—which I will do if the human does not give the sword to me."

It did not require a decision; there was no choice to make. She turned to Hugh and nodded—with a sigh, he reached inside his robe and brought forth her father's sword. Lilith hissed with displeasure but made no move to stop him. Hugh flipped the blade around, offering her the hilt. "My lady," he said respectfully.

She wrapped her fingers around the handle without hesitation. It was warmed from the heat of Hugh's body, but she felt no great power in it. Strange that she should feel so little for a thing that caused so much pain.

The nosferatu's triumphant laugh echoed through the room. She took a step toward it, and Anthony's arms came around her waist and held her fast, while his mouth pressed to her ear.

His voice was tortured. "He will betray you the moment he has the sword," he said. "We will not have time to reach you. I cannot watch you die."

Her eyes on Robert, she said, "I have to believe it will come out right."

"If she becomes a Guardian, that would be a fine conclusion," Lilith called out, her voice mocking.

Anthony's arms tightened around her. "Though I would keep you with me forever, having you die in this way would not be worth it."

With gleaming eyes, the nosferatu let go of Robert's hand. She winced as the boy's knuckles banged sharply against the floor. "Give me the sword, and I will leave you all unharmed," he said. His stare penetrated, persuaded.

Emily felt the insidious twist of his mind in hers and closed herself off from his lies.

The sword grew heavy in her grasp. "Anthony, you cannot hold me here. I am not immortal, and we do not have forever. Robert and I must move on—I must go forward." Though her chest ached to say them, every word that came from her rang with truth.

"You do not have to sacrifice yourself in this way; I cannot allow it. We will fight it—"

Anthony's voice was cut off, and his arms were pulled from around her waist. She tore her gaze from the nosferatu to see Hugh's forearm wrapped around Anthony's neck, dragging him away. Anthony's eyes burned with rage, but he could not break the grip of the older Guardian.

Hugh's face was grim and full of regret. "We cannot interfere with her actions; we must respect her free will," he said.

"The nosferatu doesn't," Lilith observed dryly. The demon's red eyes were bright with amusement.

Emily turned back toward the nosferatu. She could not look at Anthony again; she did not want to see the anger nor the entreaty— nor the grief.

I have to believe it will come out right.

She held the sword in front of her, the tip pointed at the nosferatu as if in defense, though she knew with his speed he could easily deflect any blow.

A final look at Robert strengthened her, and the trembles of fear that had made the sword an iron weight ceased. She strode forward, never taking her eyes from the creature, making plans and calculations with each step. If she dove for Robert the moment he took the sword, perhaps she would gain enough time for the Guardians to protect her. If she dropped the sword, perhaps that would give her— and them—even more time.

Stopping when the tip of the sword was inches from the nosferatu, she said, "You may take it."

And then she did none of those things she planned, because the nosferatu looked past her shoulder and his eyes widened in surprise—and in that moment of distraction, she slid the blade forward and his stomach parted like water.

He screamed in rage. She nearly fell back with the force of it, but strong, familiar hands covered hers, twisting the sword and dragging it up through bone and muscle. The scream gurgled to silence as the blade bisected heart and lungs. The nosferatu stared at them, his mouth gaping open, fangs red with his own blood. When he collapsed to his knees, Anthony pulled the sword from his chest and severed the neck with one sharp blow.

Emily crumpled to the floor and pulled Robert into her arms. Her hands smoothed over him, and a sob broke from her lips when she found him uninjured, breathing as if in a deep sleep.

Through tears of relief, she glanced up at Anthony. He stood stiffly, and she recognized his protective stance. She followed his gaze and gasped in horror.

The bloody point of Lilith's sword protruded from Hugh's chest. The Guardian's face was pale, his lips drawn tight. He gripped the blade of the sword with both hands, as if to stop the demon from repeating the same motion that Anthony had used to kill the nosferatu.

With a growl, Lilith lifted her foot and booted him forward off her sword. He fell to his knees, clutching his hands against the stain spreading across the front of his robe. She looked at Anthony and eyed Michael's sword greedily. "He was inhibiting *your* free will, after all. And mine. I was itching for a good fight. Now, be a good pigeon and give me that little toy."

Anthony's smile was like ice. "No."

Her lower lip pushed out in an exaggerated pout. "But doesn't the little doctor want to heal his friend? How will you save Hugh and keep the sword, I wonder?"

"Like this," Anthony said, and Emily felt a pulse of power, similar to when Hugh had used his Gift on Lilith. She pulled Robert closer and grinned. "I've always learned quickly."

Lilith watched Hugh doubtfully and then sighed in disappointment when the Guardian rose to his feet. "Oh, well—my father would have just taken it from me anyway." Her sword vanished, and her gaze fell on the nosferatu. "Perhaps we should go make a vampire while the blood is still warm? I may as well wreak some permanent havoc while I'm here."

ELEVEN

There is almost always another choice.
—*The (Amended) Doyen Scrolls*

Emily tipped the fourth cup of the nosferatu's blood to Colin's lips, watching in awe as his body regained its previous weight with each drink, as his hair thickened and seemed to grow. His skin paled slightly and took on a subtle luster, like light on a freshly washed face.

"This is revolting," Lilith said as she squeezed the nosferatu's body with manic glee, catching the last bit of blood in a basin on the floor.

Emily agreed, but Colin hadn't had the strength to feed himself. She and Anthony had been feeding him alternate cups. He sat quietly next to her now, his hand on her thigh, his expression pensive.

"He's rather attractive, isn't he?" Lilith set the basin on the bed, watching as Colin slowly drained the last of the blood from the cup. "Though I do wish he had killed you when I locked you in here with him."

Emily choked on a laugh. Robert was sleeping soundly in his

bed, her brother was going to live, and the nosferatu was dead. Nothing Lilith said or did now could pierce her happiness. "I wish I could say I'm sorry, but I'm not." She dipped the cup in the basin to refill it. "Where is Mrs. Kemble?"

Lilith made a disgusted noise. "At this moment, likely changing her grandchild's shit-filled nappy."

Emily smiled softly to herself. "And Aggie? The upstairs maid?"

"I had no idea who the hell you were speaking of, so I lied." Lilith shifted her gaze from Colin to Emily. "You should have been easier to manipulate, but aside from the nightmares, you resisted most of my suggestions. It's as if you are tainted with goodness. Both of you. I don't like it, and it makes me want to vomit," she said conversationally.

"You should leave," Anthony suggested, his voice hard with dislike.

"I should," Lilith agreed. "But then *you* would have to leave, and you don't really want that, do you?"

His gaze locked with Emily's. The soft glow of his blue eyes contained a wealth of emotion, and he didn't need to answer Lilith's question.

Emily's chest burned, but she was saved from tears as Colin jerked upright and blinked at them.

His eyes widened in horror when he saw Anthony.

"Good God, Ramsdell! Are you in your *shirtsleeves*? And what sadistic butcher cut your hair?"

Emily dissolved in laughter.

She found Anthony in her room, staring at her bed.

He attempted a smile when she slipped her arms around his waist, but she could see how half-hearted it was.

"He has decided that despite the unlikelihood of a vampire being accepted in London's fashionable drawing rooms, he will enjoy being immortal." She laid her head against his chest, listened to the beating of his heart. "Apparently, the prospect of a future *sans* inevitable baldness convinced him. Henry was already becoming quite thin on top, if you remember, and my grandfather's skull could have given the nosferatu a fright."

He shook with laughter and quickly kissed her temple.

"Let me see your wings," she said.

He sighed and focused, and she felt them erupt seamlessly through the back of his shirt. Stepping out of his embrace to walk around him, she trailed her hands along the sturdy, downy frame that rose from his shoulder blades to the wings' apex, feeling them quiver under her fingers.

"Take off your shirt."

It vanished, and she skimmed her fingers the length of his spine, his naked skin golden in the candlelight. His muscles were taut, the hands by his sides clenched into fists. She pressed her breasts against his back, nestled between his wings, and licked his nape. Her arms slid under his, her hands running over his chest and stomach, tracing the ridges of muscle with gentle fingers.

"Have I told you how beautiful you are?" she said.

His laugh was strangled by his arousal, and he nodded his head. "Twice."

She smiled against his skin, remembering, and quickly slid under feathers and flesh to face him again. Her fingers pulled at the front of his breeches as her mouth trailed wet kisses over his jaw, neck, and chest. Her tongue swirled around his flat nipple, her teeth nipped the small bud, and she dropped to her knees.

She felt him watching her as she drew his rigid erection from its confines and laid its pulsating length against her cheek.

His breath sucked in sharply between his teeth, and she glanced up, saw his face harsh with desire, his eyes heavy-lidded. His voice was rough, sensual, gravel and silk. "Is this when you'll make me do whatever you want?"

She held his gaze. "Yes." She whispered the word against the sensitive tip of him, lingered over it in a wet, suckling kiss.

His skin tightened across his cheekbones, and she wanted to take away the despair that warred with his arousal. "What will you make me do?"

Stay, she thought, but he could not give her that. To ask would only cause him pain, that the one thing she wanted he could not offer; it was not his choice. To voice it would be selfish, unbearable.

"Let me fly with you," she said instead, and licked the creamy drop of moisture that beaded on the taut crown. "I want to feel what you do. When I think of you, I want to be able to imagine myself with you." She traced the veins that lined his cock with her tongue, drew the heavy sac beneath into her mouth, and suckled with soft pressure.

"Emily," he breathed, and his fingers threaded into her hair. He guided her over him again and groaned in tortured bliss as her tongue stroked the sensitive underside of his shaft.

The sounds of his pleasure pulled her nipples tight and pooled beneath her womb with liquid heat. She pushed the tip of her tongue into the weeping slit to catch his flavor and felt the melting ache within her. His hips jerked as her tongue slid around the smooth head, and he thrust against her mouth. She took him deep and stroked with her lips and hands, lingering at the top with each suckling pull.

He tensed and tried to back away, but she insisted with her lips and teeth and tongue. She held him against her and drank him in and then gently licked the lingering seed away.

His chest heaved with short, shuddering gasps. She leaned in against him, wrapped her arms around his hips, and smoothed her palms over the small of his back. Their skin was slick with perspiration, her core swollen and hot with need.

"And then bring me back here, bend me over that bed, and tup me like a footman," she said, and held him to her as he laughed.

The cold night air stung her cheeks, numbed her nose, and brought tears that streamed like fire down her face.

It was glorious, she thought.

She'd screamed when they'd plummeted from her window, but it had turned to delighted laughter as they dipped and then soared. Each powerful beat of his wings took them farther, and they went over the Peaks faster than she could have dreamed possible, the moonlight shaping the stone-lined fields below into dark squares and rectangles.

How could anyone give this up? she marveled and knew that when the one hundred years was completed he would not Fall or Ascend but continue on as a Guardian. The thought brought her no pain, only a deep sense of awe and wonder and loss.

Though the wind took her words, she knew he heard them. "Will you watch after Colin?"

He tightened the cradle of his arms and banked toward the waxing moon. "Yes. And your grandchildren."

She touched her belly. "Do you think—"

He stopped her hopeful words with a kiss before lifting his head, aiming for home.

An ache spread through her at that wordless denial, but the tears that slipped from her eyes were only from the cold. The others, the ones that were hot and burned . . . those were for later.

"They told me you were here," Hugh said.

Anthony briefly nodded his acknowledgment, never taking his eyes from the parchment in front of him.

The muscles in the back of his neck tensed as Hugh silently looked over his shoulder. "I do not remember you showing interest in the Scrolls before," he observed.

Anthony finished reading the one in his hands before answering. "I spent my life in study. I did not want to repeat the process in my death." A blooming frustration started in his stomach, but he tamped it down. Yet another scroll without the answer he sought— and though he could search forever, he did not have that long to find it. It had already been a month.

It would help if I knew what to look for, he thought bleakly.

"So what brings you to the Archives now?" Hugh lifted a roll of parchment from a nearby table. He began tapping it against his opposite hand, and Anthony could not recall a moment when he'd resented his mentor more. "I have been told that when you are not decimating your opponents on the practice field, you are here."

"You should be proud," Anthony said, unable to keep the impatient tone from his voice. He picked up another scroll. "The perfect student."

"Did you promise her you would return?"

Anthony sucked in a breath. He could not erase the image of Emily's pale determination when he'd left. She had smiled and thanked both Guardians with polite gratitude; but he had heard the racing of her heart, saw how her hands had been shaking. Her face had still been flushed with their lovemaking, her lips swollen from their final, desperate kisses.

As his own had been.

"No. I did not want to give her hope if there was none."

"And yet you had already decided to search for a way."

Anthony met Hugh's gaze and held it, unwavering. "Yes. I had no other choice."

Hugh ceased his tapping and tossed the scroll to Anthony. "There is always a choice," he said. "It is a rare man who makes the right one."

Unrolling the scroll, Anthony skimmed its length. Halfway through, he paused, reread carefully, and closed his eyes against a rush of gratitude. "Thank you."

Hugh's expression didn't change. "You would have come across it. Eventually."

Anthony pushed away from the table with a burst of energy. He paused and turned. "I made a promise to Emily that I would look after Colin when she could no longer do it."

"And her grandchildren. I will," Hugh said. "For as long as I can."

My grandchildren. The overwhelming pleasure that swept through him at the thought almost caused him to miss the hesitation that crossed Hugh's features.

"What is it?"

"Lilith said you were tainted—both you and Emily." He glanced down at Anthony's hand. "And although Michael told me something was amiss, I did not know what it was until I remembered that the sword shed your blood. It must have left some of its power within you—the power that favors humanity, that rejects the divine and demonic. Lilith could not influence Emily as she wanted; you could not heal without pain and still cannot change from your human form." He gestured around them, at the massive inventory of scrolls and books. "You should have been able to read through most of this in the month you've been here."

"What does it mean?" Anthony asked guardedly.

"Once you have Fallen, it should not make a difference to you," Hugh said. "But I do not know what the effect will be on a vampire."

"The rules might not apply to Colin." Anthony nodded in understanding but couldn't let that uncertainty spoil his newfound hope. He clutched the scroll tighter in his hand. "I'm off to see Michael. Will you join me?"

When Hugh fell into step beside him, Anthony gave him a wry look. "I'm not walking; I'm going to fly there."

Hugh smiled. "Then I will join you."

Anthony materialized his wings and relished the weight of them before saying, "Do you think Michael will resist my leaving?"

"I think he planned it," Hugh said dryly.

"Do you like this one?"

Robert glanced at the rose-colored swatch of fabric and grimaced in honest repugnance, as only a twelve-year-old could do. "No!"

Emily grinned. "I think an all-pink parlor would be simply gorgeous," she said with an exaggerated, dreamy sigh.

"You're a female," Robert said patiently. He pursed his lips at her laughter. "Will you ever tell me how I came to be here from my bed at Eton?"

Emily's laughter died. She did not know if the nosferatu had made him sleep through the entire ordeal to keep him quiet, or if Hugh had removed memory of the creature afterward—and she did not care to know. It was enough that Robert would not have the nightmares she'd once suffered.

"No," she said.

"You told the messenger who arrived with the express that you had mistaken the date Michaelmas half ended and collected me too early," he pressed.

"I did." She gave him a quelling look and conceded, "I will tell you one day, Robert. Not today."

His sullen pout was interrupted by Mrs. Kemble's breathless entrance into the room. Her face was pale, her eyes wide.

"Dr. Anthony Ramsdell here to see you, ma'am."

Emily's heart twisted, and she squashed the hope that rose. Lilith could not be this cruel, could she? Would the demon pose as Anthony to cause Emily more pain?

She shook her head at her stupidity and wrestled for control of her emotions. Yes, of course Lilith would.

"I thought he was killed?" Robert said.

"Apparently not. It is not unheard of for a fallen soldier to be misidentified," Emily said mildly. "Why don't you run upstairs and see if your uncle has woken."

Robert frowned but jumped up from the sofa and scampered from the room, speeding past Anthony with a mumbled "Pardon."

He stood at the door, heartbreakingly beautiful, his hair tousled and his blue eyes seeming to devour her from a distance.

"Thank you, Mrs. Kemble. That will be all for now."

They were both silent as the housekeeper left. Mindful that Mrs.

Kemble likely listened at the door, Emily said with icy quiet, "Is nothing beneath you?"

"In a few moments, you will be." His lopsided grin made her want to believe, his words scored heated furrows in her skin.

She straightened her spine. "Lilith, you cannot expect me to be deceived by you again."

His mouth fell open, and he doubled over and began laughing as hard as she'd ever heard him. The sound made her smile against her will.

When he looked at her again, he wiped tears of mirth from his cheeks and said, "Appearances are not *always* deceiving, you idiot."

She threaded her fingers together to stop their shaking. "How?" The question left her lips of its own volition, and she hated that betrayal of the hope that lingered within her. But he sounded so like Anthony; Lilith had never perfected mimicry of Mrs. Kemble as well.

"A Guardian can Fall after his hundred years, as a reward once he has begun service," he said, approaching her with slow, deliberate steps. "I held Michael to the spirit of that rule—I had served, so I had a choice. I made a choice."

Her lips trembled. "Why?" She did not know if she asked Anthony or Lilith.

"Because I had a promise to keep," he said. Crouching in front of her, he lifted her hands from her lap and clasped them in his. They were as warm and strong as she remembered. "And because I love you. I love the softness of your breasts, and the way you shiver against me when I worship them."

Her breath caught on a sob, and he rubbed her knuckles against his cheek. The skin was rough with stubble; before, his jaw had been perfectly smooth.

"I love your navel, the little dip and shadow," he continued. "I love the taste of you. I love the way you give yourself to me, unashamed."

Heat and joy circled, gathered, and twisted deep within her.

His voice broke at her continued silence, and he whispered, "Emily, I can't keep telling you. I am coming undone."

"I want you to become undone," she said, and slid onto her knees next to him. She kissed his lips, his face. "I love you."

"Oh, thank God," he laughed, and dragged her against him. His mouth covered hers and she melted into him, met his passion with delight.

He pulled away, his breath coming in sharp pulls. "I've done all this to come back for you—you must marry me. I come with a supercilious, greedy family and a profession; I have neither title nor holdings. I will likely work long hours, delivering babies and soothing ladies' nerves. I have discovered I have a gift for it, if not a miraculous one any longer."

She laughed. "I come with a vain vampire for a brother and a nephew whom I love like my own son. I have a romantic nature that leads me into trouble. And I think your family might be made to think more agreeably of your profession when we point out that your wife is an earl's daughter and her dowry is very large."

He grinned. "We will make quite a pair, won't we?"

"That's what I told you long ago." She slid her hands to the front of his breeches and thought about the effort it took to lock the door. Then his mouth was on her and she could not think anymore.

Anthony stood at the window and lifted his face to the sun, letting the warmth soak into his skin. Behind him, the bedclothes rustled.

"Has Colin returned?" Emily asked, her voice still heavy with sleep.

His gaze traced the path her brother had taken through the garden. "He came in from the stable just after sunrise." Colin satisfied his hunger with animal blood for now. Anthony thought he did it more for Emily's sake than out of concern for the local maidens' necks.

One local neck in particular had him turning from the window.

Emily lay on the bed, eyeing him with drowsy hunger. "You have still not told me about Caelum," she said, and hid a yawn behind her hand. "I researched the name after you'd left—it is the Latin for *Heaven*, is it not?"

He smiled, slipping his robe from his shoulders as he walked back toward her. She arched back against the pillows, her gaze appreciative.

"It is like ancient Greece and Arabia melted together, and built of marble," he said, and bent his head to her nipple. "There are domes with minarets that climb into the sky, and columns topped with curling scrollwork." He brushed his lips over the skin of her belly, slid his fingers up the length of her thighs, and buried them in the curls at their apex. "It is all glistening, perfect white."

"And the food?" she asked breathlessly, the sound torn between a moan and a laugh. "Was it milk and honey?"

"I did not eat." His tongue traced the crease of her lips. "I did not sleep, nor did I dream." He slipped inside her, and she clutched at him with a sigh. "Do not be deceived, Emily—*this* is Heaven."

THE
BLOOD KISS

SHILOH WALKER

ACKNOWLEDGMENTS

Thank you, Cindy Hwang for making that call and Lora and AK for making sure Cindy and I connected.

Pam, thanks for always believing in me.

Thanks to my family, especially my mom. You always seemed to know I'd do this some day.

And last, but definitly not least, my own little family, my kids and my husband, Jerry. I love all of you more than I can possibly say. You're the reason I get up in the morning, my reason for living, and I thank God every day for giving the three of you to me.

one

Roman Montgomery was pissed. Staring at the woman in front of him, he throttled down the rage and hoped the ambassador wasn't very familiar with his kind. Behind the dark shades he wore, his blue eyes were glowing and spinning with the heat of his anger.

"The clan has done nothing to provoke this. Have your people forgotten the old law?"

The tall, slim blonde smiled, an icy smile that could freeze the blood of a lesser man, as she crossed one silk-clad leg over the other. The filmy ivory silk did little to hide their length or shape, and the dark circles of her nipples pressed tauntingly against the matching blouse.

It was just like her kind. Most likely she was testing him, the new *An Rì Mac Tire*, the wolf king of Wolfclan Montgomery, testing his strength, his control . . . and his patience as well, although he kept that hidden.

"Master," she said mockingly. "The young wolf was fool enough to dare to enter our lands. Wolfclan Montgomery has obeyed the law . . . but he has not. The House of Capiet has obeyed the law. We gave him warning; he did not leave. Now we have the right to do as we see fit with the puppy."

"Wolfclan leaves the House of Capiet alone. We have not bothered your family in ages," he rasped as his rage started to leak through.

"I believe the whelp was making too many of the cousins nervous. He didn't leave as ordered. As the old law allows, we protected our territory."

"Isabeta, you know as well as I do, a nineteen-year-old boy is no threat to the House of Capiet. Release him. Now." Roman wasn't going to leave one of his at the mercy of the Capiet. Even the thought made his lip curl.

"Nineteen-year-old boys can be very dangerous—they are entirely too tempting to our youth and the newly changed, especially the bloodkin of the new wolf king." Her lids lowered . . . until only the smallest sliver of her pale amber eyes showed, gleaming richly in the darkness of the room. "Many would risk much to have but one taste of blood as rich as his must be. Brother to the *An Rì Mac Tire,* I imagine his blood is potent indeed."

Roman bared his teeth at her and whispered, "You will not be finding out, Isabeta. None of you will. Release him."

He didn't even blink as her skin started to glow and the rich scent of her skin, her blood, and her sex grew heavy in the air. "He was too reckless, a danger to himself, so flagrantly entering our land—challenging us. Lord Eduard has done you a favor. The boy will be alive at the end of his sentence. Be thankful."

"You freely admit he was not committing any ill in your territory— that he even helped two young women, in fact. He has done no hunting, has broken no laws other than this archaic territorial bullshit. Yet you intend to lock him up for twenty years."

Isabeta smiled sweetly. "You are an intelligent man. For a dog."

Roman smiled back, a chilly one that brought a look of mild apprehension across her lovely features before she smoothed it away. "Master. I hope you recall the laws as well as your father did. Steven broke the Law. We will see our sentence through."

Roman cocked a brow at her and said, "I remember the elder laws. I know them well. Let us see how well the House remembers—of course the elders are likely to have forgotten. Senility can settle in after a few centuries."

Isabeta sneered at him. "Foolish dog." Rising, she threw her arms out, a cool smile on her red mouth and an evil look in her eyes. Wind tore the room, and her figure went misty until the vamp magick totally hid her from view.

When it cleared, a gray owl stood where Isabeta had been. She screeched at Roman, laughing, and then leaped into the air, winging past Roman, her broad wings caressing the air beside his rigid face and blowing his tousled golden hair into his eyes.

When the owl was out of hearing range, Roman turned toward his mother standing rigidly beside him. "Everything will be fine, Mama. I swear."

She shook her head. "They have my baby," she said, tears of rage, of fear filling her crystalline blue eyes.

Now that the vampbitch was gone he could actually release some of his own personal feelings. Not those of the leader, but of the brother.

Oh, he had no doubt Steve went to Louisiana to cause trouble. But he was a kid.

He certainly was no threat to the House of Capiet. One lone werewolf not even in his prime could only do so much damage. And the trouble Steven had gone searching for had been of the carnal variety. The kid had been looking to get laid. Hard and often.

Hell. It was New Orleans.

The majority of the tourists there were looking to get laid, get drunk, or both.

"I'll get him back, Mama."

She threw her head back, her eyes blazing. "But will he be whole? Sane? You know the damage a vampire can do. Do you really believe they will just let him sit? No, they will torture him, try to drive him mad."

Roman took a deep breath, trying to still the growing rage that brewed inside. "He is brother to the *An Rì Mac Tire*. Thousands of wolves bow down to me, obey my every command. That alone is enough to be sure the vampires are polite to me. They do not wish to risk an insult that will have my wolves flooding their streets, bringing about a possible war."

"You are too much like your father," she spat. "Being the wolf king didn't protect him from death, did it? It doesn't fix everything, being master."

"It kept Steve alive—they had the sense to let us know where he was, sent a very formal messenger to us, letting us know he was alive and safe. 'Safe' in their eyes, of course. But he is alive. Capiet has been known to kill trespassers. But he wouldn't dare harm my brother," Roman said levelly.

Then he turned on his heel and walked out, away from the sobbing woman, before she drove him mad with fear—hers and his as well.

TWO

They'd been in New Orleans less than six hours. Right now, the only thing Roman was doing was sitting in a bar. The inactivity was driving him insane, but stealth and subtlety weren't his strong suits.

So he'd left that part up to somebody better suited to it. But that meant he was stuck here, waiting, while he slowly went out of his mind with anger and fear. What in the hell had they done to Steven?

Closing his eyes, he breathed in slowly, trying to still the rage inside him. As he filled his lungs with the scents of beer, life, and humanity, he forced his emotions under control. He had to stay calm if he wanted to help Steven.

Running a hand through his hair, he brooded, cupping his hand around the half-empty glass before him. The amber liquid sloshed as he started to swirl it around in his hand.

Why did you come here, Steven? He'd been asking himself that question ever since the emissary from Eduard's House had entered his home with her master's message.

The bourbon didn't hold any answers for him, and with a scowl, he drank the rest of it down and gestured to the bartender for another.

Turning around, he skimmed his gaze over the occupants of the bar. It was the middle of the week, but the bar was fairly busy, with enough people milling around the small space to make him feel too confined, too hot.

After the bartender had returned with a fresh drink, Roman tossed down a couple bills on the bar before rising. Moving through the smoke-hazed air, he headed for the open-air porch that spanned the front of the building. There, he sucked in the fresher air, and with it, he caught a sweet, light, tantalizing scent.

Warm and female . . . his gaze ran over the women around him, searching for the source of that sweet scent. A breeze drifted by, bringing the scent closer. Sliding his eyes to the street beyond the waist-high rail, he found her.

A young couple vacated a table, and still keeping his eyes on her, he moved toward it, sliding into the wicker seat. As one of the waitresses cleared the table, he continued to study her.

New Orleans was full of street artists. Some of them sang, some danced, some played the blues with enough heart in it to make his throat ache. This woman was a painter.

From his vantage point on the porch, he could see the woman painting in the dim twilight. A streetlight poured over her bare shoulder, giving her more light to work by. She smiled occasionally at the boy who sat in front of her, teasing him into grinning and then moving with quick, talented hands to capture that mischievous grin before it faded and she had to coax it out again.

Damn, she was lovely.

Beyond lovely.

Her hair was a gleaming mass of black silk, yards of it hanging around her like a cape, the ends of her hair nearly to her tight, round little bottom. The skinny straps of her tank top left her shoulders and much of her back bare. Her eyes were almond shaped, blue as the Pacific, and twinkling as she smiled down at the child she was sketching.

Her hands were graceful, long, slim, and pale. And naked. No ring on her fingers, no bracelets, nothing.

As Roman's cock twitched, reminding him how long it had been since he'd taken the time to seek out a woman, she lifted her head, looking around as though she had seen or heard something. Her gaze passed right over him, a soft frown turning down the corners of her mouth.

Then she shrugged and went back to work, finishing up the sketch and rolling it up, tying it with ribbon before turning to the mother and exchanging it for the $10 bill the mother had fished out of her purse.

An innocent little fairy, wandering the Big Easy.

The monsters would have her for breakfast one of these days.

The soft, erotic scent of her body teased his senses, and he breathed it in, feeling a long-resting hunger stir within him. *Now isn't the time,* he told himself.

But maybe, once Steven was found, he'd have time to hunt her down for some playing.

As she started to gather her supplies, Roman felt a silent presence move up behind him. With a sigh, he glanced over his shoulder at the man standing there quietly, his hands linked together behind him. Jenner was the only name Roman knew him by, and he'd been around since Roman was a pup, first as his father's friend, then as his second after the Beta who had served in his position died in the pack challenge to the encroaching vampires.

They had pushed them back and protected their lands, but it had cost them dearly.

However, Roman knew it had cost the vampires of the Capiet family even more. Two-thirds of their number died in the battles four decades ago. Less than half of Wolfclan Montgomery suffered the same fate. And wolves bred so much easier than vampires.

Yes, the vampires had paid the price for their foolishness.

Murmuring into his glass, he said, "You'd think they'd learn." But here he was, because the vampires had shown their unbelievable arrogance. *Again.*

Jenner smiled, a tiny curve of his lips that for others might well be a sidesplitting guffaw. "Talking to yourself, sir?"

Roman had convinced Jenner to drop the *Master* he had used for months after his father's death. But the *sir* . . . that persisted, and he doubted it would change any time soon.

Cocking a brow, Roman said dryly, "This trip may well prove that I'm insane, but I'm not talking to myself . . . *yet.*"

Gesturing to the seat, he waited. It took the added, "Jenner, it looks weird with you standing at my shoulder like a freaking valet. *Blend,* will you?"

"I am a valet," Jenner replied levelly. "Or just about. Our purposes are the same." But he lowered himself onto the chair opposite Roman and jabbed a thumb at Roman's empty bourbon glass as one of the waitresses approached.

"So what did you find out?" Roman asked quietly, keeping his voice at a pitch too low for humans to hear. He had already skimmed the occupants, and not one of them was anything more than human. At least not yet . . . he had seen one or two walking blood banks, or vestals, as he knew the vampires called them.

They had given of their blood to a vamp and tasted it in return. Sooner or later, they'd take in enough that they had a chance to become completely vampire upon their death. They had better hope that death happened while they were young and healthy; otherwise, well, eternity was a long time to spend, and old and wrinkly wouldn't draw too many lovers.

Very few vestals crossed through the change alive, though. Too often the changed vamps were weak, and unless their creator was there to guide them through, they usually died from the blood fever that tore through their bodies in the first weeks, draining them, starving them, killing them while they slept.

That's probably why the vamps took so many vestals, to keep their numbers strong. Capiet wouldn't risk coming as close to eradication as they once had, when their house had all but died out in the battles.

Of course, the children of the vampire male and vestal female, that was the true vampire child, and they were even rarer. Good thing they had another way of making more vampires besides relying on Mother Nature. Their numbers would have died out long ago if they relied solely on breeding their female vestals.

"He's unharmed, for the moment," Jenner replied. "I had to . . . persuade some stupid blood bank to talk. Turns out Eduard is a little preoccupied at the moment. Once I finished talking with him, we decided he needed a break—he's en route to Colorado, via the baggage compartment of a Greyhound. And he's nice and unconscious, so they ought to have a long, pleasant, quiet trip before he's discovered. The bus driver was telling everybody to be ready for a long drive before they stopped."

"Find out anything else?" Roman asked, fighting the urge to gnash his teeth. Jenner was so damned . . . *Jenner*. Obnoxious and annoying as hell sometimes.

But he was as loyal and trustworthy as a saint.

So Roman tolerated the bullshit.

"Yes. He's being held at the Capiet plantation outside of town. And there's a rather large party going on there tonight, a costume party for Eduard's blood child. That's why he is so preoccupied right now. That's all the vamps are talking about now. Steven doesn't even seem to be an issue at the moment."

Roman scowled, reaching up to rub at the tension gathering at the base of his neck. "His blood child? Not just another vampire that's been brought over?"

Jenner shook his head. "No. She's rather . . . important. Truly his offspring, from what I can tell. She's twenty-five today, and for some reason, they consider that a big deal."

"She's old enough to vote with their elders and decide their laws," Roman murmured. "The men can vote at eighteen, but they make the daughters wait until twenty-five. Even those brought over have to be a vampire for twenty-five years before they are allowed a voice with their people. Or eighteen for the men."

Sending him an appraising glance, Jenner said, "You know far too much about them sometimes."

"It's the job of a leader to know the enemy," Roman said quietly, not hearing the bitterness in his voice.

It was a job. And he did it.

He would have hated it if he knew Jenner was aware of how tired Roman was of the ongoing hatred between the clans.

But Jenner . . . well, he was Jenner. And it was his job to know these things.

And he did his job supremely well.

Every bit as well as Roman did his.

Neutrally, Jenner asked, "So what do you want to do?"

With a tight smile, Roman shrugged. "Well, because they seem so focused on this party tonight, maybe we should drop in. Might be the best chance to get Steven out. Once Eduard isn't so focused on his daughter, he's going to take more interest in Steven."

He didn't have to wear contacts with the costume he had . . . "borrowed." The metal visor covered his eyes well enough.

The pre-Crusades get-up he wore was pretty authentic. Of course, Jenner had provided it, so he really shouldn't be surprised. At least he hadn't shown up with a suit of shining armor. There would be no easy maneuvering in that costume.

Although the braes he wore were trickier to fasten than jeans, there would be no difficulty running in them or fighting. Depends on what it came down to.

The music was some eerie, Celtic tune, the woman's haunted

voice creating a melody that would have had Roman stilling in appreciation, just to listen, if he had that luxury.

But he was here to find out more about Steven, his fool younger brother. And if the opportunity to free him came up . . . If he couldn't get to Steven by himself, then he was going to find himself a handy little hostage and start plotting negotiations. It would have to be one of Eduard's more valued people, but it wasn't hard to spot them.

They were holding court around the bastard himself.

Get Steven out . . . tonight. That was the plan, with or without help.

And then he'd be gone. Unless he paused long enough to find that lovely artist from this morning. A good, hard fuck was something he hadn't had in a long while.

Brooding, he stared into the crowd as he admitted he didn't have the luxury of doing that as much as he might like to. Getting Steven to safety was paramount—getting out of Eduard's territory as quick as possible.

Not getting laid. But even thinking of that pretty, black-haired artist was enough to heat his blood and make him ache.

A sneer curled his lip. There had been plenty of chances to get laid, by as many women as often as he wanted. The females in the clan flocked to the leader in droves.

And they wanted only to fuck the *An Ri Mac Tire,* the wolf king, to make her mark and hope he remembered her when he decided it was time to choose a mate.

Thus far, he hadn't met a single woman who caught his interest for longer than it took to bounce naked on the sheets.

And he wanted a lover, a friend, not just a lady wolf who was fun in bed.

He wanted . . . more. More than what his father had had with his mother. Something like what he glimpsed between some of his mated friends and their wives.

Roman took a deep breath, and suddenly an electric shock tore through him. His heart thudded to a slow stop before kicking into high gear as a sweet scent assaulted him. A familiar one . . . the artist from the street.

Closing his eyes, he swore. That sweet thing, the first woman to catch his eyes for longer than it took to guess her bra size, was here, among the House of Capiet. Shit . . . was she a vestal? A slave? A servant?

Damn it, she had *none* of their marks on her, no scent, no claim, *nothing*.

Opening his eyes, he searched the room for that black, shining sweep of hair. As his eyes glanced over an arched doorway, he heard Jenner placing himself at his back. "Are you well, sir?"

He grunted. His eyes jumped back to the arched doorway, and he froze. It was her, staring out at the crowd with grim eyes, her pretty pink mouth compressed into a firm, straight line. She didn't look happy, not at all. But neither did she have the submissive look of a vestal.

What was she doing here?

And then the music started to swell.

Roman recognized Lord Eduard, one of the lesser kings among the Vampire Clans and the head of the Capiet line. From across the room, he walked to the woman standing in the shadows, and with every step closer, the woman's face grew colder and colder.

His slave, an unwilling one, Roman decided. Fitting punishment it would be if he took the bedslave of the man who had imprisoned his brother. And he could set the girl free later. Once he had brought a smile to those cold eyes and heard his name fall from her soft pink mouth in a moan.

Yes. This would be . . . pleasant, Roman decided, a smile curving his lips upward.

But before he could explain his new plan to Jenner so they could start working out the details, the music crested and fell silent. And from across the room, Eduard called out in a clear, faintly accented voice, "People of the Clan . . . may I present . . . Julianna."

Roman froze. His breath started to burn his lungs as he forgot to breathe out.

His—

"My daughter," Eduard finished, in time with Roman's thoughts. Shit.

After Eduard's startling revelation, Roman retreated to the sidelines, keeping to himself. The more he interacted with people, the more likely they were to realize he wasn't supposed to be there. Not because he couldn't blend in as human, but because he did it almost too well. Under the guise of human, he should have been flocking to the sides of any available vampire, but he'd be damned if he'd go that far in the search for his brother. So he hung to the sides, away from watching eyes.

Jenner stood, thankfully, more at his side now than at his back. Jenner, when needed, could blend well—and right now that meant dropping his damned butler posturing.

They spoke in low tones about nothing of consequence, while mentally, Jenner relayed more information. Along the mental paths, though, their conversation was anything but lighthearted.

As always, Jenner's expeditions for information had yielded fruit. And . . . like so many times, the news he had for Roman wasn't good news—but it wasn't precisely *bad* news, either.

Steven is being kept in Eduard's lieutenant's dungeon. Apparently, they were keeping him here, but the master didn't want him here for the . . . festivities, Jenner told Roman silently. His eyes cut to the closely knit gathering in the center of the grand room, where Eduard held court and his daughter stood at his side.

Roman thought she looked rather . . . grim. Not at all like a woman happy to be here, happy for this grand party that was being held in her honor. *Did you learn anything of his daughter?*

Jenner's brow arched slightly, but that was the only reaction Roman could see. Out loud, Jenner continued to talk blithely about money. Besides blood, money was something that greatly interested the vampire population, as well as almost all who gathered around them. Roman suspected it was the vampire magick—they could attract damn near any they chose. By attracting those with money, they often added to their own wealth.

But silently, Jenner said, *Her mother is dead—she was a vestal to Eduard, but died, rather mysteriously, shortly after the child's birth. Ever since, Eduard had tried quite fervently to get his seed on another one of his vestals, but without much luck.*

Narrowing his eyes slightly, Roman said, *That isn't precisely the information I was looking for.*

Jenner chuckled, his eyes crinkling with mirth. *I do know that he is quite anxious for her to wed. And she is quite anxious . . . not to. There is a great deal of antipathy between them, from what I was able to gather.*

Roman's brow furrowed. *Antipathy?*

Jenner's shrug was all the answer the man would give.

Hissing out a breath between his teeth, Roman forced the tension gathering in his shoulders down. As his body unwillingly, but slowly, relaxed, Roman told himself to concentrate. Not on the woman . . . *Julianna* . . . but on Steven. He was the important one right now.

Where is this lieutenant's house?

Jenner's thoughts darkened. *Now that . . . I was unable to coax out of anybody I spoke with.*

At Jenner's grim words, Roman felt tension shoot straight back up his spine. Closing his eyes, he said, keeping his voice neutral, *Just how did you coax them?*

That toothy grin Jenner shot him did nothing to reassure him. Opening his eyes to mere slits, he stared at his second, his voice turning hard as iron as he said, *If you alert them to our presence . . .*

Jenner merely blinked, his demeanor as unflappable as ever. *Considering the fact that that stupid blood bank drew a blade on me and then accidentally fell on it and gutted himself, it's unlikely he will speak.*

Roman gritted his teeth. *And the body?*

Jenner gave Roman a beatific smile that did nothing to dispel Roman's unease. Finally, Jenner chuckled and replied out loud, "Have you noticed how lovely Eduard's lake looks in the moonlight? I wonder if they ever fish there."

Roman turned away from Jenner before he strangled him. So he'd dumped the body in the lake. Roman didn't bother asking him, *How do you know you weren't seen?* This was Jenner. Of course he wasn't seen.

Tension and frustration simmered inside his gut as he skimmed a glance over the throng of people. *Who is this lieutenant?*

They'd grab that damned bastard if they had to, although taking hostage one of the vampire's in Eduard's upper ranks was risky. Too many of the older vampires had powers Roman didn't trust—the mind control didn't work on werewolves, but the older vampires were damned strong. And fast.

Roman didn't want to risk a fight when he was here with only Jenner and when Steven's life was in danger.

Jenner's hand landed on Roman's shoulder, and Roman flicked a glance at him. Following his second's gaze, he found himself staring at the lieutenant. It had to be him. Next to Eduard, he was the most powerful vampire there. Hell, Roman suspected, he was actually *stronger* . . . so why in the hell hadn't he challenged Eduard?

He stood in profile to Roman, his eyes on the dancers in front of him, but Roman seriously doubted that was where his attention lay. He had dark red hair, a shade of red that Roman didn't think was natural—however, he couldn't see this man having the vanity to color it.

The waves of power flowing from him seemed to color the air around him.

He was old.

Roman could sense it—the power inside that bastard was enough to make his teeth ache. *Well, shit.* Roman had a bad feeling just looking at him. He knew his own power. That was a mark of wisdom—he'd learned that from his father. And he also knew when he was facing somebody stronger than him.

Roman's father might have been able to take this bastard.

Roman, however, was still young. A werewolf's power increased with age, just like a vampire's. And Roman hadn't even hit forty yet. The vampire across the room from him had seen a good four centuries—Roman knew that as well as he knew his own name.

And this was the bastard holding his brother.

Just when he was getting ready to turn away, the vampire turned and his dark eyes met Roman's from across the room.

Roman's breath froze in his lungs, and the entire world seemed to fall away as that vampire held his gaze. A roaring filled his ears, and his head felt strangely muffled.

Then there was a voice . . . low, soft, amused.

Hello, wolf . . .

And then the vampire blinked and looked away, pointedly turning his back to Roman.

Sir?

Roman whirled around, stumbling forward and sucking air into his lungs as the vampire's hold over him broke. No, a vampire couldn't use mind control on a werewolf, but they could sure as hell snare one with a mere look, if they were old enough.

Lifting his head, he met Jenner's gaze. Quietly, he asked, "Did you hear him?"

Jenner's brows lowered over his eyes, shaking his head. "I heard nothing, sir. What's wrong?"

Roman turned, his gaze sweeping over the crowd, waiting for some sign that the vampire had alerted his people to the presence of intruders.

But there was none.

His gut churned; his entire body tensed for battle, ready to run or fight, whatever was necessary to save his brother.

But the party carried on as though nothing at all had happened. Blowing out a breath, he looked back at Jenner and then back at the vampires circling through the room.

The lieutenant was still out there, dancing now with a human woman who gazed at him with spellbound eyes.

Eduard was holding court with two of the prettier vampire ladies seated at his knees, his hand stroking the head of one as though she were some sort of pet. All was normal . . . all was quiet.

Turning his head, Roman found Julianna, still standing off to the side, her gaze bored, her mouth set in a firm, flat line.

So damned lovely . . . of course, she was a true vampire child, which could explain some of that. The clear, glowing skin; the luminescent eyes; the shining, raven-wing hair.

Why?

Why did she have to be Eduard's child?

Child of the man who was holding his brother prisoner.

Child of the man who had signed Roman's father's death certificate.

Eduard could have saved Jacob Montgomery when that jackal of a voudon priest had started to prey on the Montgomery house. Eduard had only needed to bare his fangs at the priest, and he would have lost all interest in the werewolf clan, would have stopped hounding his father to change the priest, to make him like the clan.

The madman hadn't listened when Jacob had told him it didn't work that way. His men had captured Jacob and drugged him, using enough cyanide to kill a mortal. Cyanide had a downer effect on werekind, and it had slid Jacob into a coma. Only when the voudon priest had administered the antidote had Jacob awoke.

Roman prayed he hadn't been awake when the voudon priest started to skin him.

Eduard had assisted then, when Roman descended upon his house with the fury of hell in his eyes. Only then, he had joined them and led Roman and his wolves to the voudon priest's home hidden in the bayou country just beyond Baton Rouge.

But it had been too late.

The priest had skinned Jacob and beheaded the wolf king, the head laying on an altar as the priest chanted manically, wearing a bloody pelt Roman had recognized as his father's.

Eduard had failed. It was his job to provide safety among his territory for all. His vampires patrolled, much like Roman's wolves, feeding on those who were the true threat to humanity. Each of them, both pack and house, had unspoken agreements with local law that allowed them the freedom to live in relative peace.

Eduard hadn't taken care of the voudon priest even after he had shown that he was a threat, time and again.

And because of it, Jacob Montgomery was dead.

Rage and remembered grief tore through Roman as he remembered that night and the days that followed.

All the empty apologies and pretty words Eduard had spoken had meant nothing to Roman. Jacob Montgomery was dead, and nothing could bring him back.

And now they dared to lay hands on Jacob's youngest son, and for what? Daring to step into his sainted New Orleans?

I should have brought my wolves and razed it to the ground, killing every last cold-blooded one of them, Roman thought, unaware of how tense his body had grown, or how brightly his eyes had started to gleam inside his metal visor.

Behind him, Jenner whispered into his mind, *Sir, you must be calm. Do you want them to know you are here? Are you wanting war declared between our people?*

Roman stilled.

Do I? he thought to himself.

Slowly he turned and lifted his head, staring into Jenner's eyes.

Jenner lifted a thick, straight brow and said in that same mental voice, *If it is a war you want, then you should at least let me do my job and draft out a notice to the rest of my people.*

The dry humor in his friend's voice had him chuckling. Keeping his voice silent, speaking on the mental paths, he said, *Come . . . we have more important matters than this. I want to find Steven and leave this macabre city. Tennessee is so much more peaceful than this.*

His eyes lingered, for a long moment, on Julianna, on her raven hair and the pale green silk of her gown. She was dressed like Arwen, just waiting for Aragorn to come and carry her away, that delicate silk flowing down her body, a silver coronet at her brow. It was actually a damned good resemblance, with her top-heavy mouth and perfect oval face. Roman bit out a sigh of regret that he hadn't had a moment to taste that lopsided mouth, but a true vampire child wasn't an indulgence he'd allow himself.

Not in this lifetime.

And he wouldn't be risking his sanity by getting so close to the child of the man who had helped put his father in the ground. If he were to do so . . .

. . . he just might not have the strength to walk away from such a vision.

Then again, as Roman stared into her face, his eyes trailing over every feature as though he were trying to memorize them, he knew damned good and well he was here because he had to see her, up close, just once, before he walked away.

It didn't matter who her father was.

She could be mortal.

She could be the child of space aliens.

She could be the child of zealots here to peal his hide from his body and burn it, dousing him with salt water and shooting the rest of his sorry carcass with silver bullets. It wouldn't matter. He had to see her, closer, just once.

Of course, he was hoping it might be more than once . . . and for a little longer than a minute.

But that all depended on whether she knew what he needed to know.

"Who is out there?" a soft, tired voice asked from the balcony.

He stilled in the trees, one hand pressed against the rough bark of an oak, his entire body tensing. He hadn't made a damned sound and he knew it.

"Damn it, I told my father I wanted to be alone . . . *for once* . . . alone." Her voice was thick with tears and anger and emotion, and she was moving closer. "After twenty-five years, don't you think I deserve a little bit of peace in my damned life?"

And then she stepped into the moonlight, and Roman felt his heart stutter to a stop within his chest.

Moonlight shone silver on her face, highlighting the wet tracks of her tears, and a rage unlike he had ever known tore through him. Moving forward, he said in a voice that sounded unlike his own, "I am no man of your father's, Julianna."

Her eyes rested on his face as she studied him. Then she laughed, propping her elbow on the stone railing of the balcony. "This is N'Awlins, slick. Every man here is a man of my father's. Get off my land. I own this place. I bought it with money my mother left me, and it's mine. I don't want you, or anybody else on it."

He smiled, the grin cocking up his mouth as he studied her face. "I'm not from around here, Julianna. And I'm not your father's man." Then he said baldly, "You're the most gorgeous thing I've ever seen in my life."

She stilled and lifted her head, putting both hands on the stone railing, cocking her head and studying him, the fat black braid of her hair trailing over her shoulder as she looked at him. "Well, you're a little more blunt than his usual rats are. What is your name?"

"Roman," he replied.

Her entire body froze. "Roman," she whispered.

He heard the dry little click in her throat as she swallowed, and he laughed. "Well, I see Daddy has warned you about me," he mused, pacing in the moonlight. "Don't worry. I won't bite." Then he slid her a look. "But you're welcome to."

Her eyes widened slightly. "I'm still human," she said faintly.

"Until you die," he reminded her. "I know more about you than you could possibly dream, Julianna, how the vampire family lives, how they die, what kills them, what thrills them, what makes them happy, what makes them sad . . . but I wonder, does your father know the same about me?"

"He's scared to death of you," she said levelly. Then she winced, covering her mouth with the palm of her hand. "Ahh . . . hmmm." She started to laugh, a weak giggle at first that grew until she was all but doubled over with the gales of laughter, leaning against the balcony and wiping tears of mirth from her eyes. "Oh, damn—that's rich. All this time, he hid that from your father and then from you. And I let it slip. Oopsie."

Roman arched a level brow at her. "Really." It was a simple statement more than a question, and he just waited as she finished her last bout of giggles and then he leaped, covering the twenty feet between the ground and the balcony, hooking his hands across the railing and leaning over it, staring into her sparkling eyes. "And why on earth is he afraid of us?" he asked in a soft whisper.

She swallowed, looking from the ground, where he had just stood, to his eyes. "Wow."

He glanced down and shrugged. "I take it you aren't allowed to spend much time with your cousins," he queried.

"I prefer not to," she responded gently. Then she lifted her gaze and met his eyes. "I've never met a werewolf before."

He smiled, a slow curl of his lips, as he studied her lovely, ethereal face. "I've met dozens of vampires before. But I've never met one as lovely as you. You're more lovely than any angel I've ever seen," he murmured, taking one of her hands and lifting it to his lips, pressing a soft kiss to the back of it.

Julianna felt her heart stutter inside her chest. "I'm ahh . . . not really a vampire," she said weakly. "Not yet."

He released her hand to catch her braid, rubbing his thumb idly up and down it as he stared into her eyes. "I know," he responded. "I also know how you become one. Is he pushing you into it yet? Or would he rather you get pregnant and breed first?"

She flinched, lowering her eyes. "You really do know him well," she murmured, shame flooding her.

Roman's mouth twisted in a bitter smile. "I've had lots of time to get to know him, lots of time to see how he works," he said quietly, his head lowering. "He likes to take, and he likes to get. And what he likes to get is anything that will make him stronger. And that is more—more of his own blood under him. I suspect he would do it, even if it meant making his own daughter act the whore."

She laughed, a harsh, bitter sound. "Damn, you sure you aren't a psychic? A mind reader?" Walking away, she rubbed her arms with her hands, trying to chase away the chill such a thought caused. "I was given a choice today. Either mate with a man of his choosing, willingly, or become vampire in full, whether I like it or not. Granted, he worded it much prettier than that, but it amounts to the same thing, doesn't it?"

The werewolf with the pale green eyes merely stared at her, but she saw the sympathy in his eyes. Sympathy. When was the last time anybody had cared enough about *her* to feel sympathy? Of course, this sleek, sexy man was the last one she wanted feeling sorry for her. Heaven but he made her hungry.

She hadn't felt any drawing to the men her father constantly shoved at her, but *him* . . . She had glimpsed him at the ball, from a distance, just enough to see the thick, sun-streaked golden-blond hair and the square jaw under the half-mask he wore.

And there was that ass. The tight braes he wore revealed a body that was hard, firm, and sleekly muscled. Broad shoulders under the tunic-style shirt, and narrow hips . . . and now she could see his hands. Long-fingered, wide-palmed hands that looked as though they knew very well how to touch a woman.

She had turned away from him, instead of heeding the little voice in her mind that whispered she go to him, a dance—so innocent, and it was her party, after all. But she had ignored that voice and turned away.

And now, here he stood, and he was the man her father hated more than anybody else in the world. Hated and feared.

Julianna had to admit she wasn't above being petty. Her father would scream with rage if he knew the thoughts she was suddenly entertaining about Roman Montgomery, the king of the were-wolves, and the one man in more than half the country who didn't fear Eduard Capiet—or respect him.

But that was just a minor part. Even at the ball, staring at him from a distance had made her belly go hot and tight. Up close, the effect was so much worse.

She wanted to know how he tasted . . . how those rather beau-tiful hands would feel against her skin.

Her belly tightened at the thought, and she licked her lips, feeling the pulse in her gums as arousal grew and the ghost of the vampire lust that lurked within her rose to whisper seductively in her mind. However, for once, the ideas that demon inspired weren't unwelcome.

Going to him, wrapping her arms around his neck, and covering his mouth with hers for long moments didn't seem at all unattrac-tive. Neither did licking the skin that covered the large vein in his throat. Or undoing the lacings of his shirt, shoving it aside, and stroking the hard chest beneath.

Under the cotton of the chemise she wore her nipples tightened, and she felt the rush of blood to her face. Spinning around, she stared up at the moon, crossing her arms over her chest and cursing herself silently. He pitied her—she had best remember that.

A small, sane voice whispered, "He's your father's enemy—remember that." But that was no deterrent. In fact, the rebel part of her she had been forced to subdue all her life teased her unmercifully about how much fun she could have, defying her father in this way.

In a tense voice, Julianna asked, "Why are you here, Roman Montgomery? It's been months since your father died. If you were to come for vengeance, wouldn't you have done it already?"

He laughed, and the sound was odd enough that she turned around, facing him, looking into his hard face, seeing the alien glow of rage in his werewolf's eyes. "Don't you know? Your father is holding prisoner somebody who is very dear to me."

Julianna stilled, fear tightening her belly. *Damn you, Father. What in the hell have you done now?*

The House of Capiet could take no more losses from the hands of Wolfclan Montgomery. The wolves would slaughter them—the long line of House of Capiet would be no more. While Julianna harbored little love for many of her cousins, and even less for her father, she had no wish to see them slaughtered. If Roman desired to take offense to this and launch war upon Capiet, the wolves would destroy any and all associated with the House—vestals, servants, and perhaps even the few children. Oh, she knew her history—the war between the Wolfclan and the House had cost the lives of many, both werewolf and vampire. But the wolves bred true, much easier than the vampire. They could have very well rebuilt their numbers after forty years. Since those final battles decades ago, only three true vampire children had been born to Capiet. Only a handful of humans—less than fifty—had been brought over successfully. Oh, she was certain her father had tried to bring over more, but the change was hard, damn near brutal. Perhaps if some of the vestals were forced to come over—killed, in other words—their numbers would be stronger, but only their numbers. It took decades for a new vampire to come into full power.

She swallowed, running her tongue over her lips. Wolfclan could even decide to kill her. Although she would never become full vampire unless she took of the blood, she could be seen as a threat. If Capiet was destroyed and she left alive, she could go to one of the other vampire houses and have them change her, start the house anew, and bide her time until she was strong enough to take vengeance.

Not that she would. All she wanted was a normal life. Well, as normal as a vampire child's could be. A man to love, a life outside of what her father approved . . . *something*.

Lifting her gaze, she met the burning green eyes of the wolf king and asked quietly, "Who has he taken?"

The pit of her stomach dropped out as he responded, "My little brother."

Julianna whirled away, leaning against the stone railing of the balcony, her head spinning. *Father . . . why in the hell would you do that? How could you be so stupid?*

She didn't bother asking him if he was certain. Nor did she doubt his words.

It was exactly like her father to do something so unbelievably arrogant . . . and so unbelievably stupid. He clung to the old ways, and he thought the laws of old would protect him.

Julianna had no doubt that the Montgomery boy had done something her father saw as an insult or offense. And in turn, he retaliated, taking the boy prisoner.

Roman Montgomery, though, was clearly not one to cling to the old ways, the old rules. She doubted many outside her father's house would. The old laws were archaic, all but brutal. She knew just from speaking with her father's lieutenant, Mikhail, that many vampires and werewolves had progressed. They'd known it was necessary if they wanted to continue to live and thrive in the modern world.

But not Eduard Capiet. Her mouth twisted in a bitter smirk. It wasn't the first time he'd done something so arrogant, but it may well be his last. He'd been a fool—Eduard was often a fool in his arrogance, but this time it could cost him his life. He'd pulled the proverbial tiger's tail, striking out at Wolfclan this way. Or perhaps, wolf tail was more like it.

And this wolf was very much displeased.

Julianna forced her mind to stop chasing itself in circles. Yes, her father had done a foolish, stupid thing. But she was his daughter—his heir, if she chose to accept it—and it was her responsibility to see their people protected.

Protected . . . against an entire pack of angry wolves? Capiet was small still, although not as weak as they had once been. But their numbers were in the hundreds. She suspected Montgomery's pack was much, *much* larger.

Squeezing her eyes closed, she waited until the fear that flooded her leveled out. If she was going to talk their way out of this, she had better not sound like a blathering idiot.

"Is there a reason he was taken?" she asked, schooling her voice into a level tone. There was a formality to such things . . . always. People had died for not following proper protocol—granted, that had been ages ago, but still . . .

Roman laughed, a cool, mocking sound that did nothing to calm her fears. "Your father's emissary claims he was making people nervous. Too much a temptation to the young vampires."

She could imagine that. Life was a sweet beckoning few vampires could ignore. And if the brother had half as much life surging inside him as Roman, he would indeed be a temptation.

But not one that couldn't be ignored. *Damn you, Father,* she thought furiously. He had used old laws to his own ends. And if it had been another wolf, he might well have gotten away with it. But the king's *brother?* Not a chance.

Slowly, she forced air into her tight lungs. Lifting her head, she met Roman's gaze. "I doubt you came to New Orleans to try to talk sense into my father."

The small smile on his mouth answered that question. With a

slight nod, she murmured, "I didn't think so. Where is he being held, do you know?"

His brow arched as a speculative look entered his eyes. He moved closer, until he was just a breath away, his body heat reaching out to tease her chilled body. "Why do you wish to know, Julianna? What is my brother's life to you?"

"Life is precious," she whispered starkly, lowering her lashes to shield her eyes from him. "And if anything happens to your brother, my cousins will be the ones to pay for my father's arrogance."

His pale green eyes narrowed as his hand came up. His fingers curved around her throat, and Julianna gasped as she felt her pulse speed up at his touch. Both fear and hunger warred inside her as she fought to keep her face calm. "Wolfclan doesn't fall for vampire tricks, Julianna."

Coolly, she said, "And as I've said, I'm not yet vampire."

His hand fell away, and she stepped back, turning her back to him as she stared out into the night. No, she held no love for her father; she had no friends, save perhaps for Mikhail, among the vampires in New Orleans.

But she wouldn't see innocents slaughtered. Not all of her father's people were the mindless, cold-blooded monsters she knew Roman thought them to be.

Julianna knew what she had to do. As she ran the thought around in her head, she found a tiny smile dancing on her lips. She could even enjoy this. How often had her father forced her into things she hated? Taken things she loved from her? What a sweet revenge this could be.

Turning back to Roman, she said softly, "I'll get him out."

His eyes, that pale, pale green, narrowed as he studied her face. Vampires could sense a lie—it was a skill Julianna was picking up over time as well. She had a gut feeling werewolves could also see a lie—although whether they could sense it the same way as a vampire could, she didn't know.

But she wasn't lying. She didn't want the blood of her father's people on her hands, not if she could do something to prevent it. Coolly, she stated, "I'm not lying."

Roman smiled, a slow, confident smile that did very little to settle the nerves jumping in her belly. "Oh, I know. When a person lies, it shows, somewhere in their body. Either their breathing speeds up, or their heart beat . . . sometimes, they just start to sweat. But there's always something—even if it's a minute change, it's still there. What I want to know is why you would help me."

Julianna pursed her mouth in a frown. "I know my father—he's not a kind man. I hate to think of anybody being tortured. What's more, if your brother is harmed by him, I don't want the people of Capiet to suffer, not for their leader's stupidity."

Cocking his head, he studied her. She didn't like that intent stare; she suspected he saw entirely too much with his eyes. "You're a wise woman—how can you possibly be his daughter?"

Turning away, she laughed bitterly. "Pure bad luck, I guess." Heading for the door, she beckoned him to follow her. "Come on. I don't trust my father not to have his men out here at some point tonight. Even though he promised me time alone to think, he's lied entirely too many times for me to believe him."

THREE

Roman had to admit, she had surprised him. She was so quiet, so soft. Well, at least she looked soft. She couldn't be that soft if she was willing to defy her father like this. Vampires had been known to kill for much lesser offenses. In many ways, they were entirely too medieval.

He waited at the outskirts of the town, Jenner a silent presence at his back. The humidity was awful, the sun pounding down on them with brutal intensity, even though it was only eleven in the morning.

"What if this is a setup?"

Roman glanced at Jenner and shook his head. He had entertained the idea for a very short moment but shrugged it away as he recalled the innocence in her eyes. "No," he replied. "She is too—fresh. She is disgusted by her father. She's innocent, but rather jaded as well. Julianna Capiet doesn't care for Eduard. She fears him, but it goes deeper than that."

"Fear would be a wonderful motivator for her to stab you in the back, turn you over to him," Jenner argued.

"It would—but it's cowardly. There's nothing of a coward in her," Roman said flatly, shaking his head.

"That lovely face has clouded your mind, Roman. You're not thinking clearly."

Sliding Jenner a narrow look, he said flatly, "Nothing could cloud my mind when my brother's life is at stake. I spoke to her—I stood right next to her. If there was a lie inside her, I would have known."

Jenner's eyes dropped as he lowered his head in a slight bow. "My apologies . . . master. But it is my job to remind you to think clearly, always. I would be a poor second if I didn't look out for you and your family."

Roman rolled his eyes as he turned away from Jenner. "You never do anything but the job, Jenner. I know exactly what you are thinking, and why. And while I appreciate the intent, it's not necessary. I know what I'm doing."

Julianna Capiet hadn't been lying. Hell, as innocent as she was, he suspected any lie she tried to tell would have her blushing like a virgin. An amused grin curved his mouth. A blushing virgin—hell, were there any virgins left? He wouldn't deny the thought of an untouched woman held a great deal of appeal.

But he'd just be happy with one a little less . . . jaded. Somebody who didn't come to his bed expecting to get something in return. Who didn't fuck him just because of who he was.

Shoving those thoughts out of his mind, he focused on what was to come. No, she hadn't lied. He'd know. This wasn't some attempt to win her father's approval—hell, all she needed to obtain that was to become the broodmare Eduard wanted her to be.

Besides, it was daylight. No full vampire could come into the sun, and the servants and slaves would be fodder before a werewolf. Not that it would stop Eduard. He would risk as many as he thought were needed to get him what he wanted.

But it would stop Julianna, even if she had considered it for a moment. The goodness he sensed within her would make anything that cost lives anathema.

And he suspected that when she realized what he was planning, she wouldn't be happy.

But she deserved to be away from her father, deserved some small chance at freedom. And once Roman had made his point, he would see that she had that.

Steven was whole, if not healthy. His eyes were sunken in his face, his skin sallow, body unwashed. He stank to high heaven, and they hadn't been feeding him enough to maintain the high metabolism all werewolves had.

His eyes looked at Roman blankly for the longest moment and then he stumbled forward, rasping out, "About damn time."

Roman caught him and kept him upright as his legs started to buckle, fury ripping through him. "Taking good care of you, were they?" he snarled, his control falling to shreds as he felt the anguish in Steven's mind, anguish he was trying to hide.

"Well, you did warn me," Steven said, forcing a smile. His lips were dry and cracked, and blood welled as the skin split further.

A soft voice said, "Vampires are not known for their hospitality. Especially not Capiet. They consider him still alive and able to talk quite enough."

"He's been being starved." Roman's voice had deepened warningly, and he stared at the sky, trying to force his rabid anger under control. Jenner took Steven in his arms, sending Roman a warning glance.

He was failing, badly, to keep his anger in control. Sucking badly needed air into his lungs, he summoned every last bit of his willpower and throttled the rage into submission.

Turning his eyes to Julianna, he said, "Thank you for bringing Steven to me. I hope someday I can repay this."

She shook her head. "You don't need to. If Eduard wasn't who he was, this wouldn't have happened."

He arched a brow at her, closing the distance between them to cup her chin and lift her face to his. "Yes. And I hope you can keep in mind that if Eduard wasn't who he was, then neither would this have happened." The confusion darkened her eyes as she stared into his eyes, never down.

It wasn't until he took her hands that she glanced down. She was quick; he had to give her that. And if she was fully vampire, then he never would have been able to secure her wrists with the handcuffs. Spinning her around, he tied a gag around her face, slipping it between her lips as she opened her mouth to scream.

Lowering his head, he whispered, "I'm sorry. But know this. I'll take far better care of *you* than they took of my brother."

She turned slowly in his arms, and the fiery blue gaze she directed at him had him flinching inwardly. "I'm sorry," he repeated.

Sorry. That bastard was sorry?

Julianna struggled futilely against the steel cuffs, debating on whether she should try to jump from the moving car. It would hurt, yes. But it wouldn't kill her. She could die, sure enough, but it would take something solid to kill her. A broken neck, a bullet in the heart, having her head bashed in . . . or in time, old age.

Even a broken neck was pushing it—her bones were dense, much harder to break than the normal human's. She could survive this, if she jumped. From the corner of her eye, she studied the road speedingly by and debated.

"I wouldn't."

Slowly, she raised her eyes and met the bland brown gaze of the man Roman had called Jenner. Those were the first words she had heard out of him. Arching a brow, she flatly asked, "Wouldn't what?"

He chuckled. "Your thoughts are written all over your face, Miss

Capiet. Jumping out that window won't do you any good. Roman will come after you."

"If I make it out that door, I'm not going to be that easy to catch," she replied.

"You've never tried to outrun a werewolf." Jenner shrugged. "You may run fast, may hide very well. But you can't run fast enough from somebody who can hear your every heartbeat, who can smell the scent of your flesh on the tree you brushed against two days ago."

Julianna narrowed her eyes at him and said pithily, "So I'd be trying to outrun a bloodhound? Wonderful."

Not that knowing it would be futile stopped her. She bided her time. She wanted to be *far* outside her father's territory, which meant she couldn't try anything while she was within Louisiana.

But once they stopped around three in the afternoon, she figured she wasn't going to have a better chance. If she waited too long, they'd be in Montgomery lands. No thanks.

While she had visited the Smokys before and knew the area was lovely, she had no desire to try to run from a werewolf in his territory. She sipped at her tea while she watched Steven devour a rare steak. His third that day—he looked a lot better, actually. Barely even like the same person she'd rescued. All from three rather large meals.

Amazing.

Touching her tongue to her lip, she lifted her eyes and pasted a somewhat pained expression on her face. If nothing else, as her father's daughter, she had refined her acting skills to an art. Clearing her throat, she waited until the men were looking at her and said in a low voice, "I need to use the restroom . . . *sir*." She let some of her anger slide into that "sir," imbuing as much sarcasm into it as she could.

Her anger alone would increase her heart rate and explain why she was so tense, so agitated. And besides, she did have to pee. Arching a brow, she met Roman's stare as he studied her face. When

he didn't respond, she sniffed and added, "Or are you going to insist I refer to you as Master?"

Unless she was mistaken, Roman flushed just a bit. "How about
just Roman?" he said, lifting a golden brow at her, his pale green
eyes looking a bit sheepish, she thought.

Smiling sweetly, she said, "How about jackass, if we're going to
be informal?"

Jenner's eyes narrowed on her face—a sliver of fear settled in her
belly. She really hoped, if they decided to chase her, Jenner wasn't
the one who came after her. She'd rather not risk him catching her.
There was something very deadly about him.

Roman laughed softly while Steven chuckled, wiping his mouth
with a napkin and settling back in his chair to study her with intense
eyes. "She hit the nail on the head with that one, bro. You're better
looking than a jackass, but you're just as stubborn." Steven's mild
brown eyes caught hers, and he shrugged. "I tried to tell them both
this was stupid. You didn't do a damn thing to me, but they don't
listen."

"Sure we do. And if this was about her, that might matter,"
Roman said, keeping his voice low, too low for any human to hear.
"But it's not about her."

"Well, *her* has to go to the restroom," she said shortly, standing
up abruptly and stalking out from behind the table.

As she had expected, Roman fell into step behind her, several feet
back. *Damn, this would have been easier at the lunchtime or dinner
crowd*, she thought, searching for a throng of people. No such luck.
As she finished up in the bathroom, however, a frisson of hope
darted through her. Voices. Lots of them. She could hear them, low,
high, young, old . . . *lots* of voices.

Julianna strode out the door, brushing her damp hands on the
hips of her jeans, as she stared into the crowd, ignoring Roman. She
worked through several gaps between bodies that were too big for
him, and as he started to go around, she ducked, reversed her steps,

and hit the exit that opened into the mall. And *there* were some of
the crowds she was hoping for.

Speeding down the corridor, she dodged speed walkers and parents with kids in strollers, her eyes scanning the interior. She caught
the scent of fresh air and veered left, running into a major depart-
ment store, gracefully maneuvering her way through the shoppers,
her eyes on the door.

No footsteps yet . . . as she hit the door, though, she heard
them—light, purposeful, *fast*. Roman had entered the mall. She
could feel the pulse of anger roll from him as she ducked behind a
tour bus, hoping some of the smelly exhaust would help mask her
scent. Weaving between the buses, she thanked God for coach tours
like this one. The sudden rush of people into the mall must have
come from here.

She grinned with glee as she saw the line of trees—not a forest
or anything, just a small stand, someplace where she could unleash
the power in her body completely and run like the wind. Julianna
hit them just as she sensed Roman coming outside. He wouldn't
have seen her; she had ducked behind a bus that had parked at this
very edge. Of course, he wouldn't have much trouble tracking her,
but if she got enough distance between him and her . . .

The wind slapped stray tendrils of hair into her face and stung
her eyes. Leaping over a narrow ditch, she broke through the tree
line and found another parking lot in front of her. Another shopping
center. She ran for the entrance, shifting her path as much as she
could to keep large vehicles between her and the trees.

No sounds of his approach yet. It couldn't be this easy.

Roman fought the urge to groan as she slipped away—a lot faster
than he had expected her to be. Now he was going to have to hunt
her down—that wasn't good. Hunting her would do the exact opposite of what he wanted. He was trying to push her out of his
mind, trying to lash a growing hunger under control. He went

hunting her, and all he would want to do when he found her was take.

Take and tear those clothes from her lovely body, take her to the ground and fuck, until she wrapped her legs around his hips and screamed as he pushed her into climax. And then he'd be ready to do it over again, pushing her onto her hands and knees so that round little ass faced him and he took her from behind. What did she taste like? As sweet as she smelled? Did she like it rough? Slow?

Clenching his jaw, he focused and called out to Jenner. *She took off.*

Jenner's amusement was heavy in his mental voice as he replied, *Told you she would. You want me to get her?*

No. Stay with Steve. He's still too weak. Don't you leave him unprotected, Jenner. I mean that.

Jenner solemnly said, *I take my job seriously, sir. Steven will be fine. Go get the girl. Shouldn't be hard. She's still human.*

Still human—well, she had never been completely human, and that was what they had forgotten. Roman expected it to be much easier than it was. That was where both he and Jenner were wrong.

It took more than an hour of running before he finally ran her down, through most of the mid-size city, through several shopping centers, and into the dense mountainous forests that made up most of Tennessee. No human could run like that: unceasingly and at the speeds she had used when she was outside. No human could run like she did in masses of people and manage to totally avoid so much as touching anybody. Running in crowded places generally involved collisions, stumbling into people, things.

Not her, though. On the few glimpses he caught of her, she moved, graceful as a gazelle, weaving in and out of people and cars and trees.

But she was tiring. Though he couldn't see her dashing through the forest just now, he could hear her breathing, harsh and rasping. Anger and frustration flooded her; he could sense it in the erratic heartbeat, hear it in the occasional soft curse that drifted through the trees.

He caught up with her just as he caught the scent of civilization—the smell of exhaust fumes and fast food. She had nearly hit the I-40 with her furious run. He might have been pissed, if he hadn't been so astounded. Once he broke through the final barrier separating them, she slowed to a halt and stopped, just standing there, staring up at the sky, sweat darkening the black tank she wore. "Can't you just go away?" she said tiredly.

Roman smiled, raising one shoulder in a shrug. "Of course, I could. I just won't." He had to wonder, though, if anybody else had offered to help Steven, would he have taken such drastic measures?

Crossing the distance between them, he studied her profile and decided, *No, probably not.* He had wanted her from the second he had seen her, and he'd be damned if he would just let her walk away.

He closed his hand around the thick skein of her braid as he moved around her, staring down into her face. His mouth curved upward slightly as her eyes met his, and he found himself staring into pools of blue ice. "Don't you know better than to run from a wolf?" he whispered.

Succinctly, she said, "Bite me."

four

Roman chuckled, feeling the hunger rip through him with vicious intensity as he stared down at her. "Don't mind if I do," he murmured, lowering his head and nipping at the full curve of her lower lip.

Her hands slammed against his chest, trying to push him back. If he hadn't had a tight hold on her braid, she might have slipped away. She was fast and strong. A shadow moved through those pretty eyes, and he smiled himself as he heard the rapid change in her heartbeat. Once she had accepted the inevitable and stopped running, it had started to slow immediately, but now it was pounding, hard and steady. Covering her mouth with his, he licked at her lips, nuzzling, while he cupped her hip in his free hand and brought her against him. She gasped as his cock pressed against her belly, and he swallowed the soft little breath, pushing his tongue into her mouth and groaning as her taste exploded inside him like dynamite.

Holy hell, she was hot—sweet like molten honey on his tongue—

the taste of woman and something indefinable he knew came from her mixed ancestry. Life and death flowed inside her—he had known that, but he hadn't expected the touch of her, the taste of her, to be so addictive.

She moaned into his mouth, her fingers curling into the soft cotton of his shirt. He guided one hand up and then the other until she had her arms curled around his neck. Roman crushed her against him then, growling roughly as her breasts pressed against his chest, letting him feel the tight little buds of her nipples. He caught her braid again, pulling his mouth free of hers and tugging her head back, scraping his teeth down her neck. She shuddered against him, whimpering low in her throat. Dipping his head, he sank his teeth into the taut flesh of her neck. She cried out, her nails biting through his shirt to sink into his skin.

"Roman," she gasped as he spun them around, pressing her back against a tree.

"You taste so good." His voice was low, a hoarse growl that was barely distinguishable. "So damned hot and sweet." He pushed his knee between her thighs, sliding his hands down to cup her hips, pulling her astride his leg. Through the layers of their clothing, he felt the blistering heat of her pussy, the dampness of her panties and jeans soaking through to his.

He straightened, gripping the straps of her tank and jerking them down, totally focused on tasting more of her. All of her. The straps of her tank stopped at her elbows, the lace of her bra covering her breasts. With a rough snap, he unlatched her bra's front clasp, fire leaping through him as her breasts swung free, tipped by diamond-hard little nipples. With a hungry growl, he boosted her higher, bracing her against the tree as he caught one plump, deep pink nipple in his mouth, sucking hard, pressing it against the roof of his mouth as he tasted her.

Her breathy little moan sounded like hosanna to his ears. Switching his mouth to the other breast, he tugged on the damp nipple, tweaking it, milking it with certain, steady strokes of his fingers. Slowly, he lowered her to the ground, pulling her closer to him so the rough bark wouldn't scrape her skin. When her feet touched the ground, he dropped to his knees, pressing his mouth against the quivering muscles of her tummy. "I could eat you up," he said thickly, running a hand up the inside of one thigh, cupping her and then grinding his hand against her, pressing his fingers into the seam of her jeans until her flesh parted under the material.

Staring up at her, he whispered, "I've wanted to do nothing but this since I saw you."

The same slow flush colored her face again, starting at the smooth mounds of her breasts and rising until it had covered her face. The pink tip of her tongue appeared as she licked her lips, her head falling back to rest against the tree. Roman gave in to the gentle urging from her fingers and leaned back against her, pressing hot little kisses where her skin disappeared inside the waistband of her jeans. He flicked open the button that held her jeans closed, slowly lowering the zipper. As the material spread, he saw the black sheer cloth of her panties, and he grinned as he revealed more of the sexy little swatch of cloth. Completely sheer, hiding nothing.

Lifting first one foot, then the other, he had her shoes off and slid her jeans down her hips. "Damn, you're sexy," he muttered, staring at the sleek curve of hip, the trim little patch of silken hair visible under the see-through cloth of her panties. The crotch was wet—he could see the moisture gathering there, darkening the sheer material where it pressed against her pussy.

"Roman!"

She sobbed out his name as he leaned forward and kissed her mound through her panties, snaking his tongue out to stroke against her clit. His cock throbbed, aching within the tight confines of his jeans. Roman cupped her in his hand as he caught her clit in his mouth, sucking on it until she was rocking against him. His finger pushed inside her, the thin cloth of her panties no barrier as he breeched the first inch of her tight, wet sheath.

When she clamped around him, coming in a rush that soaked her panties, Roman's control shattered. Rising, he jerked her against him, slanting his mouth across hers and feasting on her mouth, pushing his tongue into the honey-sweet cavern.

Her hands went to his waist, jerking at the button fly with clumsy, eager fingers. Tearing his mouth from hers, Roman let his head fall back, sucking air into his lungs, trying to calm the ravenous animal that had risen inside him.

"Roman!"

His cock jerked as she dipped her hand inside his shorts, her cool, slim fingers closing around the thick, steely length. He growled low in his throat, arching in her caress.

"Roman!"

His head whipped around, following the sound of the voice. Close, too damned close. *Damn it all to hell,* he thought savagely as the sound of feet moving lightly over the forest floor penetrated the fog of lust crowding his brain. Closing his hand around her wrist, he lowered his head, brushing his lips against hers and whispering, "We have company coming."

Julianna stared up at him, her eyes blank and uncomprehending as she stared at his mouth, wanting it back on her. He tasted so good . . . but then finally, his words penetrated. More, she heard the sounds of two people approaching from the west, and fast.

Her hands closed convulsively on his shoulders, fingers digging into the solid pad of muscle before she licked her lips, feeling the cool air stroke her breasts, raising goosebumps on her flesh. She searched the ground, looking for her clothes with eyes that saw very little.

His hands caught hers, and he bent down, pressing his lips to her brow in an oddly gentle manner. Then he stooped and picked up her shirt, tucking her inside it just as Jenner and Steven broke through the trees. Julianna's face flushed as she realized she was going to have to face those two men nearly naked. But Roman brought her body against his, shielding her. She rested her head on his chest, trying to calm her labored breathing and the fire that raged in her belly.

Over her head, she heard him growl, "Go away. *Now.*"

A shiver raced down her spine at the sheer authority, the total possession she heard in his voice.

There was laughter in Steven's voice as he said, "Well, I guess we didn't need to come help, did we? Hey, Julianna, you okay over there?"

"Steve, you're going to be lucky if I don't bust your teeth out for that," Roman growled as he pulled her even tighter against him.

"Everything okay here, sir?" Jenner asked, his voice as flat and emotionless as always.

"It won't be, if you two don't turn around and walk away. Right *now,*" he bellowed.

Julianna heard Steve snicker and the sound of footsteps moving away. Seconds later, she felt Roman's hand move through her hair and then he was tugging on her thick locks again, forcing her to lift her gaze. "We're going to finish this," he said, with a finality, a decisiveness in his voice that made her shudder.

She hadn't ever wanted anybody like this. Never had this hot, raging fire torn through her, making her want nothing more than to lose herself in him, in that hunger she saw blazing from his eyes.

But she hadn't ever tolerated people making her decisions for her. And the tone of his voice made it sound as though there would be no discussion, that he had made the decision for both of them. She'd had enough of that from her father.

Julianna wasn't going to take it from this smoldering, sexy werewolf—even if part of her was tempted.

She pulled back from him slowly, bending to pick up her jeans, tugging them on. A shiver slid through her as the crotch of her jeans brushed against the sensitized flesh between her thighs, the panties sliding wetly over her flesh as she buttoned them. Sweet heaven, she was so aroused she thought she would come just from the light pressure of the seam of her jeans pressing against her pussy.

Swallowing, she forced a blank expression onto her face and turned around to face him, arching one brow with cool amusement. "Is that a fact?" she asked quietly.

His pale green eyes narrowed on her face, and she had to fight not to squirm under that direct gaze. "You know it is," he murmured.

Julianna lifted one shoulder slowly. "I don't know any such thing," she replied.

"You can't make me believe you don't want me," he said, his voice deep and rough. Roman leaned over to her, cupping her face in one palm, lifting her gaze to his.

"I never tried to say I didn't. But there's been a great many things in my life that I've wanted, or that I wanted to do. And I rarely got them. While I've been forced to accept many things I don't want," she said, her voice cold and flat. "Not everybody just reaches out and takes what they want. And I've learned that sometimes the wisest course of action is—restraint."

Roman laughed, tipping his head back as he stared up at the sky, a deep chuckle rolling from him. She flushed, shifting from one bare foot to the other, feeling the leaves crackle under her feet, the dampness of the forest floor under the layer of foliage. Her eyes narrowed to slits as she listened to him laugh for the longest time.

"*Restraint*—I didn't think that word was known by the House of Capiet," he said, his laugh abruptly stopping as he looked back at her. "They love to take, and take—and now, when it would harm nobody, you speak of restraint."

Julianna sniffed delicately. "Just like a damned werewolf. Thinking only of how it would affect the *now*." She spied her shoes and stalked over to them, sliding them on before hunkering on the ground to tug them on.

"So it's foresight you try to use?" he asked, sounding confused. "What would it hurt for you to let me finish this?" His voice dropped to a rough purr as he approached her from the back, kneeling down behind her and laying one palm on the inside of her leg, near the knee, drawing the flat of his hand up her thigh until he had reached her crotch. Cupping his hand over the covered mound of her pussy, he whispered beguilingly, "To let me slide those clothes back off you, spread you on the ground, and lick this sweet little pussy until you came, over and over? To mount you and fuck you until we both forget who we are, what we are . . . until nothing matters but what we can do to each other?"

Her breath escaped her in a shaky rush. *Nothing . . . nothing at all.* The words were frozen on her tongue, a plea to beg him to do just that locked in her throat. Julianna's heart was screaming at her. *Everything! It will hurt* everything.

Taking him as a lover, even for a brief moment, would leave a mark on her heart, she suspected. One that no other would ever be able to replace. She had felt the power this man had inside him the minute she stared into his eyes on her balcony, had felt her heart tremble and weaken with every moment spent around him. She wasn't about to compound her problem by sleeping with him.

Of course, it might be too late . . .

Julianna closed her fingers around his wrist, tugging it away. He resisted at first but then acquiesced, letting her guide his hand away from her sex, resting it on her knee as he propped his chin on her shoulder. "It could hurt nothing," she agreed softly. Squirming out of his arms, she crawled away, drawing her knees to her chest and resting her chin on them. "But it could also destroy everything. I never do anything without thinking it over, long and hard, Roman. Especially not something like this."

His hand appeared in her field of vision, and she lifted her gaze to meet his eyes. She accepted his hand, though, and let him pull her to her feet. Roman's eyes rested on her mouth for a second and then he brushed her hair away from her face, lowering his head to brush his lips against hers as he murmured, "This doesn't mean I'm letting it go."

A frisson of delight raced down her spine as he turned away. Well, she really hoped not. She was stupidly independent, not stupid.

Well, he had been wishing he could get away from the women who did little more than strip themselves naked and throw themselves at his feet, whether he wanted them there or not.

Roman walked behind her through the woods, pretty certain she wasn't going to make another run for it, but not one hundred percent sure. Of course, part of him wished she would run. If he had to chase her down again, when he caught her, he'd most likely do nothing except tear off her clothes and fuck her senseless.

The taste of her was still heavy in his mouth. His fingers itched from running over those silken curves, and his cock ached like a bad tooth, throbbing inside his jeans.

Because they were walking, they had a good four-hour hike back to where they had parked. Roman wasn't sure if he could tolerate watching the subtle sway of her ass, the way it curved in her jeans, the soft flare of her hips. The bottom of her shirt barely touched the waist of her jeans, and he kept getting teasing glances of bare skin.

His brother would be lucky if he didn't kill him. Jenner, too. Damn it, couldn't they have waited thirty more minutes before deciding to come investigating? With an aggravated snort, he muttered, "Of course not." Both Steven and Jenner probably knew what they were going to be interrupting.

Bastards.

A breeze picked up, carrying the soft scent of her body to him, and he would have fallen to her feet and begged if he thought it would have done him any good, even though groveling was something he'd never done before. Of course, he hadn't ever met a woman who made him want her the way she did.

From the first look at her, he had wanted her.

I'll have her. He knew it as sure as he knew his own name. He would have her before he had to let her walk away from him.

A niggling little voice inside his head whispered, *That's only going to make it harder . . .*

But at the moment, even though he suspected it was nothing more than fact, he didn't care.

But for now, he thought with a grimace, *I've got to get her home.* There was a dark suspicion in his gut, one that had been there since he had seen her looking so lost and desperate, walking on the balcony of her house, her eyes sad, half wild. She wasn't safe.

He didn't know what the threat was, but there was one.

Julianna wasn't safe until she was far away from her father, preferably out of his reach, his domain. His domain spread far, perhaps farther than it should. But none would dare try to touch her when she was within Roman's domain. None had the authority, or the right, save her father, and he was too much a fucking coward to step one foot into werewolf territory.

The skin on the back of his neck started to prickle, and he moved closer to Julianna, craning his head, listening. Nobody was around. But still—"Come on, darlin'. We need to hurry," he said, cupping his hand around her elbow and pulling her into a jog.

Her eyes moved to his curiously, but she fell into step. Once she had a rhythm, he sped up, keeping his hand cupped around her arm where possible, falling behind her when it wasn't, and always listening.

FIVE

Eduard stared at Isabeta as she dropped to her knees, bowing her head, as she whispered in a shaking voice, "She is gone, my lord."

"*Gone?*" he rasped, his voice icy with his rage. "What do you mean—*gone?*"

The sounds of his boyhood home, France, still lingered in his voice as he spoke. Pacing around Isabeta, he trailed his fingers over her head as he murmured, "You know how important my daughter is to me. Where do you think she could have gone, Isabeta?"

From the door, somebody cleared a throat. Eduard lifted his furious eyes to stare at Mikhail, his second. The bastard had won the right by fighting in battle, destroying any and all who had opposed him. Eduard would have loved to have dispatched him, but to do that, he would have to have him killed. He doubted he had a man among his people strong enough.

"What do you want, Mikhail?" Eduard murmured, squeezing

his hand painfully tight on Isabeta's neck. She made no sound, but he could feel the pain flowing through her. He breathed it in, like the fragrance of some rich wine, feeding on it as he stared into the cool, fearless gaze of his second.

"The wolf is gone, my lord," Mikhail said, his voice cold and mocking.

Nails bit into soft flesh, and the rich musk of vampire blood filled the air. Mikhail's eyes dropped to Isabeta's neck and then he flicked Eduard a glance, raising an eyebrow. Eduard looked down, seeing how his nails had cut through Isabeta's neck, creating deep gouges. He chuckled, slowly unlocking the death grip he had on her neck, lifting his hand and licking the blood from them. "How you managed to rise among the ranks, Mikhail, with a stomach as soft as yours, I will never know."

It was an old argument, decades old. Mikhail simply replied, "I do not see cruelty as the mark of a wise leader . . . my lord. Nor do I see the lack of it making one a soft leader."

Isabeta remained on her knees, and Eduard stroked his hand down her hair, eyeing the blood that flowed down her neck in deep, crimson red rivulets. Dropping to his knees, he licked away the blood, feeling her shudder, feeling the simultaneous desire and revulsion that coursed through her. She wanted him—she hated him— she feared him. It was a normal reaction among his females—servants, slaves, vampires alike. They despised him, one and all, yet they craved him almost as much.

"So where do you think my daughter and my wolf have disappeared to?" he murmured, savoring the last drops of blood, eyeing Mikhail over Isabeta's bowed head.

Mikhail laughed, a deep, rich laugh that echoed through the room, as he moved away from the door. "I have very little doubt about where they disappeared to. You should never have held the werewolf prisoner. Roman Montgomery is very much like his father. He doesn't back down. At all."

Eduard snorted. "That little bastard pup has no chance of getting into my lands without me knowing about it. He's nothing but a stupid boy," he snapped, shoving to his feet, using Isabeta as a crutch, uncaring that he shoved her to the floor as he rose. For one moment, though, he remembered that *boy's* eyes as Roman Montgomery stormed into his home, just a few years ago, demanding Eduard's assistance with the mad voudon priest.

And when they'd found Jacob Montgomery . . . already dead. Yes, very much like his father.

But he was young still, and foolish. Eduard had plenty of time to strengthen his ranks before Roman Montgomery became the threat Jacob had been.

Stepping over Isabeta's cowering form, he stalked up to Mikhail, staring into the cool blue eyes. "Why do you think he has her?"

Mikhail reached into the inner pocket of the black sports coat he wore, drawing out a folded piece of paper as he sardonically drawled, "Perhaps because he left a message to that effect?"

Eduard jerked it out of his hand, tearing it open. "Where did this come from?" he growled.

"One of the vessels brought it to me. Apparently a bald man who wore sunglasses even as he moved through the bar brought it to her. She said he was quite the sinister fellow—or something to that effect," Mikhail said, lifting one shoulder in a negligent shrug.

It read:

Eduard,

Your emissary was warned. By now, you already know what I told her. I can't believe you would be so stupid as to think I'd leave my brother in your hands for twenty years, over nothing. You should have released him.

You trespassed, taking the blood kin of the An Rì Mac Tire. *Had he done injury on your lands, true injury, you may have been within your rights. But he did no injury, and well you know it. Temptation my ass. I do not care if he had slit his wrists to the bone and paraded down Bourbon Street. It is your job to control your vampires. If they are weak and lacking willpower, that is your failing.*

By now, you have noticed that something is missing. Or should I say someone? Your daughter is very lovely. Know that she will have much better treatment in the hands of Wolfclan than my brother did with the House of Capiet.

No Regards,
Roman

His hand closed around the paper, crumpling it into a ball. "How dare he?"

Mikhail smirked, his mouth curved up at the corners, amusement dancing in his eyes as he moved across the room. The thick wine red of his hair was pulled back in a stubby ponytail that gleamed under the low lights as he knelt before Isabeta, using his hand to move her head around as he inspected the already-healing gouges on her neck. "My lord, if I may, he acted within his rights. You had no cause to take the pup. He was causing no harm and, indeed, saved two mortals from the rogues out of Alabama. Had those rogue vampires killed anybody within your lands, we would have been held responsible. He saved them, though he was not obligated to do any damn thing."

"I shall do as I wish in my territory!" Eduard bellowed, whirling on Mikhail and stalking to him with the fires of hell lighting his dark eyes.

Mikhail rose slowly, that same small smirk dancing on his lips, even as Isabeta whimpered in fear and scuttled away, keeping her eyes down. "You've always done so, my lord. This time, there were serious consequences."

"Serious—yes, fucking serious," Eduard purred, an evil smile lighting his eyes. "I'll have his bloody balls served to me on a platter. And watch my darling daughter eat them, if she had a bloody thing to do with my wolf's disappearance. I wouldn't put it past her, the little bitch."

Brows drew down low over Mikhail's eyes, but Eduard didn't notice as he started to pace. "She may well have assisted him—I can see it. Ah, but *ma petite amour* shall have a surprise awaiting her when she comes home to her beloved *père*."

"What, may I ask, are you planning?" Mikhail asked, in a studied tone of boredom. If Eduard had been focusing just a little less on his plans and more on his second, he might have seen the odd flicker in Mikhail's eyes.

"Hmmm. A race," Eduard whispered, his eyes gleaming. From the corner of his eyes he could see Isabeta crawling to the door, but for now, he was too focused on Julianna's treachery to care. She'd betrayed him, her father, and he *knew* it.

A hundred years ago, he could have whipped and beaten her bloody and tossed her to his men as punishment. But the Ancients had decreed too many of the old laws too brutal, and they had been abolished.

However . . . there were still a few laws . . . his eyes narrowed as a smile formed on his face. There was a way to punish the little bitch for this, and to get the offspring he wanted from her.

Spinning around, he stared at Mikhail. "I've seen how you look at Julianna. She, perhaps, is the one creature here you do not hold in contempt. Do you want her?"

Mikhail arched a brow that was shades darker than his deep red hair. One broad shoulder lifted in a shrug as he responded, "Julianna Capiet is as lovely a woman as I've ever seen. And she, unlike many others, doesn't tremble in fear when you speak. She is a very easy woman to want."

"Then you may have her. If you reach her first—and kill Roman Montgomery," Eduard purred. "I shall give you early warning. You may leave now, and if you are successful, Julianna is yours. I want more children of my blood from her. Be smart, and fuck her before you bring her back. That will save you the trouble of fighting some of the men who may wish to claim her, once I declare she is Blood Prize."

"That is a very archaic practice," Mikhail stated, his voice flat. "I prefer a woman to actually want me, not just be forced into my arms because I am the stronger."

Eduard sneered. "The ways of old are much more useful to me than modern thinking." He went to Isabeta—she froze in her tracks as she felt him approach.

Heat started to burn inside him as he studied her. Kneeling behind her, he jerked the long flowering skirt she wore to her waist and tore away the lace that covered her hips. She had almost made it to the door. Almost.

Lust flared in him, hot on the tails of his anger. Cupping his hands over her hips, he bent over her, using his weight to take her to the ground, her belly flat to the floor. He licked at the last bits of blood on her nearly healed neck before he flicked Mikhail a glance. "Well, are you leaving, *bâtard*? Or shall I let one of my other vampires claim her?"

Roman came to an abrupt halt on the threshold of his house. A tiny shudder moved through him. Turning, he pushed Julianna toward Jenner and said harshly, "Take her. Go to the sanctuary and be prepared to run. Take care of her and Steven, no matter what," he growled.

Jenner's brows rose and then his eyes narrowed. That large, powerful body tensed, and Roman knew damned well what was taking place in his canny mind. "Don't. That is an order, Jenner. Now *go*," he snarled.

There was power in the air. He didn't know who was there, but something, someone, was in his house that didn't belong. None had pursued them as they finished the journey home, but the hot, nervous tension that filled Roman never abated.

Prowling from room to room, he waited until he heard Jenner

pulling away before he called out, "Whoever is in my house, I hope you're ready to get your hide shredded for trespassing."

There was a soft laugh. Familiar . . . Roman whirled, his eyes narrowing as a soft white apparition formed in front of him, solidifying until she was all but in his house. "May I enter, full and well, Roman, *An Rì Mac Tire?*" the Countess de LaReine asked laughingly.

LaReine, one of the highest Houses in the world, and one of the oldest. She served on the Chamber of the Ancients—speaking with her was speaking with the Chamber themselves. Roman felt dread move through him, and he wanted to pound his fist through something in sheer frustration. Damn it, he hadn't broken any laws! Slowly, he nodded, his jaw clenched as she closed her eyes. When she opened them, she stood there in the flesh, her midnight blue eyes sparkling with laughter. "I've broken no fucking laws, Madame. I was within my rights—"

"Oh, do stuff it, Roman. I'm aware of that," she said, strolling away, the long white gown floating around her body. Her voice was as sexily French as she was, from her upswept hair, to the diamonds that dripped on her swanlike neck, to the designer gown that draped on her body. "I am not here to . . . ahh . . . criticize? Yes, criticize you, boy. Merely to warn you. The blood daughter of Capiet is in grave danger."

"I'm no threat to Julianna," Roman said stiffly.

She laughed, the sound as sweet as harp song. "No. You are her greatest protector, I imagine. But not the only. Many shall come hunting her, and quite soon." She paused by a stone carving of a wolf, his great maned head thrown back as he howled to the sky. Stroking her hand down it, she stared into the distance, her eyes growing distant and dark. "Her sanity could be torn apart."

Growling, Roman took a step forward, rage ripping through him. "What has Eduard done?"

The Countess said, her voice hollow and deep, "The blood children of a vampire are a great treasure. The woman even more than the man, because she can breed even more blood children, vampires born into the blood, who need only the Blood Kiss to bring them over, and they survive the change as so very few vestals do. But few of the blood daughters care to be used as breeding horses—so many of them fight it, as Julianna has fought. Ages ago, centuries, when a blood daughter refused to take a lover and beget more vampire children, she was cast out of the father's house, declared Blood Prize. Vampire, servant, and slave alike were given rein to chase her down and breed her. Whoever reached her first was the victor, although sometimes she found a protector, and to claim her, the protector must be killed as well. Once she was bred and the child born, the child would be taken, and she would be passed on to another, and another." A sad, bitter smile curved her lips. "Is there something within the makeup of a blood daughter that makes her fight the path her vampire kin lay before her?"

The rage tore through him, vicious and hot, like acid in his blood. Whirling away from her, he closed his hands into tight fists—unsurprised when long, hooked claws tore into the flesh of his palms. His skin rippled like water, bones trying to force themselves into another pattern. He sucked in air, focusing on the mirror across the room, on his reflection. *I will not change,* he said silently.

He throttled his rage into control, if not submission, before he slowly turned and met the Countess's somber gaze. There was something odd in her eyes—remembered pain, shame. She spoke from experience, he realized. Sympathy welled in him, and the wild rage inside him died, bringing the rage of his animal slowly under control.

Something shifted in her eyes, and they once more became blank, empty pools of sapphire blue. The air seemed to chill as she watched him. *Uh-oh,* the lady didn't like to have anybody reading her quite so well.

She spun away on one elegant heel. "Lord Eduard has declared his daughter Blood Prize. His second, a vampire known as Mikhail, has already left New Orleans. The others will follow as soon as Eduard makes it known what he has done."

"I can handle the vampires," Roman said, his voice cold and deadly. "She will not be harmed."

The Countess's mouth moved in a lifeless smile. "She will be in danger unless she is already mated," she said quietly. "Mikhail will be here and then others. She has protectors while she is on your land, many of them I imagine, but unless they are willing to fight every male vampire, servant, and slave of the House of Capiet, they may as well not bother. Because all will seek her."

A pulse throbbed in his jaw as the gravity of her words sank home. "Mated by anybody?"

The Countess nodded. Roman was unaware of how closely she watched him as he started to pace. "The vampire, like the wolf, know when a woman has been claimed. If they see she has been claimed by the time they reach her, they will desist. Perhaps not immediately, and definitely not happily, but they will. Having her in your possession, your control, as they see it, isn't enough, though. She must be mated, or they will fight to steal her away. The one who is successful will rape her, repeatedly, until she conceives."

Roman spat out, "That is barbaric!"

The Countess sighed, and the entire stance of her body changed, from proud and arrogant to tired, broken. Sorrow laced heavily in her words as she replied, "Yes. It is. Many of the ancient laws are barbaric, Roman. The Chamber has done a great deal to destroy many of the older laws, but too many still exist. Many who still believe in the old laws are still alive and thriving. Not so many were as forward a thinker as your father. But to abolish all the old laws, those who still uphold them must be destroyed."

With a furious snarl, Roman stalked away. "I'll destroy Eduard. He should have died when my father died, the sorry motherfucker. If he dies before it happens, is she safe?"

His gut knotted as the Countess shook her head. "No, Roman. She is Blood Prize. Until she is mated, Julianna Capiet is not safe."

SIX

Deep within the Smoky Mountains, the sanctuary of Wolf-clan Montgomery hid. The sanctuary was built within the remains of an old stone church. Long since fallen to the ages, the only things that had stood when Roman's father found it were the stone stairwell and the arched doorway. Roman's father had been buried here, along with his brother and many of their fallen dead.

The sanctuary was made of stone, built around the repaired stone of the steps and door, a great monolith of stone that towered to the sky. Hidden passageways gave the inhabitants secret ways to escape, should that need arise. And the stone protected against deadly fire far better than wood.

As he crossed through the doorway, Roman felt the presence of Wolfclan around him. Jenner had called them in. A cruel smile curved Roman's mouth. Good. If a vampire dared to try to take her from him, they'd have quite a shock waiting them. *If* they could find them.

Julianna was pacing by the stone fireplace at the northern end of the great room, rubbing her arms, her eyes cool and blank. When she sensed him, she spun around and stalked up to him, drilling her finger into his chest as she snapped, "Bad enough you have to kidnap me. But why in the hell was I brought out here in the middle of nowhere? There's no fucking TV, there's no computer . . . damn it, I can't even find some paper and a pencil."

"Bored, are you?" Roman drawled, flicking Jenner and Steven a telling glance. Jenner nodded, while Steven stood by the window, his arms crossed over his chest as he stared at them with searching eyes. "Go on, Steve."

Steven's eyes moved to Julianna's face, then to the darkness outside where cousins, friends, and other werewolves prowled the grounds. His lashes lowered over his eyes, and the younger Montgomery sighed, running a hand through his hair before he finally looked at Jenner with a forced smile. "I'm not going into hiding, big guy. Hope you know that," he drawled, sauntering out the door.

Julianna jumped as the door closed behind Jenner and Steven and the sound of a long, eerie howl filled the night air. Roman smiled slightly. Steven loved a fight. Even though they didn't know what was coming, the wolves sensed the tension in the air.

"What's going on?" Julianna demanded. Her soft blue eyes hardened to cold diamonds as she stomped away. "There was something in the air at your house, or wherever in the hell that was, something that scared you. And I don't think you scare easily. But it wasn't my father, wasn't any of his men. I would have recognized them."

Roman stared at her face with intense eyes, the words of the Countess echoing through his mind. He'd be damned if he let anybody harm her. Let anybody take her. She was his—had been from the first moment he had seen her painting in the street, smiling as a child looked up at her with delight as she captured his image on paper. *His.*

It was said that when a werewolf found his mate, part of him recognized it from the beginning. She was his. The certainty went gut-deep.

"I saw you in the street, painting a little boy," he murmured, moving up to her, catching her stiff shoulders in his hands, and drawing her back against him. "You wore a blue shirt with beads that sparkled in the sun, and it left your back bare. I watched as you smiled at that little boy, watched as you painted him for his parents, and I wanted you. I haven't wanted a woman like I want you in ages. No, in forever. I've never wanted a woman the way I want you."

Her breath caught in her chest as she lifted her head, tipping it back so she stared at him. He watched as emotion flooded her eyes, and she melted.

"Then, at the ball, I was there, I saw you, saw the sadness in your eyes. I wanted to take you away from there, make you smile, make you sigh . . . then scream out my name as I fucked you late into the night." Lowering his head, he skimmed his lips over her cheek. "When Eduard announced you to the ball, it felt like somebody had driven a knife in my gut. How could something so lovely, so pure, have come from a bastard like him?"

He kissed her, licking at the seam of her lips, pushing his tongue inside her mouth as he cradled the back of her head in his hand. Pulling back just a breath, he admitted, "Part of me knew then what I was going to do. If you hadn't offered to free Steve, I would have taken you that night, away from your home. I had to have you, Julianna. And I'm going to . . . right now."

Breath left her in a shaky rush as he gripped the front of her tank top and tore it straight down the middle, brushing the scraps away before he did the same to the lace and silk of her bra. Slanting his mouth across hers, he locked her against him, one hand fisted in her hair, the other a steel bar at her waist.

Now . . . before anybody had a chance to get to them, he would take her, claim her. And before she realized somebody was coming. He had a bad feeling that if she knew what was coming, she'd try to outrun it, try to flee. And he'd be damned if he'd let her leave him.

Julianna felt her heart melt within her chest as Roman kept murmuring to her, his voice so low, so rough, so primal. As her shirt and then her bra fell to the floor in shreds, a fist of desire hit her in the gut, robbing her of her breath and all logic. Her breasts crushed into his chest, her nipples tight, aching points of heated agony.

The cooler silk of his mouth closed over one nipple, his tongue a rough contrast to his lips as he suckled lightly, a soothing sensation—for a moment. But then hot little darts of agonized pleasure started rippling through her. Arching against him, she buried her fingers in the thick silk of his golden hair as he lifted her up, holding her feet off the ground as he straightened, his mouth still feasting avidly at her breasts, moving from one to the other, leaving the wet gleaming tip to throb hungrily for more.

One big, hard hand left her waist, guiding one leg around his waist, and she lifted the other, hooking her ankles at the base of his spine, shuddering as it opened her folds and he started to rock against her, forcing the blue denim material between her thighs to drag tauntingly across her clit. His hands cupped her ass, the fingers of one hand digging into the seam, pushing against the crevice between the cheeks of her bottom.

Slowly he lowered her down, kissing a path along her breasts, up her collarbone, until he could scrape his sharp teeth over her neck. Julianna sobbed out his name, not even recognizing that hoarse, needy voice as her own. She hadn't ever felt anything like this, this gut-twisting ravenous need for him. Her eyes opened to see his, those pale green orbs staring into hers, waiting for her to look at him. Against her mouth, he growled, "You're the sweetest thing I've ever held in my life. I don't think I'll ever get enough of you."

Then his mouth was on hers, the hot stroke of his tongue parting her lips and diving deep, stroking against the inside of her
cheeks, her tongue, pumping in with slow, steady strokes that stole
her breath, just so he could give it back again. Her hips jerked as she
heard a harsh ripping sound and then she felt the cooler air as it caressed her thighs, her butt. Roman's hands raced over naked flesh,
streaked between her thighs, and she screamed into his mouth as he
plunged two fingers inside the wet well of her pussy.

He pulled away slightly, staring at her with slitted eyes as he
pumped his fingers in and out, a maddeningly slow rhythm. She felt
a teasing pressure between the cheeks of her ass, and she sobbed out
his name as he pushed lightly against her.

"You're hot and tight," he whispered, his lids dropping down as
he sucked in air, his entire body quivering. When he opened his eyes
again, she trembled at the blind hunger she saw in his gaze. "Damn
it, Julianna. I'm not going to last five minutes when I get my cock
inside you."

The world spun around her, and she clung to him, dizzied. Now
the cold stone of the floor was at her back and he was sprawled
against her, moving down the length of her body with studied determination. The cloth of his jeans rasped against the sensitive inner
flesh of her thighs, followed by the smooth, warm cotton of his shirt
and then the grizzled flesh of his unshaven face as he lifted her hips
in his hands. He leaned down, drawing his tongue up her slit,
spreading her open before he closed his mouth around the tight bud
of her clit.

She shrieked, her hips rising to meet him, her fingers burying in
the thick silk of his dark hair. "Roman," Julianna gasped, her hips
circling against his mouth as he pushed his fingers through the tight
tissues of her sheath, pumping them in and out as he stabbed his
tongue against her clit until she was screaming, digging her heels
into his back.

One long finger stroked down from her pussy, slick with her

cream, until he was steadily pressing against the tight pucker of her ass. She exploded against him, her eyes wide with shock, bright pinwheels of color exploding before her as she came in one hard convulsion after another.

His mouth nuzzled against her tenderly, his tongue stroking soothingly against her clit as the climax tore through her. Then Roman was gone, and she was lying cold and shivering against the floor, her body still wracked with harsh shudders.

Her lashes opened, and through the fringe of them, she saw the gleaming gold of his body as he tore away his shirt, kicking off his boots. The thick, hard bulge of his cock tented the tight denim of his jeans, and he reached for the buttons at his fly with a grimace, working them loose as he lifted his eyes to meet her gaze.

She shivered at the look there, that bald, blatant hunger as tangible as a caress. Seconds later, he had shucked the jeans and now he lay down, covering her body with his, his hands spreading her thighs wide. Against her pussy, she felt the steely hard length of his cock. Her lashes fluttered closed as she felt him probing against her.

"No. Don't close your eyes," he muttered, the command in his voice driving through the fog of sheer hunger that clouded her brain.

Dragging open her lashes, she stared up at him as he pushed against her, his sex pulsing against her tissues as he breached the first tight inches of her pussy. "Yeah," he growled. "That's it. Look at me while I take you, make you mine. Watch me . . ."

His voice trailed off as she arched against him with a hungry whimper, her hands digging into the muscles of his back, trying to draw him deeper. "Holy hell, you are tight," he rasped, pulling out slightly and working his length back inside. "Tight and soft, like wet satin."

Julianna cried out then, as he plunged deeper, pulling back, driving back inside her, a tense, strained look on his face. Hot, burning pain tore through her as he drove relentlessly deeper, his eyes landing on her face, first with blind confusion and then with a soft look of wonder that had her flushing even as she tried to pull away.

"You're a virgin," he whispered, pressing his lips gently against her mouth.

Her only answer was a whimper as he pulled out, his cock rasping against swollen, oversensitized tissues. She flinched as he started to stroke her clit, and then she moaned, rocking her hips hungrily to seek out those feather-light strokes. Her nails raked his back as she threw back her head and screamed as he petted her into orgasm, half of his thick length spearing into her pussy.

Her lids drooped and she sighed out blissfully. Her entire body felt warmed from the inside out, and she sprawled boneless on the floor as his hands shifted her body, draping her thighs across his, one big hand cupping her hip and his chest coming down to crush her breasts against him.

His mouth covered hers, and she sighed as he kissed her gently, his tongue stroking against hers . . . and then he bit her, a sharp sudden pain. Her eyes flew open in shock as he used that tiny second to drive completely inside, lodging his length within her, kissing away the tears that streaked out of her eyes as he murmured soothingly to her.

Roman's entire body ached under the control he had lashed it under. Nothing had ever felt this good, the tight, wet silk of her virgin pussy rippling around him as he cuddled her against him, soothing away the tension from her body, kissing away the salty tears that dampened her face. As her body relaxed against his, he started to rock against her—not thrusting, just circling his hips in the cradle of her thighs, rubbing against the sensitive bud of her clit, one hand cupping the curve of her breast, his other hand stroking the satin skin of her ass.

As she started to move in his arms, he rose up, bracing his weight on his hands as he stared down into her flushed face, watching as her eyes widened while he stroked in and out of the gloving silk of her sex, his cock gleaming from her juices.

The scent of her hunger was heavy in the air, the perfume of hungry woman, the musk of vampire, and that nameless, sweet scent that was purely her flooding his head, tightening his gut as he started to shaft her harder.

Her tissues clenched around his cock, and he growled hungrily, shifting to cup her head in his hands, arching her face up to his. Taking her mouth greedily, he drove his tongue inside the honeyed well, drinking her down as she clenched around his dick and screamed into his mouth.

Sweat gleamed along their bodies as Roman fought back the demons inside him that whispered, *Harder, harder . . . now . . . now . . .* He sank his teeth into the curve of one sleek shoulder, marking her as he took her body higher and higher. "Again," he whispered against her flesh. "Come again. Let me feel it."

Her damp hair clung to her face as she sobbed, "I can't." Her hands fell limply to her sides, her face turning so she could press one cheek against the stone floor. Against his chest, he felt the slamming of her heart, and soft flutters in her pussy still caressed his cock.

"Yes, you can," he purred, catching her knee and bringing it up over his hip, sliding his fingers down the sweat-slickened skin of her thigh, squeezing the supple curve of her ass before stroking his fingers down the crevice between, pressing his fingers against the sensitive skin between her pussy and the cleft of her buttocks. She clenched around him, a startled wail falling from her lips.

A fiery hot-cold sensation built at the base of his spine when she contracted around him again, that sensuous little tremor of her pussy gripping his cock leaving him swearing and sucking air into his lungs. "Come for me, Julie," he rasped.

He came into her, harder, swifter, as she climaxed a fourth and final time around him, a long, slow moan shimmering out of her.

Roman howled out her name and flooded her, hot jets of semen pulsing out of him, flooding the receptive depths of her sex.

It lasted forever—and no time at all, holding him in a viselike grip as he emptied himself inside her and slowly came down atop her body with a weary, replete sigh.

She stroked her fingers up his arms, wrapping her arms around him and hugging him against her, and Roman felt his heart clench in his chest as she whispered out his name in a soft, awe-filled voice.

"Why in the hell were you still a virgin?" he muttered, trying to wrap his mind around the fact that he was her first. She had been untouched, and now she was *his*.

A soft chuckle escaped her as he rolled them, landing with him on his back against the hard floor, her cuddled against him, the flickering firelight dancing over their skin and warming them. "Do you really think I'd want to sleep with somebody who answered to my father? He'd give out a detailed report, and I'd be watched like a hawk to see if I became pregnant," she said with a shrug. "I'd rather be wanted for *me,* not for anything that has to do with Eduard."

A niggling little doubt settled in his gut, but he shoved it aside. He had taken her because *he* wanted her. Protecting her from her father and his men was just a side benefit.

Her head shifted, and he glanced down to see her staring up at him with those wide blue eyes and a smile on her lips. "Besides, until you touched me, I never really felt the need to get naked with somebody," she said cheekily.

He chuckled, pulling her atop him and kissing her quickly. "Soon as I can breathe again, I'll show you how much I appreciate that," he told her.

From all around them, a deep echoing voice, ripe with amusement, said, "Well, I'd really prefer you two waited until I've had a word with you."

*   *   *

Julianna rolled off Roman, her eyes wide, flashing with fire, anger brewing in her gut as she recognized that voice. Roman's hands pulled her to him, and he ducked his head, whispering in her ear, "I'll take care of you, Julie."

Her heart fluttered at the sound of her name, shortened, oddly sweet, on his tongue. But she swallowed and shook her head, fear crowding her mind as she slowly stood up. "I fight my own battles," she said thickly. She stared all around them, searching for the deadly man her father had sent after her. Roman came to his feet behind her, a quick, easy motion she saw from the corner of her eye as she spun in a slow circle.

Roman's hands cupped her shoulders as he slid his shirt over them, the worn white cotton button-down dwarfing her, covering her from neck to knee. His lips brushed her cheek and he whispered, "You're mine. If you haven't realized it by now, here's your wake-up call. You're mine, and I take care of what is mine."

Heat and pleasure, arrogance and awe all warred within her at his words. But she shoved it aside. Now wasn't the time.

"May I enter, *An Rì Mac Tìre*?"

Wolf king. The Gaelic rolled from Mikhail's voice, the echoes of Russia still in his voice. Julianna shook her head, her hands sliding back to grip Roman's still-naked thighs, the metallic taste of fear heavy in her voice. "No," she whispered. "Don't let him in. He's dangerous."

Roman chuckled, hugging her against him, before he kissed her temple and stepped away, flicking her a sly glance. "Julie-sweet, so am I," he replied. Then he lifted his eyes to the ceiling and called out, "You, alone, may enter, vampire. No other Capiet is welcome within my walls."

The mist settled in front of them, solidifying until her father's second stood before them, the fire seeming to set his deep red hair aflame. Mikhail's characteristic smirk danced on his mouth as he studied them for a long moment in silence. Then he shrugged. "I am not of Capiet," he said shortly, his eyes dark with secrets. "Nor have I ever been, Julianna."

His eyes moved to the windows, staring out to the south. "Men of your father's come, youngling. But I do believe they will find themselves robbed of their prize," he mused, pacing over to the windows, reaching out his hand, and resting his palm on the window.

"What prize?" she asked sourly. "I'm nobody's prize."

Mikhail's eyes rested briefly on her face, and something hot and tense moved in her belly as he slid his pale blue eyes to Roman. "I beg to differ, Julianna. Your father declared you Blood Prize just this morn. Apparently, he felt I was the one most likely to successfully tear you from Roman Montgomery, and he told me hours before he told the others."

Her knees buckled as the gravity of his words hit home. "He wouldn't," she said thickly, remembered horror stories of women declared Blood Prize racing through her mind. She tore away from Roman, grabbing a flaming torch from the wall and brandishing it toward Mikhail, not seeing the sympathy in his eyes. "He wouldn't!"

Roman's heart broke at the pain and shock in Julianna's voice. Part of her was still a small child waiting for her father's love, he realized, watching as tears rolled down her cheeks.

She might have been blind to the sympathy in the other vampire's gaze, but Roman wasn't. "Many protectors," he murmured, recalling the Countess's words. Then he moved to Julianna and gently took the torch from her hand, returning it to the sconce on the wall before he folded her in his arms. "Julie, look at me."

Her eyes were still locked fearfully on Mikhail's face, and her body shuddered with deep, wracking tremors as he stroked his hand down her back. "Look at me, pet," he ordered, cupping her face in his hand and forcing her eyes to his. "He is no harm to you. Look at him."

She shrieked out, "No harm? He is my father's fucking second. And he's twice as dangerous as my father ever was."

Yes, Roman had sensed that already. "Exactly. So if he had wanted to force you, he could have done it in New Orleans, whether your father wanted it or not. Isn't that right?"

Mikhail's shoulders moved in a restless shrug. "Rape has never appealed to me, Julianna," he said levelly. "Neither have many of the things your father has done of late. The Ancients are not happy with him." The fire danced eerily on his face as he added softly, "I should know. I've been watching him since before you were born."

Julianna stilled, her eyes narrowing on Mikhail's aquiline face. "Watching him?" she repeated, her voice cold and flat.

"Yes. Watching him," he repeated, an amused smile curving up his lips.

The answer was there, in his eyes, and he wasn't even bothering to hide it. "You fought a hundred battles to become his second. It's obvious you don't like him, but why go to so much trouble to spy on him?" she demanded, her voice thick with suspicion.

Mikhail chuckled. "There's an old proverb. Keep your friends close—and your enemies closer," he said, his voice dry. "Eduard Capiet has done many things the Ancients do not care for—many things that risk our way of life—but he has yet to break our laws. He skirts that edge very well. I was sent to watch him. If the time came that he needed to be dispatched, yet he continued to adhere to the letter of the law, then I could challenge him. And fighting those whelps who surrounded him was little trouble. I've been battling better men than that for longer than your father has been alive."

"You're not that old," she scoffed, her lip curling.

His eyes started to glow, a smile dancing on his lips. "Are you so certain, Daughter of the Blood?"

His voice echoed eerily through the room as he moved closer, bending down until his eyes were on level with hers. "I'm very good at what I do. I can hide in plain sight, and my enemies never know

I am there until I have already struck and withdrawn. Even you, who looked at me with searching, unsure eyes, never knew I was there not to take your father's place, but to protect his people. And you are the one person from Capiet I thought sure would figure me out."

"Deceit isn't something she is familiar with," Roman said from behind her. "She's very un-vampire-like."

Julianna sent him a narrow glance.

Roman gave her a roguish grin. "It's a compliment, sweet," he said, dropping one lid in a quick wink.

Julianna turned away from him, rolling her eyes as she stared back at Mikhail. "So I don't need to worry about running from you? Just the rest of his men?" she asked, rubbing her hands down her chilled arms as she scanned the room. Once she spotted her clothes, she grabbed them, turning her back to the men as she slid into her jeans, tying Roman's shirt into a knot at her waist when she saw the shreds of her shirt.

"You don't need to run at all," Roman said from across the room, folding his arms across his chest.

The firelight flickered off the long, lean lines of his nude body, distracting her for a long moment as she stared at him, her mouth going dry. "Will you get dressed?" she asked, her voice cracking at the end.

Roman's lips curved into that slow, arrogant smile of his, but he turned away, grabbing his jeans and tugging them negligently, cocking a brow at her as he finished the buttons on his jeans. "Better, sweet?" he asked.

She swallowed, running her tongue over her dry lips, ignoring his question as she concentrated on what he had said just moments ago. In a sarcastic voice, she said, "So I should just wait here for my daddy's men to come and fight over me?"

Mikhail, wisely, was silent, withdrawing into the shadows across the room. Roman didn't even spare him a glance as he moved closer to her. "They may well come, but there's nothing left for them to fight over. You've already been claimed, Julie," he said softly.

Heat flared in her belly at the look in his eyes, but in her head she heard something else. *Already claimed.* The knowledge hit her like a fist, exploding through her head as she stared at him, her throat getting tight, the knot growing there almost painful.

In a rough whisper, she said, "You knew." She blinked away tears as she tried to reconcile the fact that he hadn't been making love to her. He had been protecting her. *"You knew!"*

One brow rose over his unreadable sea green eyes and he nodded, a slow single move of his head. "Yes. A lady from the Ancients was waiting for me at my home," he said. "I knew. But all that did was change the time table, Julie. I had every intention of taking you—make no mistake about that."

One hot tear spilled out. "I don't like the idea of being a mercy-fuck," she snarled, her mouth trembling.

She never saw him move. But he was there in her face, his hands clasping tight over her arms, lifting her up until she was on her toes, arched up against him as he growled, "Don't. That was *never* what it was about. I wanted you. I'll want you until my heart stops beating. If I hadn't wanted you, I wouldn't have fucked you, no matter what the reason. I would have found a way to protect you without involving my dick in the issue."

"But that's why it happened *now,*" she hissed, trying to jerk back from him. "You had to fuck me *now* to protect me."

"You're my woman, damn it. I would have fucked you yesterday if my idiot brother and Jenner hadn't interrupted." His mouth slanted across hers, and she shoved at him for a long moment as his tongue probed for entrance to her mouth. Need tore into her with greedy hands, blinding her to everything but the taste and touch of his mouth. His hands delved into her hair, holding her still and steady for the rough invasion of his mouth. Roman's mouth moved in a line of hot, hungry little bites from her mouth to her ear, where he caught the plump little lobe in his mouth and bit it roughly before he rasped, "My woman. And you're damned right I'll protect you. But I wanted you. That is the bottom line."

Her heart broke in her chest. The bottom line . . . no. The bottom line for her was that she had slept with him because somehow, in the handful of hours they had known each other, she had fallen in love with him. Hell, she had been born in love with him, she thought. It just took meeting him for the love to explode throughout her being. That was the bottom line. And the fact that he hadn't just had *her* on his mind when he fucked her.

Another tear trickled down her cheek as she tried to get her rampant emotions in check. In his arms, she stood still, coldness radiating through her even though his hands, hot and hungry, ran over her, down her back, over her hips.

As a watery sigh escaped her lips, he lifted his head from her neck, staring down at her face. Maybe the stillness of her body got through to him. Maybe he heard the tears that had thickened in her throat.

His eyes stared down at her, his hands softening, stroking soothingly down her arms, rubbing her back in soft, slow circles. Julianna pushed at his chest, shoving free of his arms as she stumbled away, her body feeling bruised and battered.

"The bottom line is . . . I wanted you. You were the only thing in my mind when you were touching me," she said hollowly. "But I wasn't the only thing in yours."

She turned away and walked off on unsteady legs.

Roman's jaw was still dropped as she reached out and closed her hand over the door. He lunged for her and closed the door shut with a snap while she was trying to pull it open.

Something cold slammed against his mind. They were here. The men of Capiet had arrived to try to claim the blood daughter of Eduard Capiet. He hadn't given them enough credit—they had found them fast.

They wanted her very badly. He could sense their anger, their hunger in the air.

A snarl tore through him even as the alien magick of vampire reached out, trying to call to Julianna.

Mikhail grabbed her, wrapping his arms around her body in a bear hug as he spun her away from the door, kicking it closed with the heel of his boot. "This lover's quarrel will have to wait, Julianna," Mikhail said, lifting his eyes to stare at Roman over her shoulder.

"Let me go," she said faintly, pushing at his arms. "I just want to get out of here."

"And go out there, having them fight tooth and nail to be the first one to shove you to the ground and rape you?" Mikhail snapped, tightening his arms around her as she started to struggle. Finally, he just lifted her feet off the floor and let her fight ineffectually in his arms with her feet dangling in the air. "Roman has claimed you, yes, but he is werewolf, not vampire. He will have to convince them of his claim on you. He may have to fight for it. Until they acknowledge it, if you step outside this building, you are fair game to them."

Roman's eyes locked on her pale, tear-streaked face, his gut tied in knots, his heart bleeding within his chest. There hadn't been any other way, damn it! Mikhail had gotten here on the heels of their arrival, and already, the vampires of Capiet had stormed his grounds. He hadn't had time to talk to her, to convince her before he made love to her.

Women! he thought, infuriated, as he spun away from the sight of Julianna crumpling against Mikhail in defeat.

The sounds of battle—hisses, howls, and screams—became apparent. The wolves of Wolfclan Montgomery had descended on

Capiet. In waves, the scent of blood came floating to him even through the closed windows and bolted door.

His wolves were out there, fighting the men who had come to try to take his woman, and they didn't even know why.

A sour smile curved his mouth. To give him time to claim a woman who may well walk away when she was safe. Hell, she would walk away now if the vampire holding her would just let her go.

Looking at Julianna, he said, voice dull, "Stay inside, Julie. You're safe here."

seven

The odd ring to his voice resounded through her mind as she watched him walk outside, slamming the massive oak door behind him. The windows rattled their casings, and outside, she heard a wave of voices raising in eerie howl.

"He loves you," Mikhail murmured against her temple, his hands slowly loosening. "What was he supposed to do, talk you into letting him make love to you before Capiet arrived?"

"He wasn't making love to me," she said thickly, moving away from Mikhail as his hands fell aside. "He was *protecting* me."

"You're his. Why shouldn't he?" Mikhail replied easily, shrugging one shoulder as he studied her.

"I'm not *his*," she shouted, spinning away from him, fisting her hands and pressing them against her temples. Pain and indecision wavered inside her belly.

"Aren't you?"

She stood there, shaking, as she slowly turned to face Mikhail, his voice coming from just over her shoulder. His pale blue eyes gleamed at her from the shadows the dancing firelight cast upon his face.

"I was here, watching from without as he took you." A wicked smile lit his face, and he murmured, "And that was the most pleasure I've had in quite some time. But I saw a man claiming a woman, making love to her. And she reveled in it. Accepted it. Wanted it. That was lovemaking I saw, Julianna."

Her eyes burned from her tears as she tried to blink them away.

Mikhail's eyes watched her closely as he asked, "Wasn't it? You claiming him as surely as he claimed you? Wouldn't you fight anything and anyone that tried to take him away from you?"

Her voice shook as she whispered, "Yes." Her eyes moved to the window, and she felt the tears spill free, running down her face in hot tracks. An enraged shout flooded her ears, followed by a terrific crash that shook the building.

From outside the building, she heard voices raising in fury.

Slowly, she moved to the window, staring outside, wishing her hearing was as acute as her vampire cousins', or the weres who battled outside. The voices were indistinct.

A body went flying across her field of vision, followed by a tremendous cracking sound. "Why are they fighting?" she asked.

"They have only what he says—even though your scent clings to him, they want further proof," Mikhail said, lifting one shoulder in a slow shrug. "You're no small prize."

"I'm not a prize to be won," she said flatly, spinning around and glaring at him.

"That is all you are to them. To him, you're more."

Arching a brow, she said softly, "I get the point, Mikhail." She turned back to the window, staring outside with stark eyes as a pair of men came tumbling to ground just outside the window, a werewolf, his body in midshift, tearing at the vampire that had wrapped himself around the wolf's waist, sinking his teeth into the thick skin of the wolf's furred hide.

They were fighting . . . *over her*. Tearing each other apart, over her. On quivering legs, she made her way to the door, reaching out and closing her hand over the ornate scrolled metal of the door handle.

It opened, and she stared out into hell.

Blood flew, the sickening thud of bones breaking, and she watched as a shifted werewolf fell upon an injured vampire and tore out his throat, gripping the head of the fallen vamp in his hands and jerking it clear off, beheading him, very messily, but ensuring total death.

"Sweet heaven," she whispered, her eyes wide with terror.

"They would have fought each other like that—over you," Mikhail said, his voice flat, disgust rampant in his voice. "We can do so much, yet we act like animals."

"Roman." Her voice trembled as she murmured his name, staring through the sea of battling men, searching for him.

A shifted werewolf appeared ahead of her, massive, his hide a warm, golden brown, gleaming wetly in the faint light as he sank clawed hands into a vampire who lunged at him, catching the smaller man and throwing him aside.

Some instinct deep inside her whispered, *That's him.*

"Mine!" the wolf snarled, the words booming from him in a deep, possessive shout. "Julianna Capiet is *mine*. Go back to your master. Get off my lands. Or die."

From behind, she watched as a man snaked out of the woods, his fangs gleaming under the moonlight as he stalked closer to Roman—one of her father's lieutenants, Lucien. Lucien kept to Romans' back as another vampire squared off against him, his glowing eyes never once leaving the furred throat of the wolf king.

He lunged for Roman, and she screamed out his name, watching in disbelief as Roman ducked and rolled, coming up behind Lucien and grabbing him, jerking him back against him with a growl.

Lucien bellowed, his voice echoing through the clearing before the sanctuary as Roman whirled around, brandishing Lucien's captured body as the wolves aligned themselves at Roman's back.

Silence fell across them, touching first one and another and another, until all eyes were on Roman.

"I am Roman, *An Rì Mac Tire,* wolf king of Wolfclan Montgomery." His voice boomed out across the sea of people, so many bloodied and bruised. Still bodies littered the ground, and she smelled death in the air. "I have claimed Julianna Capiet, my lover, my woman."

His eyes met hers, and her heart stilled as he dropped his voice to a rough whisper, "Owner and keeper of my heart."

In a louder voice, he added, "You can have her over my dead body."

One werewolf from the line at his back stepped forward, throwing his golden-maned head back and howling to the sky, as though echoing his support of the wolf king. Jenner stepped through the throng of people, still in human skin, his jacket missing, the sleeve of one shirt torn at the shoulder, but no other signs of battle on him. He aligned himself at Roman's back as the golden werewolf moved to his side. The remaining wolves threw back their heads—some in wolfman form, others in the form of massive timber wolves—and a chorus of long, eerie howls rose from their throats and echoed through the night.

"Julianna Capiet is Blood Prize until she's been mated—and I don't care that you have her scent on you. She wouldn't have fucked a dog," Lucian snarled, struggling against the massive hands that held him. "We'll find her. We'll fuck her. Whoever gets her first claims her."

"Roman's already taken care of that."

All eyes turned to her, and she felt blood stain her cheeks as she stood in the arched doorway of the sanctuary. Lifting her chin, she said, "I was claimed. Good and well, not even an hour ago, by Roman Montgomery, *An Rì Mac Tire* of Wolfclan Montgomery.

Not one of you can dispute this, not with me standing before you."
She skimmed a glance down her body, a smug smile curving her lips
as she added, "Still wearing his scent, wearing his clothes . . . his
seed on my thighs."

Lucien's eyes narrowed and he spat, "You let a dog like him between your legs?"

She arched a brow at him. "Better Roman than you. If he is a
dog, at least he is his own dog, and not one of my father's," she
drawled back at him, a delicate sneer curving her lips.

Roman's eyes rested on her face, and she smiled, a half-hearted,
shaky smile that bloomed as she saw the answer in his.

She stepped forward, thinking of nothing but getting to him.

"No!"

EIGHT

Roman would never forget it, the look in her eyes as she started toward him, then the widening of her eyes, her head tipping up to search for the voice. The scream that tore out of her throat as her father swooped down from the sky and grabbed her, leaping to the roof of the building, holding the struggling form of his daughter in his arms.

"No," Eduard said, shaking his head as he stared out over Wolf-clan Montgomery and the surviving vampires. "I have not fought this long to ensure my Blood House to let my blood daughter go to the arms of a fucking werewolf!"

Julianna struggled in his arms, sinking her teeth into the hand that had clapped over her mouth. Eduard snarled at her, jerking her out from him and backhanding her before throwing her to the ground. His eyes met Roman's, and Roman held his gaze, aware of the wolves that had sidled off, moving through the woods on silent feet to work around to the back of the building. Jenner stood at his side still, but Steven had disappeared.

"She's mine, Eduard. Ask her. *Look* at her," Roman snarled. "She's mine, and quite likely pregnant with my baby already. A werewolf is much more fertile than a cold-blooded vampire."

"Then I'll change the bastard when she whelps it," Eduard said with an evil grin. "Unless he takes after you. Then I'll just throw him into the river, like you do with any mongrel dog."

Julianna lifted up from the ground, her eyes full of hate as she stared at her father. Roman kept his eyes from her as well, although he watched as she pushed to her knees.

He moved slowly through the crowd, leashing his power and calming the wolf, shifting from wolf to man in the span of three steps. "You hurt her, Eduard, and you are dead," Roman said flatly.

"You'd break the law over a useless bitch like her?" Eduard sneered. "She's mine to do with as I choose. My daughter, my House . . . *mine.*"

"Murder is a law-breaker," Roman replied, a chill running through him. She was a tool to him, nothing else. "She is not *yours*, not even by the old laws. You recognized her within Capiet's House just three days ago. And I've claimed her. She's my mate, my woman. She'll be my bride, God willing. And she's only useless in your eyes because you couldn't control her."

Julianna had pushed to her feet now, staring at the back of her father's head with disgusted eyes.

Eduard still never acknowledged her as he glared at Roman. "She is mine to control, you fucking dog. Just like her mother was. Just like some of the men around you—*useless.*"

Roman laughed, studying the eyes of the vampires who stared at Eduard with varying degrees of anger in their faces. "They've fought and bled to do as you ordered, to try to claim your daughter. I don't think they relish being called useless."

"Not one of them succeeded." Eduard dismissed them as he searched the crowd. "Not even that cretin Mikhail. I thought for sure he would have luck tearing your heart from your chest."

"Perhaps if I had wanted to, I would have."

Mikhail stepped out of the sanctuary and rose in the air, floating until he could step out onto the roof of the sanctuary. He smiled coolly at Eduard, his hair dark in the moonlight, his pale eyes colorless and glittering. "I was never the lackey you wanted me to be, Eduard. Tearing Roman's heart from his chest was never part of my agenda. Now yours . . ."

Roman lunged forward as Mikhail dove for Eduard. Distantly, he could hear his wolves scrambling closer to the sanctuary now, not bothering with silence as they took advantage of one vampire attacking the other.

Roman slashed through the men separating him from the sanctuary and his woman. Many moved out of the way, retreating with eyes downcast. The few who didn't move felt the claws ripping through their bellies, through their unprotected throats, until blood had painted the ground a dark, wet color.

He reached the stairs and lunged, gripping the sill of the window on the second floor. Roman busted the glass and flipped through, racing to the other side and onto the balcony where he lunged for the roof, catching the edge in his hands and hauling his weight up and over.

Mikhail had taken Eduard down, his hands wrapped brutally around one of Eduard's arms, jerking it with a sickening thud as Eduard continued to struggle. Roman ignored them, moving past them, intent only on getting Julianna.

She stared at him, her eyes gleaming . . . and then they went dull.

Roman roared as Julianna fell to the ground, blood trickling out of her lips. As she fell, the woman standing behind her was revealed. His entire body trembled with rage as he lunged for Isabeta and backhanded her, knocking the vampire from the building. She fell boneless into the throng of wolves and vampires at the ground.

The knife she had stabbed Julianna with lay on the roof, the pure gleam of it winking at him in the moonlight. Pure silver . . . he knew the scent, the sight of the deadly metal.

Kneeling beside her, he pulled her slowly into his arms, his throat locked tight as he rolled her over, staring into her dull eyes. A slow smile curved up her lips, and she gasped, "Well, I guess he lost in the end, didn't he?"

"Shhh," Roman murmured, laying his fingers across her lips.

"I didn't become what he wanted—once . . . that might . . . have been . . . enough," she said, her voice harsh, breaking, full of pain. "I wanted you, though. Now that's all I want. And I can't have it."

Her eyes closed, a stillness settling over her body. Roman moved his eyes to the side where Eduard lay broken and battered at Mikhail's feet. "Why?" he growled, his eyes flashing and swirling with rage as he stared at the vampire king.

He laughed, a wet, choked sound. "I'd rather see her dead than with you," he forced out through his mangled mouth.

Roman whispered, "Get ready to die, Eduard." Brushing Julianna's hair out of her face, he touched his fingers to her throat, searching for a pulse he knew wasn't there. Her heart wasn't beating. Isabeta had aimed her stroke well, driving it into Julianna's human heart, killing her.

"You do not have time to bother with Eduard," Mikhail said quietly. He called out into the darkness, and Roman watched as two men whom he had seen standing in the shadows during the battle floated upward, stepping onto the roof, their eyes grim and somber. "My men—not Eduard's," Mikhail clarified. "I've been seeding that house with my people for decades, and he never knew."

The men took guard at Eduard's side—the fallen vampire opened his mouth to hiss at them, but Mikhail said softly, "One word, Eduard, and I'll have them feed you to the wolves. Literally."

Mikhail knelt by Roman, reaching out to stroke Julianna's brow. "There's time left. We will bring her over."

"She's dead," Roman said hoarsely. "She had to be bitten before she died . . . it won't work now."

Mikhail said softly, "You know much of vampires, Roman, but not all. The blood children do not have to be bitten. They need only to bite . . . to drink of the blood of a creature more than human. I would give her mine, but I'm sure you would much rather she take of yours."

Roman's head pounded as he stared in Mikhail's eyes. "You had better be telling me the truth," he rasped as he shifted Julianna's inert body in his lap. He flexed one hand, released the smallest sliver of power, and his hand shifted, elongating, deadly claws forming. Roman raked one of the claws across his other wrist, watching as his blood welled. His hand melted back into human form as he slid his forearm under her head, lifting her slightly.

Blood ran down her chin as he held his wrist to her slack mouth. Mikhail moved, reaching over and tipping her head up more, forcing her jaws open. "She could hate me for this," Roman said bleakly. *If it worked . . .*

"She won't. She would have become vampire at some point—she would have had no choice, Roman," Mikhail said gently. "Better now than when she is aged."

Roman's lids flickered as he saw her throat move. Swallowing. Again. A shaky breath escaped him, and he looked up at Mikhail with wide, disbelieving eyes. "She's drinking."

She didn't open her eyes, even as Mikhail finally forced Roman's wrist away from her throat. "That will do it, Roman," he said, his fingers going white at the knuckle with the force it took to pull Roman's wrist away. "You want to bleed out? It would take longer, but even werewolves can bleed to death."

Roman clenched his wrist into a tight fist, watching as fat, sullen drops of blood flowed down his arm. Mikhail took his hand, gripping it and forcing his arm to straighten, taking a ragged strip of cloth he had gotten from somewhere and wrapping it around Roman's wrist as a makeshift bandage.

When it was done, Roman shifted his arms under her, lifting her slowly, carefully in his arms as he stood. Mikhail flicked a glance at Eduard and said softly, "Don't. He's not worth it."

Roman moved to the edge of the roof, staring down at the woman who had stabbed Julianna. Isabeta was huddled on the ground, cowering from the three oversized wolves who circled around her. "She's ours," he said shortly, not even looking at Mikhail as he spoke.

"Indeed," Mikhail said, an odd note in his voice. "At least I know werewolves are hotheaded enough to be swift in their punishments. Vampires prefer to take their time, torture—"

With a snarl, Roman bit out, "Don't give me any ideas, man." He clenched his jaw as he looked from the roof to the ground. He could jump it, no problem. But that would jar Julianna's body too badly.

"Give her to me."

Roman slid Mikhail a dark glance, but he finally slid her into his arms, watching closely as Mikhail levitated down to the ground. Roman jumped, landing on the balls of his feet. Eduard came flying down to the ground, landing in a bloody pile of limbs as his guards threw him to the ground. The other two men leaped down, taking position once more at his side.

Sliding Isabeta a narrow glance, Roman ordered, "Put her in the lowest room in the tower. She tried to kill my mate."

Growls tore through the gathered werewolves, and the three pacing around her started to tear at the ground with their claws, dropping low, prepared to lunge. "Enough!" Roman bellowed, silencing the howls and the protests. "I'll deal with her."

With that, he turned and carried Julianna into the sanctuary, striding up the stone staircase at the far end of the room, taking her to his room. Her pale skin gleamed like ivory against the dull, burnished gold of the tapestry quilt.

He hunkered down by the side of the bed, staring at her face with intense eyes. "Why doesn't she open her eyes?"

"She won't. Not until the next moonrise . . . although normally a vampire's first meal is another vampire," Mikhail said from the doorway. "I've never seen what happens to a blood child if the first meal is a child of the sun, not the night."

Roman lay down gently on the bed, curling his body around hers, the coldness of her flesh chilling him. Placing a hand on her belly, he rubbed in slow, small circles. From time to time, her heart beat, a slow, irregular sound he heard maybe five times a minute. No air stirred in her lungs. Hoarsely, he whispered, "I love you." She didn't move. She made no sign she had heard him.

Closing his eyes, he settled down, prepared to wait.

Through the long night, Roman waited for her to rise. As dawn crept closer to the horizon, he paced the room, fury and sorrow mingling inside him, tightening his throat, tying his belly in knots.

Mikhail had left. His wolves, the ones who could stay, were gathered in the great room. They took turns watching Isabeta through the narrow slit of her window. There was silver at every entrance and bowls of garlic water placed throughout the room— enough to restrict her from using vampire magick to try to escape. And to make her just miserable enough that she could find no rest, no peace.

And Roman was alone. Alone to pace the room and wonder if he could have done something different, something that might have saved Julianna. He removed the bloodied clothes she wore, washing the traces of blood from her back, his mouth tight and grim, rage pulsing red in his mind. *Isabeta* . . . a growl escaped his throat as he smoothed down Julianna's hair, easing her back onto the bed. He couldn't think of a way painful enough for him to use to kill the woman who had stabbed Julianna.

Julianna wouldn't wake from her vampire sleep. Many new ones did not. Roman had to deal with that, had to deal with the fact that he might have lost the love of his life.

In the farthest corner of the room, he brushed aside the thick, heavy cloths that had been fastened to the wall to keep out the darkness. Through the thick burgundy of the curtains and the added protection of the black velvet, no light could penetrate the room.

With the heavy velvet held aside by his shoulder, he stared broodingly out into the lightening darkness, his eyes tracking the moon as it moved through the sky. One by one, the stars were lost to view as the sky brightened. The eastern sky gleamed gold as the sun started to creep onto the horizon. Staring into the golden brilliance of it, Roman felt one hot tear trickle down his face.

She would not wake.

Forcing a breath into his tight lungs, he stepped away from the window. Soon, tonight . . . tomorrow . . . soon, her heart would stop beating altogether and she would be gone, lost to him.

With a roar, he spun away from the bed and drove his fist into the unmoving stone wall, feeling stone split and flesh rip. Sinking to his knees, he stared at the jagged break in the stone, his mind going blank.

"Roman . . ."

For a long moment, he didn't move. Then he slowly turned his head, looking over his shoulder to stare at the bed. Julianna. With his heart in his throat, he watched as her eyelids lifted.

"Sweet heaven," he whispered, surging to his feet and crossing the room in long, loping strides. Sinking to his knees beside the bed, Roman reached out, touching one hand to her face.

A slow smile curved her lips as she stared at him, her eyes puzzled. "What happened?" she whispered.

"You're awake," he breathed, stroking his thumb across her mouth.

Her brows dropped low over her eyes as she asked weakly, "Why do I get the feeling that surprises you?"

In a stilted voice, he said, "Isabeta stabbed you, in the heart. The knife was silver."

Her lids flickered as he watched memory pour into her eyes. One hand came to rest on her naked breast, pushing against the resilient flesh with a shaking hand. "I remember something hurting—it burned like fire, but it felt so cold."

He swallowed, his tongue feeling thick and awkward as he brushed a gleaming ribbon of black hair back from her face. "You took the Blood Kiss, Julie. I fed you." Roman waited, blanking his face, as she stared at him with dark eyes.

Julianna's tongue slid out, dragging across her dry lips. He heard her swallow as she lowered her lashes, reaching up with one hand to touch her mouth, probing where fangs would soon break through. "I was dying, wasn't I?" she asked, her voice soft.

Roman flinched, the image of her crumpling to the ground flashing before his eyes. Gutturally, he answered, "Yes."

Julianna's face paled as she pushed herself to a sitting position, running her tongue over the surface of her teeth. "I don't feel any different." Her blue eyes moved around the room before landing on Roman's face. She sighed, a deep shuddering breath, and Roman watched as she squared her shoulders. "Has the moon risen?"

"Hours ago," he murmured, some of the tension that squeezed around his heart relaxing a little when she didn't stare at him with hatred in her eyes. "It's dawn."

Julianna's eyes widened. "Dawn? That can't be. They rise at night, with the moon's rising."

As she spoke, though, Roman glimpsed the pearly white of her teeth, seeing the elongated tips of dainty fangs. He grabbed at her arm as she swung out of bed, her eyes on the windows across from her. "You can't," he whispered harshly.

She shrugged off his hand. "I don't feel any different, Roman. You feel it inside when you are vampire. I don't feel any different," she said, her voice urgent.

His hand fell away as she slid from bed, her eyes grim and determined. One hand caught the blanket, and Roman clenched his jaw, rising to take the blanket and help tuck it around her nude form.

He followed at her heels, ready to jerk her away from the window when the sun burned her flesh. She moved slowly, the erratic beat of her heart picking up, her mouth tight with strain. As she reached the window, Roman saw the weariness that was overtaking her. "Let me take you back to the bed," he insisted.

"I have to see." Her voice brooked no argument as she reached out with a shaking hand to draw the protective drapes away from the window. Roman watched as the sun painted her skin gold and a smile curved her lips. Those diminutive fangs flashed at him as she looked back at him, smiling. "It doesn't hurt," she said, her eyes sparkling.

Roman stared at her, confused as hell. She flung herself at him, wrapping her arms around his neck, laughter bubbling out of her throat. "It doesn't hurt!" she repeated, hugging his neck as he closed his arms around her, nuzzling his face into the thick black curtain of her hair.

Hunger tore through him as she pressed against him, the soft curves of her breasts against the wall of his chest, her soft belly cuddling the aching length of his cock.

Gathering her hair in his hands, he pulled her head back, taking her mouth greedily and plunging his tongue deep inside. With savage jerks of his hand, he tore open the blanket, revealing the long, pale lines of her body, falling to his knees to capture one beaded nipple in his mouth, worrying it with his tongue and teeth as his fingers stroked the other, milking it, tugging it with slow, thorough strokes.

Her fingers buried in his hair as he lifted his face to stare at her. "I love you, Julie," he whispered thickly, his fingers curving around the soft flare of her hips.

Her lips parted on a gasp, and Roman watched as tears leaked from her eyes, rolling down her cheeks and splashing on his face. "I love you, too," she murmured, wrapping her arms around him and bending down to cover his mouth with hers.

Julianna's tears flowed, dampening his face as well as hers as they kissed. Roman eased her down into his lap, spreading her legs so she straddled his hips, her naked breasts pressing against his bare chest. Through the fragile barrier of her ribs, he felt the slow, steady beating of her heart. His head swam with the hot, musky scent of her body, and his hands burned as he ran them over her sleekly curved body.

He shifted, moving onto his knees and spilling her onto her back. He laid his hands on her knees and ran them up the silken skin of her inner thighs, spreading her legs, his hands moving up until his thumbs met in the middle, at the apex of her thighs. He stroked one thumb down the glistening, dew-slicked flesh of her pussy, a hungry growl trickling from his throat. Roman sprawled between her thighs, holding open her folds as he pressed his mouth against her, driving his tongue into the tight well of her pussy. He alternated between stabbing his tongue inside and shifting so he could suckle on her clit.

Her hands fisted in his hair, and she screamed out his name as her heels dug into his back. Roman rose up, tearing open his jeans. Covering her, he arched his cock against her, sliding back and forth across the slick lips of her sex, groaning as she arched up against him, trying to take him inside. "Damn it, Roman, please!" she sobbed out.

He chuckled, shifting his angle and driving into her with one, breath-stealing thrust. Roman thought he'd die from the pleasure as she closed over him, the snug silk of her tissues rippling around him as her body tried to accommodate his.

"I thought I'd lost you," he rasped, cupping her head in his hands and angling up her mouth. He pressed his lips against her eyes, her nose, the elegant curve of her chin, sliding his mouth against hers, licking at her lips, teasingly sliding his tongue inside her mouth and then retreating.

"Nothing could keep me away from you." Her scream echoed off the walls as he pulled out and surged back inside her. "Roman!"

With hard, short thrusts of his hips, he pumped into her, staring down into her face. Her eyes stared up into his as she bucked under the onslaught of his thrusts. As she started to scream again, Roman covered her mouth, swallowing the soft cry as she exploded around him.

His control was shot. Too much had happened. He'd almost lost her. He reared back, planting his hands on the ground beside her face and driving into her hungrily, all thought gone, as she convulsed and shuddered around him. He howled out her name as he exploded, coming inside her with hot, vicious jerks of his cock.

Then he collapsed down and lay against her, his head pillowed between her breasts. Her fingers laced behind his neck, and he felt her satisfaction as she sighed.

"I was so damned afraid," he muttered, watching as the soft flesh of her nipple puckered and drew tight as he spoke, the air from his mouth caressing over the stiffening peak. "I thought I'd lost you—and I just found you."

Julianna hugged him tight. "I won't ever leave you, if I have a choice," she whispered.

"If you do . . . I'll follow you."

Mikhail studied her teeth with a thoughtful frown on his face. "Those aren't vampire fangs, darling," he finally said, lifting one shoulder in a shrug, his face as confused as the rest of them felt. "And you stood in sunlight. The newly changed cannot do that."

Julianna scowled at him as he continued to pace around her, stroking his chin thoughtfully, his eyes watching her carefully. "I took the Blood Kiss. I was dying, and Roman's blood saved me. If they aren't vampire fangs, then what are they?"

Roman lay sprawled on the bed, his eyes heavy with exhaustion as he listened to them. He hadn't slept. She'd tried to make him, but she had been wasting her time and she knew it. He wouldn't sleep until she did.

Mikhail laughed, a deep chuckle that echoed through the room as he slid Roman a glance. "I told him. I did not know what would happen if a child of the night took her first meal as a full vampire from a child of the day. We take so much more than blood within when we feed—hopes, dreams, desires . . . even power. A vampire can gain much from those he feeds upon. Witches were once nearly hunted to extinction because the vampires discovered what they could gain by feeding from a witch. And the first meal helps forge you into what you will be. And your first . . . was werewolf. Not vampire, as it has always been among us. But werewolf."

Julianna's eyes narrowed as she stared at Mikhail. It was Roman who spoke first. "So you are saying she's more like me than a vampire?" he asked doubtfully.

"I'd say she is more like herself," Mikhail said with a wide grin. "As she has always been. She is unique. Hmmm. I do have to wonder what you'll be capable of."

She sneered at him, turning to go to Roman, sinking down on the bed, and cuddling against him. The moon had risen. Her eyes were heavy.

She'd always feared when she became vampire, she'd want nothing more than to be like her father. Blood-thirsty, power-hungry . . . evil.

It wasn't the vampirism that had made him that way, though. Meeting Mikhail had proved that.

Eduard Capiet was just evil.

Julianna was herself. And all she wanted was to wrap herself around her lover and sleep the night away.

His eyes gleamed down at hers, and he muttered, "Mikhail—go away."

As Roman's mouth came down on hers, she had to admit, *Well, maybe that's not* all *I want* . . .